Praise for the no

MAD AB

"A cool cast of secondary characters adds much to the story, clever Plumley, who is already known for her entertaining romantic comedies, presents another winner in this humorous and engaging tale about a man who literally loses his shirt, but finds his heart."

—*Booklist* (starred review)

"*Mad About Max* kept me laughing from beginning to end. What great characters! Very highly recommended, especially for fans of romantic comedy."

—*Romance Junkies*

JOSIE DAY IS COMING HOME

"Turning not-so-perfect, unlikely characters into romance heroes and heroines is Lisa Plumley's forte, and she once again delivers a zany cast who will make you laugh!"

The State newspaper

"In this heartwarming, often humorous story, the feisty Josie proves that you can go home again—if you've got the right stuff. And once again, the talented Plumley, whose books include *Perfect Switch*, proves that when it comes to writing romantic comedy, few do it better."

—*Booklist*

PERFECT SWITCH

"There's a rising star on the romantic comedy scene, and her name is Lisa Plumley! She delivers great characters, plenty of laughs and a delicious love story. I give *Perfect Switch* a Perfect 10!"

—*New York Times* bestselling
author Vicki Lewis Thompson

"Plumley writes a funny, sexy, heart-warming romance. Add [*Perfect Switch*] to your summer reading list—it's one of the season's best."

—*The Oakland Press*

Books by Lisa Plumley

MAKING OVER MIKE

FALLING FOR APRIL

RECONSIDERING RILEY

PERFECT TOGETHER

PERFECT SWITCH

JOSIE DAY IS COMING HOME

ONCE UPON A CHRISTMAS

MAD ABOUT MAX

SANTA, BABY
(anthology with Lisa Jackson,
Elaine Coffman, and Kylie Adams)

I SHAVED MY LEGS FOR THIS?!
(anthology with Theresa Alan,
Holly Chamberlin, and Marcia Evanick)

Published by Kensington Publishing Corporation

Let's Misbehave

Lisa Plumley

ZEBRA BOOKS
Kensington Publishing Corp.
www.kensingtonbooks.com

ZEBRA BOOKS are published by

Kensington Publishing Corp.
850 Third Avenue
New York, NY 10022

All Kensington titles, imprints, and distributed lines are avail-
able at special quantity discounts for bulk purchases for sales
promotion, premiums, fund-raising, educational, or institu-
tional use.

Special book excerpts or customized printings can also be created to fit specific needs. For details, write or phone the office
of the Kensington Special Sales Manager: Attn. Special Sales
Department. Kensington Publishing Corp., 850 Third Avenue,
New York, NY 10022. Phone: 1-800-221-2647.

Zebra and the Z logo Reg. U.S. Pat. & TM Off.

ISBN-13: 978-0-8217-8052-7
ISBN-10: 0-8217-8052-2

First Printing: July 2007
10 9 8 7 6 5 4 3 2 1

Printed in the United States of America

*Thanks to all the talented and dedicated people at
Kensington Books, especially John Scognamiglio.
You help make my dreams come true!*

*Thanks to my husband, John Plumley,
for always laughing at the funny parts.
Every writer needs a reader like you!*

Chapter 1

"We're lost."

The announcement roused Marisol Winston from a fitful sleep. It was just as well. She'd been dreaming of Eames chairs and sample sales and minty mojitos, and the last thing she needed after the night she'd just spent was another cocktail. Even an imaginary cocktail. With lots of ice and a hunky bartender and a wallop to make a girl forget everyth . . .

Zzzz.

Then: "Yup. We're *definitely* lost."

Ugh. Marisol *definitely* wasn't prepared for a crisis today. She just wanted to stay in her comfy double bed in her comfy Malibu beach house in her comfy, cushy life until she got her mojo back. She'd been out late again last night, celebrating a mega-successful spree at her favorite boutiques along Third Street and Robertson Boulevard, and the last thing she needed now was a problem. She wasn't even sure she'd stashed all her finds before going out club hopping with Caprice and Tenley. That kind of carelessness meant she was slipping again, falling into that trouble zone where shopping turned into . . .

Anyway. Where was she? Something didn't feel quite right.

Blearily, Marisol analyzed her situation. Her ceiling fan must have reached Mach 1, because it felt way too breezy. The light shoved way too rudely against her squeezed-shut eyelids to be coming through her bedroom window in the form of ordinary L.A. sunshine. And despite the fact that she'd snuggled tight against something soft and pillowy, she'd swear the whole place was moving. Yikes. She opened her eyes.

Oh yeah. It all came rushing back to her. She was ensconced in the passenger seat of her all-white Mercedes SL55 AMG roadster, riding with the top down, trying to survive an impromptu mid-May road trip to a distant designer outlet mall with her stepmother.

While hungover. And possibly while carrying ninety-two shopping bags already stowed in the trunk from yesterday.

If Jamie, her stepmother, caught sight of those bags . . .

Why had they taken *her* car?

"We can't be lost." Cautiously, Marisol straightened her sunglasses, needing the refuge of their ultradark lenses but afraid of poking herself in the eye with one sharp Gucci-fied end of them. Italian designers didn't screw around. "This car has a state-of-the-art navigation system, remember?"

She pointed to the techy-looking equipment panel.

"Oh. So *that's* what that is. Huh. Problem solved, I guess."

Forehead puckered, Jamie scanned the stretch of I-40 ahead. She didn't look reassured at the sight of the stark plateau and scraggly bushes surrounding them, even though she'd occupied the driver's seat since they'd left L.A. two or three or . . . who knew how many? . . . hours ago on their way to northern Arizona. A (supposedly) fabulous new outlet mall had just opened there, and Jamie loved nothing more than discovering new frontiers.

Together they were the Lewis and Clark of retail.

Outlet shopping would be their newest adventure—a novelty for sure.

Jamie shook her head. "I still say this car ought to drive us to the outlets all by itself, considering how much it cost."

"Very funny." Especially coming from a woman dressed highlights-to-pedicure in chic Matthew Williamson originals. Jamie visited Matthew's showroom whenever she jetted to London. "Did you get that one from Dad?"

"No, Marisol. I didn't. But your father isn't the only one who's worried about your—"

"Never mind. Forget I said anything," Marisol interrupted. At the age of thirty-one, she ought to know better than to pick fights she couldn't win. Also, pot? Meet kettle. She was wearing a pretty fab Stella McCartney ensemble herself. "Just wake me when we get within stumbling distance of the Dolce & Gabbana outlet, okay?"

"Okay." A pause. "Hey, are you sure you're up for this?"

"Sure. Maybe I'll pick up a few last-season handbags for my hairstylist and her assistant. They'd like that. Trish is crazy for designer stuff." She yawned. "Also, that would have been a good question to ask *before* you dragged me out of bed at the crack of eleven this morning. You know noon is my cutoff point."

"I couldn't wait anymore. This trip is important."

"So you said. Which is why I lurched out here with only the couture on my back, ready to brave the wilds of outlet shopping for the first time. With you. I wouldn't go into the discount zone for just anybody, you know. I'm very discriminating."

She was also, at the moment, very windblown. Highway winds whipped her hair around her face, making a wreck of her long brown layers. Marisol dragged them into an impromptu ponytail at her neck, then nestled beneath her cashmere pashmina, a shopping victory from a million seasons ago. She'd gotten twelve more just like it for her friends and one for Jamie too. Sales on gifts were the best. So was this pashmina.

Ahhh. Sleep, wonderful sleep. The only thing better than sleep was sex. And with certain people, even that was debatable.

"*Really* important." Jamie's voice broke through, earnest and a little . . . tense. "I hope you'll remember that later."

"Um, okay." The grateful glance her stepmother threw her in reply made Marisol decidedly uneasy. "I will. I promise."

Jamie nodded, her bejeweled fingers tightening on the steering wheel. The white leather cover squeaked.

"Hey, is something else going on?" Snug in her cashmere cave, curled sideways in her seat, Marisol peered more closely at her stepmother. "You seem upset. Did Dad—"

"I'm fine! Just fine. Too much caffeine from that triple latte, probably." Jamie nodded at the Coffee Bean & Tea Leaf to-go cup stashed in the holder. "Isn't this exciting though?"

Dubiously, Marisol examined the windswept highway— mostly deserted. The stumpy juniper bushes on the hill ahead—mostly bedraggled. The interior of her car, with its hi-tech doodads, deluxe leather seating, and assortment of road trip supplies—mostly untouched.

They were on their way to an outlet mall in Podunkville, Arizona, and she had yet to see another living soul, much less anyone interesting (aka male). Yeah. Really exciting.

"It's awesome." No point stirring up trouble.

Something was definitely going on with Jamie though. Marisol studied her stepmother next, trying to figure out what.

All she saw was the same wavy blond hair Jamie had always had. The same California-girl salon tan and the same strong, lean arms and torso from lots of yoga. The same combination of openheartedness and realism that no younger woman could have pulled off. Jamie made fifty-five look amazing.

She was too good for Gary Winston.

Probably too good for Marisol too.

Marisol had loved Jamie almost from the moment Jamie had married her father and moved into the Winston mansion. Against all odds, Jamie had always been there for her. It had been Jamie who'd held Marisol's hand while her braces were adjusted. Jamie who'd helped her through her first date (a country club dance), first bra (a swanky couture training bra number), and first heartache (damn you, Brandon Hollister!).

It had been Jamie who'd comforted her when her mother had married a twenty-four-year-old bullfighter in Madrid (olé!)—leaving her daughter to discover the news via the society column in *Harper's Bazaar*. It had been Jamie who'd supported Marisol when she'd moved from the family mansion to Malibu six years ago, Jamie who'd coaxed her tightfisted, workaholic father into releasing enough trust fund money to pay for it. It had been Jamie who'd first introduced Marisol to duty-free shopping in Europe—to all the wonders of Italian textiles while (ostensibly) on scouting trips for Home Warehouse, the family's booming chain of home-improvement super centers.

Basically, Marisol decided, she and Jamie had bonded over their shared love of loud music, Cool Ranch Doritos, and Marc Jacobs' grunge collection for Perry Ellis almost fifteen years ago, and they'd never looked back.

Which explained this. The outlet mall trip.

Still in über-chipper mode, Jamie consulted the GPS readout on the Mercedes' instrument panel, then peered down the road. A hand-painted sign marked a junction—probably offering homemade cactus jelly or Kachina dolls or other touristy bargains. A ponderosa pine

blocked part of it from view. More pines marched along-
side the highway too. Marisol yawned again.

"So how was last night?" Jamie asked. "Did you have
fun?"

"Sure. We went to dinner at Koi, then hit a couple of parties in the hills. Tenley met someone. We drank mojitos."

They turned, jolted across a cattle guard—Marisol
could tell by the cow on the sign—and continued
through the pine trees along a curving blacktop road.
The Arizona high country pushed closer. Wow, the Pinetop Prestige Outlets really *were* remote—practically all
the way to the Grand Canyon. Jamie would get the jump
on everyone in staking her claim.

"Well, I'm glad you girls enjoyed yourselves." Jamie
sighed. "You have to make the most of every moment,
you know. There's no telling when the fun will stop."

"For me? Never."

"Still . . . you never know." Jamie shot her a serious
look. "Someday you might get a job. Discover a calling."

A calling? She meant join the family conglomerate,
Marisol knew. Spend the rest of her days helping suburban-
ites meet their cookie-cutter home-improvement needs.
Devising new and thrilling ways to market melamine, poly-
wood, and composite plastics. Toeing the Winston family
line that had begun with her entrepreneurial grandfather
more than fifty years ago and had ended—for now—with
her mega-successful father.

"Ugh." Marisol made a face. She had no interest in becoming a Home Warehouse corporate drone. Her style
was more town, less country. More sleek single, less
sloppy family. And even though lately she *had* given
some thought to what else she might do with her life besides scour the racks at Fred Segal, date cute boys, and
party till dawn—such as open her *own* chichi home-furnishings boutique someday—she still hadn't quite
worked out how to make her dreams happen. Or how to

approach her father about financing them. Frankly, he was intimidating. "Not likely. I've never felt a 'calling' to do anything besides have fun."

Jamie frowned.

"I don't remember 'fun' being quite this debilitating though," Marisol added. Another bump. Reminded of her hangover, she groped behind her seat for her purse. "Ouch. Do you have any aspirin? I can't even find my wallet in here."

Not that that was unusual. Marisol was notoriously disorganized. Or as she preferred to think of it, famously *unfettered*. Thankfully, her stepmother wasn't.

"Take this." One-handed, Jamie produced a bottle of aspirin. Like the inveterate nurturer she was, she carried a whole arsenal of practical items in her Prada tote. "Go ahead and keep the bottle." She gestured. "You might need it later."

"Thanks." Gratefully, Marisol chased three aspirin with a swig of iced coffee, then tossed the leftover pain relievers in her bag. She slumped in her ergonomic leather seat again.

Ahhh. The salesman had been right. This car really did cradle you. Maybe not $150,000-plus worth of cradling, but still. It was nice. And cuddly. And she needed all the cuddly comfort she could get today. Her temples throbbed with a killer headache. Her ears rang. Her tongue felt fuzzy. She'd swear her knees were still wobbly from last night too.

Her knees. Wobbly!

Sheesh, she wasn't that old. She was in her prime! A simple night of ordinary club hopping should not have this effect on a smart, fun, *happening* woman like her. So what if there was a whole new batch of quasifamous twenty-something socialites cluttering up her favorite nightspots? The editors of *W* magazine had named *Marisol Winston* the Hot Heiress of the Moment, hadn't they?

Although come to think of it, that glossy spread had been published almost *six* years ago now. . . .

Jamie glanced over and tsk-tsked in the motherly way she had, effectively diverting all of Marisol's gloomy thoughts.

"You've got low blood sugar," she diagnosed. "It's affecting your mood. You should've had some turkey jerky, like I said. My nutritionist just started marketing her own brand. Try it." She waggled the snack bag on the sleek console between them, sending up a meaty aroma.

Marisol stared at the bag. Geez. Her own brand? Even Bree "The Terminator" Jones had more ambition than Marisol did.

But hey, so what? She didn't yearn to be the jerky queen of L.A. County. "Please. Stop. Coyotes are following my car now."

"You'll need a new car soon anyway. I know you just bought this one, but—to no one's surprise—it isn't exactly practical." From beneath the last unBotoxed eyebrows in California, Jamie cast her a meaningful look. "I should have come with you. You can't even fit a baby seat into a tiny roadster like this."

Oh God. First the realization that she was an over-the-hill slacker. Now this. Well-meaning lecture number twelve.

Marisol held up her hand to ward off what was coming next. Too late. Her stepmother was off and running. This was her latest obsession, ever since her book-club posse had started bringing pictures of their grandchildren to meetings.

"—no backseat at all," Jamie rattled on cheerfully, "not to mention room for a diaper bag. They have such cute ones now too—with masculine styles made just for daddies, even. You're lucky. Daddies are so much more involved these days than in—"

Marisol groaned. "Please stop calling them 'daddies.'"

"Why? That's what you'll need, you know. A daddy. A man to father your children—"

"Come *on*! I'm already queasy."

"One good man is all you need," Jamie announced with relish. "One who will slip you the big salami."

"Oh. My. God."

"Okay, fine. I read that last part in my April book-club selection. It was very gritty." Red-faced, Jamie waved her hand. "What I *mean* is, you just need one man who understands you—who understands why you don't like Sundays and why you do like wrapping paper. Why you don't like to be alone and why you give the best hugs ever. Just for instance. That's all I'm saying."

Awww. Jamie was so wonderful! Momentarily (and despite the salami comment), Marisol felt downright misty. She *did* want a guy like that. A stand-up guy who wouldn't let her down. A guy who would love her and cherish her and—

Hang on. One measly hangover and she'd gone all schmaltzy? What the heck had been in those mojitos?

She snorted. "As if."

"What are you, thirteen years old again? It's true."

Marisol shook her head. "I've been there, done that. None of those guys were keepers."

"Well, in your heart of hearts, you know there's someone out there for you. All you have to do is find him." Jamie eyed the custom-designed steering wheel dubiously. "Although once you do, I'm not sure you could fit behind this thing while pregnant. It's just too small."

"Stop. Just stop, okay? There's nothing you can say that will change my mind. I'm not the 'kid' type. Just try taking a first-grader to a club. They get carded *every* time."

"Marisol!"

"Kids don't like spas." Marisol ticked off the drawbacks on her fingers. "Or shopping or sashimi—"

"Admittedly, three of your favorite things. But—"

"—and they're noisy and whiny and grimy." Marisol examined the pristine white leather seat beneath her trendy white skirt. Kids? In *her* life? No way. It just didn't add up. "Thanks, but no thanks. Even *you* didn't get suckered into having any babies. You just had me. And *I* eventually grew up."

"Hmmm. 'Grew up' is debatable."

"Aside from which, giving you grandbabies would put a serious crimp in my madcap lifestyle." *No matter how unsatisfying it's become lately.* Wait, did she really just think that? Shaking her head, Marisol made her voice sound as stern as possible. "And no more dragging me into Baby Benetton either."

"But those tiny sweaters are so adorable!"

"Enough." Ahead, a welcome diversion caught her eye. As they drove closer, a series of low-slung buildings came into view, with meandering landscaping, au natural colors, and façades of river rock and peeled logs. Très rustic. Maybe too rustic. All the same . . . thank God. Especially if their arrival put an end to the babies-and-kids talk. "Look. We're here. Bargain hunting, here we come!"

Chapter 2

Her stepmother slowed the Mercedes to a prowl, hugging the blacktop as though reluctant to reach their destination. Which was really weird, because Jamie lived for shopping. Everyone knew that. Especially Marisol, her frequent partner in purchasing. But she wasn't complaining. Not now that the promise of diversionary shopping loomed so near.

Pine boughs whooshed past the convertible. The smell of evergreens and soil grew stronger. Marisol caught a whiff of mossy earthiness, more genuine than even the most organic Diptyque Feu de bois candle. She'd never experienced anything like it, especially not in her polished and manicured life.

"Wow, it's really, um, all-natural out here." She tilted her face to the dappled sunlight, grateful for this momentary respite from the pressure to procreate—or to allow a random baby-maker to slip her the big salami. Ugh. Marisol cast off her pashmina, letting her hair catch the breeze. "Did you know it was going to be like this?"

"Um, sort of. I did some research beforehand."

Preshopping reconnaissance was always good. But Jamie sounded kind of strained. Worried, Marisol gave her a curious look. She decided that Jamie probably just needed a healthy dose of civilization, especially after such a long drive.

Vowing to treat her stepmother to a relaxing espresso after they got inside—and to call for the Winston family Learjet for the return trip, for sure—Marisol gazed at the scenery.

They glided along the edge of the grounds, then passed through a pair of tall iron gates bordered by well-tended greenery. Jamie waved to someone at the security station. The gates swung shut behind them with motorized grace. At least those were sleek. Smooth. Easy on the hangover headache too.

Although now that Marisol considered it, it seemed pretty improbable that an outlet mall would be situated within a gated compound. Weren't those for exclusive estates? Or private schools? Or euphemistically named "recovery centers"?

But before she could make sense of the dichotomy, especially with her mojito-impaired analytical ability, Marisol realized something else was wrong. Jamie had slowed the car even further. At this rate, the Versace outlet would lock its doors for the day before they set a single stiletto inside.

"Hey, are you okay?" Marisol gave her stepmother a friendly nudge. "I've never known you to drive this slowly to a sale."

"I'm fine. It's just that—" Jamie's ominous gaze met hers. "Before we get there, I have something to tell you. I promised I wouldn't, but it's only fair that you have some warning."

In Marisol's experience, that could only mean one thing.

"Oh my God. Dad's divorcing you, isn't he?"

Tight-lipped, Jamie shook her head.

"He's neglecting you then." Undaunted, Marisol leaped to Jamie's defense. "I should have known something was up, the way he kept talking about the competition's lawn mowers at dinner the other night." Her father was obsessed with beating the big two: Home Depot and Lowe's, and he had the work hours to prove it. "Don't worry. You can't take it personally, trust me. A little retail therapy, and you'll feel so much better."

"Your father and I are fine. Honestly."

Okay. That wasn't it then. But what could be wrong? Just contemplating the idea of Jamie in trouble made Marisol feel even queasier. A hangover she could handle. A problem with her stepmother . . . maybe not so much. She steeled herself.

Okay. Think positively. Maybe you can help.

"Did you forget your AmEx card? Is that it? Because this can all be my treat. You deserve it. You've done so much for—"

"You're *not* buying anything for me today," Jamie snapped.

Okay. Fine. Sheesh. Jamie was usually so calm. Today she was definitely prickly. Which could only mean . . .

"You've finally caved! You're having Botox, aren't you? And you wanted to go waaaay out of town to do it in secret." It all made sense now. The hasty trip. The unlikely interest in outlet shopping. "Oh, Jamie. Please don't do it. You're beautiful just the way you are. Maybe a little spray tan to lift your spirits—"

"Marisol, stop!" Jamie sucked in one of her yoga-fied Ujjayi Pranayama breaths. She breathed out slowly. "I'm *not* getting Botox. But this isn't the Pinetop Prestige Outlets either."

"It's a plastic surgery center, isn't it?" Marisol raised her face to the sky in exasperation. "I swear, if Dad is making you get liposuction to impress his Fortune 500 business cronies and their Barbie-wannabe wives, I'll karate-chop him."

"Please listen. You might as well find out now." Jamie's

expression pleaded for understanding. "We're not here for me. We're here for you. This is . . . it's—it's—" She gestured helplessly. "Well just look around you. You'll see."

Bewildered, Marisol scrutinized their surroundings. She spied several clustered structures, meandering walkways—even wind chimes. The stone-façade building to their right looked distinctly lobby-like too. The truth walloped her.

"It's a resort! Of course!" Awww, it was *so* like Jamie to plan a surprise like this. She must have sensed that Marisol had been feeling down lately. This was her way of helping. Hadn't she just said *we're here for you?* "You're *so* sweet. Thank you!"

"Wait. Just wait. I want to explain before you—"

Marisol muffled her words with an impulsive hug. "You're the best. We'll go shopping later just like you wanted, okay? Maybe after a nice massage. I promise. There must be shopping nearby, right? There's no way you'd plan a trip that didn't involve shopping."

"Umm . . . this definitely involves shopping. But—"

"You are *so* smart to plan this." Marisol beamed at her as they parked. "I mean, blame my hangover, I guess, but I can't believe I didn't realize something was up!"

"Something's up, all right. But before you go inside—"

Marisol couldn't wait. After one iced coffee and several hours in the car, she needed to move. She spied three uniformed men moving to meet her car. Impatiently, she signaled them.

"Wow!" she squealed in an undertone to Jamie. "Studly valets too! They look as if they could bench press my Mercedes instead of park it. This is my kind of place for sure."

Hurriedly, she gathered her pashmina and purse. She smoothed down her hair, then rearranged her cute Stella skirt and matching white top. It was time for pampering, and not a moment too soon. If there was one thing Marisol Winston understood, it was having the best of everything.

Almost everything, at least.

A uniformed employee appeared, holding out both hands to greet her. He smiled. "Miss Winston. We're so happy you're joining us. Will you let me show you the way, please?"

"Of course." Happily, Marisol let him take her elbow. He chivalrously offered to carry her huge handbag too, so she let him. It *was* pretty heavy, and she didn't have any other luggage. The poor man probably just wanted to feel useful.

Keys jangled—Jamie handing them over to a valet, Marisol assumed. She strode toward the lobby entrance with her escort, drinking in the atmosphere. Everything looked rustic, yet peaceful. Birds chirped in the pine trees. Water splashed beneath a nearby footbridge, then meandered away.

They'd really done a nice job with the whole outdoorsy vibe here. The rocks and plants—even the artistic sprinklings of dirt on the pathway—all seemed authentic. Which was how Marisol knew they weren't. After all, what kind of people wanted *real* dirt?

"Here we are, miss." At the lobby threshold, her escort paused. He gestured to the flagstones underfoot. "Most people like to take this first step alone. It's part of the experience here at Dzeel."

"Dzeel? That's the name of this place?"

Her escort nodded. "It's the Navajo word for strength, miss. You'll understand once you get inside."

"Excellent." Marisol beamed. All resorts needed some kind of shtick these days. Merely offering five-star service was no longer enough. "I can hardly wait."

She didn't quite get the *first step alone* bit, but . . . whatever. She was game. Marisol walked inside.

Instantly, a peaceful aura surrounded her. Wildflowers

bloomed in an arrangement on the lobby table. More stood along the reception desk, where several uniformed employees waited. Sofas and slipper chairs upholstered in nubbly fabrics and soothing colors formed the basis of two seating areas, each of which contained interior waterfalls backed by shimmering copper.

Behind her, hurried footsteps rang across the au natural flooring. Marisol turned to see Jamie headed her way, an apologetic look on her face. "I'm sorry. I didn't mean to leave you alone. I hope I'm not too late."

"Too late for what?"

From the closest seating area, three people stepped forward. They must have been shielded by the fountain and foliage until now. To her disbelief, Marisol recognized all of them.

"Dad? What are you doing here? Caprice? Tenley?" She stared at her friends, belatedly walking toward them with her arms outstretched. A wobbly smile spread across her face. "What's going on? Why are you all here? How did you get here?"

Humph. No doubt *they'd* taken the Learjet.

Tenley, her very best friend, hugged her. "I love you."

Utterly confused, Marisol hugged her also. Caprice joined the hug next, wrapping her skinny arms tight. "I love you too!"

What in the name of Ferragamo was going on here?

The resort employees kept a discreet distance. Dimly, Marisol noticed two of them standing at the entryway with their arms folded over their burly chests, Mafioso-style. They looked, all of a sudden, as if they belonged with that huge gate outside. With the security guard and the hush-hush atmosphere.

Jamie hugged her next. "Please don't be mad."

"Mad? Why would I be mad? What is going on?"

Trying to get her bearings, Marisol looked for her escort—the man with her handbag. She spotted him nearby, still holding it. He seemed to be—hey! He was searching it!

She lunged in that direction. Her father stopped her. "Don't. He's supposed to do that." He wore his usual custom-tailored suit and tie, and his demeanor was identical to the Soprano wannabes at the door. "Listen, the first thing you need to know is that this is for the best. The second is that I missed an important meeting to be here, so you'd better take this place damned seriously."

Hey, where did he get off taking over this way?

"This is Jamie's surprise," Marisol said hotly, "so—"

Suddenly, Jamie was there, gently taking her arm. "Maybe you'd better sit down. You look a little unsteady."

She did? But—but she was in the middle of a tirade! She was—oh, cripes. She was downright wobbly, all of a sudden. Damn those thirty-one-year-old knees. Gawking at her friends and family, Marisol dropped to the nearest sofa. They all encircled her—Caprice and Tenley on either side, Jamie on the closest chair, and her father standing by.

"You guys, knock it off. You're scaring me."

Jamie squeezed her hand. "We want to help you."

"Freaking me out doesn't help!"

"You have a problem," Caprice said. Everyone nodded.

"A shopping problem." This, from Tenley. "And we're here to help you face it. To help you face your shop-aholicism."

Marisol blinked. "This is a *shopping intervention?*"

They nodded solemnly. That was all she needed.

"That's it. I'm out of here." Marisol surged to her feet.

Freakishly, they must have prepared for that, because all four of them tackled her. She flopped back on the sofa with a whoosh, her hair flying in her face. She blew it away.

"This is ridiculous! So I shop. I like to shop. Big deal!"

Marisol flung her arms sideways, filled with disbelief and irritation. "Is it hurting anyone? No. So let's drop it."

"It's hurting *you*." Jamie's eyes looked teary.

For an instant, Marisol's eyes stung too. "I'm fine. Look, let's go scope out the resort boutique and forget all this happened, okay? Dad, you need a new tie, if that one's any—"

"You're not going anywhere," he said. "Not right now. Not until we get through this."

Even he looked a little choked up. That gave her pause. Her father had a famous poker face and a knack for making a person feel invisible. If even he were moved enough to do this . . .

"You didn't like your new golf clubs? Is that what this is about?" Marisol blurted. "I know I'm no expert, but I thought they'd be a perfect gift for you. That's why I got them."

Her father shook his head. "Don't be ridiculous."

"Whatever." As usual, he'd completely dismissed her. "I don't have a problem," Marisol insisted. "I'm not staying here."

"Miss?" An employee tiptoed nearer. "I'm sorry to intrude, but shall we put these in your suite, or would you like them delivered home?"

Marisol glanced sideways. Four employees stood nearby. But they were nearly invisible behind the single piece of luggage she definitely hadn't packed—and the roughly ninety-two shopping bags she'd left in her trunk after yesterday's spree. All the bags were emblazoned with the names of her favorite boutiques; all overflowed with items she'd simply *had* to have.

Those bags were glossy and familiar and safe. For one bizarre moment, Marisol wanted to dive inside one and vanish.

Her family and friends gazed at those heaps of incriminating evidence, then at her. Marisol looked away, her hands shaking. She just couldn't face them.

"Stay here for a little while," Jamie urged quietly. "It's a good place. A good program, with experts and a multiconceptual two-part treatment that's supposed to be revolutionary. Maybe they can help you, if you let them."

"Yeah," Caprice encouraged. Beside her, Tenley nodded

"You're staying." Her dad crossed his arms, typically plain-speaking. "Because you're not getting another dime from your trust fund until you do. And that's a promise."

What? Instantly outraged, Marisol leaped to her feet. It was bad enough that her father was in charge of her income until she turned thirty-five—a provision laid down by her overly cautious grandfather. Now he was cutting her off completely?

"You can't do that."

"I can," her father said, "and I will."

Even Jamie nodded in agreement. Feeling betrayed, Marisol averted her gaze, only to catch sight of that double crossing staffer rifling through her handbag.

"Contraband." He held up her aspirin with a disapproving sniff. "We'll have to confiscate this," he informed the desk.

"What, my aspirin?" Marisol swiveled to see. "My Splenda packets too? You can't be serious." Without her favorite go-to sweetener, she'd pack on five pounds overnight, for sure. "What kind of sick place is this?"

"It's the kind of place that can help you," Jamie said gently. "It comes very highly recommended. At Dzeel, they treat addictions of all kinds, from shopping to drugs to Internet porn. It started as a treatment center for athletes with painkiller addictions, but since then it's expanded to—"

"Hmph," Marisol said. "Internet porn, huh? Nice wholesome niche they'd got going here. I should fit right in."

Jamie closed her mouth. Her grasp went limp on the brochure she'd picked up from somewhere. An awkward silence descended.

She could wait them out, Marisol decided. Surely her need to avoid this place overrode their plans to leave her here.

"This is for the best," Caprice urged. "You need help."

"If I do, so do you!" Marisol snapped. "I wasn't the only one buying multiples of those cute skirts at Lisa Kline."

"It won't be that bad," Tenley coaxed, not the least bit chagrined by her own participation in that particular shopathon. "Everybody could use a little *dzeel* now and then, right?"

Dzeel. Strength, Marisol remembered. She stared at the accusing faces of her family and friends, still unable to believe it had all come down to this. A shopping intervention. A total cash-and-credit cutoff. And a killer hangover, all at once. Talk about your bad days . . .

Well, if she was going to prove them wrong about her, she'd need plenty of *dzeel*—plenty of strength. Because they were wrong about her, Marisol swore. She didn't need shopaholic rehab—whatever that entailed. She needed boutique-to-home delivery service to avoid messes like this one. Then no one would have found those shopping bags, and no one would have been the wiser to her latest spree.

She hesitated, still looking for a way out. She was Marisol Winston, darn it! She didn't have to put up with this.

Jamie reached out to smooth a stray lock of hair from Marisol's face, exactly the way she had all those years ago—all those times when Marisol had needed her.

"Try it for me?" her stepmother asked.

For Marisol, that was all it took.

"Okay." She sighed. "I'll do it."

Chapter 3

Three weeks later

"All right, everyone." Imelda Santos bustled into the Wednesday morning therapy session with a bulging paper grocery sack clasped to her chest—a sack so large it almost obscured the *Dzeel Oniomania Counselor* badge pinned to her chest. Imelda beamed at Marisol and her fellow rehabees with unyielding good cheer. "Welcome and good morning! How is everyone today?"

Murmured replies echoed around the circle of chairs.

"Good. Excellent. Today we'll be learning about cues." Imelda shifted her sack. "You might remember from our Tuesday afternoon session that cues are the precursors to all disordered shopping behaviors. An important part of your recovery will be learning to recognize and resist your own personal cues."

Marisol slumped in her chair and yawned, wishing she could recognize and resist a billowy feather mattress and 800-thread-count sheets. Despite her hopes, the beds at Dzeel were hardly five-star-resort worthy, even though she'd coaxed one of the maids into giving her two additional mattress pads. The favor had cost her one of her favorite white skirts—an Alice Roi original packed into

Lisa Plumley

her luggage by Jamie on the day of her shopping intervention—and she still hadn't decided if the loss had
been worth it.

Probably not. That skirt had been really cute. But thirty-
one-year-old heiresses should not be plagued with back-
aches like the ones she'd suffered during her first few
nights here. Even after retrofitting her mattress, Marisol
would've paid a hefty chunk of her fortune for a professional massage. She would have even treated all rehabees
in her group while she was at it.

Unfortunately, massages weren't allowed at Dzeel. Neither was treating anyone. Aside from which, her father
had flatly refused to authorize any trust-fund transfers—
exactly as threatened—until she completed shopping
rehab.

Period. Finito. End of story.

It was so unfair. Without access to her trust fund,
Marisol couldn't go back to her old life or try to start a
new one. She was stuck. She'd decided that she'd just
have to grit her teeth and get through this idiotic shopaholic therapy. It had begun with phase one (counseling
and workshops) and would be followed with phase two
(job placement assignments).

Ugh. The sooner—and more successfully—she finished, though, the sooner she'd be back to her own
normal, footloose-and-fancy-free life. No matter how far
away it seemed right now.

As a result . . . another mind-numbing counseling session.

At the front of the sunlit room, Imelda cleared her
throat. She regarded her group members with a smile,
obviously thrilled by whatever was inside her rumpled
Shoparama grocery sack.

Sunglasses on, Marisol rolled her eyes. She still hadn't
quite forgiven Imelda for keeping her here after their initial evaluation meeting—or for refusing the impromptu

gift of one of Marisol's nicest pair of chandelier earrings two days later.

They hadn't been a bribe to get out of "sessions," damn it.

"The only way to learn resistance is to practice it in a calm and safe environment." Imelda said everything in pseudosoothing counselor-style tones. "To learn to tolerate negative feelings, stop seeking approval, and develop alternative behaviors that will help you resist the urge to shop excessively. Strategy is the key to success."

Marisol examined her manicure. This whole thing was so booooring. Sure, she shopped a lot. Sure, she enjoyed it. Sure, she spent plenty. But she was a bona fide heiress—she could afford it. Shopping didn't hurt anyone. And if a few splurges now and then meant she was some kind of cuckoo . . . well, in that case there were a whole lot of high-living crazies in the world.

The plain truth was, after too many sessions and workshops and tests and exercises to count, Marisol hadn't recognized herself in any of the descriptions of oniomania—compulsive shopping—and she didn't think she ever would.

"Before we begin with today's exercise," Imelda droned on, "let's have everyone turn in their spending journals. Okay?"

As if that were optional. Ha! Marisol handed her notebook to the woman next to her in the circle. Everyone else did the same, first-grade style, until the last woman placed the pile on the designated table. Marisol's journal lay right on top. She'd tried to use one of her favorite Kate Spade agendas at first, a stroke of motivational genius that had been soundly refused.

Now her spending journal was identical to everyone else's—and probably contained similar entries too. Dzeel offered three minuscule on-site stores from which rehabees were allowed to purchase necessities—their snacks, toiletries, and other items. Payments were on a voucher basis now. They'd switch to a strict cash-only system halfway through the on-site treatment program, then to an expanded credit-inclusive payment scheme during the work placement phase of the program. It was a series of tests, really. Every week, the counselors scrutinized the journals and brought up their contents in sessions.

Marisol found the whole process demeaning. Being grilled on shampoo and snack-size Doritos purchases? Please. Judging by the resigned looks of the other six women in her shopping disorders therapy group, they felt the same way. The women here varied in age from nineteen to sixty-three, she'd learned. Some had checked themselves into Dzeel; others, like Marisol, had been ambushed into the facility.

"Everyone," Imelda announced, "brace yourselves."

She upended her grocery sack. Its contents spilled to the center of the therapy circle in a jumble of color and pattern. The scent of hand-finished leather filled the air. Gold and brass fittings gleamed; imported Italian silk jacquard contrasted with woven metallic leather and dyed snakeskin.

"Oh my word! It's handbags," breathed Georgia, a blond coed from South Carolina. "Dozens of handbags!"

Other murmurs went up. A few women shifted nervously in their seats. Several averted their eyes. One wrung her hands.

"For this exercise, we're each going to choose a handbag." Imelda gestured to the pile. "Go ahead, ladies. Don't be shy." Then, in a slightly firmer tone: "You too, Marisol."

"No, thanks. I already have tons of handbags."

"Possessions are irrelevant. This is about recovery."

Marisol made a face. "If that were true, my trunk full of shopping bags wouldn't have landed me here."

"Hmmm. Still feeling feisty, are we?" Imelda met her gaze with a nonconfrontational, yet completely no-nonsense stare. A stare like that one would have been pretty useful when negotiating with her dad for a bigger trust fund allowance. "Please don't keep everyone waiting."

"Fine." Barely looking, Marisol snatched a handbag. The moment its buttery Venetian leather met her fingertips, she felt her resolve slip. Just a little bit. Oh cripes.

"Now then. Let's begin." Imelda strode around the circle, making sure everyone held a bag. She nodded. "Place your handbag on your lap, please. Now clasp it. Lightly!"

Everyone complied. Marisol pretended she held something utterly ordinary—a newspaper, for instance. The weight of her make-believe newspaper barely made a dent atop her thighs. Feeling more assured, she waited for Imelda's next instruction.

"Bobbi, you only need one bag for this exercise. Please put the other one back in the pile. Thank you." Imelda clasped her hands as she trod around the circle. "Lynda, open your eyes."

The woman next to Marisol gave a soft groan. She focused her gaze on the handbag on her lap. Everyone else followed suit.

"For many women, handbags are a particular object of compulsion," Imelda explained. "They're feminine, appealing, and variable. They come in a range of prices. They feel like an essential. But for you—starting now—they are not essential."

The only sounds were the shuffling of nervous feet and the occasional throat clearing. Sunlight filled the room, hot and bright, leaving Marisol feeling bizarrely exposed.

"Take a deep breath. Focus all your attention on your handbag of choice. Really see it." Imelda padded past Marisol, leaving a trail of antiseptic scent. "Touch it. Is it soft? Or structured? Natural or colored? How do the straps feel?"

"Like I want to wear it!" shouted a homemaker from Topeka.

"We won't be wearing these handbags. Take your time, Rhonda. Change doesn't happen overnight." Gently, Imelda touched her shoulder. "Marisol, you're not paying attention. You don't like the bag you chose? Feel free to select another one."

"This one is okay."

"Are you sure? You should have one you really like."

Something in Imelda's tone—something teasing and secret—suddenly seemed to promise more. Were they going to be able to keep these bags? Maybe there was an upside to therapy after all!

Excitedly, Marisol glanced at her chosen handbag. Oh God. That was a mistake. The buckles were adorable, all hard-edged and rocker-chic against the sleek leather. So cute! That bag would make a perfect gift for Caprice's birthday next month. Marisol had already scouted out a really fantastic spa package for her friend, and an adorable Missoni scarf, but if she added this bag to her gift, it would be so much better. Yes!

No. *Newspaper, newspaper,* Marisol reminded herself sternly. *It's a newspaper. An uninteresting, recyclable newspaper.*

"Everyone, focus in on your handbag. Do you want it?" Imelda's voice seemed hypnotic. All six women nodded.

Marisol dared herself to confront her handbag again.

Mmmm. The workmanship was superb. The leather felt supple, the finish perfect, the buckles cool against her fingertips. She imagined the handbag's heft, pictured the tasteful designer box and protective drawstring bag it would come in. In her mind's eye, Marisol could already see that handbag boxed and nestled in a shopping bag—could see herself having it gift wrapped.

"*Feel* that wanting," Imelda urged in a husky voice. "*Commit* to it. Let yourself indulge in *wanting* that handbag. Go ahead—want it. Really want it. Smell it. Touch it. *Need* it."

Marisol raised her brows. This session was veering into handbag porn, but she didn't really care. She wanted that bag! She needed it. The gifts she'd already gotten for Caprice's birthday would never be enough. She realized that now.

"Now . . ." Imelda stopped beside Marisol again. Something crinkled. Her grocery sack. "Let go of your handbag."

"Huh?" Marisol blurted. She had to be kidding. After all that wanting? All that needing? All that seductiveness?

"Let it go." Imelda waggled the sack. "Put it in here."

"But I want it." Marisol hugged her handbag. "I need it!"

"You can't keep it. You're practicing resistance to an important cue—desiring something without needing to possess it. That's what we're learning today, everyone." Imelda nodded at the women in the circle. "This is a healing step."

It was a dirty trick. That's what it was. Feeling bamboozled, Marisol bit her lip. She'd been doing so well! She'd wanted. She'd needed. She'd smelled and touched. She'd actually thought she was making progress—at long last—with something her counselor expected. Crushingly now . . . she wasn't.

Five women's gazes swiveled to center on her.

Imelda smiled encouragingly. "You can do it. Go ahead."

Marisol wanted to. She really did. Hey, maybe it would help spring her from this place faster. Or maybe, at the very least, she could set a shining example for the other rehabees.

But then she'd never been very good at being selfless, had she? Just ask anyone. Innocently, Marisol widened her eyes. She pointed out the window. "Hey, is that Jake Gyllenhaal?"

Everyone looked, including Imelda.

Marisol clutched her handbag and bolted for the door.

Jeremy Fordham, Dzeel's residential program director, steepled his hands. He looked at Marisol, then shook his head.

"Miss Winston, this behavior really has to stop."

Marisol slumped in her chair, feeling like the school delinquent being hauled to the principal's office. It was a new experience for her. Usually no one gainsaid a Winston—or imposed many rules on them. "I offered to pay for the handbag. It's not my fault your security didn't catch me until I reached the gate. I have an excellent personal trainer."

Fordham sighed. "Your fitness level is beside the point."

"Don't tell that to Bjorn. He'd be crushed."

The program director wasn't amused. Maybe he'd had a tragic Pilates accident and still had a grudge against personal trainers. After all, the man was built like a string bean. A glasses-wearing, sober-looking, possibly organic string bean.

"Miss Winston, let me explain something to you." Again with the grave look. "While developing our treatment program here at Dzeel, we've learned that some people simply don't respond well to clinical intervention. Often those people perform best in the more interactive work-placement component of our program. For your sake, I certainly hope you're one of them."

Well, that didn't seem plausible, did it? She was as likely to excel at an actual job as she was to start wearing discount denim culottes and highlighting her own hair.

Marisol smiled serenely. "I hope so too. As a matter of fact, I've been meaning to talk with you about that work placement thing." She arranged her hands identically to his, hoping to achieve a matching gravitas that would advance her cause. "When it comes to my placement, I'll need a special assignment, please. Something that isn't too taxing. I know we're supposed to learn real-world coping skills to help with our treatment, but . . ." She wrinkled her nose in thought. "Do you have any positions in Antigua? I'm very good with beaches."

"This is not a vacation, Miss Winston. Not even for you."

Not even for you. Ugh. She hated that phrase.

"Yours is going to be a trying case as it is." Fordham flipped open a file—undoubtedly hers—then consulted the chart inside. "As it happens, you're psychologically and socially sound. Well adjusted. Friendly. Talkative and actually quite intelligent—"

"Try not to sound so surprised."

"But you're uncooperative in treatment, and your practical skills, if you can call them that, are meager at best."

"I'm excellent at scoring the perfect stilettos."

"Your skills don't quite lend themselves to practicing real-world coping ability in a job placement situation—"

"I can max out my Platinum Visa like nobody's business."

"—yet here at Dzeel we don't believe in giving up."

"Um, partying till dawn is a skill. Most people get tired by two or three A.M. I could be an events coordinator!"

Fordham gazed out his office window, beyond which lay a bucolic view of pine trees. A vein in his temple throbbed. "I'm afraid there isn't a great demand for that around here."

"That's what *you* say. Everybody likes parties."

"Miss Winston, I'd suggest you take this treatment more seriously." Fordham's expression gentled a bit.

"Resistance is not atypical. But as things stand right now . . . you're failing."

Marisol couldn't accept that. "Wow, somebody needs treatment for chronic pessimism." She offered up her most winning smile. Usually she could cajole people out of moods like this one. "Are you having a bad day, Dr. Buzzkill? You know, you really should get a masseuse in here. A professional. It could help you. And others. Staff. Rehabees . . ."

His stare could have frozen a triple espresso.

"Okay. I can see that you're more of an acupuncture guy. I'm sorry. Forget I said anything." Marisol held up her hands in surrender, then searched the office for a diversion. Clearly it was time for a little damage control.

Her gaze landed on the framed photographs lining Fordham's office credenza. One of them featured a shot of Fordham with a burly football player. Both men grinned for the camera, but the football player had special charisma. They appeared to be at a ribbon-cutting ceremony. As a Winston, Marisol had participated in more than her share of those.

"Are you a sports fan, Mr. Fordham? I could probably arrange for season tickets to the sport of your choice, if—"

"No, thank you."

"It would be my treat. Really, it's no trouble."

Fordham eyed her. "That's more than we can say for you."

Stung, Marisol looked away. She rubbed her thumbnail along the arm of her chair, examining its unraveling tweed, until she felt sturdier. "You know, Mr. Fordham, I'd be happy to arrange for new office furniture for you. Something to replace these Jonathan Adler knockoffs. I happen to know a number of artisans and antique dealers on a personal basis. They're friends of mine. It would only take one little phone call."

The program director nudged his phone out of reach. "Your father warned me you might try a bribe like this."

Oh God. She preferred to think of her offer as a favor, but still . . . Had her father thought of everything to keep her here? Warning the program director about her? In advance? What kind of head case did he think she was, anyway?

Unwilling to admit defeat, Marisol directed an unswerving gaze at Fordham. "Listen, what's it going to take for us to come to terms? I want to leave here. You want me gone. It should be easy-peasy, right? So come on, Jeremy. Help a girl out. Tell me how we can make a deal."

His answering stare made her feel downright naked. In the right circumstances, that sometimes worked . . . but Marisol wasn't that kind of girl. All she wanted from him was a bargain. An honest bargain that would give her her life back. Her good-time life of partying, shopping, and perfecting her luxury surroundings—one Karl Springer or Tommi Parzinger original at a time.

Fordham sighed. "Try actually believing in this treatment."

Marisol made a face. He really was Dr. Buzzkill. In a single sentence, he'd reduced her successful negotiating percentage—earned the hard way through hours of dickering with dealers and suppliers and retail clerks— to the pathetic range.

"Try actually giving this program an honest effort." Fordham closed her file, then stood. "Try doing your best."

Oh boy. Had he honestly had to go there?

"Then we're really in trouble." Marisol stood too. "Because my best has *never* been good enough for anybody. I can't believe my father didn't tell you that."

Without another word, she raised her chin and sashayed away.

Chapter 4

The wide, fluorescently lit aisles of Phoenix's newest Shoparama grocery store were ready—stocked and swept and clean. The staff was ready—checkers and carryouts and managers—and the in-store bakery crew had even whipped up a special cake. The PA system was ready, booming out announcements of the upcoming event every fifteen minutes. The main attraction, however—he damned well wasn't ready, and he didn't think he ever would be.

"Grocery store openings?" Cash Connelly confronted his personal manager and sports agent, Adam Sullivan, standing toe-to-toe with the man who'd seen him through draft days, game days, play-offs and practices. Plus two Super Bowl appearances. "How the hell does it all come down to grocery store openings?"

Adam straightened his tie. "Ask your ex-wife."

Cash leveled him with a look. "Fuck off."

"Hey, you asked. Don't shoot the messenger." Adam buffed his shoe on his pant leg, then checked his hair. "I'm making the best of the situation. I suggest you do too."

Cash offered another glare, then turned away. Filled with pent-up energy, he paced the length of the cold storeroom they'd been directed to wait in until it was time for his appearance. He clenched his fists. Unclenched them. Loosened his shoulders.

He confronted Adam again. "You're supposed to handle things like this."

"You're supposed to be a superstar. Guess we both suck."

Cash consulted his watch. "Screw waiting. I'm going out there."

He made it past a forklift full of toilet paper packages before Adam smacked him in the chest, stopping him. At six three and two hundred and twenty pounds, his manager had the muscle to back up his actions. He also had the nerve. Most men avoided hitting Cash unless they were on the field.

"I'd forgotten what an asshole you can be before a game."

"This. Isn't. A. Game. You dickhead."

Adam sighed. "It's still a game. Like it or not."

Cash didn't like it. He didn't have to say so.

"Look, don't blow this." Adam gave his shoulder a squeeze, half commiseration and half warning. "You've got enough problems as it is. Remember, this is the first step to the rest of—"

"Yeah, yeah. Whatever. You've got to lay off the self-help stuff." Cash shrugged off his hold. The last thing he wanted was to have a long, crybaby conversation about the events that had landed him here. In the local Shoparama, waiting to make a bunch of housewives very, *very* happy. "Maybe you forgot. It's Friday."

Adam's answering look, filled with something Cash refused to recognize as pity, let him know his longtime friend hadn't forgotten anything.

His manager held up his palm. "Hang tight. I'll go see if I can shake something loose."

"If you don't, I will." Cash didn't tolerate lateness—or less than one-hundred percent effort—in himself or others.

Adam peeked out the door, then left. Wimp. Was he afraid the produce manager would bean him with a cantaloupe?

Left alone in the storeroom, Cash paced faster. Jesus. A freaking grocery store opening? When he'd retired from the NFL two years ago, it sure as hell hadn't been to make personal appearances with rutabagas and yogurt. He'd planned on bigger and better things. More important things. Things that *mattered*.

Now look at him. Stuck in the back of the Shoparama like yesterday's Wonder bread.

He had to trust Adam to do his job, Cash reminded himself, dredging up some of the discipline he'd relied on during his football career. He forced himself into a patient posture, knowing that he had to give Adam some time. They were a team. Each of them had his assigned roles. Cash didn't have to carry the entire load on his shoulders this time.

On the other hand, trust had come a whole lot easier before the upcoming season's free agency signing period had come and gone at the end of April. And trotting out this dog-and-pony show had felt a whole lot more doable before he'd realized it fell on a Friday. Damn it.

Beyond the storeroom doorway, a PA system whined. The manager began a long windup to the store's grand opening event, talking about the Shoparama chain in general, the Phoenix location in particular, and something called e-coupons.

Apparently Adam had made something happen.

Cash's foot twitched. So much for his patient posture. He shook the tension from his shoulders instead.

"And now, direct from the NFL," came the manager's voice, "I'm proud to announce our special guest. He's a Heisman trophy winner, a five-time Pro Bowler, and a two-time Super Bowl player. He's the man with the golden hands—"

Inside the storeroom, Cash groaned. He hated that phrase.

"—the man with the plan—"

Damn. They'd left no cliché untouched.

"—the man who led the Phoenix Scorpions to their first NFC championship since the team began—"

Christ. He was going to hurl. Barking at his shoes had been a pregame locker-room ritual for Cash since his days at USC, but he hadn't expected it to follow him to a civilian event.

"—the man who is going to sign autographs—"

Eager squeals rose from the housewives.

"—and chitchat for a while with our Shoparama guests—"

Oh screw it. Cash yanked open the door before the manager could promise he would kiss babies and go tampon shopping too.

"—retired but not forgotten, please welcome—"

The announcement faded as Cash stepped into a glare of bright lights, streamers, balloons, and screaming. Dozens of cameras clicked; video phones recorded his every move along the roped-off path the Shoparama management had erected for him.

Cash forced a smile, still walking. He waved. Faces jogged into view as the crowd shoved closer. Men grinned as he passed, some hooting "Scoooorpions!" in booming voices. Women clutched his jersey—his old jersey, number seven. They yanked his hair. Someone grabbed his ass, fingers gouging his jeans.

"Leave a little bit for the next gal, sweetheart," Cash cautioned, throwing out a trademark wink. The women giggled.

Someone else hurled him a pass. Cash caught the football automatically, then tossed it into the crowd. A near stampede ensued as everyone tried to make the catch. Holy shit. If Tyrell, his wide receiver, had been that eager for a pass, Cash's entire final season with the team might have been a lot different.

He stepped onto the packing-crate platform and leaned toward the microphone. "How's everyone doing today?"

More shrieking. A woman in the back jabbed her CASH CONNELLY 4EVER sign higher, endangering a pyramid display of Hormel chili. Her friend noticed him looking and blew a kiss. Then she reached for the hem of her pink polo shirt. Oh hell. Cash knew what came next. This was *not* the venue for a tittie autographing.

He caught Adam's eye. Nodded toward the flasher. Then, confident his manager would handle everything as usual, Cash launched into the rest of his spiel, pissed at himself for having developed an actual patter for a grocery store grand opening.

Adam hustled to the woman—out of long practice chivalrously ignoring her baby blue lace bra, now visible about three-quarters of an inch from the band up—and whispered something to her. She nodded, beaming from ear to ear.

"Thank you all for coming out. It's good to be here." Cash removed the mic from its stand, then headed toward the crowd behind their taped barrier. Both security guards gave him death looks. "The Shoparama security will probably tackle me for this, but since you people were so good to come out here today, I want to meet as many of you as I can before we get started."

Eagerly, the whole crowd shoved nearer. Cash reached the edge and started shaking hands with people. Men laughed like boys. Women blushed like girls. Standing near the store manager, Adam pursed his lips like a constipated tax accountant.

"You know, I live in Phoenix myself." Reaching the end of the line, finished with his initial meet and greet, Cash took up where he'd left off. He aimed his ESPN-ready grin at the crowd. "So I shop here too. After all, a man's got to eat."

Squeals of approval. Offers to feed him. Laughter.

Except from the store manager and Adam. Both of them gave Cash distinctly menacing looks. The manager pantomimed speaking, giving him the *keep going* arm twirl and a nervous grin.

Knowing exactly what they wanted, Cash stalled. He might be easy, but he wasn't sleazy. And he wouldn't be pushed around either. If not for everything that had happened since his divorce, he wouldn't even be here.

But so far, this was just people. He liked people. They usually liked him. Remembering that, he took his time bantering with the crowd. For a few minutes, he actually forgot his script.

Adam's pleading expression finally bored through.

"But all that aside, there's still no place I'd rather buy my groceries than Shoparama." Cash gritted his teeth in a pseudosmile, gesturing toward the waiting aisles. "So take those shopping carts and fill them up the Cash Connelly way . . . all the way to the top!"

The crowd cheered. The store manager practically pulled out his wallet on the spot. Adam offered a double thumbs up.

Cash only took a deep breath and gave the audience more of what they wanted. Him. Or at least the man they thought he was.

He'd finally sold his damned soul. It was official. And it wasn't even to win at football. It was just to survive.

"That was a fucking joke." Cash snarled the words as he and Adam strode through the parking lot after his Shoparama personal appearance. "Housewives? Retirees? Coupon clippers?" He hurled his Sharpie into the nearest trash bin, disgusted with himself for using it. For caving in. For knuckling under. For selling out. "Next I'll be doing ribbon cuttings at garage sales. Christ, Adam!"

"Look. I know how desperate you are—"

Cash stomped onward. "You don't know anything."

Adam jogged to keep up. "I know that last woman was pretty happy to see you." He jabbed his elbow sideways. "Right?"

"The one with the blue bra? In the storeroom?" Cash frowned at Adam's waggling eyebrows and hound dog look. "I'm not sure she was as thrilled as *you* were, pal."

His manager sighed. "I miss the good old days. When the baby blue bras were lined up as far as a man could see—"

Cash stopped him. "I can't believe you promised her I'd 'do her' in the storeroom. She almost cried when I stopped beside that pallet and whipped out a pen instead of my dick."

"I was *talking* about autographing her. In whatever area she chose." Adam grinned. "Not getting busy on top of the Charmin. Any reasonable woman would have realized that. She was caught up in the excitement of meeting a real live star quarterback for the first time. Of meeting the famous, underwear-modeling—"

"Bite me, you perv." Digging out the keys to his Range Rover, Cash realized his hands were shaking. "I was demoing goddamned Fruit Roll-Ups in between autographs. Fruit Roll-Ups!" He wrenched open the driver's side door, then yanked off his number-seven jersey and threw it inside. It landed in a crumpled heap. He stared at his manager. "You've got to do better."

"Those people *loved* seeing you," Adam insisted. "Even you must have realized that. They couldn't get enough. Men, women, little kids—everybody. You've still got it, Cash!"

Cash shook his head. "Don't say that to me."

"—and soon enough, another team is going to want it. They're going to want *you.* I've got feelers out to Seattle,

San Diego, and Baltimore. If you'd been willing to take that offer from the Eagles—"

"You know I can't move to Philly."

"—you wouldn't be here right now. Come on. Trust me."

Rather than admit he couldn't—not the way he used to—Cash slid inside his Range Rover. Silently. Stubbornly.

"Things will happen," Adam said, "It'll just take time."

Time. As if he had tons of that. Scowling, Cash locked his hands on the steering wheel. Feeling them tingle an instant later, Cash deliberately eased his grip. He had to take care of those "golden hands," didn't he?

There was still a chance he could score a spot in the NFL again. He refused to admit there wasn't. It was still months before the preseason started.

He stared straight ahead. "What about Ed?"

At his mention of the Scorpions' head coach, Adam hesitated. For a good ten seconds, the only sounds were the passing traffic, the chattering of nearby shoppers, and the sigh of the Range Rover's leather interior as it fought a losing battle with the hundred-degree June afternoon.

"I'm still waiting on Ed. The Scorpions drafted that rookie from Miami State—Johnson—and they've still got backups. The way you left . . ." Adam gave a gusty sigh. "Things move on."

"Just make it happen. Soon. You know what's riding on it," Cash said. "I'm out of here."

"I'll do my best. You know that."

Jaw clenched, Cash nodded. But even as he peeled away from the parking lot, technically leaving the whole debacle behind him, he couldn't quite shake the sight that lingered with him. The sight of his manager—his friend—standing there on that new striped asphalt. Standing alone. One big man. One huge job.

One gigantic screw up just waiting to happen.

Again. Just like Cash.

Chapter 5

Rush hour was a bitch. It took forever to fight traffic across town. By the time Cash drove up into the foothills, pushing the speed limit around elegant curves and past multimillion-dollar houses, the whole Valley of the Sun lay shadowed in deep blue below him.

As he parked and pocketed his keys, the only brightness left was a vivid slash of orange cutting across the mountains. In the big bowl in between, streetlights and porch lights and lighted houses studded the dusk like stars.

He took big strides up the walkway, his gut tightening with each step. His head felt strange. His hands too. He didn't believe in psychological mumbo jumbo or New Age bullshit, but something about approaching his former house hit him like a 350-pound defensive tackle with a grudge against QBs and a bad case of mean. Maybe it was because he didn't live in that house anymore.

His ex-wife did. With her new boy toy.

Stephanie opened the door before he could raise a hand to knock. Outfitted in a cocktail dress and lip gloss, she no longer had the ability to make him want her. But she did have a serious knack for making him feel like crap. Still.

She stood on the threshold. "You're late."

Cash nodded in greeting. "Are they ready?"

"For the past half hour."

Stephanie turned slightly to look inside, offering a view of his former foyer. The custom-made chandelier in its center cast sparkles onto the imported tile she'd been so eager to install. He'd felt like a hero for getting it for her, years ago now.

A shadow passed in the living room. Her new man.

Deliberately, Cash turned his gaze to the grounds outside. Landscaping them had cost a bundle. More than one lost weekend during the off-season too. He inhaled a tangy, creosote-scented breath. "You want to tell them I'm here? I'll wait."

"You don't want to come inside?" A pause. "Okay. Have it your way. You usually do." Stephanie stepped away, then came back. Her fingers touched his. "Hey, did you get a call? We were in Orlando when the free agency signing period passed, and I've been meaning to ask ever since. It's just so crazy around here. You know."

Against his better judgment, her softhearted expression got to him. It reminded him of better days and loosened his tongue when he would ordinarily have shut the hell up. "Not yet."

She sighed. Pursed her lips. Gave him a pitying glance that made Cash wish he'd remembered to guard his back.

"Well, if you do get called up, let me know, okay?" Stephanie glanced over her shoulder, then leaned closer. "Since Tyrell is franchise player this year, we were thinking of going to Venice after offensive mini camps are finished. He's always wanted to ride in a gondola, I guess. Isn't that cute? And since we'll be traveling anyway, we thought you could take a little extra time with—"

"Dad! Dad! You're here!"

The shouts interrupted her. Three pairs of stamp-

eding feet hurried to the foyer. The door slapped open
wider, startling Stephanie and throwing her off balance.
She glanced down, saw what the ruckus was, then surrendered to the inevitable.

"Have a good time, kids," she said as she got her high-
heeled feet beneath her again. "See you on Sunday."

Smooches all around. Gathering of backpacks, toys,
snacks, and suitcases. Last-minute hunts for stuffed animals. Mild bedlam, even as Cash dropped to his knees
on the porch.

He caught all three of his children in a giant bear hug.
They squirmed and squealed and giggled like no one
but six-year-olds could, talking over each other and
squeezing him back.

"Dad! Dad! I got my face painted with a flower. See?"

"Look, Dad. I can do a karate kick just like Superman!"

"Why were you late, Daddy? We waited and waited
for*ever*!"

Emily, Jacob, and Hannah. All of them born on the
same day, but each completely unique. They were love in
pint sizes, a three-part blitz on his unprotected heart.

Wrapped in their embrace, still on his knees, Cash felt
his breath leave him. He waited for this moment all week.
Every time, a part of him expected it not to be there for
him anymore. For *them* not to be there anymore.

"Listen, about next month—" Stephanie began again.

"Whatever you want." Cash looked over his children's
heads at her. "I'll do it. Just say the word."

His ex-wife looked surprised. Cash couldn't imagine
why.

He wasn't the kind of man to wonder about it either.

He said good-bye to her, avoiding another glance
toward that indistinct figure inside, then hustled the kids
to his Range Rover. It was going to take eons to get them
loaded up with all their gear, but Cash didn't mind. The
good part of his day had finally gotten here. He would

have signed a thousand autographs, demoed a million Fruit Roll-Ups, to make it happen.

He pulled a handful of leftover Roll-Ups from the console and tossed them into the backseat. Giggles erupted as Jacob, Hannah, and Emily grabbed the packages from the air.

"Hang on," Cash warned. "Don't open those. Dinner first."

"We already ate dinner!" they chorused.

"Hot dogs!" Jacob elaborated. "With grape jam!"

Cash shuddered. His son was the king of bizarre food combinations.

"And apple slices," Hannah added, distaste clear in her prim little voice. "Ugh. Tyrell makes us eat them. 'Cause Tyrell always says, 'If you—'"

"Well, don't eat all those Fruit Roll-Ups at once," Cash interrupted in a hearty voice. He set the Range Rover in motion. "Because we've got a drive ahead of us tonight. This weekend, I've got a surprise for you."

Two hours later, just outside Flagstaff in northern Arizona, Cash turned onto a bumpy stretch of blacktop. It wound through the darkness into a dense forest of ponderosa pines, then leveled onto an expanse of private property. A two-story log cabin hunkered in the middle of it, its wide porch like a grin against the house. Landscape lights showed off a fenced yard and gnarled oak tree; a porch light cast a welcoming glow.

Cash peered over his shoulder. His kids had crashed about forty miles ago, after a million rounds of "Row, Row, Row Your Boat" and about fifty-nine requests for Fruit Roll-Ups, potty breaks, and juice boxes—not to mention frequent refereeing of squabbles. Now they slumped belted in with their eyes closed, all three of them leaning against the pile of pillows and blankies and stuffed animals on the left like dominos ready to drop. Man, they were cute. Like some kind of miracle.

Leaning his cheek against the seat, he watched them sleep. Just for a second. There was something ridiculously satisfying about looking at them. About seeing their cheeks all flushed, their hair all crazy, their little hands grasping their ratty stuffed animals. The three of them had identical brown sea otters, souvenirs from an aquarium field trip. God only knew how they could tell them apart, but they could.

Jacob mumbled in his sleep. Cash shot into action before anybody caught the big, tough, former football player mooning over his kids. Moving stealthily, he opened the driver's side door and stepped into the night. The dirt scuffed beneath his feet. The mountain air felt chill on his bare arms. The scent of pine filled his nostrils. Keeping his eyes trained on Hannah, Emily, and Jacob, Cash eased open the backseat door.

Nobody moved, not even when he accidentally jammed the door on his thigh and all but collapsed in a fit of silent swearing. Whew.

He pulled Emily into his arms, then grabbed her backpack too, leaving it to dangle from his elbow. Emily snuggled against him, forty-five pounds of sweet-smelling little girl, and went on sleeping. Cash could have probably tossed her in the air like one of the Flying Wallendas without waking her. It was one of the peculiarities of having children, that they trusted so completely. Even in their sleep.

Cash couldn't remember ever trusting anybody that much.

Probably he never had.

The house was exactly the way he remembered it, roomy and comfortable. It was the kind of place where a man could kick off his shoes, grab a beer, and rule the remote. Navajo blankets draped the leather sofa and chairs. A few pieces of southwestern artwork hung on the walls. Fishing poles tangled in a bucket near the kitchen, warring for space with a set of golf clubs and a mop. Cash tiptoed up to the bedroom loft once, twice, three times, until Emily, Hannah, and Jacob were securely tucked in.

Afterward he lingered under the eaves, leaning his shoulder on the doorjamb as he studied his slumbering kids. Coming here with them had been risky—pushy, even. Cash didn't even know if he'd *need* a place near the Scorpions training camp this summer. But if the kids didn't like it here, nothing else mattered.

He hoped they liked it here. Hoped it with an intensity that might have freaked out a lesser man. Because if everything went the way he wanted, this place could be key to his future—and theirs.

If everything went wrong . . . He refused to consider it.

Yawning, Cash tromped downstairs again. There was a lot to do before the weekend officially kicked off. Even as a part time bachelor dad, he'd learned it was better to plan for things. He organized all the toys and snacks for tomorrow, made sure the Cartoon Network was still on cable here in the boonies, turned on SportsCenter, then put his cell phone on the kitchen counter.

His voice mail icon was flashing.

With his heart in his shoes, Cash punched it up.

"Cash, where the hell have you been?" Adam bellowed, as clearly as if he'd been standing there. "Ed called. Johnson tore his biceps during rookie mini camps today."

Ugh. Poor bastard. Even though Cash didn't know that punk Johnson—a second round draft pick out of Miami State—he felt for the guy. An injury like that was a major setback for any player.

"He's questionable for the season," his manager went on. "The Scorps still have McNamara"—Cash's old backup—"but the number two QB spot is yours if you want to fight for it in training camp. Ed's messengering contracts." A pause, loaded with meaning. "Told you so, you asshole."

Cash grinned. *Yours if you want to fight for it.*

Who the hell did Adam think he was talking to? Cash Connelly *lived* to compete. There wasn't anything in the world that would stop him from winning this time.

Because this time, everything he had depended on it.

Chapter 6

With three weeks to go till the start of training camp, Cash entered crunch time on Independence Day. He needed a nanny, and he needed one fast. He'd already been through four promising candidates, and he wasn't sure where he was going to dredge up a fifth. Raking his hand through his hair, he took in the mayhem of his household—the TV blaring cartoons, the snack wrappers, the basketballs and toy fairy wands, then picked up the phone.

Hannah tugged his sleeve, her face solemn. "Daddy, are we in trouble? Me and Emily and Jacob?"

Cash hunkered down. He scrutinized his daughter's worried expression, her chocolate-smudged cheek, her pink tutu worn over her PJs. He shook his head. "Nah. You're not in trouble."

"Because we scared away M'lissa, and she quit."

Melissa. The fourth nanny. Cash had come home after a workout and six mile run today to find her up to her eyeballs in soapsuds and goo after the triplets had decided to machine wash their crayons to "make the colors color better."

"She said we were hooligans." Jacob looked up from his snack of crackers, applesauce, and pickles—all stirred together in a plastic bowl. His little forehead crinkled as he marched his army men across the counter. "What's a hooligan?"

"It's a word grumpy nannies use when they can't do their jobs." Cash rumpled Jacob's hair, then smiled at Hannah. "Don't worry. We'll find somebody even better than Melissa."

Starting . . . now. Hell. Feeling lost, Cash fisted his cell phone. He'd been frankly overjoyed to take custody of the kids during July and August, freeing Stephanie to traipse all over Venice with Tyrell—and allowing *him* to spend extra time with Jacob, Hannah, and Emily. He'd been even happier when Stephanie had hinted that they might rearrange their custody agreement permanently if things went well over the summer.

But with training camp looming and his workout schedule intensifying . . . Nope. None of that mattered. He had to make this work. He *would* make this work. He was a man who made things happen. The man with the plan. This was an opportunity that wouldn't come again. The Scorpions wouldn't give him two second chances. Neither would Stephanie.

Steeling himself, Cash dialed the child care agency.

Ten minutes later, he slammed down the phone.

In front of the TV, Emily jerked. She looked over her shoulder at him, her eyes wide beneath her brown bangs. She was still wearing her nightgown, he noticed. With, for some reason, a pair of purple fuzzy mittens. And *his* sneakers. On her tiny feet, they looked like clown shoes.

Hell. The latest nanny had only bailed out forty-five minutes ago, and already chaos ruled. Cash had to take charge.

He started by pointing up to the loft, commando style. "Go get dressed. All of you! It's eleven thirty."

Hannah took off instantly. "I'm first!"

Her tutu-clad behind disappeared upstairs as she reached the loft. Aside from being the most obedient of the three, Hannah was also the most competitive. Thuds sounded. A door slammed. Satisfied, Cash eyeballed his other two children.

"No fair!" Emily shouted. "You got a head start!"

She ran toward the stairs. Kind of. His size thirteen shoes seriously cut her speed. Clomp. Clomp. Cash plunked his hand on her snarled hair and stopped her. "Leave the shoes."

She pouted. "But I like them. They make my steps big."

"They make *my* steps barefoot."

"So? Your feet are *way* too tough for anything to hurt them." She clasped her hands. "You're like, magic or something."

Cash gaped at her. "Did you just bat your eyelashes?"

"Maybe. Can I keep your shoes if I did?"

God help him. He held out his palm. "Shoes. Gimme."

Nearby, Jacob dunked two army men into his applesauce-cracker pickle goop, oblivious to Cash's command. He was busy making high-pitched "Geronimo!" sounds.

He'd get back to Jacob later. Right now . . .

"Shoes." Cash wiggled his fingers. "Take them off."

Emily wound her hair around her fingers. She did not reach for his contraband shoes as ordered, but wiggled her feet in them instead. She eyeballed him with outrageous sincerity. "You know something? You look very nice in that shirt, Daddy."

Aww. He did?

Wait a minute. He looked down. Sweat-dampened white T-shirt. Running shorts. Hairy legs. Bare feet. Huh? What the hell was going on here? He wasn't sure what to make of his daughter's cherubic grin or her new sweet talk routine. He scanned the coverage, took a read, then made a play to Jacob instead.

He motioned sternly. "Upstairs. Change. Now."

His son groaned, then poked a spoon at his bowl of army men. "We're siiiinking!" he piped up. "Siiiinking." He gave Cash an appalled frown. "Great. Now they're all drownded, Dad."

"Throw them a cracker and get going. Brush your teeth too."

"Okay. But I'm only brushing the ones I chewed with." Wearily, very, *very* slowly—*glacially* slowly—Jacob climbed the stairs to the loft, testing Cash's authority with every step.

"Double-time!" Cash yelled.

Jacob hurried up, his stuffed sea otter bumping along behind him. Upstairs in the loft, another door slammed.

There. Two down. One to go. Cash folded his arms.

"You too—" he began.

At the same time, smacking noises came from hip height.

Emily.

"Mommy does this when she wants Tyrell to do something." Puckered lips. Walleyed fish expression. Kiss, kiss. "It always works. Always. Tyrell gets this funny look, kind of like Pepé Le Pew when he sees a girl skunk. And then he—"

That did it. Fed up, Cash plucked her right out of his shoes. "Say good-bye to the shoes, Princess."

"Good-bye shoes! Whee!"

Emily squealed, giggling as she squirmed against his arm. Leaving his sneakers behind in a stubborn pose on the kitchen floor, he hoisted her over his shoulder and tromped upstairs.

"Daddy! This is *exactly* what Tyrell does to Mommy!"

He'd just *bet* it was. Arrgh. When had he signed up for on-the-spot updates of his ex-wife's love life? However it had happened, Cash wanted out. He wanted out, he wanted a nanny, and he wanted his life back again. Not necessarily in that order.

Especially not after the doorbell rang.

* * *

Steadfastly ignoring the banging and hollering going on in the loft—not to mention the running water—Cash deposited Emily at the top of the stairs, then hurried to the front door. Against all reason, he hoped someone at the child care agency had wised up and sent a replacement nanny. A super nanny. A nanny who wouldn't run at the first sight of goo.

He opened the door. "Hell. You're not Mary Poppins."

"Then we're even." His former mother in law, Leslie, put her hand on her hip. "You're not Tom Selleck."

"Tom Selleck?"

"Handsomest mustache *ever*. Mmm, mmm, mmm." She shook her head and wiggled her hips. "I looove that man. Love him."

"Oh, man." Cash shielded his eyes. "Grandmas Gone Wild."

"Is that the one where the girls take off their tops? Because in the case of Mr. Selleck, I might make an excep—"

"Stop." Cash held up his hand, daring a single peek. Good. No more gyrating. "Quit it before my imagination kicks in."

He opened his arms wide. Leslie laughed and stepped into his embrace, leaving him ridiculously glad to see her, even with the bump-and-grind routine. "Hey, thanks for coming over."

"No problem." Her gaze searched his, earnest beneath her cropped silver hair. "So . . . you got another shot with the Scorpions, huh? It won't be easy. How are you feeling?"

Desperate. For an instant, Cash almost confessed as much.

Fortunately, he was saved from making an ass of himself by the appearance of his oldest friend. Dump was fourteen years old, about two feet high, and sixty-five pounds. He had bad hair, worse breath, and a habit of humping your leg. He was a German shepherd with two gimpy knees, and he was perfect.

Freed from the leash Leslie had been holding, Dump galloped forward. Sort of.

"Hey, boy! How you doin'?" Cash crouched, cooing a greeting in an embarrassingly high-pitched voice. The dog was practically deaf, so talking to Dump required either a megaphone or a willingness to look like a total idiot. "Did ya' miss me? Huh?" Ear scratching. Muzzle grabbing. Petting. "Did ya'?"

Dump wagged almost hard enough to topple over.

"I guess you did!" Cash boomed. "I guess you did!"

Leslie laughed. "A little louder. I'm not sure the neighbors heard you"—she angled her head—"four acres over."

Cash threw her a quelling look. Most grown men cowered before that look. His mother-in-law only laughed harder.

But she was one of the few people, aside from Adam, who knew almost everything and still stuck by him. Also, she'd taken care of his dog while he'd set up everything for his summertime stay here. That earned major points, so he let her get away with it. "Get in here, Dump." He paused. "You too, Leslie."

Three minutes later she was ensconced on the sofa for her usual midweek visit, mostly buried in grandchildren, chatter, and books. "So, where's the latest nanny?" She raised her head expectantly, midway through passing out cherry Life Savers. "Melissa, is it?"

Cash tried to look as deaf as Dump. "Well, it looks like you've got everything settled here." Blinking innocently, he rubbed the shoulder of his threadbare Scorpions T-shirt. "I'm headed for the shower. Back in a minute."

He almost made it. Family room . . . in sight of the kitchen . . . almost to the downstairs master bedroom . . .

"Hang on, mister. I asked you a question."

Cash stopped. Damn it. If word got back to Stephanie

that he couldn't even keep a nanny for more than three days . . .

"M'lissa quit," Hannah informed Leslie piously.

"Uh-huh. She said we're hooligans," Jacob added with gusto.

"Yeah." Emily ratted him out without a qualm. "When Daddy got here and found her packing her stuff, he said a bad word." Her eyes twinkled. "*Loud*. He said—"

"You lost another one?" Leslie gaped. "How? That's four!"

"Uh—" Stalling, Cash frowned at his kids.

"You would *never* say that word, Grandma." Emily snuggled nearer, gazing up from her book with an angelic expression. "You're too pretty and nice to ever say a word like—"

"I'm taking care of it," Cash interrupted before his six-year-old daughter could demonstrate The Naughty Word out loud. So much for stalling. "I already called the agency."

"Yes? And . . . ?"

"And they don't have anybody else to send right now." Technically, the woman at the agency had lectured him on his kids' behavior, then instructed him not to call again. Ever. "This is a small town. There's not a huge demand for nannies around here. I guess most people hire teenagers to babysit."

"Well," Leslie said, "that might not be so bad."

Cash aimed an incredulous glance at her. He indicated Jacob, methodically pulling every book from the shelves for no reason at all. Hannah, attempting to put a sparkly tiara on Dump. Emily, trying on lipsticks cadged from Grandma's purse. "They're triplets. It's a lot of work, even for an adult."

"So hire *three* babysitters. I've been retired here for nine years, give or take a few years serving on your foundation's board. Even I know teenagers are a dime a dozen in Flagstaff."

Annoyed at her breezy tone, Cash folded his arms. He was backed against a wall here. Couldn't she see that? His kids were apparently Nanny Kryptonite. The last four nannies had proved that much. He wasn't enough of a Superman to do it all himself.

"Besides." Leslie squinted at Emily as she helped her apply Day-Glo pink lipstick. "They're not *that* much work."

"Oh yeah? Tell that to the nanny who's probably still scrubbing off the permanent-marker tattoos these three gave her. She looked like a multicolored Maori tribe member."

"But she smelled *really* good when she quit," Emily said.

Right. They'd been scented markers, Cash recalled. "Or explain that to nanny number two," he pointed out. "She's probably still recuperating from her sprained ankle."

"That was an awesome obstacle course!" Jacob's face lit up. "I got really tired dragging all those logs inside though."

"The snake shouldn't have come in with them," Hannah said.

Emily squirted perfume. "Or the skunk either."

Cash raised his eyebrows at Leslie in a "see?" expression. She only waved him off. "So they have a lot of energy. So what? They're too lovable to be too much trouble."

All three kids scrambled over for hugs. Shaking his head, Cash watched them huddle up, clamoring for more Life Savers. The sight of his children, all contentedly munching, perfuming, lipsticking, and reading, gave him an idea. A brilliant idea.

Cash leaned his hip on the sofa. "So . . . why don't *you* do it? Everybody knows grandmas are the best babysitters."

Leslie snorted, then opened another book.

He went on watching her. Patiently. As patiently as he'd ever watched a defensive lineup on the field.

She glanced up. "Oh great. You're serious, aren't you?" An eye roll. "Now I know where Emily gets it from."

He tried to look clueless. "Gets what from?"

"Her penchant for blatant charm." Leslie clapped her hands over Emily's ears. "This little girl could talk the white off of snow and make it happy to melt too, and we both know it. As soon as she learns subtlety . . . wham! There'll be no stopping her."

She moved her hands. Emily grinned. Cash shook his head.

"It's a good idea. The kids love you," he argued. Everything else was beside the point. Especially now that he had a plan. "They'd love to spend more time with you. You've always been great with them, ever since they were babies."

Leslie arched her brows. "Well, God knows Stephanie needed the help back then. One woman, three tiny babies . . ."

She gave a weary sigh, clearly baiting him. Cash refused to bite. The past was over with anyway. Trying to make amends for it had been a debacle, despite his best intentions.

"You won't do it? Okay. I get it. You're busy. You can't help out." He strode to the kitchen peninsula and grabbed the cordless phone. "That's all right. I just remembered—a couple of the Scorpions cheerleaders are sharing a cabin up here near Lake Mary. They'd probably be great nannies. Two's better than one, right? All that enthusiasm. And energy."

"And boobs," Leslie said in an undertone, snatching away the phone with warp speed. "Don't forget those."

Cash gave her his most eager grin. "How could I?"

Groaning, she shook her head. "You can't be serious."

"How did you get over here so fast anyway?" He gazed past her shoulder. "Ah. You gave them your whole purse to work over."

"Who cares?" She didn't so much as glance at the wreckage of her belongings. "You're a Neanderthal. I can't have you hiring bimbos to babysit my precious grandchildren."

"Sure you can. It's easy—just give me my phone back."

Leslie shook her head. "Forget it, pal. Not if you're going to call the hotsy-totsy twins with it."

"Hey. Bambi and Brandi are professionals."

His mother-in-law's face turned red. "That's it! You've had your chance, and you blew it." She jabbed him in the chest with the phone, punctuating every word. "I'm taking over."

Finally. Damn, she was tough.

Cash mustered up a scowl. "Nobody takes over. Not from me."

"Oh yeah? Just watch me."

He did. But he tried not to seem happy about it.

Leslie paraded to the sofa and started scooping up her things. "I'll babysit for now," she announced, "*and* I'll find you a new nanny—*my* kind of nanny—and you'll *like* it!"

"I don't know how you're going to do that." Cash spread his arms in a helpless gesture. "The agency won't send anyone. Teenagers can't handle the job. After everything that's happened"—he didn't have to say what, not with her—"I can't afford to bring in a professional from the city. I'm all out of options. And I'm *not* telling Stephanie I blew it. This summer is my last chance—for everything."

Leslie stopped in midscoop. She stared at him. All at once, her expression softened. Cash had the distinctly uneasy feeling he'd misread the coverage—and stepped right into a trap.

He hooked his thumb toward the bathroom. "I still

need a shower. You'll stay until I'm done, right? The kids need lunch—"

Shaking her head, Leslie stepped nearer. She'd set up Emily, Jacob, and Hannah with more toys, he realized as he glanced behind her. Whew. That meant she was staying awhile.

"Look," Leslie folded her arms, gazing intently up at him. Way up. "Listen. Heck, take dictation, I don't care. Just believe me—you don't have to prove anything this summer. To me or anybody else."

"Right. I know," Cash agreed. "People have been telling me that my whole life, from Pop Warner football to the pros." He met her serious look with one of his own. "It wasn't true before, and it's not true now. I have everything to prove."

Leslie peered at him, probably gauging his sincerity. "No wonder you can't keep a nanny, if you're this bull-headed."

"Don't worry about it." Grinning, he waved her off. "Just find somebody equally stubborn to match."

"It would serve you right if I did, you big galoot."

Sure. As if *that* would happen. He doubted Leslie would even bother to search for a nanny replacement. Not when she could do the job better herself. Satisfied the situation had been handled, Cash leaned sideways, whistling to get the kids' attention. "I'm headed for the shower. No fighting, no nonstop flushing"—he saw Jacob redden guiltily—"and no tying up Grandma. She doesn't want to play *Pirates of the Caribbean* with you."

"Awww," came a trio of disappointed moans.

"And neither did nanny number three. Behave," Cash warned. "Somebody get Dump some Dog Chow too."

He turned, confident the situation was well in hand. He'd only reached the kitchen before a little voice piped up.

"Um, Dad? It looks like Dump already ate lunch."

"My bubble blower!" Hannah cried. "It's all chewed!"

"Ewww." Emily pointed. "Dump urfed on the rug."

"On top of my army men!" Jacob shouted. "Awesome. They'll need a Hummer to get out." He ran to fetch his toy vehicles.

Cash met Leslie's gaze. He hoped she knew what she was getting into. He headed back to the kitchen for the cleanup job.

"No, you go shower." Leslie shooed him away. "I'll do it."

"Nah. Dump's my job," he insisted.

In the end, Cash took care of everything disgusting— much to Jacob's chagrin when he arrived bearing an armload of toy vehicles, including a tow truck, a fire engine, and a dump truck, and learned the rescue operation was already finished.

Cash checked his dog, let Dump outside for a chomp through the grass, then scrutinized Hannah's well-scrubbed bubble blowing set.

"See? If you bend the wand this way, it makes even better bubbles," he told her, demonstrating. "Dump made a new design."

She quit moping. "Cool. Thanks, Dad!"

Cash gave Hannah a hug, then escaped. Mission accomplished. The kids were okay, Dump was okay, and Leslie would take care of babysitting—or she'd find a new nanny. Either way, he had a lot of work to do in the meantime if he was going to get football ready in only three weeks.

Grinning, Cash reached his bedroom and dragged off his shirt. Suddenly the summer looked a whole lot easier to handle—thanks to his quick thinking and a little finesse.

As usual, discipline and strategy were key to everything worthwhile. Cash was just lucky that Leslie understood how important both were to a man like him. Especially now.

Chapter 7

Darn it. Another bump in the road. Marisol frowned, glancing up from her mirrored compact and lip gloss. When she arrived at her work placement assignment, she was going to look like a demented cosmetics counter beauty consultant. But that was better than looking like someone who'd been stuck in shopaholic rehab—sans facialist and hairstylist—for weeks. She tried again.

The Drexel courtesy van lurched sideways, traveling over a country pothole that had to be the size of a disco ball. Bracing herself, Marisol peered out the backseat window. What she saw there made her forget all about looking her best for the second phase of her oniomania treatment program. Instead, she started worrying about becoming an hors d'oeuvre for coyotes. Or worse.

"Excuse me." She leaned toward the gray-haired driver in the front seat. In the rearview mirror, his expression looked stoic. "You must be lost. Do you have a map?"

"Not lost."

"But this can't be right." Marisol gestured outside with her pen of Stila pomegranate lip glaze. "We're in the middle of nowhere. There's nothing but pine trees and dirt out there."

The driver didn't budge. "Not lost."

Marisol shook her head. This was all new to her, and she wasn't exactly wild about the whole idea of phase two (the work-placement program), but still . . .

"My assignment can't possibly be out *here*. The program director and I talked about this. We had an understanding."

This is not a vacation, Miss Winston. Not even for you.

Okay. So maybe she and Jeremy Fordham hadn't reached an understanding as much as they'd suffered a breakdown in negotiations, she decided, remembering their meeting in his office. At Dzeel, for the first time in her life, she'd come up against a situation that she hadn't been able to wiggle her way out of, and it was about to get even worse. She could feel it.

Marisol glanced outside again. Nervously.

More pine trees, almost close enough to slap the Dzeel van's sides. A mountain looming in the distance. A lonesome unmarked road, which couldn't possibly be leading to her work assignment. She was *not* the outdoorsy type. She didn't even like terrace dining. Clearly, it was time to break out the big guns.

"Um . . ." She squinted at the driver's name badge. "Tom? Maybe you didn't realize this, but my work assignment was arranged for by one of the Dzeel board members personally. You probably know her. Leslie Neil?"

Tom steered around a stump in the road, stone-faced.

"Okay. That's fine. I'll just call her up myself. Leslie's supposed to meet me at my assignment anyway. She's probably just running late. I'm sure she can clear up any confusion."

Marisol nudged aside her suitcase and tote bags, then searched her handbag for Leslie's card. She found her cell phone too. "See?" She waggled it at the driver, offering him a chipper grin. She might be down, but she wasn't out for the count. "This will all be settled in a jiffy."

"Don't bother." Tom aimed his grizzled chin down the

road, indicating . . . more trees. And more dirt. "We're almost there."

With the cell phone squashed against her ear, ringing up an obviously unavailable Leslie Neil, Marisol pressed closer. Just in case she'd missed something. She squinted. She took off her sunglasses and squinted again. "I don't see anything."

Tom chuckled. "Just wait. You will."

Oh God. Suddenly his tone sounded downright ominous. Marisol abandoned her phone call. "Um, Tom? Are you working for *Us Weekly*?" This wouldn't be the first time the tabloids had ambushed one of the Winstons. They'd probably love to reveal Marisol's stay at Dzeel, with all the gory details of her group therapy sessions and handbag resistance training. Her pathetic shopping journal would be worth big bucks all on its own. It would probably become an instant book. With a tawdry cover and a foreword by Paris Hilton. "Because if they paid you to set up some kind of photo op, I'll pay you double to avoid it."

She'd assumed that, aside from warning Jeremy Ford Liam and the entire rehab center staff about her potential bribery attempts and overall uselessness, her father would have done something to keep away the media too. Maybe she'd been wrong. She'd misjudged her father before.

Tom didn't take the bait. Sheesh. Did Dzeel give their employees mandatory bribery-resistance training, or what?

More pine trees flashed by. Some of them weren't even green and lush—a few of them looked broken and black. Yikes! It was positively primordial out here. Marisol had thought that being stuck in a hush-hush shopaholic rehab facility in the middle of Nowheresville had been bad. Coming out here was a thousand times worse. And that was nothing compared with what having her stint in Podunk rehab plastered all over the glossies would be like.

More urgently, Marisol dialed Leslie again. This could *not* be her assignment. She was supposed to be acting as a temporary nanny and part-time housekeeper to three adorable children and their football-star single dad— one of the few tasks that Fordham and the Dzeel board had felt she was equipped for, given her extensive network of little Winston relatives. Not to mention her vast experience with maid service. Marisol wasn't exactly thrilled about the nanny/housekeeper combo, but still. Supposed shopaholics couldn't be choosers.

Her assignment did beat some of the alternatives her fellow rehabees had gotten, and she didn't have the skills for much else—especially since Fordham had shot down her fantastic party planner idea. With her back against the wall, Marisol had had to accept this work placement. It might actually be fun to hang out with three cute kids, she figured. They were only six years old—they probably napped a lot. At least that was what Leslie Neil had implied when she'd stepped in to make it happen, just like a rehab fairy godmother.

Tom braked suddenly. The whole van lurched, sending Marisol's suitcase, totes, and handbag crashing to the floor.

"This is it," he announced gruffly.

Marisol peeked. There was no sign of paparazzi. No evidence of electronic news gathering vans from the E! network. No tabloid reporters shoving microphones at the windows. There wasn't anything else either—only dust. Miles and miles of dust, billowing all around the Dzeel van in a choking brown cloud.

No *way*. No way, no way, no way—

Tom met her dismayed gaze in the rearview. "I said, this is it. You might as well get out. I'll be back in two weeks to take you to your next therapy session."

Two weeks? That was a lifetime! She'd be dead from dust inhalation by then. Either that or she'd be grizzly sushi. Neither option appealed to her. Marisol hesitated, feeling an urgent need to straighten her skirt and matching nanny-ready tank top. It didn't even have spaghetti straps, that's how modest it was.

She planned to really ace this work placement, the better to get back to her real life in L.A.—before those runner-up socialites totally replaced her. As it was, things back home appeared to be going on without her in a very alarming way.

She'd been able to reach Caprice and Tenley only twice on the phone. And the one time she'd spoken with her dad, all she'd gotten was a Home Warehouse stock update and a stilted weather report. Only Jamie had stayed in touch reliably during Marisol's stay at Dzeel.

Tom sighed. "I'm not hauling your luggage, if that's what you're waiting for." Impatiently, he gestured outside. "Go on."

It was no use. She couldn't do it. "I can't! It's filthy out there." She gave him a plaintive look via the rearview mirror. "I'm wearing white. It's my signature color."

Tom seemed unmoved. "Look, I've got other places to be."

Marisol tried again. "Do you know how special this skirt is? Parisian women sewed for hours to piece together the laser-cut leather for it. I'm not disrespecting all that work."

Stubbornly, she sat there. Tom could kick her out if he was that eager to get rid of her. Some of the dust had settled, but it still looked ultrarustic out there. Plenty of trees, ten or twenty malls' worth of open space . . . and a rambling two-story log cabin with a traditional fence and a huge oak tree, just visible at the edge of the road.

Hey, there was civilization out here after all! That must be where her work assignment was. There was nothing else around. Apparently not for miles. But even on closer inspection, that house and yard still looked . . . so . . . *naked.* So raw. So untamed.

People who lived like this couldn't possibly relate to an heiress like her. What if they wanted her to chop wood? Grind wheat? Brew coffee all by herself?

"I think I need a new assignment," she blurted.

For the first time, Tom actually turned around in the driver's seat. His gaze—his *compassionate* gaze—met hers squarely. "Don't be afraid. You can do it."

"I'm not afraid." Marisol clutched her handbag. Oh God. *I'm terrified*, she realized. She swallowed hard, then chanced another look at the house. "Do you really think I can do it?"

"Sure. You bossed me around plenty, didn't you?" He grinned, displaying startlingly white teeth for a wizened old guy. "You can probably handle a few little kids."

A few little kids. Tom was privy to her assignment then! She couldn't *believe* he hadn't warned her. Told her to wear combat boots and a bush helmet, at least.

"Well . . . I do like kids," Marisol ventured. "They're cute. And easy to talk to."

Biting her lip, she stared at the house, trying to imagine herself standing on that rough wooden porch. She failed. In her white clothes, she'd look like a blobby bleach spot on a Ralph Lauren bedspread from the American Frontier collection.

"See there?" Tom's smile broadened. "If you like kids, you're halfway to being a good nanny already."

"Do you really think so?"

"Yeah. Why not? I mean, I wouldn't want you to babysit my kids, but from what I hear, this guy's pretty desperate. So—"

"Desperate?"

"Uh, he just needs help with those kids, that's all."

Marisol pictured them—adorable urchins with hand-whittled toys and photo-ready smiles. The image took hold, blossoming into a magazine-style montage. Yes! She could be like Christy Turlington in those perfume ads, frolicking on the beach with her perfect children and their gorgeous male model father.

Really, she liked frolicking as much as the next girl. This would involve trees instead of sand, of course, but the idea was starting to grow on her. If that's all there was to it . . .

She could do it. She had to do it, Marisol decided. For the kids' sakes. They were probably counting on her to bring them some modernity. A glimpse into the twenty-first century. Even six-year-olds from the boonies needed that. Raising her chin, she gathered her things.

Okay. She was ready. Sort of.

"All set?" Tom asked.

"I think so." She scooted across the backseat and grabbed the door handle. It really wouldn't kill him to help her with her luggage. "Here I go. See you in two weeks."

"I'll be here. Bright and early at seven in the morning."

He had to be kidding. "Can I convince you to make it noon?"

Tom laughed. "Always haggling, aren't you?"

It usually worked too. "Well?"

"I might be able to arrange to be late. Eight work?"

"Sure." Marisol smiled at him. Aside from being untalkative and unwilling to haul her bags, he'd been pretty nice. And rules were rules at Dzeel—something she'd loathed about the place. The way she saw it, discipline and structure were seriously overrated. "Thanks, Tom. Thanks for everything."

He saluted her, still grinning. "Good luck."

The van door creaked as she opened it. She stepped onto the dirt outside, instantly smudging her sandals. Her DIY pedicure—her first amateur primping in years—was probably ruined too. But none of that mattered next to the task that lay in front of her.

Making an excellent first impression.

Mustering all the bravery she could, Marisol picked up

her suitcase. She added her handbag and both tote bags. Then she eyed that rambling country house, plastered a smile on her face, and marched toward the gate.

Damn it. He was going to be late again.

Cash punched up Leslie's number on his cell phone, pacing across the cluttered kitchen while he did. He reached his mother-in-law's voice mail.

"Where are you?" he barked into the receiver. "I'm meeting with Ed and the Scorpions' front office in forty-five minutes. It's important. Don't call me back. Just get here."

He snapped his phone shut. Cast an impatient glance at the clock. Jangled the keys to his Range Rover. Across the family room, Hannah, Jacob, and Emily were constructing something elaborate out of Legos. Two-thirds of it was pink; the other third was blue. Peaceful cooperation all around, despite the screaming TV, the scattered stuffed sea otters, and the seventy-nine abandoned water bottles lying around.

Except for his being late, the whole scene was picture perfect, straight out of *Family Harmony Monthly* or something.

It occurred to Cash that he must have been hiring dumbass nannies all along. Otherwise, what the hell was their problem? His kids weren't hellions. They were adorable damned urchins, full of smiles and teamwork. Even though Stephanie sometimes seemed overwhelmed with caring for the three of them, Cash had never had any trouble. Period. On his watch, they were like angels.

Probably that was because he didn't put up with any guff, he decided as he patrolled the family room one more time, still on the lookout for Leslie. The nannies he'd hired so far had all been too wishy-washy. Too undisciplined. Too soft. Clearly, he'd have to make sure the next one—if Leslie ever turned up nanny number five—was different.

In the meantime, he was grateful for Leslie's help, especially on such short notice. Even though training camp hadn't officially kicked off, Cash still had to attend meetings, fit in workouts, and run routes with his receivers, a few of whom had arrived in Flagstaff for early training. He had to get ready. He wasn't twenty-two anymore, full of hotshot arrogance and able to rebound for the season in a heartbeat. At thirty-four, a man had to work harder.

Especially if he was working for his second chance.

And his kids' future.

Making it in the NFL again would kick off a whole new beginning for the four of them. Without his ex-wife around to Hoover up the proceeds, Cash could give Hannah, Emily, and Jacob the life they deserved. He was determined to do it.

Still waiting, he shot a scowl at his gym bag. It stood for every grueling lifting session, every nagging old injury, every single year that separated a veteran player like him from the up-and-comers like Johnson . . . and Tyrell. But it was his chance to come back too—his chance to bankroll enough money to support Jacob, Emily, and Hannah, no matter what happened.

He had to make the most of it. On freaking time.

Aiming another impatient glance at the clock, Cash dialed Leslie again. While he listened to the phone ring, he covered the mouthpiece with his hand. "Hey, turn down the TV, I can't hear a thing."

Obligingly, Jacob hit the remote. The noise didn't quit altogether though. Frantic barking came from outside. Dump had probably found a cat to chase. Being out here—and not cooped up in the modest Phoenix bachelor pad Cash had moved into after his divorce—really got the dog revved. Out here, Dump probably got in touch with his wild dog roots or something.

"If you're not here by the time I hang up the phone," Cash growled into it, "I'm taking the kids with me. Meet us there."

He gave directions to the pertinent areas of the Northern Arizona University campus, which the Scorpions traditionally took over every summer for training camp. Players practiced on the football fields, kept their gear in the locker rooms, and lived for eight weeks at a local hotel with the team staff and management. Rookies had it tough, with huge playbooks to learn, the occasional good-natured hazing, and a strict curfew after practices were done for the day. Things were looser for veterans—many of whom kept houses near Flagstaff for the summer.

Cash strode to the window, still booming out directions to the university for Leslie. He shoved aside the curtain. Outside in the yard, Dump barked and jumped at the big oak tree in a frenzy of doggie territoriality.

He hung up the phone. "Did one of you give Dump a can of Red Bull again? He's going crazy out there."

The kids all murmured denials, still Legoing.

"I gave Dump some of my Wheaties this morning." Jacob stuck his tongue out, concentrating on snapping wheels onto Mr. Potato Head. Lately he turned everything into a vehicle. "He liked 'em. I put on extra sugar."

Great. His dog was having a sugar buzz. Cash let the curtain fall, then went to the front door. "Get your stuff," he told the kids over his shoulder. "You're coming with me."

Their disappointed moans followed him as he stepped onto the porch. Cash couldn't cave in. A man had to lead by example, even if it wasn't fun. A man had to take charge.

A man had to find out what the hell his dog had treed in the yard.

Poor Dump was barking himself hoarse now. And his double ACL injuries couldn't stand much more jumping.

"Dump." Cash motioned toward the German shepherd. "Come."

The dog deigned a glance at him. Then he went on barking with renewed intensity, as though he liked having an audience. His canine body stiffened, his muzzle pointing toward the tree's upper branches. Cash trooped over there and grabbed his collar.

"I've got to hand it to you, boy." He caught hold and gave a tug. "You might be old, but you're still on the attack. Let's see what's got you all riled up."

Cash peered up through the branches. Behind him, he dimly heard Hannah, Emily, and Jacob thump onto the porch, dragging backpacks behind them. See? he thought in satisfaction. You told kids what you expected, you expected a lot, and you got it. Simple as that. Holding Dump's quivering body, Cash squinted.

He blinked and squinted again, dumbfounded.

There was a woman in his tree. A hot brunette with long hair, acres of bare skin, and some skimpy white clothes.

Great legs, was his first thought.

What the hell? was his next.

"Get him away!" The woman pointed at Dump with one shaky hand, using the other to clutch a branch. She looked terrified—until her eyes narrowed. "And quit looking up my skirt!"

"I'm not." He kind of had been, Cash realized. Shit. She was cute though. What he could see of her. "Look, I've got the dog. See? You can come down from there now."

Wide-eyed, she shook her head.

"I'll help you." He held up his arms. What was she, a new neighbor or something? There were mostly retirees and football wives living nearby, but Cash hadn't met this woman before—and he didn't know of any teammates who'd gotten married during the off-season. "Come on down. Take it slow."

"No way." She scrambled higher. "Put away your dog first."

"Who, him?" Cash looked down. Dump sat on his haunches, tongue lolling as he watched the action. "He's harmless."

"Tell that to my handbag." She held it out with an expression of pure obstinacy, showing him the damage. "It was all I had to defend myself with. It's a genuine Birkin too."

Whatever that meant. Stephanie would have known, but Cash didn't care about much beyond his family and football.

He looked. "That's just a little dog slobber. It won't hurt anything."

She made a disgusted face. "Just put him inside, okay? I'm really, really afraid of dogs. Especially big ones like that."

Hannah appeared at his side. "Who's that, Daddy?"

"I dunno. But why don't you put Dump in the house for me? I'll find out."

His daughter shrugged. "Okay."

The kids herded Dump indoors. His treed visitor watched, biting her lip, never taking her eyes off the dog. When the front door shut, she looked at Cash. "Is it safe now?"

"It was safe before." He held up his arms. "Come on down."

"I'm serious." Suspiciously, she squinted toward the house. Her eyes were blue and wary. "Do you have one of those doggie doors? He might come out again."

"Nah. Dump can't get out. Besides, he's hardly a threat." Cash kept his arms up—uselessly, as it turned out, because she started climbing downward, picking her way from branch to branch with frequent flashes of long, bare legs and no help from him. "He's got two bad knees. Tore both ACLs years ago."

She paused on the lowest branch. Primly handed him her purse, then took a deep breath. Seeing the outline of her bra beneath her skimpy white tank top made something tingle to life inside him—something Cash instantly tamped down. He wasn't here to ogle lost Avon ladies. Or freaked-out, slightly disheveled Welcome Wagon representatives. Or whoever she was.

While she jumped to the ground, Cash grabbed his T-shirt hem and used it to mop the dog slobber from her purse. It was the chivalrous thing to do. Even though she'd been trespassing.

He handed it back. "There. Good as new."

"Thanks." Gingerly, she examined it, then she pointed her chin toward the tree. "Good thing Bjorn had me doing all those rock-climbing drills at the gym. They probably saved my life just now."

Ah. She *was* a football wife then. Cash knew the type. They usually had personal trainers, personal stylists, and too much time on their hands. They lived to gossip, to get manicures, and to spend, spend, spend. Stephanie had been friendly with more than a few of them over the years. Not that all the wives of Scorpions players were silicone-pumped, high-maintenance airheads . . . but this one sure looked as if she fit the part.

She stared at him, probably expecting him to applaud.

"Uh, you looked good up there," he said, gesturing to the tree—and earning himself another "don't look up my skirt" frown in the process. He tried again. "Strong, I mean. Strong."

Her expression softened. She seemed pleased and a little flustered. "Thanks. Again." Her gaze met his. Held for a single weird, electric moment. She sucked in another breath, looking nervous all of a sudden. "I—"

Don't look at her bra, Cash ordered himself as his brain

registered the implications of that deep breath. *Or anything underneath it.*

For the first time in a long time, his famous self-discipline failed him. He whipped his gaze upward quickly.

Just as he did, a car roared up the road. He looked toward the sound, saw Leslie behind the wheel, and remembered what he was supposed to be doing. His meeting.

"Hey, sorry about the dog." He smiled at the woman, preparing to make his exit. "You're okay, right?"

She nodded, also watching Leslie.

His mother-in-law braked in a cloud of dust, then jumped out of her Prius and hurried toward the gate. "Hey, you two! Sorry I'm late. I got stuck behind an RV pulling a fishing boat to the lake, and I couldn't get here any faster."

Leslie bustled into the yard. She stopped in front of Cash and his unexpected visitor, beaming at them both.

"I see you've already met! Good!"

Ah. The reality of the situation hit Cash in an instant. His treed visitor wasn't a football wife at all. She was one of Leslie's nanny candidates, here for an interview. Well, if she was afraid of poor old Dump, she didn't stand much chance going toe-to-toe with his supposedly hellacious triplets, did she?

"Yeah, we've met," Cash said, "but I've got to run. I'm already late." He eyed the brunette one last time, sorry he wouldn't be able to stay for the interview. She was exactly the kind of woman he liked too—leggy, dark-haired, and not too big on top. All smiles also, now that the threat of his ancient dog had been removed. He might have been able to make something happen with her—a commiseration drink at least, to make up for her not getting hired. "Good luck, ladies."

"Thanks," not-the-new-nanny said, looking surprised. "But we haven't even—"

"Just stay for a minute," Leslie said. "I want to explain—"

"Can't stay. Gotta go." Cash headed for the house to change and grab his gym bag, hauling off his dog-slobbered T-shirt as he went. "Don't worry, I'll pen up Dump while I'm in here."

It was the least he could do. After all, it wasn't every day being late for a meeting was so damned entertaining.

He sure did like a lacy bra too.

Chapter 8

Hands shaking, Marisol fluffed her hair in the house's bathroom, then applied more lip gloss. Her stomach felt fizzy, sort of the way it did when she spotted a terrific, can't-miss gift for someone's birthday, and her eyes looked all dark in the mirror. Her whole body zinged with leftover adrenaline.

Way to make a stellar first impression. Not.

Treed like a monkey. Did it get any worse?

In her defense though, she hadn't expected to see that huge dog come bounding up at her the moment she'd stepped inside the gate. She hadn't expected to find it necessary to climb a tree in her totally cute Moschino strappy sandals. And she *really* hadn't expected to find herself staring down at the man of the house, gallantly—if grudgingly—come to rescue her.

Marisol still couldn't get over the sight of him strolling away after Leslie had arrived. He'd casually stripped down to the waist, all dark hair and miles of muscles, before entering the house—and what a sight *that* had been! She'd probably still been gawking when Leslie had offered to let her freshen up. Now here she was. Practically slobbering like a dog herself.

She gazed around, hoping to pull herself together.

She hadn't been sure what to expect, but this wasn't it. The bathroom had log cabin walls. Seriously. Log cabin walls!

Marisol spied two knots in the varnished wood and a few places that looked as if they'd been gnawed on by bugs at some point too. Sure, the sink and fixtures were deluxe, and the tub was lusciously deep, and the vanity was made of mahogany and—to her trained eye—appeared to be a repurposed authentic Stickley original cabinet. It was all very comfortable. But still. This whole place was way more back-to-nature than she was ready for.

Then again, she hadn't been ready for anything so far. She figured she was doing pretty well just winging it.

Murmured voices outside the closed door made her perk up her ears. Leslie's sophisticated, good-humored tones were instantly recognizable. So was the deep, rumbling voice belonging to the man of the house. Footsteps sounded.

She had to move fast if she wanted to salvage this situation. If this was Fordham's and Dzeel's best shot at her work assignment, she didn't want to experience their runner up.

Marisol grabbed her handbag and whipped open the door. She hurried down the hall, emerging in the open-planned kitchen and family room just in time to see her treetop rescuer pulling a clean T-shirt over his tousled hair, his shoulders, and his perfectly muscled torso. Much too quickly, his chiseled abs disappeared from view.

She almost sighed with regret. Or longing. Or some stupid mixture of the two. Geez, she had to get a grip. She'd only been penned up at Dzeel for a few measly weeks, and already she was dying to jump on the first male she saw?

Okay, so technically speaking, Tom the driver had been the first male she'd seen outside the rehab complex. But Tom hadn't possessed quite the same twinkle in his eyes . . . or the same raw energy. Or the same magnificent musculature. It was really breathtaking. The bizarre part was, the single dad of the house—let's not forget the *single* part—acted as if there was nothing at all unusual about looking like a billboard come to life.

He caught her gawking. Still saying something to Leslie, he smoothed out his shirt—as though she might be the Wrinkle Police, about to cite him for excessive rumpling—and went on giving some sort of instructions about the kids. The man honestly was clueless about how fantastic he looked.

Also, time was wasting. Marisol spotted her tote bags and suitcase leaning against a nearby chair and grabbed the top bag.

"Thank you, Leslie, for setting all this up. I really appreciate your help." She shook hands with her benefactor, not at all surprised to feel an instant camaraderie with her now that they'd finally met in person. "Before we get started, I have a little something for you. I'm sorry it's not wrapped."

Marisol rooted around in her bag. She emerged with a triple pack of soap, embellished with a ribbon. It had been the best she could do while limited to the offerings at the Dzeel shops. She'd had to forgo Doritos for three days to save up for it.

Leslie smiled. "Oh, thank you! That's very thoughtful."

"You're welcome. And for you"—she turned to the king of this rustic castle—"something special. I hope you like it."

He accepted his gift. Turned it over. "Huh. Shaving cream. Every guy needs that, right? Thanks, um—"

"Marisol." She hesitated, then decided to go for broke. He might as well know the whole truth. "Marisol Winston."

Her famous name didn't appear to ring a bell with him. Didn't super macho football players read *W*? *In Style*? *People* magazine?

"Marisol," he repeated. "Good. Well, gotta run."

He turned. Leslie smacked him on the shoulder. "Stop! Aren't you forgetting something?"

He eyed her. "Like what?"

"Like introducing yourself, you big dumb jock."

Every bit of him seemed impatient to leave. Recognizing that, Marisol stepped in. "It's okay. We'll get to know each other later. Right?"

Her sunny smile made him blink. Abruptly, as though remembering something, he set down his shaving cream gift.

It sat on the counter. Lonesome. Abandoned. Forgotten.

"Cash Connelly." He shook her hand. "Good luck, Marisol."

With effort, Marisol dragged her gaze from her forlorn attempt at a gift. Two days without her afternoon Cheetos snack, gone for good. "Right. Thanks. It's been nice to meet you. Thanks again for the rescue."

"Any time. Now I'm *really* leaving." Cash offered a brief wave, then grabbed a gym bag and keys. He whistled. "Bye, kids!"

Within seconds, they all piled on. There were shouts and noisy kisses and tightly squeezing hugs. It was the most boisterous good-bye Marisol had ever seen. In the midst of his three children, Cash Connelly seemed a different man. A gentler man. A man who wouldn't dump a gift, no matter how lame it was.

Still surrounded by his children, Cash stood. He pointed to one of them, a little boy with brown hair and mischievous eyes.

"Jacob, you're in charge of Dump. You can let him out of my bedroom, but keep an eye on him. Understand? Hold his collar the whole time if you have to, or take him outside to play. It's up to you to make sure he doesn't bother Marisol while she's here."

The boy, Jacob, stared at her in obvious puzzlement. "Why?"

"She's afraid of dogs," one of the little girls piped up.

"Even old Dump." The other rolled her eyes. "That's why she was up in the tree. To get away. I heard it all. Daddy, you would *never* have to climb a tree to get away from a dog. You're too brave and too strong to *ever* be afraid of anything."

"Let's take it down a notch, okay, Emily?"

"Well, it's true, isn't it? You're tough and smart and you even rescued her." The little girl, Emily, pointed to Marisol.

Cash shared a meaningful look with Leslie—one Marisol couldn't quite decipher. He seemed pleased though, to be thought of as brave and strong and tough. It was ridiculously endearing, that he was so affected by his children's opinions.

"She saved herself," Cash disagreed. He put out his arms, gym bag and keys dangling. "Now who's got Dump? Jacob?"

"I'll do it." Jacob nodded, sticking out his scrawny chest proudly. "I've got your back while you're gone, Dad."

"Good. Now all three of you . . . behave."

"We will!" they chorused, then scattered.

A second later Cash was out the door, taking a huge portion of the room's energy with him. When Marisol moved her gaze from the spot he'd just filled, looming broad-shouldered in the doorway, Leslie was watching her.

With sort of a knowing expression too.

Or maybe Marisol was imagining that part.

"He's quite a presence, isn't he?" the older woman asked.

"Um." *Yes, and I want to rub myself all over him. Maybe lick him a little too.* No, admitting that probably wouldn't make the correct professional impression. No matter how accurate it was. Marisol settled for a different truth. "He obviously loves his kids a lot. It's adorable."

"Yes, he does. My son-in-law might have come late to the fatherhood party, but he's hell-bent on making up for lost time now." Leslie gestured to the kitchen. "I'll give you a tour of the house in a minute and explain your responsibilities. Then you can meet the kids. But first . . . how about a cup of coffee?"

Oh God. This was it. "Do I have to pick the beans?"

Leslie gave her a curious look. "No, Juan Valdez already did that."

"Then yes, that sounds fantastic." Relieved, Marisol followed Leslie past a sweeping black Durat peninsula into a kitchen that was a mishmash of old and new. Aged Craftsman-style cabinets. State-of-the-art Viking range. Antique glass inlays. Ultramodern track lighting. A Remington bronze and other artwork. A gigantic plasma TV. Log cabin walls. She'd swear that was a Philippe Starck chair in the corner too.

Overall, the place looked a lot like one she'd stayed in at Sundance a few years ago, when she'd been dating an actor. Except here—unlike in Park City—there wasn't any shopping or dining or nightlife, and your neighbors weren't major celebs.

Her gaze fell on the shaving cream can. That same crushing feeling returned. "Cash doesn't like gifts much, does he?"

Leslie shrugged, puttering around with the coffeemaker. "He didn't mean to be rude. He's late for a big meeting with the Scorpions management. There's a lot riding on it. Which is why you, my dear, are so important." A mysterious smile played around her lips as she slid the glass carafe into the coffeemaker. "I hope you're ready for all this."

"I am." With a firm nod, Marisol perched on a stool. She hefted her tote bag atop the peninsula counter.

"And I appreciate the opportunity too. I'm *so* glad to be out of Dzeel. It's just . . ." She couldn't let it go. She had to explain. "I know those gifts are awful, but I can't bear to go anyplace empty handed."

Serenely, Leslie took down two mugs. They looked hand-crafted. "You brought *you*, didn't you? That's all you need."

Marisol scoffed. "Clearly Jeremy Fordham didn't brief you."

"I've read your whole file." Leslie gave an airy wave. "Psychological profile, intelligence tests, personal history, transcripts of sessions . . . the whole shebang. It's a board member's privilege, you know. I needed to be sure about you."

Suddenly, Marisol felt completely naked, from her IQ to her shoe size. Leslie knew *everything*? From the hand-bag rebellion to the escape attempts to the time she'd set up a forbidden slumber-party clothing swap among the other rehabees?

"I still wanted to meet you in person, of course," Leslie was saying, "but now that I have, I don't have any doubts at all. As long as Hannah, Emily, and Jacob like you—"

She had to audition for the kids now? Oh God. They already thought she was a complete wimp for being scared of their dog. And something told Marisol they would be about as impressed with their gifts as their father had been. Meaning not impressed at all. This family was a tough crowd for outsiders.

"—you're in. My intuition tells me you're the right choice, and I always pay attention to that." Leslie bustled to the counter, then raised her voice to be heard over the sounds of the dog barking in a distant room. "Kids, leave Dump alone for now. Come meet your new nanny!"

Chapter 9

Steadying the ice pack taped to his shoulder, Cash got out of his Range Rover. The house and yard were quiet around him as he grabbed his gym bag and trod up the walk, squinting against the setting sun. His meeting with the Scorpions' team management had gone well enough— if inconclusively, as far as his future was concerned, since they'd wanted to know how he would "interact with" Tyrell during the upcoming season. Cash had had to grit his teeth and insist that he'd handle working with his ex-wife's new boy toy just fine, thanks.

No matter how it rankled his competitive nature to feel bested by a baby-faced punk who'd started sniffing around his wife years earlier, when he and Cash had first played together. No matter how much it pissed him off that team management was still hung up on a years-old issue. No matter how idiotic it had been to beat out his frustrations afterward on a hard workout practicing passing routes that had seriously kicked his ass.

All he wanted to do now was hug his kids, grab a slab of whatever fifties-style meat-and-potatoes dinner Leslie had whipped up, and collapse on his deck chair until he quit feeling quite so bruised. Wearily, he opened the front door.

That incredible beefy smell he'd grown used to wasn't there to greet him. Neither was Dump. Or Hannah, Emily, and Jacob.

"Hey, Daddy's home!" he called.

Poised on the threshold, Cash listened.

Nada. Where the hell was everyone? He glanced over his shoulder. Leslie's car was still parked out front. She had to be here. Or maybe she'd walked the kids to a play date at the neighbors' house. That wouldn't be unusual, though she probably would have told him about that. He snaked his cell phone out of his gym bag, then dropped the bag on the oak floorboards.

No voice mail message. No text message. No missed calls.

Confused, he stood there for a minute. Usually everyone watched for him to pull up in the driveway—Leslie, because she wanted to get to her swing dancing club meetings; Dump, because the dog liked the bacon chewies Cash gave him; the kids, because . . . hell, just because they loved seeing their dad at the end of the day, just like he loved seeing them.

It was so quiet too. Cash tilted his head. The TV wasn't even on. They definitely weren't home then. Disgruntled, he stomped inside. First stop was the refrigerator for a long slug of Gatorade—straight from the bottle, man-style. Then the freezer, for a cursory check of the groceries. Then the bathroom, for a fresh layer of tape that would secure his ice pack until it was too melted to be of further use. He had to watch out for his throwing arm, especially now.

Bare-chested except for his strapped-on ice pack, Cash wandered down the hallway. He stopped in the kitchen, debating if he should grill up a hunk of chicken and nuke some frozen broccoli—a standard training meal— or just call Leslie and find out if she was making dinner. Her cooking was better than his.

His gaze fell on the shaving cream can on the counter. He couldn't help but grin as he picked it up. What kind of kook gave out shaving cream? As a getting-to-know-you gift?

It was too bad Marisol hadn't made the cut as nanny number five, Cash mused. Weird gifts or not. It might have been hilarious to have her around. She was easy on the eyes too.

Her legs were incredible, he remembered. Long and shapely and smooth, with just enough curve to suggest their owner was all woman. Cash didn't go for scrawny legs—legs that looked like they belonged on a teenage girl. He didn't go for cheerleader-style instant-fake-tanned legs—legs that looked like they belonged on an Oompa Loompa. The truth was, he liked legs like Marisol Not-the-Nanny had. The kind that were strong enough to climb a tree . . . but sexy enough to look amazing while doing it.

Really amazing.

He bet Marisol knew how to use those legs to her advantage too. Feeling his groin tighten, Cash imagined her using them to straddle him instead of a tree branch. He imagined her dark hair wild and loose, like it had been today . . . only cascading down her naked back. He imagined himself peeling off that little white tank top and revealing her lacy bra. Thinking about that bra (and the glimpse he'd had of it) had tortured him all day.

If not for his idiotic daydreaming about what lay beneath that bra of hers, he'd never have gotten hit in practice today. He would have seen Tank coming, would have gotten out of the way once he'd realized the rookie sharing the football field with Cash and his backup wide receiver was off his defensive drill route. Way off. But had he? Hell, no. He'd stood there, tongue lolling, while he thought about sliding his hands over Marisol's bra, and he'd gotten his ass handed to him on an accidental tackle.

It had been worth it though, Cash decided.

He thought about the way Marisol had looked at him when he'd called her strong—the way she'd smiled. There'd been something special there. Something unique. Women oohed and aahed over him all the time—at games, at press events, even at that lame-ass Shoparama store opening Adam had set up—but none of those women had ever looked at him the same way his non-nanny had.

A look like that one made a woman dangerous. Fortunately for him, Marisol had seemed too wigged out by his dog to realize the way she'd affected him. And Cash had gotten out before that feeling had gotten any worse. Still . . .

Damn, she'd gotten under his skin somehow. When she'd handed him that shaving cream can, when her fingers had brushed across his and she'd stood near enough for him to smell her sweet, spicy perfume, he'd felt something. Something jolting and unexpected.

Probably years' worth of stored-up lust, Cash told himself. He hadn't exactly dealt with his newfound bachelorhood by screwing his way across the Southwest. But even if that was all it was, he couldn't believe that a workout and a hard tackle hadn't knocked it out of him. Couldn't believe he still wondered what Marisol wore beneath a skirt like the outrageous white leather one she'd had on.

Did she wear anything? White panties? A thong? Did it match her bra, lace for lace? What would her expression look like if he slid his hands up her legs, if he touched that lace, if he dragged those panties down to her ankles?

He wanted to find out.

Instead he heard laughter coming from the back deck. What the . . . ? Still distracted, still dying of curiosity and an impossible-to-fulfill craving, Cash headed that direction. He spied multicolored Christmas lights wound around the deck railing, shadowy forest beyond it, and four people sitting on the floorboards. Jesus. It was Marisol and his kids. What the hell was she still doing here? And where was Leslie?

He opened the door. They all looked up from the hunk of white fabric they were sitting on. Jacob, Hannah, and Emily wore identical cheerful expressions. But nobody budged.

"Hi, Daddy!"

"Look, Daddy! I finger-painted a butterfly!"

"Dad! You're home!" Jacob waved his blue-and-yellow-tipped fingers, his face lit by the glow from the holiday lights. "We're making a new shower curtain! Marisol showed us how."

The woman in question nodded, peering at the fabric. "It's sort of Jackson Pollock-esque," she explained. "With a little touch of Basquiat to keep it fresh."

Hmmm. If she said so. To Cash, it looked as if Dump had had another accident. In Technicolor this time.

Smiling, Marisol got up. She tugged her skirt, spoiling a fantastic (and probably illicit) view of her thighs. "The kids are doing a great job. They took to the paint like decorators to tchotchkes." She beamed at Hannah, Jacob, and Emily over her shoulder. "Keep going, you guys!"

"Yeah. Good work, kids!" Cash said gruffly. What the hell did a guy have to do to get a welcome-home hug around here? Still feeling bewildered, he took Marisol's arm. He led her to the edge of the deck where they could talk. "Where's Leslie?"

"She had to—" Marisol broke off, frowning in concern. "Hey, are you okay? You look all hot and flushed. And naked." She slapped her hand over her mouth, darting an embarrassed glance toward the kids. They seemed too absorbed in their finger painting to listen to the adults. "I mean, obviously you're not *naked* naked. You're still wearing shorts, right?"

As if to confirm that observation, she glanced down. Cash watched as her eyes widened. A positively radiant smile crossed her face. One of her hands twitched too. The way she scoped out the fit of his workout shorts didn't make him feel any less hot and flushed, that was for sure.

Marisol jerked up her head. "I mean, obviously you couldn't fit your shirt over that ice pack, right? And that's why . . . Um, how did you get hurt anyway?" Brightly, she peered at his taped-on pack. "That's, like, a five-pound bag of ice! Are you crazy?"

"It's effective," he managed. Jesus, three minutes ago he'd been entertaining X-rated fantasies about her. Could she tell? Was that why she was grinning that way?

"I guess it must be," Marisol nattered on. She checked on the kids, as if doing so were second nature, then continued. "For margaritas at least. You're like a bar on two feet. If you stuffed an ice pick down your shorts, you'd be all ready to go."

He felt like he already had an ice pick down his shorts. And he was rapidly headed toward ready to go, too. She had to quit giving him that eager-plus-innocent once-over. It was killing him. Scrambling his brains too. He'd had a question for her—a question she hadn't answered yet. But . . .

"Uhhh." Cash worked to come up with more words. It wasn't easy. What was wrong with him? He needed to find out where Leslie was, he remembered, find out why Marisol was still here, and find out why nobody seemed to care that he was home.

Him. The man of the house, damn it.

Marisol gazed in apparent fascination at his chest and arms. Even his hands. Or his ice bag. Probably his ice bag. After all, his chest was just . . . his chest. And his arms were just ordinary football player arms.

"I see you kept your shaving cream." Her smile broadened even more. Her whole face lit up as she nodded at the can.

He stared at it. He'd forgotten he'd been carrying it. But judging by Marisol's expression, the stuff was like solid gold.

"Yeah. The shaving cream," he said like a moron.

Because he was too busy with a sudden and compelling vision of Marisol lathering him up. Slowly. Completely. Anywhere she wanted. In a steamy, soapy, private mirrored bathroom where they could be alone. Really alone. Get-naked-and-get-happy alone.

She leaned nearer. Winked. "I won't tell anybody you like it, you know. Your secret's safe with me."

"Uhhh." He liked it all right. But his brain had completely gridlocked. He wasn't sure what they were talking about anymore.

"A lot of tough guys like you can't admit they enjoy being spoiled a little." Marisol rose on tiptoes, almost bursting with satisfaction. "But *everybody* likes to get something nice."

"I like to get something nice." Screw it. He was lost.

"See? I knew it the minute Leslie explained you were just distracted this morning." Marisol touched his ice. "Uh-oh. You're getting slushy."

The hell he was. Cash had never felt less slushy in his life. Despite that fact, he tried to stay focused. "I thought Leslie would be here."

"Oh she was. But she had to—"

"Marisol!" Hannah interrupted. "Look at what I painted!"

"Sorry, I'll be right back." After a single apologetic glance, Marisol headed for the other side of the deck. "Wow, that is a really excellent fairy princess." She leaned over, examining the shower curtain. "I can see her wand, and her crown, and her pretty dress. You have an eye for detail."

Hannah, Cash's quietest child, positively glowed at Marisol's praise. Cash couldn't stop staring. Emily tugged Marisol's wrist next, guiding her to the other side of the shower curtain fabric. With very Emily-like bossiness, she positioned Marisol for a perfect view.

"Stand here," she said, her toy tiara gleaming. "And look at mine too! I put stars all over! Here and here and here."

"Nice choice with that yellow paint," Marisol told her, smiling. "Those stars look very real and sparkly. I'd say you have a flamboyant side. That's very useful for an artist."

Now Emily glowed too. While Jacob hurried to show Marisol what he'd been up to during the past few minutes, Cash watched in growing amazement. He'd never seen his kids seem so animated, so eager, so . . . content. Marisol had cast some magic spell over all of them, it seemed. Maybe that was why Leslie had allowed her to babysit tonight. It couldn't be that his mother-in-law had actually hired Marisol to be nanny number five. After all, she was hardly ideal nanny material.

Particularly because Cash couldn't quit having *Penthouse*-ready illicit thoughts about her. Even now, while Marisol dipped her finger in green paint and added a swoosh to the shower curtain fabric, demonstrating some technique to Jacob as she exclaimed over his masterpiece, Cash couldn't help but admire the curve of her ass, the fit of her tank top, the brilliance of her smile.

There was no way he could survive training camp and this test-run, supersize version of summertime custody of Jacob, Emily, and Hannah, plus a tempting nanny, all at the same time. He'd crack. It was as simple as that. Someday, Marisol would bend over to grab a box of macaroni and cheese from the cupboard, Cash wouldn't be able to stand it anymore, and he'd take her, right there on the kitchen counter.

He was halfway through imagining the scene—enjoyably

and vividly—when Marisol waved her hand in front of his nose.

"You really should do something about that flush on your face. Come on, let's go inside and get you a new ice bag." She led the way, her hips swaying hypnotically (and not the least bit nannily), then opened the freezer.

"Anyway," Marisol went on, her voice muffled as she rummaged inside, "as I was saying, Leslie had to leave to catch her flight to Puerto Vallarta. Don't worry though—she took an airport shuttle and left me her Prius to use while she's gone, so I won't be without wheels, *and* she gave me a complete rundown of everybody's schedule, including yours, before she left. She gave me a list of chores to be done too. Plus a very long dos-and-don'ts list. So I'm fully equipped to take care of everything." Something clattered. "Ah, here we go."

Cheerfully, she emerged with a container of ice.

"Leslie's . . . gone?" Cash felt stunned. "For how long?"

"Three weeks, I think she said."

Three weeks? *Three weeks?*

"That's why she was in such a hurry to bring me out here for my work assignment." Marisol peered at the tape holding the ice pack on his arm. She plucked at it, frowning in concentration. "So it looks like from here on out, I'm your gal. Your go-to gal. This summer, it's just you and me—"

"And the kids," he blurted. Damn. Damn, damn, damn. How could Leslie *do* this to him? Without any warning? Without a hazmat suit and a pair of blinders? Without, at least, a dowdy, head-to-toe uniform for Marisol to wear?

A sudden vision of her dressed in a racy French maid's outfit tucked itself into his brain. Ooo-la-la! Très sexy.

No. That kind of uniform would never work.

Cash scowled. "The kids will be here all the time too."

"Of course. That's what I was about to say." Marisol

gave him a curious look. "They're great, by the way. We've been getting along so well. Like we've known each other forever. Emily, Hannah, and Jacob haven't been a bit of trouble."

That was a first. "You're a miracle worker then."

"Maybe." A dazzling smile. "Maybe I'm just a big kid at heart myself, and that's why the kids and I get along. Oh, and they loved their gifts too. I was so happy."

More gifts? "You didn't have to do that."

"I guess not. It's just . . . I've never seen three kids who were so *excited* to get new toothbrushes! It was really cute."

She had to be kidding. "Toothbrushes, huh?"

A nod. Cash still felt bewildered. His kids loved getting new toothbrushes? Loved sitting quietly—with no TV—and painting?

Either Marisol Winston was some kind of genius nanny savant or he was being Punk'd. He wasn't sure which. The only certainty was that Hannah, Jacob, and Emily were crazy about her. He hadn't seen them look so contented for a long time.

Cash wasn't sure how that could be. Why that would be. While he puzzled over it, Marisol worked at loosening his tape. She bit her lip, drawing his attention to the fact that her mouth was just as luscious as the rest of her.

Oh man, he was doomed, he realized. Doomed to crumple beneath his nanny's inadvertent sex appeal. Doomed to behave inappropriately somehow. Doomed to get himself stranded with no child care before training camp even began. How was he going to survive the summer? The long, hot, sultry, nannified summer?

He had to stay on target. That was all there was to it.

For his kids' sakes.

He struggled to remember the conversation.

Oh yeah. Tooth brushing.

"Usually I have to practically hold them down and brush their teeth for them," Cash confided.

Marisol shrugged. "They've already brushed their teeth twice. Hannah wanted to go three times—I think just to get a jump on Emily and Jacob—but I told her she should wait. That little girl is supercompetitive, isn't she?"

Well, so was he. Nothing wrong with that, because—wait a minute! Again Cash stared at her. How did she keep doing that? Having insights into his kids most people never even tried for? Outsiders usually assumed triplets were identical in every way and never considered that their personalities were unique.

"Well, I really wanted to help, but I can't get this loose." Marisol threw up her hands, shaking her head in exasperation at the twisted tape on his ice pack. "We'll have to try something else. Maybe if I rub you down with some lotion or something? That might loosen the glue."

Immediately, Cash imagined cold lotion, warm hands . . . and himself coming completely unglued beneath her ministrations. "No! It's all right. I can handle it myself."

She gave him a saucy look. He'd swear it.

"I'll bet you can. But with me around, you won't have to."

God help him. He wasn't even going to survive the night.

Shouts suddenly came from the deck. Just what he needed—a diversion. "Marisol, Marisol! Come look!" the kids yelled.

"Just a minute!" she called. "I'm helping your dad."

Clearly intent on ignoring his instructions—and finding a creative solution to removing his ice pack while she was at it—Marisol delved into the cupboards. She flipped open the top row. She bent over to check the bottom row. Cash felt momentarily transfixed by the tempting shape of her derrière. If he put his hands right *there* on the curve of her ass, she might—

"Oh look! Macaroni and cheese." She plunked the box on the counter. "I should *totally* make that for lunch tomorrow."

Yep. He was screwed, Cash realized. Blitzed by a sexy nanny, a local child care embargo—and his own damned body, which seemed determined to make a joke of his strict hands-off-the-nanny policy. What the hell was he going to do now?

Well, he knew one good way to start.

"I'm taking a shower," he announced, headed that way with his shaving cream firmly in hand.

"But . . . your ice pack!" Marisol called after him, sounding confused. "Wait! Don't you want me to get it off for you?"

Cash groaned. Get it off. She meant his ice pack of course. He knew that. He was a smart guy. But his dick seemed intent on misinterpreting. Cash Jr. *loved* the new nanny already.

"I'll get it off myself," he called over his shoulder.

Yippee! a certain part of him responded.

Cold shower, cold shower, cold shower, he told it sternly.

When he got there though, his shower curtain was nowhere to be found. Cash guessed he'd be getting a new hand-painted "Jackson Pollock-esque" version sometime soon. Or a Basquiat-influenced one. In the meantime, the plastic liner would have to suffice. It was either that or an ice bath, straight up.

Stripping off his shorts and untaping his ice pack, Cash got in the shower. Then he turned on the water, ripped open his discarded pack, and let the partially melted cubes and frigid water rush over him. Brrr.

Better safe than sorry though . . . especially when facing the kind of temptation he did. In fact, a jumbo-size ice machine might make an excellent summertime investment this year.

Chapter 10

After a fitful night spent tossing and turning (and dreaming of a certain husky-voiced quarterback) in her downstairs "guest" bedroom—aka, the maid's quarters, an irony that wasn't lost on a genuine heiress like her—Marisol awakened to the patter of tiny feet. She smiled groggily. The kids had obviously come to wake her up, the little sweeties.

Well, she wouldn't spoil their surprise. Instead, she kept her eyes closed and stayed still, pretending to be asleep.

She was good at it too. Very convincing. Marisol had lost count of the number of times she'd used this maneuver on her dad, whenever he'd tried to confront her about her spending, her night clubbing, or her "frivolous outlook" in general. As a man who'd pulled himself up by his bootstraps to expand the family chain of hardware stores into a worldwide megaconglomerate of home improvement supercenters, Cary Winston had no patience for anyone who didn't even know what the heck bootstraps were.

Like, for instance, his only daughter.

Determinedly, Marisol kept her breathing steady. She sensed movement in the bedroom, then someone nearing the bed. She heard breathing—heavy breathing, like the combined breath of three excited tiptoeing triplets. She felt someone bump into the bed.

Someone landed on the bed.

Marisol yanked off her pink sleep mask.

The dog! The dog was on her bed!

Gripped by total panic, she clutched the bedcovers and screamed her head off. "Help! Help! Jacob!"

He was in charge of the dog, right?

Her whole body tensed. Yet she couldn't bring herself to move. Were you even supposed to move when confronted with a dog? Marisol wondered fearfully. Were you supposed to stare into the dog's eyes or look away? Make small talk or pretend to be aloof? Maybe offer a compliment?

"Um, *nice* doggy?" she tried.

Dump seemed unimpressed. He gave her a blast of Alpo-scented breath and padded nearer, making the whole mattress dip beneath his weight. His feet—his paws—okay, his claws looked gigantic. So did his teeth.

Now what? Snippets of advice she'd gotten from people over her dogphobic lifetime whooshed into her mind. Maybe she should just stay still and think about this first. Yes, definitely stay still, so as not to seem threatening to the dog. As if.

Also, scream some more. "Help! Help!"

Dump had the gall to look offended. Giving her one doleful glance from his big, brown, sizing-her-up-for-breakfast eyes, he jumped down from the bed. Slowly. He did seem vaguely arthritic, Marisol realized. He gave a whuff of displeasure as he forced his shaggy German shepherd body across the room.

Gimpy or not, he still had those teeth. Big ones.

Marisol wasn't moving. She kept the covers bunched up for extra protection, trying to strategize a way out of this. Maybe if she slipped out the other side of the bed,

moving underneath the blankets, the dog wouldn't realize she'd escaped?

Before she could make her move, thumps sounded
down the hallway. Shouting. The bedroom door smacked
open all the way, making the wall thud, and then Cash
was there. Soaking wet. Sexy. Dressed in a hip-slung,
loosely wrapped white towel and nothing else. Carrying
a golf putter.

"What's the matter?" he demanded. His gaze swept
the room.

"Dog." Marisol pointed. Her teeth actually chattered.

All the tension drained from Cash's body. He aimed
an exasperated look at the German shepherd. "Get out,
Dump."

With clear reluctance—and equally unmistakable
obedience—the dog left. Actually, he kind of sauntered
out. Marisol would have sworn Dump tossed her another peeved look too.

"You've got to calm down." Cash leaned his putter
against the TV armoire. He shook his head. "Dump isn't
going to hurt you."

"He jumped on the bed!" It was hard to make her
point about exactly how terrifying that had been. Especially while she couldn't help gawking at Cash's incredible body. Did the man ever go any place fully dressed?
Not that she minded, but . . . Back to her point. "He
jumped on the bed with *me* in it!"

A shrug. "I think Dump's been sleeping in here."

"On *this* bed?" Appalled, Marisol scrambled out of it.

Cash's eyes widened. Too late, she remembered her
sleeping attire—a pair of girly boxer shorts and a match
ing camisole. Neither left much to the imagination, but
they'd been the most modest she had, thanks to Jamie's
hasty prerehab packing job.

Marisol decided to work it, just like the time she'd found
herself paparazzied at an L.A. party, leaving because her

dress strap had broken. A week later, she'd been pictured accidentally flashing all the readers of *Star* magazine, of course, but hey—she'd never been a person who backed down. So who cared if she and Cash were both practically naked? They were adults. Adults who could handle a little seminudity without making a big deal out of it. Europeans did it all the time.

Aside from which, she was afraid to grab a robe. The dog might come back any second. Instead, Marisol raised her chin and pretended she was fully dressed. In something fabulous.

"Well, thanks for coming to my rescue again—" she said.

"Well, you look all right—" Cash said at the same time.

They both gave awkward smiles. He gestured toward the open doorway, keeping his gaze unwaveringly above chin level.

"You're not hurt or anything, so I'm going to go—"

"Wait." Without thinking, she grabbed his damp arm.

He stilled, his whole body stiffening. His gaze zipped from her hand on his arm to her face. His eyes darkened dangerously.

Wow. All Marisol could think about—aside from how inappropriate it probably was to grab your boss (not that she'd ever actually had a boss before)—was how huge his biceps were. She couldn't even wrap her fingers all the way around his arm, it was so muscular.

Given his expression though, she wasn't sure it was smart to keep hanging on to him. After one good-natured squeeze—just to prove she wasn't going to be cowed by mere muscles, authority, and the fact that Cash really was the boss of her—she let go. "Um, you'll make sure the dog stays out there with you, right?"

For one long instant, Cash only went on looking at her. His face was handsome and sort of sculptural, she noticed, with an aggressive nose and a pair of hazel eyes that seemed positively mesmerizing. What was he waiting for? Should she apologize for grabbing him? Thank him again for rescuing her? What?

Trying to decide, Marisol glanced downward. Which was a mistake. She would swear that his towel—the entire two square feet of white terry cloth covering him—had slipped a little.

Hubba hubba! It was going to be really tough to concentrate on nannying while Cash was around. Especially if he kept on showing up seminaked like this. She was only human after all.

The bedroom door slammed, making her jump.

Marisol glanced up just in time to realize Cash had kicked it shut with his foot. And his face looked stormier than ever too. Either he planned to seduce her—which seemed unlikely, given his deliberate above-the-chin-only way of looking at her—or he was going to fire her—in private—for grabbing him.

Firing her seemed more likely. He'd probably read the Dzeel dossier Leslie had left for him, and her dogphobia plus the arm grabbing had been the last straw. Why couldn't she just succeed at something besides shopping for once?

She'd tried so hard too. Last night, it had taken all the determination she had not to rub herself all over him while she'd been trying to remove that stupid jumbo-size ice pack from his amazing, macho, hard-bodied self.

Stricken, Marisol stared him down. Her sacrifice wouldn't be for nothing, darn it. Maybe she could still change his mind, her dismal negotiating session with Jeremy Fordham notwithstanding. "What did you do that for?"

"The kids." Even as Marisol gawked in confusion, Cash hooked his thumb toward the hallway. "They're on their way here. A minute ago, you screamed loud enough to fell timber."

"What are you, a lumberjack?"

"Nah. Just a dad." He eyed her skimpy sleeping attire once more, then pressed the lock button. A genuine—and dazzling—smile crossed his face. "A dad who'd rather keep this"—Cash gestured from his towel to her boxers and camisole—"between us."

Marisol was still puzzling over *between us* when feet scuffled on the other side of the locked door, proving him right. One of the kids crashed into the door. The knob turned this way and that. Squabbling could be heard. Muffled arguments about who should open the door and how.

Then . . . a timid knock.

"Yes, Hannah?" Cash folded his arms, head tilted to listen.

"Is Marisol okay?" his daughter asked.

"She's fine," Cash replied. He winked at Marisol.

"Is she coming out soon?" Hannah persisted.

"We have a surprise for her!" Emily added eagerly.

"A great big one!" Jacob said. "It's breakf—"

"No! Shut up, Jacob!" one of the girls cried.

More thumping and banging.

The door shuddered as someone bumped into it again.

"Are they all right?" Marisol asked, getting worried.

"Yeah," Cash told her with an amused look. "They're muffling Jacob so he can't tell what the big surprise is, I bet. And he's fighting back." Then, more loudly, "Stop arguing. Go finish your surprise. Marisol will be out in a little while."

"But Daaaad . . ."

"Go." His tone accepted no arguments.

Evidently, the kids knew it. "Ooookay," they moaned reluctantly. "We're going. Hurry up, Marisol!"

The hubbub faded. Marisol glanced at her bedside

clock. It ticked away merrily beside her rumpled, *doggy* sheets. She groaned. "Oh my God. It's only six A.M.!"

"Yeah." Apparently not on the verge of firing her, Cash lifted his gaze from her boxer shorts. He took his time moving all the way up to her face, beneath her undoubtedly bed head hair. "That's what time they get up."

"At six o'clock?" She scoffed, feeling marginally more comfortable now that she wasn't about to be pink slipped on the second day of her work assignment. "Be serious."

"I am."

"Humph." Marisol eyed him skeptically. He was serious. He was also wet, gorgeous, and one hundred percent male. And the two of them were alone. In her bedroom. Almost naked.

Despite the fact that she'd woken up earlier than she typically went to bed, Marisol realized that her powers of observation were remarkable today. For instance, she observed right now that Cash didn't seem in any particular hurry to leave. Also that drops of water had fallen from his freshly showered hair to his big, broad shoulders.

She wondered what it would feel like to lick them off. One at a time. Slowly.

A rogue drop made a getaway, zooming down the plane of his chest, past his dusky flat nipple, over those abs . . . It delved beneath his towel. So did her curiosity. She glimpsed a hint of his hip bone, the intriguing indentation of a few taut pelvic muscles, the shape of his hands as they hung loosely at his sides. She didn't know what she'd done to deserve an assignment like this one, but she was done fighting it.

Halleluiah! Thank you Dzeel!

The work might not be great, but the scenery was fine.

Even if she did intend to remain platonic and professional and Mary Poppins-like the whole time. The whole

tempting, sexy, nearly naked time. She wouldn't do a thing.
Except look.

Mmmm . . . .

Just as Marisol finally managed to lift her gaze from
Cash's towel, she caught him staring at her camisole with
an expression of utter absorption. That dark look was back
in his eyes too, promising things a proper employee had
no right to hope for from a diligent boss. Nevertheless . . .

Hey, party's on! her body declared. Her nipples decided
to send out a pair of perky invitations.

No. That wouldn't do at all.

Marisol crossed her arms and tried to pull herself together. She had to focus. The kids were waiting for her,
she reminded herself sternly. She didn't want to let them
down or blow this assignment. Right now, finishing
shopaholic rehab was all that stood between her and a
lifetime of pennilessness. Not to mention eroded self-
respect and discount denim. Ugh. To succeed though,
she had to stop ogling her boss.

Starting . . . now.

"Okay. So. Thanks again for rescuing me from the
dog," she said. "That was really brave of you."

"Any time."

"I really mean it. I was totally scared."

"No problem."

Marisol examined him. She wasn't sure he was paying
attention. It was as if now that the kids had come and
gone, Cash had forgotten his intentions to leave the
room altogether.

"Still," Marisol said, her resolve growing, "for all you
knew, there might have been a crazed killer in here or
something. You really charged in, ready to handle things."

This time, he only nodded. His gaze wandered from
her chest to her bare legs. Something carnal leaped into
his eyes.

"Um, so, thanks. You'll watch out for the dog, right?"

"Sure." With no warning at all, Cash touched her camisole strap. He rubbed his finger over its silky fabric. His brow furrowed. "Is this all you ever wear to sleep in?"

Was he criticizing her? Implying she wasn't nanny-ready? Even after her diehard efforts to stop ogling him? To stop imagining herself pulling off his towel with her teeth?

"All I wear to sleep in?" Marisol repeated. Her natural rebelliousness shoved its way to the fore. She heard herself say, "No. If it's hot, I sleep naked."

Whoops. A veritable heat wave flared between them at her admission.

Cash raised his eyebrow, looking intrigued. Or maybe annoyed. She didn't really know him well enough to decide.

"You'd better keep your door locked then."

"I will." She nodded, biting her lip to keep another reckless statement from slipping out. "I promise."

"Good idea."

"Right."

They stared at each other for another long, awkward moment. The scent of toasting bread wafted through the air. The TV turned on in the living room. Both reminded Marisol of the kids—and her mission here.

But the man in front of her . . . well, he was unignorable.

All on its own, her gaze slipped to his towel again. It looked a little loose, like it might fall off. She started rooting for gravity to take its course. So much for ultra professionalism. Maybe she didn't have it in her.

This was going to be one long, hot, tempting summer.

"I'm sorry to interrupt your shower," she said primly, hoping to cover her lapse in decorum. She gestured toward him. "You didn't, um, even have a chance to dry off."

"It's okay. I didn't have to go far." Cash tilted his head to the left. "My bedroom's right down the hall."

Right down the hall. Hmmm.

"Still, I really appreciate your coming to help me."

"No problem."

"It was very brave."

"You already said that."

"I know. But you were amazing." And she wanted to prolong this somehow, no matter how stupid doing so would be.

Testing the waters, Marisol stepped nearer. When Cash didn't move away, she darted a glance at the locked door. The heck with it. She'd never been very good at self-discipline anyway. Maybe she should just get this out of her system.

"Especially all wet and everything," she murmured.

Wholly unable to resist, she thumbed away a water drop.

She pressed it to her mouth.

She'd swear Cash's knees crumpled.

"Yeah. I'd better go." He sounded strangled. He didn't take a single step, but he did reach out with one big hand to steady himself on the TV armoire. His gaze never left her. "I've still got to . . . uh, dry off. And shave."

Of course. He must be dying to use his new shaving cream.

But his beard stubble was fascinating, Marisol thought now. Burly and dark and a little dangerous. His hair was appealing too, all damp and spiked up and mussed. "You look good to me."

With typical equanimity, Cash took that in. Then he nodded, seeming to reach some sort of decision. "Marisol—"

She eyed another tasty water drop, barely listening.

He nudged up her chin, forcing her to meet his gaze. "We're going to be spending a lot of time together this summer. But you're here for the kids. So if this is going to work out—"

"I know. I'm sorry." She held up her hands. "I just—"

"Couldn't help it?"

His knowing grin made her gawk.

"*You* too?"

"Yeah." Cash nodded. "But I have to focus on Hannah, Jacob, and Emily. On training camp. It's not—"

His raspy voice scarcely penetrated. Holy cow. If Cash felt this *zing* between them, if he was dying to touch her the same way she was dying to touch him, then what were they waiting for? There was a bed not four feet away. Plus, she wanted him. And in most instances, what Marisol Winston wanted, Marisol Winston got. It had been that way most of her life.

"—so don't take this personally," Cash was saying in an earnest and no-nonsense way, "but nothing is going to happen between us."

She mulled it over. "That sounds like a challenge."

He disagreed. "Only because you want it to."

Despite everything, his eyes lit up. He seemed to like her take on things. But before Marisol could ponder the matter further—before she could just be up-front and honest and admit that now that she'd actually touched him, she was going to have a completely impossible time stopping—she sniffed instead.

"Is that smoke I smell?"

A shriek cut off whatever reply Cash made.

The smoke alarm was blaring.

"Stay here," he commanded, his face hard.

He unlocked the door and bolted for the hallway, everything else forgotten. Marisol lunged for her clothes and followed.

Chapter 11

"We're sorry, Dad!" Hannah shouted as Cash ran into the kitchen. "We didn't mean to. It was an accident!"

"I wanted really toasty toast for our surprise breakfast for Marisol," Emily explained at a fever pitch, tagging along as Cash followed the smoke to the farthest end of the countertop. "Toast like *you* make, Daddy, when it's extra yummy and perfect and toasty—"

"Quiet." Growling with combined worry and aggravation, Cash surveyed the scene. One, two, three safe children. One manic dog scampering around. No flames. He could see immediately what had happened—some bread had gotten stuck inside the toaster, then caught fire. White-faced beside him, Hannah reached for it.

"Don't touch that!" Cash commanded.

Shouldering past her, he yanked the toaster plug from the outlet. Smoke curled up from the blackened bread trapped there, rising in a leisurely plume to the house's raw-beamed ceilings. The smoke alarm still screamed. Now there was pounding too.

Cash turned. "Jacob, quit that."

Not listening—or maybe unable to hear him—his son jabbed at the squealing smoke detector with his plastic ninja sword, his small face determined as he smacked high on the wall shared by the family room and kitchen.

"Don't worry, Dad." Jacob jumped, grunting with the effort. "I've got it covered. This is what Tyrell does when Mom burns the bacon on Sundays. Tyrell always says—"

"Stop!" Cash roared. "That's enough."

He wheeled around, his whole body pumping with adrenaline, and spied Hannah reaching for the damned toast again. She was trying to put the charred slices on a plate—a plate which Emily, her nightgown splattered with chocolate milk, diligently held. The kitchen looked as if an entire horde of first graders had gotten a hold of it, not a measly three of them.

"Are you trying to wreck the whole place?" he demanded. "This isn't even *ours* to burn down, damn it. We're just borrowing it."

They stared at him, looking perplexed.

"We have to give it back?" Jacob asked.

"Not exactly." Hell. Cash couldn't believe he'd admitted that. Even to them. But with his finances shot to pieces, he'd been lucky to get this place from a friend who'd been traded to the Chargers and still hadn't sold his training camp digs—and he wasn't the kind of man who asked for favors lightly. Or who took them that way.

"Just *don't* burn down the house!" he yelled.

They all gawped at him. Hannah's chin quivered, Emily's rose in a defiant pout, and Jacob clutched his sword. The smell of scorched bread, boiling coffee, and . . . Kool-Aid? . . . reached his nostrils. The smoke detector still blared, making his ears ring.

Cash shook all over with . . . He decided it was anger.

"Go to your rooms." He pointed fiercely. "Now."

The kids only stood there gawking, blinking at the smoke in the air. On the heels of his order, Marisol skidded into the kitchen dressed all in white, crushing spilled Cap'n Crunch beneath her impractically high-heeled feet. He caught a glimpse of her bewildered expression. An instant later, the shrieking stopped.

What the . . . ? In astonishment, Cash saw that Marisol had nudged past Jacob and snapped out the smoke detector's batteries. She set them down, then reached for the cordless phone, simultaneously herding the kids in front of her.

"Come on, everybody. Outside. Here we go."

"No," Cash said. "They're going to their rooms."

In complete defiance, Marisol calmly guided the kids to the front door. She flung an over-the-shoulder glance his way. "You too, tough guy. Come on. I'll call the fire department."

The fire department? It took him a second to process what she said. By the time he did, he had to hustle outside across the dew-damp grass to catch up. The four of them had huddled together by the mailbox, Cash saw, Dump included.

How the hell had they managed to evacuate his *dog* without him noticing? Feeling befuddled, holding his sagging bath towel with one fisted hand, Cash stomped toward them.

"This is some kind of adventure, right you guys?" Marisol gave Jacob, Hannah, and Emily a reassuring grin. She spotted Cash, then nodded. Seriousness flashed in her eyes. "I'm on hold. The fire department is on its way."

"Nothing's burning," he said. "It was just toast."

He gave the kids a fatherly glare. All three of them knew better than to mess with the stove, the microwave, or the toaster when there wasn't an adult around to supervise them. They must have *really* wanted to make that surprise breakfast. Already Marisol's presence was screwing with his usual rules.

"I know, but it's a good idea to have things checked out anyway, just in case." Marisol smiled at Jacob. "In the meantime, we just had our first fire drill! Neat, huh? You guys were great. Hey, who wants to see a real fire truck?"

"We do!" the kids yelled. Whatever trauma they'd suffered from setting off the smoke detector had clearly been forgotten.

So had Cash's punishment of going to their rooms. They'd all defied him, possibly for the first time ever.

"Can we go for a ride in the fire truck? Can we?" Emily jumped up and down in excitement. "And meet some firefighters?"

"Sure, we can probably arrange that," Marisol promised. "I'll ask when they get here. I have a way of getting what I want." She peered upward at Cash, looking astonishingly pert, given the situation. Then her brow wrinkled with concern. "Are you okay? Your face is as white as my wardrobe."

He wasn't one of the kids. She could damned well quit caring about how he was doing.

"I'm fine," Cash barked.

He didn't feel fine. He felt as if he'd been kneed in the gut by a defensive lineman, as if he'd landed at the bottom of a twelve-player pile on—and then left on the sidelines for a crucial third-down play. What if the kids had *really* started a fire? Would he have sent them to their damned rooms?

What was wrong with him?

He looked down the street. "Here comes the fire truck."

Sure enough, it careened around the bend in the road, moving past the pine trees with its siren blaring.

"Awesome!" Jacob breathed.

"Look, Daddy! Isn't it neat?" Emily asked. "It's so big."

Hannah only squeezed Marisol's hand, gazing at her in adulation. "You saved us, Marisol. You're the best nanny ever!"

"Aww, thanks Hannah." Marisol beamed. "But I just did what anybody would have done to keep you safe."

Except him, Cash thought. This time, he didn't need Stephanie to tell him how badly he'd blown it with the kids.

Marisol, on the other hand, had performed like a trained rescuer, he realized as the fire truck stopped and firefighters started piling out, rushing to assess the scene. The same woman who'd climbed his tree to escape Dump, turned his shower curtain into a homemade art masterpiece, whipped him into a sexual heat not even five pounds of ice had cured, and enchanted his children within twenty-four hours had proved to be someone Cash could count on . . . but couldn't figure out at all.

Who the hell was she?

The dog whined, wanting to get free—probably to defend the house against marauding firefighters with funny hats.

Jacob pointed. "Hey, Marisol! Look. You saved Dump too! You're not scared of him anymore."

Cash, Emily, and Hannah stared. Marisol looked down at herself, clearly astonished to find her own hand gripping the big German shepherd's collar.

"I guess I wanted to make sure he was safe too." Marisol tilted her head, blinking at the dog. Tentatively, she patted Dump with her free hand. She waited a second, then patted him again. "Maybe he likes me now. Right, Dump?" she cooed.

His traitorous dog—the same dog Cash had raised from a wiggly, big-footed, abandoned puppy—wagged his tail. His tongue lolled in an unmistakable doggie grin too.

"We *all* like you, Marisol!" Emily chimed.

"We want you to stay forever," Hannah added adoringly.

"I'm going to give you my ninja sword," Jacob announced.

Okay, that was it. Jacob's ninja sword was his second most prized possession after his stuffed sea otter. Marisol had hypnotized his kids somehow. Next thing Cash knew, they'd be picking up their own socks and giving away their Game Boys.

Before this went any further, he had to find out more about his new nanny. Starting with the dossier Leslie had left, and ending with . . . a person-to-person interrogation. In bed. With no clothes, lots of time, and an earnest desire to learn everything about Marisol Winston. Yeah. That sounded better and better and—

One of the firefighters returned. He doffed his hat, his fireproof coat flapping open. "Okay, everything checks out, Mr. Connelly." The man's gaze dipped lower. He chuckled. "You might want to put on some clothes before the press gets here though. I hear they're right behind us."

Cash groaned. He'd forgotten all about his towel. Adam wouldn't be thrilled if he wound up in the paper seminaked. Again. Neither would the Scorpions' front office. Given their concerns about how Cash would react to being on the gridiron with Tyrell again, he couldn't afford to borrow trouble.

"I'll take care of it," he said. "Thanks."

"The press?" Marisol's eyes widened.

"Probably just the local paper," Cash told her. "It's no big deal."

But his new nanny had already grabbed the kids, looking panicked. She caught Emily and Hannah by the hand. "Come on, you guys. Let's go find out about that fire truck ride, okay?"

She hustled after the firefighters, her hips swaying in her white miniskirt, halter top, and high heels. The firefighters all stared, nudging one another. The kids trooped after her like lovesick ducklings, scrambling to keep up. Sure enough, within minutes Marisol, Hannah, Jacob, and Emily were climbing into a nearby fire truck. They grinned and waved to him.

"Bye, Dad! See you later!" Hannah called.

Cash waved. The gesture proved too much for his

towel. It started to slip. At the same time, an SUV turned around the distant bend in the road. The logo of the local daily paper showed proudly on its side. Shit. The press was here.

Cash hitched up his towel and raced into the house, whistling for Dump as he ran.

Chapter 12

An hour and a half later, Cash met Adam at a downtown Flagstaff diner, an old Route 66 place that still hadn't knuckled under to the Starbucks-style homogenization of suburban restaurants. He strode in, spotted his manager-turned-agent at a window booth, then headed that way, determined to ignore the heads that turned—as usual—at his approach.

Whispers followed him. He ignored those too.

"The bad news is, I made today's evening edition of the *Arizona Daily Sun*," Cash announced when he reached Adam's table. "The good news is, I wasn't naked this time."

Adam glanced up, probably remembering all those times Cash—and various starlets—had wound up in the papers during his BMOC years at USC. "Thank God for small favors."

"Yeah." Cash smacked down his morning's discovery on the table, ready to get down to business. "I guess that makes me older and wiser. Lots wiser, after this."

"What is it?" Adam turned the large manila envelope Cash had dropped, idly glancing at the handwritten label on its face. He recognized the letterhead in the corner. "Paperwork from Dzeel? Come on, Cash. Give this stuff to your accountants, not me. My job is setting up and publicizing your charity foundation—and *you*—not holding your hand while you have a mathphobia meltdown over your financial statements."

"Bite me." Flipping up his middle finger, Cash slid into the opposite seat. "I told you before, I didn't *need* math tutoring at USC. I *wanted* math tutoring at USC. Or have you forgotten Bethany already?"

"Ah. Bethany." Adam's eyes lit up. "I would've faked an inability to comprehend the ABCs if she'd have helped me."

"Bingo."

"Then what's this?"

"My nanny's dossier."

Adam choked on a mouthful of scrambled eggs. "Your nanny has a *dossier?* Where did she come from, the United Nations? I know you like to do things big, but—"

"She came from Dzeel." Cash ordered an iced tea, took a minute to chat with his waitress—and autograph a blank guest check—then took a slug of his brew before leaning forward again. "Leslie set me up. She got me a nanny from Dzeel—"

"A nanny from Dzeel? One of the work-placement clients?"

Cash nodded. "Then she skipped town to go to Puerto Vallarta. Bye-bye backup babysitter."

He'd been counting on his mother-in-law too. Especially after having tapped out the local agency four nannies ago. But Adam didn't seem nearly as indignant as Cash expected. He sat there for a minute, looking thoughtful. Then he nodded.

"You're the one who put Leslie on the board," he reminded him. "You shouldn't be surprised when she takes advantage of it. Besides, you knew she wouldn't babysit for you all summer."

Cash only scowled at him.

"Don't tell me." Adam held up his hand. "You did think she'd babysit for you all summer, didn't you? Jesus, Cash."

"Why not? They're her grandkids. She loves them." Cash sat back, his arms folded. "I was going to be home a lot of the time too. It was all settled, damn it."

"Settled for you, maybe. I guess Leslie saw things differently." Adam accepted a refill of his coffee. He thanked the waitress, then gave Cash a shrewd look. "Come on. Don't be such a crybaby. Just because Leslie got the better of you doesn't mean—"

"She did *not* get the better of me."

"—that this isn't a good plan. And not just because it's got your shorts in a bunch, either." He offered a teasing grin. "That's just a bonus."

"Oh hell." Cash rose, tossing his manager an appalled look. "I'm leaving. I don't know why I came here."

"You came here," Adam said evenly, "because even 'the man with the plan' isn't bulletproof—"

"I hate that nickname."

"—and sometimes even the mighty Cash Connelly needs advice." Adam caught Cash's undoubtedly fierce expression. He raised his hands in a gesture of surrender. "That goes no further than this table, of course."

"Damned right, it doesn't." Grudgingly, Cash sat again. He did feel relieved now that Adam was involved in the situation too. But he'd rather eat Astroturf than admit it. He tapped the dossier, key to his nanny situation. "So . . . what do you think?"

His manager steepled his hands. "Truth? I think hiring someone from Dzeel is positive PR *and* a solution to your babysitting problem, all at the same time."

"What are you, crazy?" Cash blurted. "The last thing I need is a nanny trainee, probably with no experience at all"—except an ability to enchant his kids, a clear head in a toaster-fire crisis, and a distinct knack for firing him up, he reminded himself—"and a link to my foundation.

Now if I fire her, I'm screwed. It would be like admitting the rehab program doesn't work. And Leslie must have known that."

She'd probably been counting on it to make her getaway, he groused to himself. She knew how important Dzeel was to him. The heart of the foundation was its unique two-part rehab program, designed by a group of specialists Cash had trusted when he'd first set up the charity during his rookie years in the NFL.

At first, Dzeel had been intended to treat drug addictions—like the ones pro athletes sometimes developed to painkillers. Since then, it had branched into other areas . . . including a nanny with the potential to mess up his whole summer.

"You're looking at it backwards," Adam argued. "You need a nanny, even if she's inexperienced, right? Now you've got one. You need positive press, especially now that you've got another shot with the Scorpions. This could be it."

"This could be a disaster."

"Nah. You're just pissed this was sprung on you all of a sudden. You've got to think positive."

That was easy for Adam to say. He wasn't the one with toaster fires and a sexy nanny and a continuing visitation-schedule issue and eight grinding weeks of training camp still to complete.

"Listen. If this nanny of yours finishes her work assignment successfully, it makes your foundation look fantastic. And it encourages local businesses to hire Dzeel's rehab patients themselves. It's a win-win." Adam slid the paperwork from the envelope and flipped open the dossier folder. "Oniomania treatment, huh? Compulsive spending disorder. Better keep a close eye on your checkbook."

"Right." Cash rolled his eyes. "Marisol might clean out the last five hundred bucks in my bank account."

"Five hundred bucks? What happened to your signing bonus?"

"That's invested." Cash stared at his iced tea glass, rubbing his thumb along its condensation-beaded sides. He didn't look up. "We both know there's no more coming if I get cut. If I don't make the Scorpions' final fifty-three after training camp."

For a minute, Adam was silent—probably contemplating the team roster . . . and the pathetic state of Cash's finances these days. Ten percent of nothing was no way to make a living. Even longtime friends needed to keep themselves in peanuts and beer.

"You're going to make the final fifty-three. And you're going to have a winning season too," Adam insisted. "Which is why this whole nanny situation is a step in the right direction." He looked out the diner window at the street and railroad depot-turned-historical museum beyond, obviously strategizing. "Do you think this nanny of yours would do interviews? You know, talk about what a great dad you are—"

"Leave my kids out of your PR spin," Cash warned.

"—or what a bighearted charitable opportunity you're providing people through Dzeel, that kind of stuff?" His manager squinted at the dossier. "Even if she won't, we can definitely work this opportunity. Well done, Leslie." He mimed a salute.

"Hold on. Don't do anything crazy with PR," Cash warned. "Give me some time to get a handle on things first."

Still disgruntled, he knocked back more iced tea. He needed a minute to get his feet under him. A minute to think, to react, to . . . hell, to become "the man with the plan." Ever since Marisol had shown up, he'd been thrown off his game, and it hadn't quit yet. Obviously the tight ship he usually ran at home had sprung a few leaks since Marisol's arrival.

When he'd picked up that dossier—only minutes after throwing on some clothes, dealing with the firefighters, giving an unenthusiastic statement to the newspaper, and opening every kitchen window to air out the house this morning—he sure as hell hadn't planned on learning that he'd accidentally hired a nanny with no verifiable experience, a shopping obsession, and a link to his charitable organization, to boot.

She sure was cute though, Cash remembered, relaxing a little. Sweet and generous. Marisol had actually choked down the kids' reassembled Cap'n Crunch, Kool-Aid, and burned toast breakfast after the fire truck ride, and she'd smiled the whole time too. She also had a talent for choosing shaving cream.

Absently, Cash stroked his jawline. No stubble. Nice.

"Marisol Winston . . ." Adam mused, frowning at a memo. "Why does that name sound familiar?" He flipped pages, searching.

"I haven't read the whole thing yet," Cash admitted. The folder was thick with egghead details like a psychological profile, intelligence tests, a personal history, and transcripts of counseling sessions. He was a bottom-line kind of guy. "The upshot is, I'm stuck with her, and I need a way to deal with it." He grimaced. "There's evaluation paperwork to do too."

He shoved his thoughts from pencil pushing to something else—how excited Jacob, Hannah, and Emily had been to ride on that fire truck today. How happy they'd been to finger paint—even to brush their teeth. How they'd all conspired (however disastrously) to surprise Marisol with breakfast in bed. How even Dump loved the new nanny enough to want to sleep with her.

There was definitely something special about Marisol.

"You don't sound nearly pissed enough about all that paperwork." Adam glanced up, brows raised. "Ah. I get it. She's cute, right? You like her, don't you?"

Cash bristled. "That's beside the point. I wouldn't hire a damned nanny just because she was hot."

"Then . . . yes. You do like her." A hearty grin, then another bite of scrambled egg. After a slurp of coffee, Adam ducked his head to peruse the dossier again. He waved his hand carelessly. "I wouldn't worry about it. The fact that you're here at all tells me your conscience is working harder than your dick. You won't jump the nanny anytime soon."

"Who said anything about—" Cash stopped stubbornly.

Assface. It was time to launch the most brilliant part of his plan, he decided. The whole reason he'd come here at all, when he should have been doing bench presses at the gym.

"Right," he said. "I won't be jumping the nanny, because you'll be there to make sure of it."

"Hmmm?" Adam plucked a photo from the dossier, examining it in the sunlight from the window. "*Hey*, I see what you mean."

Cash grabbed the picture. Marisol smiled up at him from its glossy surface, but he wouldn't let himself be swayed. Not by her lovable smile or her unbelievable knack with his kids.

"You'll be there to make sure of it," Cash repeated firmly. He waited until he had his manager's attention. "I want you to visit the house. Stay for a few days. Keep an eye on things."

Adam stared at him. "You've got to be kidding me."

Cash stared right back. "Nope."

"I'm not spying on your nanny for you. Especially if it's just to keep you out of her pants."

Cash let that crass comment fly. This time, he'd be the bigger man for a change. This was too important not to be. Also, he wanted Adam around mostly to provide his usual enthusiasm-dampening, no-nonsense influence—not to double-team Marisol.

"I don't want you to spy. I just want you to . . . oversee things for a while. Just until I get a handle on the situation." He gave Adam his best persuasive grin. "It'll be easy. You can say you're from out of town."

"I *am* from out of town. I'm only here because of training camp. And I do have other clients besides you, so—"

"See? It's settled." Feeling better, Cash scooped up the dossier. He tucked its assorted papers under his arm, drained his iced tea, then stood. "Don't be late," he advised, nodding to a waving fan in a nearby booth. "I already told Marisol you're coming to dinner tonight."

Adam frowned. "You were that sure I'd do it?"

Cash couldn't help but grin. "Hey, I'm still me, aren't I?"

"Yeah." Looking resigned, Adam pushed away his picked-over breakfast plate. "But we'd better get our stories straight first. Who am I? Who'd you tell her I was?"

"Yourself, dickwad." Cash frowned. "I might be a lot of things, but a liar isn't one of them."

Adam seemed to think about that. Then he stood too. "Okay. I'm still not wild about spying—"

"Don't think of it as spying," Cash urged. "Think of it as being a professional third wheel. Three's a crowd. You know."

A sigh. "Aren't the kids enough for that?"

"The kids have bedtimes," Cash reminded him. Bedtimes when it was dark and quiet and he and Marisol would be alone. All alone. He needed someone like Adam there—someone dependable and studious and inclined to launch into discussions of grocery stores. Talking about cauliflower would dampen anyone's libido.

"Fine. I'll do it. For the kids' sakes," Adam said. "Jacob, Hannah, and Emily need somebody else around besides their crazy daddy."

"Very funny."

"This is only temporary though." His manager—his friend—stilled. "If you really think you can't handle this situation with the nanny, end it now, Cash. Use your head for something besides memorizing a playbook for a change. There's too much at stake here to screw around."

Cash hesitated. There'd only been one other instance when Adam had given him a similar warning. But by the time he'd realized that granting Stephanie an uncontested divorce—for the sake of the kids—was a colossal mistake, his ex-wife had already cleaned out their joint bank accounts, gotten herself the house and a huge settlement, and skipped town with Tyrell for an end-of-season fuckfest on some tropical island, leaving Cash sorrier, poorer, and a hell of a lot wiser. And determined to avoid romance for a while too.

"Don't be such a pessimist," he told his manager, slapping Adam on the back. Cash grinned. "Nobody's a sucker twice. This time I've got everything under control."

Chapter 13

If there was anything trickier than cooking, Marisol didn't know what it was. Except maybe finding a perfectly fitted pencil skirt. Or, come to think of it, finding an accessory that would look right on her fantastic Le Corbusier coffee table back home. She'd been working on that particular conundrum for a while now, and she still hadn't unearthed the right objet d'art. Something ultramodern was too obvious. But anything too rococo was jarring, like daisies in a Ming vase.

However, if she didn't pull off this dinner for Cash, she might never make it back to her beach house at all—and then perfecting her design vision wouldn't matter, would it?

Resolutely, she picked up the nearest cardboard package. Frost melted from its colorful, glossy sides, chilling her fingers as she read it out loud, concentrating hard.

"Place chicken nuggets on a baking sheet. Bake at 350 degrees until golden brown and crispy."

Yum. Golden brown and crispy sounded good. Marisol searched the cupboards, unearthed a pan, then dumped in the nuggets. Weird. They didn't look at all like the French food she got at her friend Henri's bistro in L.A., despite the *chicken cordon bleu flavor* banner emblazoned on the package. Oh well. She tossed the empty box in the general direction of the trash.

On to the additional entrees . . .

"Okay," Cash said, striding into the kitchen with a businesslike air. He put his palms together, examining things. "How's it going in here? Adam will be here any minute, so—"

Caught by surprise, Marisol looked up . . . and then couldn't quit looking.

Cash wearing a towel, Cash wearing workout shorts—those had been fantastic. Admittedly. But they were nothing compared with the sight of Cash wearing a nice white shirt and dark pants, obviously showered and dressed for dinner. And that was nothing compared with the way Cash looked while smiling. At her.

Or maybe he was laughing. At her. Oh man . . .

"What's so funny?" Marisol demanded. Whoops. The Fritos she'd been pouring had overflowed the bowl, spilling onto the countertop. A few landed in the tub of refrigerated dip.

"You. Cooking." He gestured toward the cluttered counter. "Are you sure you're up for this?"

"I volunteered, didn't I?" When Cash had mentioned inviting his friend Adam to dinner, Marisol had jumped at the opportunity to make a good impression. If there was one thing she understood, it was entertaining people. "I'm totally up for this. What you see here is my process at work."

"Your process?" His smile widened. Adorably.

"You know, like an artist. This is my canvas!" She waved her handful of scooped-up wayward Fritos, indicating the appetizer platters. It had taken her half an hour to skewer the pizza rolls alone. "And you're my guinea pig. Here. Taste this."

She came at him with an hors d'oeuvre.

Cash looked dubious. "I'll wait for dinner."

"Don't be silly. They're tasty. The kids and I made the little ruffled flags for the toothpicks out of construction paper and Elmer's. It's a good effect. Very French café. You eat with your eyes first, you know." She nudged his chin. "Open up."

He eyed her, possibly impressed by her entertaining skills and foresight. Or maybe awed by her gussied-up appearance. She couldn't tell, but she had made a special effort with her ponytail today. Or maybe Cash was just procrastinating. He had sounded pretty skeptical about her cooking abilities.

He blocked her just as she neared his mouth with the pizza roll . . . maybe because she had to reach way up. Or maybe because she stopped for a nanosecond, mesmerized by the slight curve of his lips, the seductive semi-pout of his mouth, the thrill of being *this close* to him with a perfectly verifiable, professional reason. Either way . . . no dice on the tasting.

"You look nice," he said, stealing her attention even further. He nodded toward her skirt. "I like the apron."

"You do?" Marisol patted its white ruffled edges.

"It's very appropriate. Adam will be impressed."

"I know, right? I thought so too. I found it in the closet in my room, along with a whole maid's uniform. But the rest of the outfit was black, with a little short skirt and stuff. You know, like one of those crazy French maid outfits at a costume shop? And my signature color is white, so—hey, are you okay?"

She paused, just about to perform a runway-style twirl, and laid her free hand on his arm instead. He'd gone completely rigid, from his taut cheekbones to his motionless hips. He didn't seem able to tear away his gaze from her apron either.

"You have an entire French maid's uniform in your room?"

Marisol nodded. "Ohmigod—was I supposed to wear

it? Do you want me to wear the French maid's uniform? I tried it on—"

Cash gulped. One of his hands fisted.

"—and it fits perfectly. What are the odds, right? It fits just like a glove. Like a French couturier's tight, short—"

Cash fisted his other hand. He bit his lip.

"—sexy glove. It's a little racy to wear around the kids though. Maybe when I'm cleaning up at night? After all, you're the boss, so if you want me to wear the French maid's uniform while I'm dusting or something . . ." She bent over, pantomiming waving a feather duster around. "See? I'm game for it."

"No! Uh, I think I hear the doorbell," Cash blurted.

"Oh. Okay." Hmmm. No uniform then, she guessed. Good.

Marisol shrugged and popped a pizza roll in her mouth, barely tasting it as she savored the view of Cash walking away instead. Mmmm, mmmm, mmm. If there was any justice in the world, he'd be required to walk everywhere butt first, just for the enjoyment of every woman within eyeshot.

Satisfied, she went back to work.

Twenty minutes later, Marisol was running out of oven space and out of pans. All six burners on the stove held simmering, spattering pots. The microwave held a contingent of potatoes, all spinning in a pile on the turntable as they microbaked. The oven was jammed on every rack with baking sheets of frozen mini pizzas, pot pies, enchiladas, and onion rings.

Those items didn't quite go together, she knew. This meal would hardly be a gourmet extravaganza. But if she had anything to do with it, Marisol vowed, it would be *fun*. And the kids would definitely like it. And that's what mattered most. Not whether Cash would take a bite, moan in ecstasy, and proclaim her the greatest gastronomic genius since Chef Boyardee.

Although she still hoped he would. Her first Dzeel evaluation form was due back to Jeremy Fordham at the end of the week. She wanted to knock the socks off that organic string bean—and maybe make him realize she *did* have some skills. Make him realize that he—and everyone else—had underestimated her.

Because of that, Marisol had decided it would be savvy to prepare some backup food. Just in case. That way if something burned or blackened or exploded (it sounded less likely than it actually was, she'd learned), or fell on the floor, she was covered. Truth be told, her most recent culinary accomplishment back home had been reheating some leftover seared monkfish with chanterelles from the Tower Bar. She wasn't exactly confident about preparing an entire meal—from scratch!—for the first time.

Dump sat patiently near the pantry door with his doggie gaze fixed on her every move. He'd already been the gleeful recipient of two scorched pigs-in-blankets and one wayward onion ring, still frozen but chomped with gusto all the same. Marisol had the feeling Dump was watching over her. It was nice.

Hannah tugged her arm. "Marisol, can we help?"

"Sure, sweetie." Frazzled, Marisol surveyed the kitchen. By now, it looked almost as bad as it had during this morning's breakfast surprise. Of course that might have been because she'd forgotten to load the dishwasher. She hadn't quite figured out how to, you know, open the thing yet. "Why don't you assemble the sandwiches? We're having mini grilled cheese squares."

"Okay." Hannah skipped off to grab a package of Wonder bread. "I'm helping!" she announced to the kitchen at large as she peeled the plastic from some Day-Glo orange cheese slices. "I'm practically doing *everything* for the dinner."

"Hey, what can I do?" Jacob put down his toy dump truck.

"Umm, do you know how to use the grill?"

He glanced toward the tabletop model. "Yeah! Tyrell makes stuff in his George Foreman grill all the time. I can do it."

"Then you can cook the grilled cheese sandwiches—carefully—after Hannah puts them together. How about that?"

"Okay!" He scampered off to the opposite counter.

"Use some oven mitts!" Marisol cautioned. She'd learned that one the hard way herself. Jacob nodded and pulled on some gigantic quilted mitts. He beamed from ear to ear, wielding a purple silicone spatula almost as long as his arm.

Only Emily remained. She stared at the hors d'oeuvres. "Are you sure we need all this food? It's really a lot."

"I know," Marisol admitted. "But I've never cooked for so many people before. I wanted to be sure we had enough."

"Well, I could eat that whole pan of pizza rolls! Just me. 'Cause I *love* them." Emily rounded her skinny arms around her belly. She stomped across the floor like a sumo wrestler, making her assorted plastic playtime necklaces swing to and fro. Her fairy princess shoes clomped. "I'm starving!"

"You're dramatic too." Marisol smiled. She saw a lot of herself in this little girl. Which was impossible of course, but still true. "There's never a dull moment when you're around. Also, you have a flair for fabulous accessorizing."

Emily posed like a cover girl. They shared a laugh.

The little girl peered at her, tilting her head in a thoughtful pose. "You laugh a lot. Daddy doesn't."

Uh-oh. "Well, that's probably because he's a big, tough football player. With lots of responsibilities."

"I think it's because he's lonely. My mom has Tyrell to keep her company, but my dad doesn't have anybody."

Marisol stopped. This was more than she strictly needed to know about her work-placement boss. She hated to think of Cash being lonely though. All by himself, with just his tight tush and dynamite smile for company. It just wasn't right.

Besides, he'd been nice to her so far. A lot of people would have fired her the minute they'd found her up in that tree hiding from Dump. Her father had once dismissed a gardener for trimming the mansion's bougainvilleas an inch too short.

She snapped out of her reverie. "Sure, he does!" she told Emily. "He's got somebody. He has you, and Hannah, and Jacob."

A shrug. "I guess. But only some of the time."

Some of the time. Marisol had said those words herself, to her mother, on the day her cruise to Spain had launched. She'd only been eight years old. Too young to recognize the gift wrapped, limited-edition Barbie Beverly Hills playhouse her mother had pressed into her hands for the blatant bribe it was.

Be a good girl and don't cry. Look at your pretty gift!

"Some of the time is better than none of the time," she assured Emily, pushing that memory aside. "Besides, you guys are the ultimate. Even though you don't actually take naps anymore." She couldn't believe Leslie had misled her that way. "Also, you have the biggest, most jam-packed fridge I've ever seen."

"We do? The biggest ever?"

Marisol nodded. As conversational detours went, that one had been clumsy, but apparently effective. Mission accomplished.

"You bet," she said. "Back in L.A., my fridge usually doesn't contain much more than a few bottles of San

Pellegrino, a couple of limes, a takeout box of sushi, and some Cristal."

"Ooh! What's Cristal? That sounds neat."

"It's like Kool-Aid for grownups. It's really good."

"Let's buy some! Next time we go to Shoparama."

"Maybe when you're older. In the meantime, why don't you help me put these bananas in the blender? I'm making smoothies too. We're a little short on beverages, and my caterers always say you should plan for twenty-five percent more guests than you expect to attend." Of course, her caterers also refused to coordinate any event less grandiose than a party for three hundred. And someone on their staff usually drank part of the profits in Stoli vanilla. Marisol shrugged. "Drinks are important, you know. Almost as important as goodie bags."

"Goodie bags? Wow." Emily's eyes shone. "And twenty-five percent extra too?" At Marisol's nod she sighed, still unpeeling bananas and cramming them into the blender. "You're so smart, Marisol. Even with math, and that's my favorite subject in school. When I grow up, I want to be just like you."

"You do? Aww, that's sweet." Marisol hugged her. These kids honestly were special. "Whatever you do though, don't ever try to outrun the paparazzi. They'll just take bad, sweaty photos of you. Then the magazines will publish them and say you're dying of some mysterious disease. Or you're pregnant. Or both."

Emily nodded solemnly.

"Also," Marisol told her, settling into her newfound woman-of-wisdom groove, "don't ever believe anyone who tells you boy-cut jeans look good on anybody but boys. Because they don't. Period. If you have any hips at all—and you should, because you'll be a woman someday—you'll look wide as a Pasadena Bowl float in boy-cut jeans."

Another nod. Marisol felt downright fulfilled. This was so neat, imparting her wisdom to another generation!

"Finally," she said, hunching down to put herself on eye level with Emily—because it was weird and rude to tower over someone you were talking with unless they were an obnoxious groping boor and you were a woman in fab peep-toe pumps, "and you should remember this one carefully, because it's something my stepmom shared with me when I was little—"

"You have a stepmom?"

"Actually, I've got three. My parents got divorced when I was a little younger than you. My mom married a bull-fighter and my dad has this thing about never wanting to be alone"—actually, they sort of had that in common, it occurred to her—"so he kept on getting married and divorced until he finally got it right."

Emily looked kind of freaked-out. "Your dad got married *three* times?"

Marisol nodded. "At first I used to think that if I were *really* good, he'd be happy with just the two of us. But now that I'm an adult, I know that was silly."

Emily didn't seem reassured. "I hope my dad doesn't get married three times."

Hannah and Jacob glanced over, looking worried.

"I'm sure he won't," Marisol assured them, straightening to spoon yogurt into the blender. "He's much too smart for that."

"He is very, very smart," Emily agreed. "And hand-some too."

"Yes, he is." *Especially when he smiles at me.*

An insightful glimmer came into the girl's eyes. "Do you want to marry my dad? Because you're very, very smart. And you're pretty, even without a tiara on. And you're nice too."

"Really nice!" Hannah piped up, still looking on.

"Yeah," Jacob agreed. "Especially with TV time."

"Well . . . getting married is a serious thing," Marisol hedged, her finger hovering above the blender's start button. She could hardly tell such sweet kids that all she wanted to do was boff their daddy's brains out, could she? No.

But she'd never been a woman for settling down. Chad, her longest-term boyfriend, had only precipitated the beginning of the end between them when he'd proposed a few years ago, forcing her to confront her fears that she'd be genetically terrible at family life. And parenthood. Obviously those fears had won, because she was still single, despite Jamie's urgings.

"I'm sure if your dad ever asked me to marry him, I would just have to say yes," Marisol said. "What girl wouldn't?"

Emily nodded emphatically. "*Exactly.*"

Thank God it would never come to that.

"So anyway," Marisol continued, finishing with the blender at last, "What my stepmom used to say, and what you should always remember, is—"

"Never wear white after Labor Day?" Emily volunteered.

"No, sweetie. Although that's a good one too. Very old-school *Vogue.* What my stepmom, Jamie, always used to say was, 'You can only fail if you give up. So just keep trying.'"

Then she snatched the last clean pan from the cupboard and dumped a rock-solid hunk of frozen lasagna on it. Next she prayed. Finally she bent down in front of the dishwasher, determined to figure out the darn thing once and for all.

His dinner plans—and especially his buffer-between-him-and-Marisol plans—didn't exactly go as Cash expected.

"Wow, Marisol. That was amazing." Adam rubbed his stomach happily, gazing around the table with a smile. "Who'd have believed 'smorgasbord à la Connelly' could taste so good?"

"Yeah!" Jacob rubbed his stomach too. "Especially

when you squish together the enchiladas and the apple-sauce. Yum."

"It was super extra scrumpdillicious good!" Emily said. "Nobody ever made such a yummy dinner as you, Marisol."

"And *I* helped!" Hannah added proudly. "So I think the grilled cheese squares were a very, *very* good idea."

"Aww, thanks, you guys." Marisol's face looked luminous. Especially in the glow of the Christmas lights she'd transported from the deck outside ("Safer than votives!" she'd said) and arranged on the table as a centerpiece. "And thank you too, Adam." She gave him a beatific smile. "The name goes a long way toward setting expectations, I think. Smorgasbord à la Connelly!" She spread her arms as though picturing it on a marquee. "So do the garnishes. It's just like when you walk into an apartment or a house for the first time—the foyer sets the tone, doesn't it? Like here. The minute you see all the toys and stuffed animals all over the place, you just *know* there are three fantastic kids living here."

Marisol beamed, gesturing toward the mess beyond the dining table. Everyone nodded and grinned, practically hypnotized by her asinine theory. Could no one resist her? Cash wondered.

He couldn't exactly call himself immune though. He'd nearly passed out over all that French-maid-outfit talk. In fact, he'd had a semiboner ever since. But he refused to let Marisol walk all over him or his household. There was a lot riding on his staying in control of things.

"Speaking of toys and stuffed animals," he said, "this place looks like crap, Marisol. It's time you did some of that housekeeping you're supposed to be here to do."

Everyone gawked at him.

Doggedly, Cash persisted. "I know it's only been two days, but you're supposed to keep things clean. This is not—"

"Daddy!" Hannah and Emily protested, frowning.

"Not cool, Dad." Jacob shook his head. "Not cool."

"Can't that wait?" Adam shafted him an annoyed look. Cash kicked him under the table.

His manager retaliated with a sidelong glance at Marisol.

One look at her crestfallen face made Cash feel like an ass. He had to stick to his guns though. First she made him want to strip off her frilly apron and get busy on the kitchen counter. Next . . . who knew? He had to stay in charge.

He ignored the assembled accusatory looks around the table.

"Marisol, you don't have to—" Adam began.

"No, Cash is right." She stood, her hands fluttering as though in search of a job to do. She picked up her plate. "I've got a lot to do. A dishwasher to battle, for one thing." Her smile wobbled. "Thanks for letting me join you, everybody."

"Wait," Hannah urged. "Daddy didn't mean it."

His daughter bit her lip, casting him a hopeful look.

Stubbornly, Cash refused to take the bait. He was still king of this castle, damn it. It was too late to buckle now. If he caved in at this point, he'd lose all his authority.

"Yes, I did mean it," he said.

Disgusted looks all around. Several sighs. He could read the *buzzkill* sentiment in their faces as plainly as he could read a second-string defense, but he had to stay strong.

Marisol's chair slid. Her movements stirred the air, teasing him with the scent of her . . . was it perfume? Shampoo? Cocoa butter body lotion? Whatever it was, it made Cash want to lick it off before she passed him. Slowly. With long, careful sweeps of his tongue and maybe a nibble or two. Mmmm.

Oh hell. Now he had a full-on hard-on.

"I'll be in the kitchen," Marisol announced.

"We'll help too!" The kids bolted from their seats.

They carried their plates with a swiftness Cash had never seen before, like mini speed walkers. On speed. As Emily, Hannah, and Jacob passed him, they all pouted. Pointedly.

Cash turned to Adam, lifting his gaze from the scraped-clean platters of pizza, Easy Mac, onion rings, and enchiladas. Even the exploded microwave potatoes had been gobbled up by this crew. "That's impressive. No nanny ever produced those kinds of results before," he joked. "Next they'll be cleaning the house."

His manager only glared at him. Then he picked up his plate too. With exaggerated dignity, Adam added his silverware and banana smoothie glass and carried the whole mess to the kitchen.

From his place alone at the table, Cash heard Marisol murmuring thank-yous. Running water. Scraping. Laughing.

Oh screw them all. Discipline had gotten him where he was, and discipline would get him to the next step too. He didn't have to kowtow to the new nanny, no matter how much he wanted to beg her to let him touch her. He was the boss, damn it!

Besides, he'd brought Adam here to act as a blocker. To help lessen Marisol's appeal. Not to become her newest cheerleader. Her fan club. Her freaking knight in shining armor. From the moment he'd shook her hand, Adam had been like a gawky science geek with a crush on the popular girl in school. His adulation didn't appear to be dwindling anytime soon either.

"So, Marisol." Adam's voice drifted from the kitchen—which, given the house's floor plan, was right behind Cash's back, after all. Not that *he* was going to participate in the nanny revolution. "I heard you were a real hero this morning when the toaster fire broke out. It was all over the newspaper."

"She was awesome!" Jacob yelled. "Pow, pow!"

Cash could picture his son's little fists punching, superhero style. Emily and Hannah broke into applause.

"Marisol was very, *very* brave," Emily enthused with her usual charm. "The bravest nanny *ever* in the world!"

"I was scared, 'cause Daddy was yelling," Hannah added, piously jabbing home her point, "but Marisol just scooted us outside. And the fire truck was super neat. I sat the highest and I got to ring the siren. It was so fun!"

"Marisol even saved Dump," Jacob added. Woof!

Grumpily, Cash stared at the remains of the dinner.

Marisol had scattered pinecones artistically across the tablecloth—which, if he didn't miss his guess, was actually his Pollock-esque-with-a-touch-of-Basquiat shower curtain doing double duty. He might never get it back for its proper purpose now. He picked up his fork, which was wrapped in a froufrou ribbon she'd gotten from someplace. He scowled.

He wasn't sure how she'd done it, but Marisol had made the table look great. She'd garnished all the food, making it look even better than it had on the boxes. She'd chatted and laughed and told stories about how helpful the kids had been while cooking, and she'd made Adam feel more welcome than the damned turncoat had a right to. She'd been perfect. Absolutely perfect.

Even the kids had been well behaved. And Adam had swooned.

So what was *his* problem?

"It sounds as if you handled the crisis magnificently, with real presence of mind," Adam was saying in his best please-can-I-carry-your-geography-book voice. "How did you stay so calm?"

"Oh that." Marisol chuckled. "Well, *you* try getting a hold of the last pair of Ferragamo boots with fifty other women on your tail at an end-of-season sale. You learn a few things about grace under pressure."

Adam guffawed. Cash never knew his manager had such a grating laugh. This was the guy he'd chosen to negotiate his latest—and probably last—NFL contract? Hell.

"Plus," came Marisol's voice again, filled with warmth and affection, "I guess I was motivated to make sure everybody was okay. These kids are pretty great, you know."

"And you're great with them," Adam said. "Anyone can see that." He raised his voice. "Anyone. Right, Cash?"

That was it. Game over.

Cash raised his head. "Adam, let me show you the deck."

"No, thanks. I've already seen the deck, back when Dozer used to throw those—"

"Deck." Cash gritted his teeth. "Now."

Chapter 14

Cash rounded on Adam the minute his manager stepped onto the darkened, quiet deck and closed the door.

"What's the matter with you?" he demanded, jabbing Adam in the chest. "Are you *trying* to screw things up for me?"

"Not really," Adam said. "Are *you*?"

An exasperated sigh. "What the hell does that mean?"

"It means you're being pretty hard on Marisol, Cash. Remember, if she quits, you're in deep shit. No nanny."

"She can't quit. She's on work assignment from Dzeel."

"That's not true. She can request a reassignment." Adam shook his head. "You, as usual, haven't read the paperwork."

Cash offered an expletive. He never read paperwork. It wasn't his job. He was the talent, not the management. He operated on instinct and skill, not red tape.

"Just knock off the love fest and start being boring, damn it," he ordered. "That's what you're here for."

Adam arched his brows. "Boring?"

"You know." In frustration, Cash waved his arms around, trying to come up with something suitably Adam-like. "Talk about tofu or mutual funds or chick flicks. No wait.

Not chick flicks. You're supposed to be boring to Marisol, not me."

"And the point of all this is . . . ?"

Cash would have thought it was obvious. "To keep her out of that damned French maid's uniform." He paced faster. "It's right in her closet. Twenty yards away! You know how fast I can cover twenty yards," he reminded his manager earnestly. "Fast."

"You're crazy."

"And you're not helping."

Oh man. Cash could see Marisol moving around in the kitchen, framed by the doors to the deck in a perfectly lit tableau of nanny-plus-kids harmony. Somehow she'd even convinced Jacob, Emily, and Hannah to wipe down the countertops, with gusto and near precision. That was voodoo for sure. If he didn't miss his guess, they were all singing too.

He wheeled to face Adam again. "You're *definitely* not helping. 'That was amazing, Marisol,'" Cash mimicked, making prissy hand gestures. "'You're great with the kids, Marisol.' 'You look really hot tonight, Marisol.'"

"Hey. I never said she looked hot," Adam protested.

"You didn't have to. You said it all with your eyes."

"Again—you're crazy." Looking aggravatingly calm, his manager leaned on the deck railing. He gazed up at the star-filled sky. "Wow. It's like a blanket of diamonds up there. There's nothing like a Flagstaff sky at night, right? That's why they put the Lowell observatory up here, you know."

"That's it!" Excitedly, Cash grabbed his arm. "Just like that. Don't use up all the good stuff at once though. Keep some of that poetic crap for Marisol. Talk about the observatory too. Like when it was constructed or what astronomy programs they have. She'll be dying to get away from both of us."

"You want her to want to get away from you? Invite her

out here for this conversation," Adam said dryly. "That ought to do the trick."

Cash didn't know why his friend was being so uncooperative. To him, this seemed a very obvious and urgent plan.

"Tell you what—just pretend Marisol is Stephanie," he said. "Or one of my old girlfriends from college. Remember? Then do whatever you used to do to make them dislike you."

"Like what? Interfere with your make-out sessions?"

"No, you idiot." A tantalizing vision of himself making out with Marisol, pushing her against the refrigerator and kissing her until she begged him to undress her, almost blindsided him. Cash nodded. "I mean yes. Also do that. But make sure you're critical too. Tell her she's wrong for me. Be a macho prick."

"Wow." Adam smiled. "You really like this girl, don't you?"

More than he'd ever expected to, Cash realized. Which made her a triple threat—dangerous to his life, his heart, and his future.

Or maybe he was still affected by the junk food extravaganza they'd all shared for dinner, he told himself. Maybe he was hallucinating because of artificial-flavor overload and only thought he was falling for his babealicious nanny.

The bottom line was . . .

"I have to make sure she thinks of me as her boss. Period."

"I dunno. You might be underestimating her." Adam delivered him a gallingly dubious look. "Marisol is pretty remarkable. She's funny, and the kids love her. I still can't figure out where I know her from though. In person she looks even more familiar than her photograph, but I can't quite place her."

"Screw that. Just be unreasonable. Okay, buddy?"

Another sigh. "I'll do my best."

"That's all I can ask." Cash slapped him on the back. "Thanks for coming up here. I really appreciate it."

"I've got to find another job," Adam complained.

Then, after one final glance at the stars, he turned and left the deck with Cash trailing eagerly behind him, ready to implement his latest foolproof plan to keep his hands off the nanny.

When they stepped inside, Marisol glanced up. She smiled, surrounded by a kitchen peninsula still full of wrappers and packages and pots and pans, despite the fact that Jacob, Hannah, and Emily were enthusiastically running around filling trash bags. Seeing him looking, she made a goofy face, comically rolling her eyes at a stack of dishes. Damn. She was going to be a good sport about all of it. His calling her out on the cleaning, his dragging away her rabid helper—Adam—and his grumpy demeanor too.

Marisol gave a little hip wiggle, joining the kids in a song from a Nickelodeon TV show. She winked, raising her arms in the air while she performed the accompanying hand motions, just like Emily and Hannah and Jacob did as they dumped their trash bags and cha-cha-ed out of the room. Of course, Marisol's arms were sheathed to the elbows in yellow rubber gloves, but somehow she made the *hausfrau* look work for her.

Cash could tell she wasn't the world's greatest dish washer, because she appeared to have sprinkled Cascade Lemon powder across every plate on the countertop, instead of in the dishwasher itself. And she'd squirted Jet-Dry in all the glasses too—every one had a little blue puddle in the bottom.

Just at that instant though, and maybe because of that song and that dance and that silly look on her face,

Marisol seemed so at home there—so right—that Cash had to stop and stare.

For a single breath, just that, he wished this really was his house, not a summertime respite from his cramped bachelor apartment. He wished the kids really were that angelic all the time, not squabbling about SpongeBob versus the Angry Beavers most days. He wished Marisol really was his. His alone.

She held up two bow-tied sandwich bags, waggling them enticingly. "I've got goodies for you two! Come and get 'em."

Without a second thought, Cash and Adam bolted for the kitchen. They collided. Cash elbowed his manager and took the lead. Adam tripped him and surged ahead. They scuffled. They had to leapfrog over poor Dump. After numerous scowls and several dirty looks, they made it past three of the most contested yards in kitchen history. Cash gave Adam one final shove.

Victory! He offered a champion's smile to Marisol, then accepted the goodie bag she held. "Thanks. This looks good."

"Looks *great*." Adam maneuvered in front to accept his bag.

"The kids already got theirs, but they're saving them for later." Marisol looked amused. "Go ahead. Open them."

Cash did. Doing so required working past two thick layers of stickers—some metallic, some scratch-n-sniff, some featuring Shrek and others featuring My Pretty Pony—one multiply wrapped ribbon with curled ends, and a few stick-on bows.

"The goodie bags are the pièce de résistance for the dinner," Marisol explained. "You can't have a successful event without a little take-home gift, right? I hope you like them."

"I know I will." Cash unearthed two foil-wrapped Hershey kisses, one comic strip carefully snipped from the newspaper, three polished pebbles, and a miniature pine cone. Clearly Marisol had made do with what she could find for goodies, without violating the rules of her Dzeel no-shopping program.

"The kids helped decorate." She bit her lip, watching him. "They did a really good job too. You can see how they took their time with all the stickers."

Cash could, having spent countless hours with Emily, Hannah, and Jacob with coloring books or Magna Doodles or craft projects. Usually, their artistic zeal—and accompanying hand-eye coordination—waned after the first five minutes. He didn't know how Marisol had motivated them to stick with goodie bag making.

Impressed, he glanced up at her. She met his gaze, her whole expression suffused with excitement and generosity.

In that moment, Cash was a goner.

Marisol was too sweet, too giving, too good for the kind of evasive tactics he had in mind. All at once, they struck him for what they were—completely stupid.

He didn't even know if Marisol felt the same way he did, but Cash did know one thing—having Adam here as a buffer hadn't stopped him from recognizing the truth. He felt something when Marisol was around. Something he never had before. And he wanted more of it. More than countertop nookie. Just more.

"Eh, I'll open mine later." Carelessly, Adam dropped his goodie bag on the counter. He didn't give it a second glance, but he did offer a big, manly snort. "How about I beat your ass in a game of pool, buddy?" He slung his arm around Cash's shoulder.

Cash glared at him, trying not to see Marisol's disappointed expression in his peripheral vision. He shrugged off Adam's arm. "Hang on. I want to put this away first—"

Adam grabbed Cash's bag. He flung it on the counter. "Hey!" Instantly, Cash went for his throat.

Only his manager's hard, meaningful look stopped him. *You asked for this*, that look said. *You got it.*

They froze for a second in that awkward pose—Cash with his arm pulled back for the first punch; Adam staring him down.

"It's okay." With a stilted-sounding chuckle, Marisol scooped up the bags. "These will keep. You boys go have fun."

Incredibly, Adam swiveled to wink at her. "Hey, you should come along." He offered a cheesy double finger-gun salute. "It won't be fun without you, dollface." He leered.

What the f—? *Dollface?* Cash mouthed, disbelieving.

Meeting his incredulous expression, Adam only offered the tiniest shrug. He never had been the most diehard macho of men, it occurred to Cash. He was only doing what he thought Cash wanted him to do.

The only plus side was that Marisol wouldn't be on the receiving end of Adam's attempts to set up a screen between her and Cash for much longer, because she would never agree to shoot pool with them. She had cleaning up to do, trash to take out, kids to corral . . . a whole bedtime routine to engineer. Cash knew better than anyone what a handful it could be to get Emily, Hannah, and Jacob settled down for the night.

"Hmmm." A smile played around Marisol's lips. "I've got some things to do right now, but maybe later I'll join you."

"Don't join Cash," Adam blurted. "He's bad for you."

Marisol gave them both a quizzical frown.

Oh Christ. Enlisting Adam in his hands-off-the-nanny plan had been the king of bad ideas. Before he could make anything worse, Cash clamped his hand on his manager's neck. He steered him toward the back of the house, giving Marisol a helpless "Who knows what's wrong with this clown?" look in the process.

* * *

"Dollface?" Cash repeated. He shoved Adam across the trophy room toward the pool table, completely exasperated. "What the hell is that? Who are you, James Cagney all of a sudden?"

"Hey, it was your stupid idea. Don't blame me."

"You hurt her feelings!"

"No, you hurt her feelings," Adam retorted. "You just used me to do it, dumbass. If you don't like it, call it off."

Cash stalked around the pool table, with its gaudy overhead lamp, tacked-on fringe, and purple baize covering. Maake "Dozer" Anapau, the defensive tackle who owned the house, believed in making a statement with his decorating whenever possible. Cash just believed in making sure he was always the strongest, the fastest, and the best at whatever he did. Including this.

"You know I can't do that," he said.

"Good. Because as pathetic as this plan of yours is, it's all we've got." Calmly, Adam racked several balls. "You're not the only one with his future on the line. Remember that."

"You think I'm not? You think I'm just screwing around?"

"No, I don't. Not now. That's just the problem."

Cash glared at him.

"If you were just screwing around, you wouldn't have gone all mushy in there a minute ago with Marisol."

Mushy? Cash rolled his eyes. He knew he could cover his tracks better than that. "You're delusional."

"The hell I am." Adam racked the last two balls, then slid the rack into position. He lifted it away, leaving the balls in place. "I've known you a long time. I can see the signs. You like this girl. A lot. But she's your nanny, Cash. You need her."

"I know that."

"So all I'm saying is, keep your hands to yourself. Okay?"

"I have been!" And it had cost him too. Five pounds of slushy ice-water shower wasn't easy on a man. "I have been."

"Good. Keep it up. Ride it out. Be a man." Adam slapped him on the back. "In the meantime, I'll do what I can to separate you and Marisol. God knows you need it. The two of you are like lovesick puppies in heat."

"Oh screw you."

Blandly, his manager selected a cue. He examined the pool table with an air of determination. "So are we playing or not?"

"Are you going to be nicer to Marisol?" Cash demanded. "Are you going to take advantage of her?"

"Take ad—" That went too far. Cash stalked closer, giving his manager an assessing stare. "When have I ever taken advantage of a woman? Tell me."

Adam rubbed the back of his neck. He didn't meet Cash's eyes. "Well, actually . . . you're more inclined to fall in love with them than take advantage of them."

Cash scoffed. Fall in love? His manager didn't know squat.

"And then there is the fact that your ex-wife cleaned your clock in your divorce, right after you'd become a full-time family man. So I guess Stephanie took advantage of you."

Low blow. That one definitely deserved a middle-finger salute. Cash obliged with both hands.

"But on the other hand, you *have* been living like a monk these past two years, so I'd say all bets are off." Adam chalked his cue. "Besides, Marisol is special. I don't want her to buy your line of bullshit and get hurt."

"What, you're defending her now? From me?"

"Hey, whatever it takes." Adam spread his arms in a conciliatory gesture. "Because you know those ex-girlfriends you were talking about? The ones you said didn't like me?"

Cash didn't like the sound of this. Grudgingly, he nodded.

"Well, after you were through with them, guess who they came to for answers?"

"I don't believe this." Cash grabbed a cue of his own. He used it to point at Adam. "You're telling me that my ex-girlfriends cried on your shoulder when we broke up?"

A nod. "Once or twice."

Unbelievable.

"So I know what a guy like you does to a woman," Adam said. "And it isn't pretty. I wasn't wild about this idea in the first place, but now that I've met Marisol . . . she probably does need help staying away from you, pal. For her own good."

Shaking his head, Cash shut his mouth. He pocketed two balls on his first shot, but he was too preoccupied to enjoy his early lead. Adam made him sound like the freaking Toxic Seducer, ready to wreak havoc everywhere he dropped his pants.

Well, screw him. Adam was wrong about him. Cash wasn't that bad, and he wasn't going to go all goo-goo eyed over his nanny either. Not if he could help it—and he could. He would.

Aside from which, he didn't fall in love all the time. Sure, he liked women. He *loved* women. But he'd only been in love once—with Stephanie—and that had ended disastrously. He'd have to be some kind of moron to sign up for more of the same now.

Especially when his life was still so screwed up.

If only Marisol hadn't looked so damned welcoming when he'd come back in the house tonight. If only she hadn't winked at him. If only she hadn't unearthed a French maid's outfit (of all things) to tempt him with. Everything would have been different.

If you don't like it, call it off.

Well, Cash didn't like it. But he couldn't call it off.

"Look, just try to be more subtle, all right?" he instructed Adam. He banked a ball off the left-hand rail, then sunk it. "Don't hurt Marisol's feelings. All you have to do is make sure she doesn't think I'm too irresistible—"

Adam chortled. "That should be easy."

"—and definitely make sure she knows I'm off limits," Cash persisted. "I told her that already, told her she's here strictly for the kids, but—"

"But a little reinforcement couldn't hurt. Gotcha." Adam nodded. They each took a few more shots, circling the table. Then Adam glanced up again. "Listen, it's not like I can't see why Marisol would be hard to resist. I can. Not just because she's beautiful, but also because she's got this other quality, you know? This thing that's special and unique and—"

Cash cut him off. He didn't need to be sold on Marisol's better qualities. He could see them for himself.

"Now who's a lovesick puppy?" he asked, forcing a grin. He edged around Dozer's wall-engulfing customized trophy case, then pointed his cue to the right. "Four ball, corner pocket."

He sank it cleanly. Take that. Cash Connelly was still in control of his game, his life, and his destiny—and no nanny, however enticing, was getting in his way.

Chapter 15

Marisol got the kids settled in with a DVD of *Cinderella*, doled out blankies and stuffed sea otters for each of them, then checked the dishwasher before hauling out four bags of trash. Given Jacob's sketchy directions, it took her a while to find the Dumpster, hidden way around the corner of the log-cabin-style garage, and even longer to work up the courage to open it.

She stared down the hulking green plastic tub. Set down her bulging trash bags. Tiptoed closer. In the feeble glow of the yard lights, that Dumpster looked like a perfect hiding place for raccoons. Which might be pretty cute actually. But didn't bears like to scrounge through people's trash out here in the country too? A bear could probably fit inside that Dumpster : . .

Nah, she was being silly. If there were some kind of wild critter out here, she'd hear it first. Right? With her toes growing chilly in her sandals, Marisol edged toward the Dumpster. She held her breath. She listened carefully, wishing she'd brought something sturdier than four plastic trash bags with her, in case defending herself was necessary.

Also, that Dumpster looked gross. She didn't want to touch it, even with her rubber-gloved hands.

Well, she'd just have to be resourceful. She'd proven she could improvise with dinner, right? Glancing around, she spotted a big stick lying nearby. Marisol picked it up—quivering dried branches and all—then bravely poked the Dumpster's lid.

It creaked upward. She cringed, then pushed harder. It flopped open all the way, its momentum nearly knocking her off her high heels. *Whump.* A faint smelly odor wafted out, competing with the grass and the pine trees, but it wasn't too terrible.

Maybe Cash had ordered his trash not to stink. She wouldn't doubt it, given how high handed he'd been after dinner.

Of course, she knew the reasons behind that now. Adam had confided to her—whispered to her over the sink full of dirty dishes—that Cash sometimes had trouble delegating authority. Which explained his overbearing way of demanding she start cleaning up, Marisol figured. Tension could do that to a person. Even a person as big and burly and improbably reticent as Cash apparently was, underneath all those muscles of his.

It was interesting. According to Adam, if she wanted to deal with Cash successfully, she'd have to really assert herself. Be in command. So Marisol had decided to do exactly that. She was a strong woman. She had no trouble taking charge.

Or charging something—but that was a whole other issue.

The bottom line was, if Cash thought he was scaring away Marisol Winston with a few blunt orders and the threat of a little hard work, he'd better think again. There was no way she was quitting. Not after she'd come so far.

Seriously, she'd never taken out the trash before. Heck, she'd never even wondered where it disappeared to after she tossed her latte cups and empty mascara

tubes in the bin. And she'd definitely never thought
about how scary a big, darkened Dumpster might be in
the middle of the wilderness.

The important thing now was, she'd succeeded!
Woo-hoo!

The Dumpster yawned open in the moonlight, ready
for phase two of her kitchen cleaning. Only two days out
here in the boonies, and already she was mastering new
challenges.

Proudly, Marisol planted her stick in the ground, high
on her dinner triumph and her defeat of the Dumpster.
She felt like an adventurous explorer—like the first
woman to cast a ballot, or the first woman to wear pants
and declare them fabulous.

Greta Garbo? Or maybe Katharine Hepburn. She
wasn't sure. The one thing Marisol *was* sure of was that
nannying and housekeeping might be new to her—but
so far, she rocked.

A yowl came from the bushes. Something streaked
across her path—something furry and fast. A wild
animal! Maybe a bear!

Marisol freaked. She hurled the trash bags hastily into
the Dumpster and bolted for the house, feeling one
thousand percent less Garboesque than before. Stupid
Mother Nature. She really did a number on a person's
sense of style.

"Tada! I brought refreshments." Marisol poked her
head inside the log cabin's trophy room, having calmed
her postmarathon-level heart rate (after the bear scare),
reapplied her lip gloss (her Stila supply was getting dangerously low) and finished an excellent first-time job of
kitchen cleanup (thank you, all-purpose blue spray stuff!).
Now with the kids settled in, she was ready to relax.

She spotted Cash and Adam, apparently engaged in a

highly contested poolroom battle, and carried in her tray of after-dinner drinks—lemonades, because of the kids—without being invited. "Who wants a nice cold drink?"

She held up a glass.

Their jocular attitudes vanished. Both men looked at her as if her innocent lemonade were a live snake—and they were wimpy men who were afraid of live snakes. Marisol seriously doubted anything that low to the ground could scare Cash.

Maybe she'd startled them or something. They had been acting pretty weird right before they'd left the kitchen to play pool. For a second, it had almost looked as if Cash and Adam were going to have a smackdown over the goodie bags. As if they weren't both fully equipped to get all the goodies they wanted.

She clinked the ice in the glass, trying to entice them with her superior hostessing skills. "It's really good."

As she might have expected, Cash got brave first.

"Thanks, I'll take one." He strode nearer, his gaze lingering over her bare legs with every step. He moved upward, past her frilly white French-maid's apron, then reached her breasts just as he reached her. He gave her a wholly irresistible smile. "Looks great. I'm really thirsty."

He paused, holding her momentarily spellbound. Marisol felt a little dizzy. She wasn't sure how one man could have such an impact on her, but when she got within reaching distance of Cash, somehow all her good intentions fled.

This time, she yanked them back, trying urgently to remember Adam's words of wisdom. *Be aggressive. Take charge.*

Okey-dokey. She thrust a glass at Cash. "Here. Take this."

He lifted his eyebrows but did what she said, all the same. He took the glass. He even raised it to drink. Unfortunately, his heated gaze never left her. So Marisol

didn't feel any less entranced by the details before her—
the firm grasp of his hand, the subtle shadow of his
beard stubble, the greedy movements of his Adam's
apple as he slaked his thirst.

Mmmm. She did like a man who went for what he
wanted.

Suddenly, Adam snatched the glass away, nearly stepping on Marisol's toes in the process. He wedged himself
between her and Cash like a clipboard-wielding PR
person kneecapping the riffraff when they tried to sneak
behind the velvet rope.

"I'll take that." Adam chugged his pilfered lemonade
in a few huge swallows, then exhaled noisily. "Ahhh.
That's good!" He set down the glass, then elbowed Cash.
"No more for you though. You know that stuff's off limits
for you." He leaned toward Marisol. "I've got to keep this
guy on the straight and narrow."

"It's just lemonade," she protested, her gaze darting to
Cash. He didn't seem unduly affected by her lemonade.
She set down the tray, making the remaining glasses
wobble only a fraction. "I didn't even spike it. It's practically all fruit."

At least that's how it looked on the frozen tube.

"I know, but Cash is in training." Adam shouldered
past a disgruntled-looking Cash to confide in her further, hooking his thumb toward his friend. "He's got a
pretty shaky grasp on what's good for him, actually.
Always wants what he can't have."

"Really?" Marisol would have sworn Cash was a pretty
disciplined guy. "That's surprising."

"I know." Adam nodded. "But if I don't keep tabs on
Cash during the off-season and training camp, he gets in
all kinds of trouble. Especially when it comes to anything
sweet."

The two men exchanged prickly glances. Marisol would

have sworn that Cash surreptitiously gave Adam the finger, but she couldn't be sure.

"Really?" she asked Cash, fascinated by this unexpected information. So far, she hadn't glimpsed any real weaknesses in him—aside from that authority-delegating thing. That he was actually vulnerable to something made him seem twice as real somehow. Twice as approachable. "You've got a sweet tooth?"

Cash smiled. "Sure, you could call it that."

"Me too." Marisol nodded, suddenly swept away by a vision of herself and Cash—alone together with nothing but whipped cream, a few spoonfuls of chocolate fudge body paint, and hours to spend. Mmmm. Since she was being the aggressive one, she'd probably have to tie him down before licking off all that creamy goodness. But she figured she could handle it pretty well.

She wondered if he could. Or if he would beg her to let him loose so he could take charge instead. *"Please,"* he'd cry in a husky voice, straining at his ties. *"I have to—"*

"Oh yeah," Adam confirmed, blithely puncturing her fantasy bubble. "Cash has got a major sweet tooth. If I don't get between him and whatever goodies he's after, he, uh, balloons up like Homer Simpson. It's ugly."

Bug-eyed, Cash gave a sound of protest.

"Well, you must be doing a good job, Adam. Because Cash looks very fit to me." In demonstration, Marisol moved close enough to pat his chest. He felt warm and enticing beneath her fingertips. He stiffened a bit too, as though she'd caught him by surprise. Belatedly, it occurred to her that if faithful nannies-slash-housekeepers weren't allowed to grab their bosses' biceps, they were very likely completely forbidden to manhandle their bosses' muscular chests.

With a mighty effort, she lowered her hand. "You know," she said breezily, "fit in a professionally athletic sense."

Cash lifted his eyebrow. "In every sense."

Oh wow. She eyed him, imagining exactly what other senses he meant. Sight. Smell. Touch. Mmmm. Yeah. Maybe he'd pictured that whipped-cream-and-chocolate-fudge scenario too. If not, she could explain it. Or demonstrate in detail. Whatever he wanted.

They'd probably need cherries too. Just when Marisol was starting to get swept away again, Adam shoved between them.

"Come on you two!" he said jovially, grabbing Marisol's hand and dragging her aside. "Since I've got to be here to keep Cash away from the goodies anyway, let's play pool!"

Moments later, Marisol found herself with a pool pole in hand, staring down at a gaudy purple felt-covered table while Adam explained the finer points of billiards—including carom, pool, and snooker. Midway through Adam's instructions about solids, stripes, and scratching, she stole a glance at Cash.

He smiled at her, giving her another intense look that somehow combined warmth, humor, and hang-onto-the-headboard cockiness in equal measure. He'd definitely divined her fantasy whipped-cream-and-chocolate set-up somehow. It was all there in his eyes. Marisol waved her pole, trying to fan herself.

"And that's how the game evolved historically from a form of French croquet played with a *bille*, or ball, to what we call pool today," Adam was saying. He stopped abruptly, caught Marisol and Cash exchanging glances, then frowned. "Marisol, why don't you come over here and try racking the balls?"

"Um, okay." Gamely, she pulled the triangular thing closer and started piling in balls. There was no way she was going to be able to color-coordinate them in any aesthetically appealing fashion, but she decided to give the job her best anyway. Never let it be said that Marisol Winston wasn't a good sport.

She glanced up. Cash's attention had swerved to Adam.

An unreadable look passed between the two men.

"Am I doing it wrong?" she asked. "I know you said to mix up the solids and stripes, but artistically speaking, they look better like this." She pointed to her arrangement.

"That looks fine," Adam said.

"Let's just play." Cash put his hand to the small of her back, casually guiding her. "I'll show you how to break."

Marisol listened intently. No amount of concentration could override the stimulating effect of being right next to Cash though. When he placed his hands over hers, showing her how to form a bridge with her fingers, she felt tingly all over. When he smiled at her, praising her efforts to hit the cue ball, she wanted to sigh. When he touched her hips, positioning her just so for her next shot, she couldn't help pushing herself a little more firmly into his palms. She'd swear he groaned in response.

"Have I told you about the observatory nearby?" Adam blurted, striding closer. "It was established in 1894 by a mathematician and amateur astronomer named Percival Lowell."

Marisol shook herself. "No, you didn't."

"It's a real piece of local history. In 1930, astronomers at the Lowell Observatory discovered Pluto—the planet, not the Disney dog." Adam gave Cash an indecipherable look. He wet his lips. "Also the stars outside are like a big bowl of diamonds, all scattered on a piece of uh, black velvet."

Marisol tried to share an isn't-he-cute? glance with Cash, but he was already frowning at Adam. She settled for, "Really?"

"Yes. You should come check out the view sometime." Adam's gaze shot to Cash, then to Marisol, then to the few feet separating them. "Like right now, maybe. I'll take you out to the deck myself."

"It's her turn right now."

As he said the words, Cash moved into her airspace again, charging up all the molecules that surrounded them. Whatever Adam said as a rejoinder was lost. His voice dropped to a steady background murmur, something Marisol could scarcely focus on while Cash was near. She felt herself drawn to him, pulled to stand closer, to savor his voice, to stare raptly into his face.

It was a nice face—honest and tough and appealing. She wanted to look at him for hours. She wanted to touch him, to be with him, to know him. It hardly seemed possible they'd met such a short time ago. The connection between them felt inevitable.

"Go ahead." Cash guided her hands. "Go for it."

Oh, wow. *Go for it.* She really, really wanted to. But with Adam right there, lecturing about solar systems and historical events, she knew that dragging Cash onto the pool table and ripping off his clothes would not be polite. Not even out here in the boonies.

Instead, Marisol tried another shot and actually hit the ball this time. Hurray! Pleased, she gave a little wiggle, then high-fived Cash. Their gazes met. He clasped her hand, then interlaced their fingers and squeezed. From that single point of connection, a tremor shot through her whole body.

Oh boy. They were going to be *fantastic* together.

Or at least they would be, Marisol reminded herself, if not for some restriction that she couldn't quite remember right now. Not while touching him. She might have known Cash would have nice hands . . . and a firm, commanding grip to go with them. Men who were confident about touching were her favorites.

". . . but of course, other scientists didn't agree!" Adam

shouted. He must have been droning on about astronomy and constellations all this time. "Only Lowell thought so!"

Discomfited, Marisol dropped her hand from Cash's.

Equally chastened, Cash made a fist. "Your shot, Adam."

His manager gave him a hard stare. Something else passed between the two men, something that felt like more than training camp issues. More than pool-playing rivalry. Just more.

After all, a girl didn't live through a childhood divorce, a judgmental father, and three varied stepmothers without picking up a little something about body language. All that eyebrow waggling, impatient gesturing, and meaningful gazing that Cash and Adam were doing definitely added up to something.

Just as he'd done before, Adam inserted himself right between her and Cash. He actually nudged her aside a little too, the way autograph hounds sometimes did to Caprice and Tenley when the three of them shopped the Promenade in Santa Monica.

Marisol stepped away, feeling baffled

"Remember, you're in training," Adam told Cash, grabbing his arm to make his point. "You promised you wouldn't do this."

"Do what?" Marisol asked. "Play pool?"

Both men turned as though remembering she was still there. Cash growled, hurling his manager a frustrated look.

Indignantly, Marisol put her hands on her hips and waited for things to start making sense. Maybe Cash and Adam were just really competitive. But she didn't think that explained the way Adam kept butting in between her and Cash—or the way Cash kept casting his manager vaguely guilty looks. Not to mention the way the two of them kept talking about being *in training*—it was as if they were speaking in code or something.

Then it hit her. She couldn't believe she'd been so blind.

Why hadn't she realized what was going on?

"Listen, you guys go ahead and play." Marisol waved them toward the pool table. "One of you can take over for me right? I've got to go shuffle the kids off to bed anyway."

She smoothed down her skirt and apron, gave both men a slightly unsteady smile, then headed for the door.

Chapter 16

It took Cash two days to track down Marisol so he could find out why she'd disappeared so abruptly after their pool-playing lesson. Even then, he only caught up with her because she was in between coordinating teddy-bear makeover sessions and serving up triple fudge ripple for breakfast.

"Ice cream?" he asked, boggling when he came upon the kids digging into cereal bowls piled high with the stuff. "Who let you eat ice cream for breakfast?"

Mouth full, Jacob pointed a spoon. "Mmm said we could," came the garbled response. It looked as if he'd garnished his ice cream with crumbled-up potato chips and black pepper, and was digging into the mixture with relish.

"It's healthy," Emily informed him, glancing up from her Polly Pocket play set. "Some studies suggest that three daily servings of dairy foods may help people lose weight."

"That's right." Hannah nodded. She rearranged her teddy bear—currently sporting hoop earrings, a newsboy cap, and shiny gold shorts—so it sat on top of Emily's and Jacob's bears. "So far, I'm winning at eating the most dairy foods."

"It's not a contest." Cash eyed the drippy container. It

looked dented, as though all three of them had wrestled over it.

"Marisol ate ice cream too," Jacob said.

"She did?" Cash would have liked to have seen that.

Instantly diverted, he pictured her licking the spoon, closing her eyes in ecstasy as she tasted the first frosty bite, shimmying in delight as the ice cream melted in her mouth. Mmmm. There was no doubt in his mind that Marisol was a woman who knew how to savor a treat. Slowly. Sexily. With every last bit of attention and intensity focused on pleasure.

Adam cleared this throat, deflating Cash's fantasy.

Disgruntled, Cash frowned at him.

His manager only lowered his newspaper, then pointedly shook another two Shoparama store-brand pain relievers from the jumbo-sized bottle on the table. He washed them down with a swig of coffee, making his displeasure more than evident.

Adam didn't think his presence at the house was helping, even after all the butting in and the boring conversations he'd started over the past forty-eight hours. Clearly, he wanted Cash to know it. He wanted Cash to know that he didn't find the sofa very comfortable to sleep on either.

"Oh go buy some Bengay, old man," Cash snapped.

Adam merely raised his newspaper again.

The kids went on plowing through their ice cream "breakfast," completely ignoring every rule he'd ever laid down about healthy eating. Cash wasn't even sure where they'd gotten ice cream. When he was in training, he didn't keep it on hand. Come to think of it, he'd noticed several new items popping up in the pantry lately . . .

Suddenly, a voice from the other end of the house caught his attention.

"Remember to put your bowls in the dishwasher,"

Marisol called. "I don't want to play hide-and-seek with them again."

"We will!" the kids chorused. They giggled, undoubtedly planning to do anything but. "In the dishwasher."

With no time to spare for his offsprings' shenanigans, Cash swiveled toward the master bedroom. He'd found Marisol. Now he'd get to the bottom of the ice cream situation—and more, besides.

Hurling his gym bag and keys onto the peninsula, Cash went in search of his MIA nanny.

The first thing he did was stub his toe.

Cash yelped and grabbed his bare foot, hopping in the hallway. Who the hell had moved that table there?

Marisol popped out of his bedroom, looking inquisitive and unreasonably saucy. She had a feather duster in her hand. If he hadn't been in pain just then, he might have spanked her with it. As it was, all he could do was clench his jaw, trying to ignore the tingling in his big toe.

How had this happened anyway? All he wanted was a nice, predictable summer so he could excel in training camp, cement his spot with the Scorpions, and convince Stephanie he'd earned expanded custody of Emily, Jacob, and Hannah. Instead, Cash had gotten rebellion, confusion, and a potentially broken toe. Not to mention an irresistibly sexy nanny.

He pointed. "What the hell is that doing there?"

"The table?" Marisol blinked. "Well, that console was underutilized in the foyer, so I moved it here to the hallway. It really completes that space, don't you think so?"

"No."

"Hmmm. I do. Especially with that vase on top." She gave him an appraising look, seemed to decide that his toe wasn't broken, then folded her arms. The feather duster poked out from beneath her elbow, reminding him that it probably went with the French maid's uniform. "I don't know who your decorator was, but they clearly didn't have much of an eye for proportion or color. I'm planning a few improvements, if you don't mind, now that I've gotten in a groove with the kids."

"Whatever." He waved his arm. "Fine. Go crazy."

Marisol crinkled her nose. The gesture looked adorable.

"Are you all right? You seem cranky." She leaned sideways, as though trying to see down the hallway to the dining room. "You probably didn't eat breakfast yet, right? You always get a little grouchy when you haven't had your regulation six-egg-white omelet with feta cheese, spinach, and Pop-Tarts."

She smiled, as though the combination were hilarious.

Cash didn't know what was so funny about that. "So I like having the same breakfast every day. Eggs are healthy. So what?"

"So . . . I see where Jacob gets it from, that's all."

"Gets what from?"

"The weird food fetish." She nudged him. "Come on, you seriously never noticed? With you polluting your Cool Ranch Doritos by dunking them in strawberry jam, and Jacob feasting on bologna-and-raisin-bread sandwiches with salsa?"

"I never noticed," Cash said squarely.

Right now, he couldn't help noticing *her*. She had on another one of those short white skirts he liked. High heels too. And a fluttery white top that, unfortunately, wasn't sheer enough to offer a glimpse of her lacy bra.

"Okay, be in denial," Marisol told him. "At Dzeel they'd call that ignoring your triggers, then hustle you into therapy."

Dzeel. Hell, he still had that evaluation paperwork to do.

"Anyway, I won't rat you out to Jeremy Fordham." Marisol's eyes sparkled. "But I have been meaning to talk to you." She stepped closer, the subject of his eating habits apparently put aside for now. She gazed up into his face solemnly. "I'm sorry about the other night. When we were playing pool? I didn't mean to make things awkward or make anybody uncomfortable."

She'd made him uncomfortable, no question. But he doubted she was talking about the fit of his black pants. Cash nodded.

"It's just that—" Marisol broke off, gazing down the hallway again. She faced him once more. "I didn't realize you and Adam were so close. But don't worry. While he's here, I'll do my best to leave the two of you alone together."

He blinked. "Alone?"

"You know—" She elbowed him in the ribs, waggling her eyebrows. "Alone. For a little private time."

"Private time to do what?"

"Whatever you want." Marisol grinned, giving him a sisterly squeeze on his biceps. "I think you two are sweet together."

"*Sweet?*"

"I can't say I'm not disappointed," she went on, "because I am. And I can't say I'm not embarrassed not to have picked up on the signals earlier. But now that I know where things stand with you and Adam, I promise I won't get in the way."

Cash frowned. What the hell was she talking about?

Oblivious to his bewilderment, Marisol perked up. "In fact, we could probably work out some kind of signal so I can keep the kids occupied whenever you and Adam want a little grown-up time together!" She gave a broad wink. "Just give me the sign, and I'll hustle them off for T-ball or something."

Grown-up time together? Dumbfounded, Cash gawked at her.

"You think Adam and I are a *couple?*"

"Well . . . yeah. Of course." She gestured toward the

kitchen. "The way you two keep exchanging glances, sending each other those covert looks . . . it's all very romantic."

"*Romantic*?"

Marisol nodded. "I'm telling you, when Adam swatted you on the butt yesterday, I almost cried. I swear to God."

She raised two fingers in what approximated a Girl Scout salute, still looking a little misty. Cash couldn't believe his eyes. Or his ears.

"Adam and I are just friends," he said.

Marisol gave him a no-nonsense look. "Come on, Cash. You don't have to feel weird around me. I know that maybe things are touchy because of your football career and everything, but—"

He pressed his fingers to her mouth, stopping her. He shook his head more emphatically. "You have the wrong idea about me."

"It's okay! I mean, I'm a little embarrassed about having such a big crush on you," Marisol admitted, "since it's one-sided and all. And I guess I imagined some things were more—"

"Things *are* more," Cash said. "For me too."

She stopped, staring up at him.

"I'm not interested in Adam. Especially not that way."

"You're not?"

He shook his head. He could practically see the gears grinding in Marisol's brain. Her lips turned downward, looking no less luscious in the process. She had a realization.

"Oh Cash. It's just Adam, isn't it?" Fervently, she clutched his arm, her eyes wide. "Adam is the one with a crush on you, isn't he? And it's one-sided too." She clutched her heart. "Oh, poor Adam. I know just how he feels!"

"No!" The word came out in a hoarse whisper, the most intensity Cash could manage with his manager and three kids just down the hallway in the kitchen. "Listen to me for a second—"

"You should be nicer to him." Marisol gave him a disapproving look. "I've heard you calling him names, you know. You ought to be sensitive to Adam's feelings, even if you can't return them. It's the decent thing to do."

Cash fisted his hands, summoning patience. "Stop. Listen to me. Adam doesn't have feelings for me. I don't have feelings for him. We're just friends. That's all. Friends."

"But—" Marisol paused, then gestured in the direction of Dozer's trophy room. "The significant looks. The butting in. The jealous glances and the code words—"

"Code words?"

"'In training'?" She raised her brows. "'Sweet tooth'? You can't tell me those weren't code words."

"Remind me never to give you a Scorpions playbook." She scoffed, still waiting.

Cash swore. Damn Adam. He didn't want to be in this position. Not now. "Adam was only trying to help."

"Help with what?"

"Keeping me away from you." Cash rubbed his palm across his forehead, reluctant to meet her eyes—or admit the truth. But Marisol deserved no less, and he was a man who laid things on the line. "Adam is here to remind me to stay away from you."

For a second, there was only silence. He raised his head.

Marisol looked even more baffled than before. Then, "You need all that help just to stay away from me?"

Humbled, Cash nodded. "You're the nanny." He couldn't face her. Not if he expected to say what came next. "I'm not supposed to take advantage of the situation. Of you."

"Oh." Marisol nodded as she absorbed that information. "That's right. We did talk about that, didn't we? 'Nothing's going to happen between us,' you said. I didn't know you meant that you didn't want to take advantage of me."

"I don't." He mustered more of his famous self-discipline. "I won't." He sucked in a breath. "So now that that's settled—"

"Settled? Says who?" Marisol looked at his hands, fisted at his sides. She caught them in her soft grasp, squeezing gently. "What if I'm the one who takes advantage of you?"

He held his breath, all his attention focused on the union of their hands. Her touch was as gentle as she was—but as persistent as she was too. He liked it. He liked it all over.

"You can't take advantage of me. I'm too tough for that."

"Oh yeah?" Marisol arched her brow. She centered her gaze on his mouth. "Watch me."

An instant later, her lips touched his. Incredibly, the whole world rocked. Slowly, gently, sweetly, Marisol kissed him, still holding his hands steady at his sides. She levered upward, smiled, and tried it again.

Cash shook with the impact of her mouth on his, with the knowledge that she wanted him the same way he wanted her. It was in her kiss, her touch, her indrawn breath as she crashed against the hallway at her back and pulled him nearer.

That was all he could stand. Cash pushed closer, working toward the same goal Marisol had in mind—complete surrender. He teased open her mouth, slipped his tongue inside, moaned in bliss as their lips slid faster. He'd never experienced such incredible friction, such hot suction, such mind-blowing need in a single kiss . . . much less the several that came after.

When he finally raised his head again, he'd pressed himself all the way against her, their bodies flattened against the hallway as they kissed. He couldn't believe the peeled logs at Marisol's back hadn't ignited already. She gasped and stared up at him, her hands tangled in his hair.

"Don't stop," she demanded. "I like it."

He obliged, tipping her head back for another, deeper kiss. There was something completely necessary about that contact, something mind-blowingly right about kissing her. Cash didn't know what it was, and he didn't care. Not so long as he had both arms full of hot, eager Marisol, and not so long as she kept on kissing him back. Her little moans drove him crazy. They were so sexy, so husky, so uninhibited . . .

All the need he'd pent up demanded release, and Cash knew exactly how to satisfy it. He dropped his hands to her derriere and cupped her, pulling her hard against him as he went on kissing her. Yes. *Yes.* He could stay here all day, all night, all the time. All his attention filled with the feel of her in his hands, with the slide of their mouths and the urging of his body to move closer, closer—

"Daddy, your phone is ringing!" Hannah shouted.

Her steps pounded down the hallway.

Cash panicked and thrust Marisol away. Their mouths popped apart with a comical sound. He jerked himself backward and spun around, feeling his hair stand on end. Shit, shit, shit!

Hannah skidded to a stop. Her gaze darted between him and a rumpled-looking Marisol. She thrust his cell phone toward him. Its lights flashed as it played a Scorpions ringtone.

There was nothing else to do. He took the call.

"What?" he barked into the phone.

"Step away from the nanny," came a familiar stern voice. "Put your hands up. Or maybe in a straitjacket. Come on, Connelly. What the hell is wrong with you, anyway?"

Cash wheeled away, clutching the receiver. "*Adam?*"

"Who else? Jesus, why don't you carry your cell phone on you like a normal person? I didn't mean for Hannah to grab it."

Peering down the hall, Cash looked for his manager. Nada. Somehow the man had eyes everywhere. Had he installed hidden video cameras or something? "What are you doing, you perv?"

"Saving your ass, that's what," Adam replied crisply. "Just like you wanted me to. Remember?"

Cash groaned. He saw Hannah watching him with wide, innocent eyes. He patted her hair, offering a reassuring smile. "Thanks, honey. You can go finish your ice cream now."

His daughter skipped away, neatly avoiding the relocated table. Apparently only females possessed the redecorating survival gene. And he'd just given Marisol carte blanche to do whatever she wanted with Dozer's place too. He was screwed.

"Hey, are you there?" Adam demanded in his ear, probably pacing. "Because I just remembered where I've seen Marisol before. And you're in *way* over your head this time, buddy."

"No, I'm not." The reply was automatic. He could always handle everything. And okay, so he hadn't exactly reacted in a mature fashion when he'd first found out his ex-wife was banging his wide receiver. But what man would have? "Quit spying on me."

"She's *Marisol Winston*," Adam said urgently, ignoring his command. "Marisol freaking Winston. Of *the* Winston family. The multibillionaire Winston family with the Home Warehouse empire."

"So?" Cash glanced to the side. Marisol had dropped her feather duster at some point during their kiss. Now she bent over to retrieve it. She smoothed her skirt. Her short, sexy, driving-him-crazy skirt. He gave her an appreciative nod. "It's not her balance sheets I'm interested in."

"She's tabloid bait," Adam declared. "Trouble with a capital T. She's in the papers every other week."

"Not this week." Mmmm. He really loved Marisol's legs.

"No. Listen to me," Adam droned through the phone. "The last thing the Scorpions front office wants you to do is bring more notoriety to the team." He paused, probably to let his warning sink in. "It was bad enough when you and Tyrell were feuding. Bad enough when the whole team was divided. But this—"

"That's over with," Cash bit out, starting to get mad.

"You can't get involved with your nanny," Adam declared, "especially when she's also a famous heiress. You just can't."

"Hey, maybe you can't," Cash said with a grin, "but I—"

"Don't go there. You're losing perspective."

"No, *you're* losing perspective. This isn't a big deal." Now Marisol was feather dusting the hallway sconces. She reached higher, making her skirt ride up tantalizingly. Cash caught a glimpse of lacy white panties. Oh man. "And I'm busy. Turn off your spy cams and go buy yourself some Bengay. My treat."

"Cash." It sounded as though Adam were gritting his teeth. "I can say this because I'm out on the deck where the kids can't hear me, so I'm just going to let you have it. You're getting stupider by the second. Don't let your dick run your life. This is a volatile situation. Remember why I'm here—"

Marisol closed her hand over Cash's, muffling the sounds of his manager's diatribe. "Hang up the phone," she murmured.

Cash balked. First Adam's freak-out and now this? Usually women didn't tell him what to do.

"Do it," she urged. "Call him back later."

"No! Don't you hang up this phone!" Adam yelled, his voice reduced to a tinny screech. "I'll come back there if I have to! You're the one who wanted me here! I'm a buffer, damn it!"

"I'll call you back later," Cash said, eyeing Marisol.

"No! Listen to me," Adam squawked. "Get your head on straight. Don't let the heiress boss you around, damn it. You don't even like take-charge women! You don't have to—"

"No, you don't like take-charge women." Adam always got that mixed up. Cash smiled at Marisol. Damn, she looked good. Especially now that Hannah had gone and his kids were occupied. "I love them. I've gotta go."

He snapped shut his cell phone. He pocketed it, feeling an eager grin spread across his face.

"Very good." Marisol nodded approvingly. "That was easy. I wonder what else I could make you do if I asked?"

He eyed her pert face, her mile-wide smile, her long, long legs. *Right now? Just about anything.*

"Well, if you said please first," Cash hedged, lazily spreading his arms to the sides, "I guess the sky's the limit."

Something new was starting between them. Something unstoppable. He felt it with every step Marisol took.

"Hmmm. In that case . . ." Her eyes sparkled as she looked him up and down. She nodded. "Please kiss me again."

Cash moved forward. He cupped her cheek in his hand, marveling at the softness of her skin. He smiled, then lowered his mouth to hers. Marisol met him with equal fervor. It was as if they'd waited years to share this kiss, eons to feel their bodies touch. One kiss became two. Then three.

"Awwww!" came Emily's sigh.

"So romantic!" Hannah added on a girlish squeal.

"Yuck." Jacob scraped his spoon against the last of his ice cream, potato chips, and black pepper concoction, talking around a gigantic mouthful of the stuff. "I'd rather play Hot Wheels."

Huh? Cash drew back, startled. His three children stared

back at him with perfect equanimity from the other end of the hallway, lined up like spectators on the sidelines.

"That was even better than the way Tyrell kisses Mommy."

This came from Emily. Hannah agreed with a nod. Jacob made gagging sounds, balancing his now-empty bowl in both hands.

"How long have you three been there?" Cash asked.

"Long enough," Hannah said.

The other two nodded. Evidently, she'd gone straight from delivering the phone to ratting out her father. Nice.

"Hi, kids," Marisol said. "All done with your breakfast?"

They nodded, still staring expectantly at Cash. There was no hope for it except to own up to the situation, he decided. He was a stand-up guy. He knew how to do the right thing, even without Adam perched on his shoulder like Jiminy Cricket.

"Kids, listen to me." Cash hunkered down to meet them on eye level. "Sometimes when a man and a woman like one another, they, uh, want to spend time alone together—"

"Yeah. *Kissing time.*" Emily giggled.

"Well, maybe kissing time," Cash agreed. *Oh yeah, kissing time!* his body cheered. "But also adult time, when they can talk and share their feelings and get to know one another—"

"And suck face!" Jacob said gleefully.

Manfully, Cash mustered a serious expression. "Okay . . . and suck face," he agreed solemnly, casting a glance at Marisol. Maybe she'd help him out here. He didn't want to stunt his kids' development by treating them like babies. He didn't want to get all clinical either. But he did want to be respectful.

Geez, this fatherhood stuff was tricky.

Marisol gave a solemn nod. "Swap spit," she concurred.

She had to be kidding.

Cash flipped her a *that isn't helping* look.

She shrugged and elaborated. "Do the tongue tango."

Hannah, Emily, and Jacob nodded sagely. "Lock lips."

"Get to first base."

"Play tonsil hockey!"

"Have a little kissy poo."

"Enough!" Cash shouted. Were they all crazy? He gave the four of them a severe look. "Bottom line is, it's nobody's business but mine if I want to mack on Marisol."

They gawked at him.

"Well, it's kind of my business too," Marisol said.

"Yeah, Dad!" Emily nudged closer to her nanny. "It's Marisol's business too. She's got girl power."

"Are you two going to get married?" Jacob interrupted.

"Ooh! Can I be the head flower girl?" Hannah asked.

"No, I want to!" Emily cried, jumping up and down.

"Me, me!" Hannah objected. "I'd be the best at it."

"Don't make me a flower girl." Jacob backed up, his spoon clattering in his bowl. "I'm not doing it."

They were planning his wedding now?

Cash looked at Marisol for backup. No help there. She seemed to be enjoying all the chaos. She looked deliciously disheveled too. He would have liked to pick her up, carry her into his room, and make her a little more tousled for good measure. Maybe in three or four days he'd let her out . . .

Ahem. What the hell had happened to his self control?

Deliberately, Cash cleared his throat. He teed his hands in a time-out signal, needing to regain control of the situation.

Mayhem. He put his fingers in his mouth and whistled.

Everyone shut up. They looked at him expectantly.

"I've got to get to the gym," he said, and bailed.

Chapter 17

"No, I'm being dead serious." Marisol adjusted her cell phone's hands-free headset, being sure to keep an eye on Jacob, Hannah, and Emily as they cavorted down the Shoparama aisle ahead of her. "We shared this incredible moment together, and then Cash just bolted. What do you think that means?"

"Maybe it means he had to get to the gym, like he said," Tenley offered. She usually had the most optimistic slant of all of Marisol's friends. "Men are simple. They say what they mean."

"Right," Caprice scoffed on the other end of their three-way call. She sounded breathless, probably because she was doing her usual Thursday shopathon. "Men are so straightforward. Like when they say, 'I'll call you.' Then don't."

"Sometimes they do call," Tenley insisted.

"Ooh! A new Rebecca Taylor top!" Caprice squealed, obviously having gotten sidetracked. "So cute!"

"I wish I could see it." Forlornly, Marisol wheeled her grocery cart past an array of Hamburger Helper. Hmmm. She could use all the helpers she could get. And who didn't need a product that sounded so nurturing and supportive? She added two packages to her cart. "I haven't been shopping—really shopping—in for-*ever*. Did you get your birthday presents, Caprice?"

"Yup. Special delivery just like you ordered. Thanks, hon. Everything was perfect."

Warmth glowed in Marisol's chest. She squeezed her cart handle a little tighter. "I miss you guys."

"I miss you too," Tenley said.

"Me too." Caprice dropped the phone. Clunk. "Sorry. I just wrestled somebody for the most adorable pair of skinny jeans."

"Did you win?" Marisol asked.

"Of course. Wow, you *have* been gone a long time."

Her friends laughed. But suddenly Marisol felt strangely distant from both of them. She had been gone a long time, and her whole world was going on without her.

"Don't worry, Tenley." She forced a cheer she didn't quite feel into her voice. "I'll find something perfect for you too."

"I'm fine." Her friend sounded bewildered. "You don't have to give me anything. It's not my birthday, you know. Just come home soon, okay?"

"I will." But Marisol knew that wasn't enough. She looked up from her shopping list, searching for a poten-tial gift.

Too bad the Shoparama didn't stock spa packages.

"And have fun with that hottie quarterback of yours in the meantime," Caprice urged. "If you're stuck out in the boonies, you might as well boff Daniel Boone, right?"

More trills of laughter.

"Actually, I think it might be more than that," Marisol admitted. She cruised past a row of multicolored cereal boxes, each one claiming superior vitamins and antiox-idants. Everyone knew those were good for your skin, and complexion care was important, even for kids. She picked several varieties. "There's something about Cash. Something special. I really want him to like me. To think well of me. To respect me. You know?"

"Of course he will. Who wouldn't?" Tenley asked loyally.

"I'll put that on my AmEx card," came Caprice's muffled voice. "And I'd like it delivered too." She returned to the line. "Sorry about that. Where were we?"

"In the middle of Marisol's crush on her boss."

"Right. Well, I say go for it. Be all you can be."

"Thanks, you guys." Marisol spied the kids as they rounded the corner. If she didn't hurry, she'd lose them. She hustled down the aisle, past a tempting display of cookies, her high heels clicking. Wow, she really had her *Desperate Housewives* mojo going on. "It's just that Cash is a really hard worker. He's gotten where he is through blood, sweat, and tears—"

"He's a crier?" Caprice interrupted. "Oh, honey—"

"It's an aphorism," Tenley said. "Keep—"

"A what? That sounds gross. How old *is* he anyway?"

"Never mind Caprice. Just keep going, Marisol."

Marisol smiled. "And he's not going to be impressed with the magnitude of my trust fund. Or the number of party invitations I receive. Or the size of my shoe room."

Even if it *was* six hundred square feet of footwear nirvana, with custom shelves and a climate-controlled atmosphere.

Geez, she missed that shoe room, Marisol mused. The rest of her beach house too. It was so sleek, so clean . . . so austere.

Huh? *Austere?* Where had that come from?

Her place was sophisticated and luxurious, she reminded herself. Unlike the grape-jelly-splattered, gooey, toy-strewn wreck of a log cabin she was living in right now.

"You're a hard worker too," Tenley said, breaking into her thoughts in a chipper voice. "Look at all the fantastic gifts you scored for everyone last Christmas. It took you days to hire and supervise the gift-wrapping staff alone."

"Plus you're awesome at interior decorating," Caprice added. L.A. traffic sounds came from her end of the line. She'd left the boutique. "Nobody we know has a showplace like you do."

That was true. Marisol had worked long and hard to collect and arrange the various pieces in her beach house. She'd even fancied herself a designer of sorts, and had actually thought she might open her own home-furnishings boutique someday. Sort of an anti-Home Warehouse kind of place, where things weren't practical or plastic, and nothing was machine washable. A place she could be proud of. A place she could develop all by herself, where she could become more than a boldfaced name with stealth ambitions.

The one time she'd broached the subject, her father had quashed her ambitions, saying Marisol didn't have what it took to start a business. And rightly so, she supposed, since a couple of weeks later she'd wound up in official shopaholic rehab. Dzeel was hardly junior entrepreneur boot camp.

At least Tenley and Caprice were on her side though.

"Aww, you guys are the best. Thanks for being there."

Her friends murmured more sympathetic and encouraging things, making Marisol feel glad she'd called them. Even if it was tricky to wheel around a grocery cart, stockpile responsible food items, make entries in her required Dzeel shopping log, and talk on the cell phone at the same time. Oh, and keep an eye on the kids too. This nannying gig required a distinct ability to multitask. Good thing she was getting so adept at—

The kids were gone.

She rounded the corner, expecting Hannah, Emily, and Jacob to be waiting in the next aisle. They were nowhere to be seen.

"I've got to go," Marisol cried.

She hung up her phone and literally ran down the aisle.

Two frantic minutes later, Marisol still hadn't found them. Her heart raced as she hurried through the produce section one last time, feeling sick to her stomach. How could she have let Emily, Jacob, and Hannah out of her sight? Even for one moment? Where in the world had they gone to? How would she find them?

She stopped dead, her hands shaking. How was she going to break the news to Cash that she'd lost his children?

Oh God, oh God. Panicky, Marisol scanned the huge piles of apples and bananas and carrots. Why did they stock things so tall here? She had to race around every single bin, swiveling her head right and left, to see if there were any tiny people standing behind them. The kids were so small. So helpless . . .

She accosted a produce manager in the midst of spraying down the romaine lettuce. Wild-eyed, she grabbed his arm. "Have you seen three little kids? They were just here."

"Sorry, lady." He shook his head. "Try the bakery. Sometimes kids wander over there looking for the free cookies."

Free cookies. Brilliant! She raced that way.

"Have you seen three little kids? Two girls and a boy, about this high?" Marisol held her hand at waist height, fighting back tears. "I just took my eyes off them for a second. Maybe you gave them free cookies?"

"Yeah." The woman in a hairnet nodded. "They were here."

Marisol wanted to weep with relief. Her whole body sagged. "Oh my God. Thank you!" She looked around. "Where are they?"

"They went that way." Ms. Hairnet pointed toward the deli.

No. No! Desperately, Marisol scurried toward the cold cases. Behind them, a scrawny teenager manned the bologna. He looked scarcely burly enough to pick up the microphone behind him near a list of specials (a sale that, for once in her life, Marisol didn't care about at all), much less an entire salami.

"Have you seen—" she began, then stared at that microphone. She had a better idea. She lunged past the teenager and grabbed the microphone. Where was the darn switch? There.

"Attention all shoppers!" Marisol boomed. Her voice sounded shaky, still on the verge of tears. She strengthened it. No one would listen to a hysterical lunatic. Her bargaining-for-Achille-Castiglioni-chairs voice might come in handy here though. "Would Emily, Hannah, and Jacob Connelly please report to the deli at once?" she said evenly. "There's a free slushy here for you. I repeat, there's a free slushy here for you."

Anxiously, she shut off the microphone. She waited.

She clicked it back on. "The blue kind. Blue slushy."

Off again. A moment crawled past. Then another.

A hesitant voice interrupted her vigil. "Ma'am, I think that's mine." The teenager tried to take away the microphone.

Marisol tightened her grasp. "Just turn on the slushy machine, junior. I'm not letting go."

Marisol's strategy didn't work. Three agonizing minutes after her announcement, Hannah, Jacob, and Emily were still nowhere to be seen.

Other shoppers wandered the aisles, oblivious to the drama going on. Marisol wanted to scream at them. *Can't you tell there's a crisis happening here? I just lost three adorable children!* Several stopped by the deli counter, shooting her curious looks as she paced in front of the potato salad display.

Two teenage girls in particular pointed and whispered. One of them opened the magazine she'd been holding, peered at its pages, then stared at Marisol again. Finally she approached.

"Um, aren't you, like, Marisol Winston?"

"Yeah," the other girl agreed. "You totally look like her."

"Except in real life you look fatter." The first girl held up the magazine, a copy of *Star* opened to a paparazzi shot from three months ago. "See? I love those shoes, by the way."

They both waited expectantly. Marisol shot them a brief smile, still wringing her hands as she scanned the Shoparama for three little dark-haired children. This was not the time to be recognized. If her dad were here, he'd tell her to leave. Being seen in public—especially in Podunkville, Arizona—would raise questions none of the Winstons wanted to answer. Beginning with why Marisol wasn't in L.A., and why she'd gone to Dzeel.

Maybe if she were polite, they'd leave her alone.

"Yes, that's me." With a valiant effort, Marisol broadened her smile. "Would you like me to autograph that for you?"

"Would you? Yeah!" The first girl thrust forward the magazine. The other unearthed a mini Sharpie from her purse. With a shaky hand, Marisol scrawled her name across a wildly unflattering photo of herself munching through a salad on the Urth Caffé patio. She handed back the magazine. "Here you go."

"Ohmigod! It really is you!" The first girl nudged her friend, her smile showing off purple braces. "Thank you!"

"You are, like, my *idol*," the other girl gushed. "This is so freaking incredible! *I* met Marisol Winston!"

Marisol leaned forward and lowered her voice. "Actually, I'd really appreciate it if you could keep the news to yourself. I'm kind of here on a secret project, and if word gets out—"

"Oh. Oh, okay." The first girl looked solemn. She crossed her heart, her hands tipped by chewed fingernails and chipped pink sparkle polish. "We won't say anything. We promise."

"It's a reality show, isn't it?" The other girl clutched her hair and looked around, probably searching the store for cameras. "I knew it! Are we going to be on MTV?"

"Sorry, I can't say." Marisol grabbed the deli counter microphone again. "I've got to get back to my project though, before I get in trouble. Nice meeting you."

They took the hint. After a few more comments and a giggly good-bye, they skedaddled, casting her knowing backward glances as they went. They waved, then disappeared around the corner.

Whew. That was a close one. Time to get serious.

"Attention all shoppers." Marisol spoke firmly into the microphone, ignoring the deli counter clerk's dirty look. "We have a special offer right now—free slushies for all kids under eight! Exclusively at the deli counter. Come on over for your free slushies! Especially you, Jacob, Hannah, and Emily!"

She set down the microphone, her stomach in knots. If this didn't work, she didn't know what to do. Calling for help would come next. She could always dial 911 on her cell phone, but a hasty check of her watch revealed that it had still only been a few minutes since she'd lost sight of the kids. For all she knew, the three of them were simply wandering around the store, and they'd just missed each other during her frantic search.

On the other hand . . . Was it possible to file a missing-person's report after only nine minutes? Marisol didn't care if the whole police department laughed their heads off at her—she'd do whatever it took to get Emily, Hannah, and Jacob back safely.

"Remember folks. Those are blue slushies. Blue slushies!"

Kids of all sizes began streaming toward the deli counter, most of them dragging parents in their wake. Marisol scanned their little faces, searching for those three familiar ones. She stood on tiptoes, straining for a glimpse of them.

"Lady, who's paying for this?" the deli clerk asked as the kids approached. "This looks like a lot of slushy orders."

Marisol glanced down at her grocery list, then at her Dzeel shopping log. She was under strict orders to stick to her list and to record all her purchases for review by Imelda Santos, Dzeel's oniomania counselor. Any deviation from her prescribed plan could result in flunking out of shopaholic rehab—and *never* getting her trust fund back.

"I'm paying," she said. "Just keep those slushies coming."

The whole crowd pushed forward, eager to get their freebies. Two junior soccer teams showed up too. Apparently, blue was a popular flavor with all kids, not just hers.

Well, hers as in the kids she nannied for.

Suddenly, two stroller-pushing moms parted. Jacob, Hannah, and Emily darted between them with Hannah in the lead.

Marisol *knew* she was seeing things. Her heart stopped, then kicked into high gear. Could it be . . . yes! It really was them, making their way toward the deli with eager faces. Jacob jostled Emily, Emily pushed him back, and Hannah zeroed in on the lineup for free slushies. She dragged her siblings that way.

At the same moment, they all spotted Marisol. She glimpsed their faces turning toward her, saw the recognition in their expressions . . . saw them wave at her and continue blithely on.

Wave at her? What was the matter with them? How could they be so matter-of-fact about having disappeared?

Completely freaking out, Marisol rushed toward them. She didn't even care that she was wearing one of her cutest Behnaz Sarafpour skirts. She just dropped to the grimy grocery store floor and pulled them into her arms.

"Thank God!" she cried hoarsely. "Where have you been?"

"Right over there." Cavalierly, Hannah pointed toward the Shoparama checkouts. Jacob craned his neck, probably inspecting the status of the free slushy line. Emily hugged her back, saying, "You smell really pretty, Marisol. You must have the best perfume ever. Can you help me find good perfume sometime?"

"I'd be happy to share mine with you." Marisol heard her voice crack. Weak with relief, trembling all over, she hugged them even tighter. They felt so great, solid and perfect in her arms. She never wanted to let them go.

"Um, you're squishing us a little," Hannah complained.

"I want a free slushy," Jacob said.

Marisol leaned back, delighting in their small, lovable faces. She'd never really noticed those freckles Emily had before. Or the long, long eyelashes Hannah had. Or the cute button nose on Jacob. Someday it would turn into a tough, rugged nose like Cash's, but for now, it was adorable. They all were.

"Hey." Emily peered into her face. "You're crying."

"Am I?" Swiftly, Marisol swiped at her cheeks. She gave a relieved laugh. "I guess I'm just that excited about free slushy day. Let's go get some, okay? Everybody hold hands."

She stood, careful to stay within touching distance. When she'd gotten herself together, she looked at them.

Hannah, Jacob, and Emily stared back at her as if she were crazy.

"Hold hands?" Jacob made a face. "We're not babies."

"I know. But just for today, I thought—"

"Darlings!" interrupted someone from nearby, crashing into their conversation. "I *thought* I heard your names being called."

At the sound of that melodic voice, all the kids turned. Marisol did too. She'd have recognized that tone anywhere. It said *money*. It said *privilege*. It said *I can do whatever I want*.

A well-dressed blonde sashayed nearer, her curious gaze fixed on the Connelly kids—and on Marisol. She held her chin high, moving in a way that somehow made everyone nearby step aside. In her wake came three similarly dressed women, all of them about Marisol's age—but none of them familiar. They all looked stylish, perfectly coiffed, and ready to gossip.

In short, they looked like Marisol's kind of people. And they were the first women she'd seen who'd dared to challenge the rule—apparently a law out here in the boonies—that everyone wear polyester, shun makeup and highlights, and embrace comfortable footwear.

After an inquisitive but not unfriendly glance at Marisol, the blonde smiled down at the kids. "I haven't seen you three in ages! It sounds as if *somebody* got lost though."

Her mischievous tone didn't seem to impress Hannah.

"We were playing that old video game machine." She pointed to a dingy corner of the grocery store. "Our dad lets us."

"Yeah." Emily's attitude dared the blonde to disagree. "Because he's the best, handsomest, most wonderful dad around."

"Isn't that sweet? Familial loyalty." The blonde shared a glance with her designer-clad posse, all of whom were busy inspecting Marisol's shoes. She rumpled Jacob's hair, then pinched his cheek. "You've certainly gotten bigger since I've seen you, Jacob. Are you going to play football too?"

He glared at her, jerkily straightening his hair. He was fussy about it, and Marisol had already learned to leave his 'do alone. "Maybe," he said. "My dad will teach me if I ask him to."

"Cash is pretty busy getting ready for training camp these days," Marisol volunteered, making a mental note to find a way to grant Jacob's apparently hidden wish to play sports. "But I know he'd be great at teaching Jacob anything he wanted to learn." She stuck out her hand. "Hi, I'm Marisol. I'm—"

The kids' nanny, she'd been about to say, but Hannah piped up instead. "She's our dad's new girlfriend."

"Really?" The blonde reared back, taking in Marisol's appearance with newly interested eyes. "I didn't know Cash was seeing anyone since the divorce. The two of you are dating?"

"They're living together," Emily said.

"And *kissing*," Jacob specified. "All the time." He grabbed Marisol's wrist. "Can we go get some slushies now?"

"Sure, Jacob." Marisol patted his shoulder, deciding against straightening out the mix-up about her and Cash. It was nobody's business but theirs anyway—no matter how incredible Cash's kisses had been. Or how much she wanted more of them. Soon. "Let's go get in line." She paused, nodding to the women. "It was nice to meet all of you."

"Well, we haven't really met." The blonde chuckled.

So did her cohorts. They all exchanged another cryptic glance—and the four of them checked out her handbag too. Then, as though some decision had been made, the blonde nodded.

"I'm Cassie," she said, gesturing to indicate her friends,

"and this is Amanda, Ashley, and Lindsay. We're football wives—you know, Scorpions players' wives. Our kids used to have play dates with Emily, Hannah, and Jacob all the time during training camp. Right now they're at enrichment ballet-and-karate camp in Phoenix, getting a jumpstart on their social networking."

The other three women nodded earnestly, as though this were a real achievement. The whole idea of six-year-olds actually networking was unfathomable to Marisol. What did they talk about? The best way to eat crayons? The chicest grade schools? Who was grounded and for what?

Clearly she had a lot to learn about the world of parenthood. "Um, good for them," she said, trying to play along. "Do they have little business cards too?"

The four women exchanged glances. "Of course not."

One of the women rolled her eyes.

"They have customized *calling cards* at this age."

That was the most ridiculous thing Marisol had ever heard. But maybe she was supposed to be securing designer calling cards for Jacob, Emily, and Hannah too. Maybe she was supposed to be setting up play dates and ensuring their future networking opportunities and—she spied Jacob picking up a discarded jelly bean from the floor, then rubbing it on his shirt—keeping them from contracting botulism from grubby candy. Sternly, she held out her hand. He dropped the jelly bean into it.

"Well, you won't let me have a slushy!" he complained.

"We'll get one in a minute," Marisol promised, stepping aside to avoid being jostled by more children sprinting toward the deli counter. "When the line slows down a little, okay?"

Her mind raced at the opportunities these women presented. They clearly knew Cash. They knew the kids. They knew how things were supposed to work in the realm of families and children. If she wanted to avoid further missteps like today, succeed at her work assignment, and make Cash respect and admire her, she'd have to do more. She'd have to do child care reconnaissance.

"I'd love to buy you all a slushy," Marisol offered, gesturing gamely toward the burgeoning line. "My treat."

Cassie, Amanda, Ashley, and Lindsay shared glances. If they took her up on her offer, Marisol realized, she might be able to make some new friends and gather some hints, all at the same time. These women were just like her. She could relate to them. Without Caprice and Tenley nearby, she had nobody to talk to.

Plus, football wives had to know what it took to keep a football player happy, right? It would be in Cash's best interest if she made friends with these women.

"I could really use some help with the kids' summer itineraries," Marisol said, hoping to sweeten the deal.

That did the trick.

"Sure, why not?" Cassie said with a smile at her pals. She hoisted her Louis Vuitton handbag smartly. "I'll bet we could all learn a thing or two from each other. Let's go."

Chapter 18

Cash slung a towel over his shoulder and carried his clipboard into the NAU gym, which had been set aside for Scorpions training. The place was empty except for a few early-bird returnees like him—players who wanted to get a jump start on training camp. Someone had cranked up a boom box to set the right atmosphere, and weights clanged in the grasp of a two-hundred-pound running back and a three-hundred-pound tackle alike. The whole place stank of sweat and metal and old work-out mats, but for Cash that smell was like coming home.

He nodded to one of his fellow players, then got on the treadmill to warm up. Soon he was back in the groove. More players were showing up every day—all veterans like him—and everyone had work to do. They just had to saddle up and do it.

Usually, Cash didn't mind this part of his day. Maintaining his strength was simply something he did, like brushing his teeth. But today   today he felt rattled, unable to focus on the lat pulldowns he did next, or the biceps curls that came after.

That kiss with Marisol had felt like more than a kiss. It had felt like a homecoming, crazy as that sounded. And when the kids had happened upon them, ready to start playing

"The Wedding March" on their karaoke machine . . . well, Cash hadn't known what to make of it. Jacob, Hannah, and Emily loved Marisol, so he shouldn't have been surprised by their reaction. But still, he damned well wasn't ready for a wedding. And he apparently wasn't ready to explain kissing to his nosy brood either.

He sat on a free bench, checked off everything he'd completed on his clipboard of trainer-assigned work-outs, then lay back. He stared at the bar, psyching himself up for bench presses. He wrapped his hands around the bar, ready to lift.

Another player stepped into position at the machine beside him, getting ready to work his quadriceps. He spotted Cash. His mahogany face broadened into a grin. He held out his hand.

"Hey, Connelly. Good to have you back, number seven."

"Thanks, Darrell. Good to see you too." Cash returned the greeting, slapping his palm and then offering a low handshake. He nodded at Darrell's dark stubbled jaw. "Getting geared up for the preseason, I see. Playing it safe."

"Damn right! After the season we had last year? We need everything we've got." Darrell believed he played better when he hadn't shaved—and because of it, he did play better scruffy. Now he stroked his chin, offering a wicked grin. "Sheryl hates all this stubble. She won't leave me alone about it. She's even got the kids nagging me to shave. 'Daddy, you look like a grizzly bear,' they say. But you know how it is—you need every advantage."

"Tell me about it." Cash pushed out his first set, both men by rote falling into their routines. When he'd finished, he dropped his hands to his thighs. "Family's doing good then?"

"Yeah." Darrell grunted, curling his leg on the machine. As an offensive lineman, he needed plenty of

power on the ground. "They're all good. They're getting
settled in at our summer place by Lake Mary. You and
the kids should stop by—let the little monsters have a
sleepover or something."

"Maybe we will." It occurred to Cash that Stephanie
had handled all the play dates with her posse of vacuous
football wives. He didn't even know how it was done, but
he didn't want the kids to miss seeing all their buddies.
"Later this week sometime."

"I'll tell Sheryl." Darrell paused, shaking his head in
wonder as he gazed at Cash. "It's good to see you again,
seven. That whole thing with Tyrell was bullshit. Things
haven't been the same around here without you. That's
God's own truth."

With a nod for acknowledgement, Cash went on lifting, pumping out reps. He added a few more for good
measure, shoving away the rush of emotion he suddenly
felt. He'd been training here for weeks now. Lots of veterans had welcomed him, slapping him on the back as
they relived old times and past games.

But until Darrell, everyone had pretended that his tu-
multuous break with the team hadn't happened. That
he hadn't retired, gotten slapped in the face, and lost
everything.

"It's good to be back." Cash swabbed his face with his
towel, catching his breath. "First time Ed lets me take a
snap, I'm taking my starting spot back from McNamara,
that punk."

Both men grinned. Trash talking was common in football. It didn't lesson the respect Cash felt for his former
QB backup.

They changed stations, consulting their clipboards
and then moving past rows of burly steel weights, tread-
mills, and various rehab machines. By habit, they settled
in at adjacent machines.

"Yeah, I guess retirement didn't suit you," Darrell said,

hoisting a bar to perform squats. "I wish you'd opened that damn sports bar you talked about though. That would've been sweet."

Cash grunted, not wanting to discuss his former post-football dream. He'd wanted it. It hadn't happened. The end. He selected a pair of dumbbells and started on hammer curls.

"Big-screen TVs, free beer . . . no out-of-town games away from the family. What's not to like?" Darrell continued as he stretched between sets. He rubbed his hand over his bald head as though shining it up.. "You should still do it."

"Maybe."

"But this time, wait until you're *really* too old to play." Darrell wagged his finger. "You quit too soon last time."

Cash shook his head, feeling sweat drip in his hair. He couldn't work out hard enough to end this conversation.

"Big shock when you retired." Darrell tightened his grip on the bar, then fell silent for another set of squats. He groaned as he finished the last. "The front office thought you were milking them for more money. So did some of these losers."

With a nod toward the fellow players present, Darrell offered a choice expletive to show what he thought of that. The lineman set down his weights, then cheerfully rubbed his head dry. He consulted his training clipboard, ready for more.

"It wasn't about the money," Cash said.

The truth was, when he'd been a star quarterback, he'd sucked at being a father. And at being a husband. Constant training, injuries, rehab, team meetings, film study, practice, two-a-days, home games, away games, and even required promo appearances had all taken their toll on his home life.

Professional football wasn't the game-a-week easy ride outsiders assumed it was. It was a grueling, everyday, in-your-face load to be lifted, and Cash had felt that responsibility strongly. Probably too strongly, after Emily, Jacob, and Hannah had been born. Raising triplets had been a challenge sometimes. Even a struggle some days, especially when tackled alone. But Stephanie had confided her struggles to her mother, Leslie, not him. Not until afterward when he couldn't do squat to change it.

Not until the damage had already been done to his marriage.

All his life, teamwork and discipline had been Cash's saving graces. But both had failed him at home. All he'd ever wanted was a kick-ass football career, a house in the 'burbs, and a happy family. When the family had come along, he'd tried to do his part by working harder, working longer, making sure the people he cared about had a secure future. Instead he'd accidentally left Stephanie alone too much of the time, and screwed up the whole damn thing. By the time he'd realized that his efforts to do the right thing had meant doing exactly the *wrong* thing—and tried to fix the whole mess with a hasty early retirement so he could be home more—it was already too late.

Not long after Cash's final season had ended, Stephanie had run off with Tyrell and a big chunk of their joint bank accounts, crushing his hopes for that happily-ever-after for good. Not to mention KO-ing his sports-bar plans and leaving him in exactly the same damnable situation as before—because now he *had* to play again to stockpile some cash . . . but playing again meant being away from the kids for much of the regular season.

Wanting to shove away that reality, Cash pumped out a few extra hammer curls, breathing hard with the effort. Beside him, Darrell gave a camaraderie-filled guffaw.

"Hell, I know it's not about the money, seven." He

grinned even more broadly, polishing up his Super Bowl ring. He sniffed in his usual macho fashion. "Once you've made your first big paycheck, who needs to push for more?"

Technically Cash did, but he remained silent. It would have crushed him to admit that Stephanie—his former sports agent—had screwed him over on most of his contracts. That he'd trusted her enough to let her do it. That he'd wanted their divorce over with cleanly and hadn't even argued when she'd insisted upon a huge settlement for herself. That he'd trusted her at all.

"I know *I've* got more scratch than a poor kid from Alabama ought to have," Darrell was saying, "and all for the love of the game, dawg. Once I bought my mama a Cadillac and got my house paid for, I was set." He cocked his head. "I still like that sports bar idea though. I might try it myself."

Cash nodded, then tried to focus on his next several sets as they lifted awhile longer. Whatever work he skimped on here would only come back to haunt him later on the field—kind of like the way Marisol haunted his thoughts these days, whenever he let down his guard. He often found himself thinking of her. Wondering what she was doing. Wondering how an heiress—of all people—had wound up working as his nanny. Wondering what kind of life a genuine Winston (as Adam had so stridently put it) expected or wanted or needed.

Could Marisol's kind of life happen in the 'burbs?

Hell. Cash put away his dumbbells and slung his towel around his neck. He had to quit thinking about this stuff. Especially when he was trying to concentrate on work.

The only problem was . . .

"Hey, Darrell. You talk to your kids about kissing?"

The lineman made a face. "Hell, no. That's Sheryl's job."

Another lineman passed by. "Give 'em a book," he advised Cash. "That's what I did. The birds and the bees or some shit."

Cash nodded, swabbing his sweaty forehead as he thought about it. A book might work. His kids liked books. Maybe if they read one of those birds and the bees stories, they'd realize there was a big difference between kissing a woman and wanting to marry her. Especially for their dad.

"One more set." Cash checked off hammer curls on his list, then bent to equip a barbell for deadlifts. He hefted a forty-five-pound plate, twisted awkwardly to affix it to the end of the barbell . . . and felt a tweak in his leg. His hamstring.

Swearing, he clutched it. Darrell raised his brows, saw Cash's pissed-off expression, and knew instantly what had happened. "Looks like a few days off for you, seven."

Cash glared at him. Training camp started in five days. *Five days.* That was all that stood between him and his chance to impress the coach, the team, and the front office with his playing. He didn't have time to screw around with injuries.

Mulishly, he grabbed another plate anyway, then hobbled toward the other end of the barbell. The back of his thigh hurt with every step, making him grimace.

"Don't make me report you to the training staff." Darrell blocked his path, arms crossed. "I will, if you endanger our next championship season by being a stubborn butthead. We already lost one backup quarterback when Johnson went out. McNamara might be good, but we still need you healthy."

Cash glared at his friend. "Fuck off. I'm fine."

Another jolt of pain made him wince. Hell. How had this happened? He wasn't that freaking old! Only thirty-four. Montana had played until he was thirty-nine. Elway had started a damned Super Bowl at thirty-eight. Flutie had kept going until he was forty-one. Cash intended to be one of the lucky ones—the guys who stayed in the game as long as they wanted (or needed) to be.

"You gotta learn to take it easy, seven," another player jibed as he passed by, "now that you're an old-timer."

"Hey, my fist isn't too old to find your face."

"Oh yeah? Why don't you prove it?"

Cash lunged for the man, a fullback-size asshole who probably outweighed him by sixty pounds. He must have been traded to the Scorpions recently, because Cash didn't recognize him. Darrell grabbed his arms and pinned him.

"That won't help, man. Just get checked out and go home."

Cash struggled, fury welling up in a hot rush. The full-back fought back too, held in a similar lock by his training partner. It would probably feel pretty good to beat the crap out of somebody, Cash thought, and vent his frustration somewhere. Losing it on somebody equally spoiling for a fight would be perfect. He shoved Darrell.

"Take it easy." His friend angled his head to the side, indicating a member of the front office staff who'd stopped nearby and was curiously watching the drama unfold. "Last thing you need is pressure from the higher-ups. I hear they've got you on a pretty short leash since you came back."

Darrell was right. Damn it.

Cash issued a final warning glance at the fullback, then relented. He felt his face harden. "Watch yourself," he said.

Then he hurled his towel across the room and stalked in the opposite direction—toward the trainers' rooms to have his damned hamstring checked out . . . and his fate for the preseason decided.

* * *

Marisol puttered around the log cabin, keeping one eye on the kids at all times. Right now they were lounging in front of the TV, securely in the grips of some Japanese anime cartoon. With a few minutes to spare for herself, she cradled the phone, happy when someone picked up on the other end.

"Home Warehouse Enterprises. How may I direct your call?"

"Oh." Marisol blinked, startled to have gotten the switchboard. "I'm sorry, I must have misdialed. This is Marisol Winston. I was calling my father, but his direct line seems to be out—"

"I'm sorry, Ms. Winston. Mr. Winston changed his extension a few months ago. I'll put you through."

"Thank you." She paced, listening to the company Muzak. She was really getting out of touch, if she didn't even know her own father's phone number at the family business. More Muzak.

"Gary Winston's office," a woman answered.

"Hi, Mindy! This is Marisol. How are you?"

"I'm sorry, Ms. Winston. Mindy left us last year. This is Sophie, Mr. Winston's new assistant. How may I help you?"

"Oh. Well then . . . hi, Sophie! I'd like to speak with my father, please. He said he'd call, but it's been a few days—"

"Thank you. Please hold, Ms. Winston." More Muzak.

Hmmm. She didn't know her father's new assistant either. Hadn't even realized he'd changed his staff. Sure, her dad could be tight-lipped at times—reluctant to confide in her about business—but this was absurd. He could at least have given her his new phone number. Was he hoping to ditch her or something?

All of a sudden, it felt that way.

Marisol paced further, trying to keep her spirits up. She dragged a catalog nearer from the Connellys' stack

of mail, looking for distraction. While she flipped
through the glossy pages, she straightened her posture
and stuck her shoulders back, the way she'd learned in a
Dzeel relaxation workshop. She breathed deeply, striving
for a soothing yoga-style inhalation.

Her own father was dodging her calls. Ugh.

Nope. He couldn't possibly avoid her forever, Marisol
reminded herself. She'd just keep calling. Also, a nice
little memento might help keep her on his mind. Maybe
one of the leather-bound desk sets in this Restoration
Hardware catalog?

She circled one and felt a little better. She added a
counterpoise task lamp in polished nickel to her mental
wish list, and her mood boosted further. She circled a
silver picture frame—perfect for a desktop photo of her
and Jamie. Even better.

Sophie came back on the line. "I apologize for the
delay, Ms. Winston. I'm still trying to locate your father.
Would you like to wait a little longer or leave a message?"

"I'll wait, thanks."

As Sophie offered another crisp promise to keep
trying, Marisol angled the phone against her neck and
shoulder, barely hearing the Muzak anymore. She circled
a nostalgic-looking mantle clock, then a desk fan straight
out of an old black-and-white Humphrey Bogart movie.
Her dad would love these! She pictured his delighted
face when he unwrapped everything, and figured she'd
better check delivery options too. The faster the better.
And gift-wrapping! She'd definitely need that.

Yes, this was much better. She didn't mind waiting for
her dad—not when she had a surprise package to plan
for him. Marisol scrutinized the catalog more closely,
searching for anything else that seemed special. Her
credit cards had all been confiscated at Dzeel, of course,
but new accounts were easy to open over the phone.
She'd already blown her rehab plan at Shoparama

today—why not go crazy? If she was going to wash out of Dzeel anyway, she might as well go out in a blaze of glory.

She wondered if Cash received any other catalogs. Still on hold, she pawed through his mail, looking for anything that might yield another few gifts for her father. Maybe for Jamie too. She didn't want Jamie to forget about her while she was stuck here in Arizona. A gift package delivered to the mansion would be just the thing to brighten her stepmother's day.

The Muzak ended. "I'm sorry, Ms. Winston," Sophie said, "it seems that your father is in a meeting and can't be disturbed."

"Oh. Really?" Marisol stopped, her hands going slack on the piles of mail. "Did you tell him it was his daughter calling?"

A pause. "I'm sorry. I did tell him that, Ms. Winston."

And he still didn't want to talk to her.

"Did he say when he might call me back? Or maybe I should call him again later?" Marisol heard the plaintive note in her voice. Embarrassing as it was, she felt powerless to stop it. "I've been . . . um, away for several weeks, and I've been expecting to hear from him. It's important."

"Is it an emergency?"

"Well . . ." Briefly, Marisol toyed with the idea of saying it was. She just wanted to hear her dad's voice—to let him know she'd been doing her best with the whole rehab stint and had been kind of succeeding . . . at least until today. This time he might have been proud of her. "No, it's not urgent. I'll try back later."

"Thank you, Ms. Winston. I'll remind him to call you back."

Dispirited, Marisol hung up. Even her father's assistant sounded sorry for her. It was pathetic.

But once Marisol sent this fantastic gift package to his office, Sophie would see things differently—and so would her dad. Shoving that disastrous phone call from her mind, Marisol picked up her gift-circling pen again, ready to go into action.

Emily tugged her sleeve. "Marisol? Are you really going to share your perfume with me? 'Cause it was so pretty."

"Um, sure. In a minute. I'm kind of busy." More circling.

"Okay." Emily slumped at the kitchen peninsula, waiting.

Jacob bounced over too. "Can we play a game?"

"Just a sec. I'm almost finished." Gift wrapping options . . .

"Wow, that's a lot of stuff." Hannah arrived and peered past Marisol's arm at the order form she'd started filling out, flipping back and forth between her circled selections to check their item numbers. "Yuck. That clock looks about a million years old. You should get a better one, I think."

"It's a gift for my dad. He'll like it."

"No, he won't. Not if it looks prehistoric."

"It doesn't look prehistoric. It looks *aged*. That's different." Marisol paused, getting annoyed. All she wanted was to order these gifts for her dad and Jamie. "Look, can't you three amuse yourselves for five minutes? Please?"

At her snappish tone, the kids stared back at her. Jacob's mouth was an O of distress, and Hannah looked on the verge of tears. Even Emily, usually boisterous and sweet-talking, seemed hurt. The three of them exchanged injured glances.

"I'm sorry," Marisol said. She'd never yelled at them. She didn't know what had gotten into her. Holding out her hands, she softened her voice. "It's just that I wanted—"

"Don't worry, we're going!" Emily interrupted in a tear-filled voice. "And you can keep your stupid perfume too."

"Yeah, never mind." Jacob jerked his chin in a bona fide huff. "We can play a game all by ourselves. We don't need *you*."

Hannah only gave her a sad look. Then all three of them flounced away toward the loft stairs, leaving Marisol alone with her catalog—and a deep sense of regret to go with it.

Chapter 19

Well. Nobody pushed Marisol Winston around. Especially a trio of first-graders who wouldn't know a good surprise package if it sat up and barked.

At least she had some peace and quiet now. It had been too long since she'd experienced *that* here in Kiddie Town.

Desperate to secure her gifts, Marisol wrote more item numbers on the order form. She filled the first side and started in on the back, scrunching her handwriting. Her eyes burned with unshed tears and her throat hurt too, but she refused to let herself be distracted. Emily, Jacob, and Hannah just didn't understand. They didn't know how important this was.

She picked up the phone again. It was hard to read the toll free number for placing orders, because it was sort of blurry. Gamely, Marisol punched in the first few digits anyway.

"Here. You'd better take Stuffy." Emily shoved her tattered toy sea otter under Marisol's arm. "You need him more than me."

Where had Emily come from? Marisol hadn't heard anyone coming down from the loft. But then she'd been preoccupied . . .

"Take Mr. Munchington too," Hannah ordered, cramming her plush sea otter beneath her other elbow. "He's the best."

Awkwardly, Marisol squished them both against her sides. She wasn't sure what else to do. Everybody knew you couldn't refuse to hold a stuffed animal. It was like being offered a baby to cuddle—the only right thing to do was smile and coo.

"If you sit down, you can have all my army men." Jacob stood beside her, his arms gripping a bulging bucket of plastic soldiers. "You have to sit down though, or they'll all fall."

Marisol stared at them. The kids stared back patiently. It was impossible to hold both stuffed sea otters, sit on the floor to play army men, and place a gift order from Restoration Hardware, especially if she had to open an account to do it.

She hesitated, unsure what to do.

"We talked about it." Hannah squinted at the catalog lying open on the peninsula. "For somebody who's getting a whole Christmas's worth of stuff, you don't look very happy."

"It's because that clock is from caveman days," Emily diagnosed. "Hug Stuffy," she urged. "You'll feel better."

"Yeah. And sit down too." Jacob rearranged his bucket, then put his little hand on her shoulder and tried to coax her downward. His army men rolled together, two of them dropping to the floor. "Do it." His domineering tone was a pitch-perfect imitation of his father's. "These guys are so much fun."

Numbly, Marisol eased downward, the phone still in her grasp. She wouldn't be able to read the phone number or her order form from here, it occurred to her. But before she could remedy that problem, Jacob grinned and upended his bucket.

Her lap filled with a shower of little green men, some

of them wielding plastic weapons and others simply posturing in macho positions. Marisol selected one. He looked like her old boyfriend, Chad. Except Chad wouldn't have been caught dead in an outfit so plebian or so lacking in designer labels.

Jacob brightened. "They do anything you want them to do. Look!" He set to work arranging a fighting tableau by her knees.

"I think Stuffy likes you." Emily plunked on the floor too, then scooted closer beside Marisol. "See? He's smiling at you."

He was a stuffed sea otter. With pretend whiskers. He was always smiling, Marisol felt pretty sure. But somehow, suddenly, she was smiling too. How could kids be so forgiving? So smart?

How could they have known this was just what she needed?

"You could hold Mr. Munchington better if you hung up the phone." Deftly, Hannah plucked away the phone, then replaced it in its stand. She brushed off her hands and sat on the floor with her legs crossed tailor-style. "There. Isn't that better?"

Strangely enough, it was. Marisol breathed in deeply again, gazing at the kids—*her kids*—in wonder. They'd surrounded her with a buffer of caring and helpfulness. Without even knowing it, they'd stepped in just when she needed someone—someone to let her know not *everyone* in the world had forgotten her.

Some people were just discovering her.

And she was discovering them too.

"Boy, you three are bossy—just like your dad," she joked.

But Marisol loved them for it. She didn't know how she'd lucked out in winding up here, with this family, with these kids, right now. But just then, she was grateful for it.

She was better for it too, she guessed. Because after they'd played awhile—the army men taking on Godzilla and T-Rex (aka Stuffy and Mr. Munchington) in a heated fight to a solid tie—and after she'd stood again, and after she'd spied her catalog order still waiting by the phone, Marisol finally felt an inkling of what Dzeel had been trying to give her all along—and what these kids had given her completely by accident.

Strength.

She turned her back on the catalog for good and looked at Jacob, Hannah, and Emily instead. "Come on, kids! I have a great idea for something fun to do."

Cash burst in sometime later, making the front door fly open with a force that startled Marisol. She looked up.

"Hi. You're home early." She smiled. "Slacker."

For some reason, her joke didn't hit its mark—or at least Cash didn't think so. His face actually reddened another shade, his gorgeous cheekbones mottled with color beneath his tousled hair. His eyes flashed too.

"Why didn't you answer the phone?" he demanded, slamming down his gym bag. "I called to say I was on my way."

"Oh that." Marisol waved, airing her fingertips. She blew on them. "I heard it. We were giving ourselves mani-pedis."

Catching his confounded look, she nodded to the girls. Proudly, Emily and Hannah flashed their freshly painted peony pink fingernails and toenails. They giggled at the cotton still wedged between their toes.

"We look pretty and stylish and the most shiny ever!"

"*I* learned how to do it all by myself!"

Cash stared. Gradually comprehension dawned,

although he still frowned at the cotton. "Oookay. What about Jacob?"

"A man is never too young to have attractive feet."

A groan. "Tell me you're joking."

Just then, Jacob ambled in, awkward in a pair of Marisol's flip-flops. "Look at my feet, Dad! I'm a real man now."

Cash only gawked. Marisol beamed approvingly. Someday future young women would thank her for this.

"I've been buffed, clipped, sanded, scrubbed, and had lotion put all over my feet," Jacob announced. "It tickled."

"All that? Did you get into my Black and Decker toolbox?"

"Nah." Jacob admired his clean toes. "Maybe next time."

Cash scratched his head, staring at the lot of them.

"Would you like me to do you too?" Marisol showed him the emery board in her hand. "I'm getting really good."

He smiled for the first time. "I'll bet you are."

And yeah, I'd like you to do me, flashed in his expression, but Marisol didn't think Cash was contemplating a mani-pedi. All of a sudden, neither was she.

Mmmm. Their first kisses had been wonderful, she remembered. Their next kisses would likely be even better. Especially now that she was feeling comfortable with him and this whole domestic scene. She was practically a natural at it—an until-now undiscovered talent.

"Grab your sleeping bags, kids." Cash rubbed his palms together eagerly. "I've got a few days off from football, and we're going to use them to get dirty." He pointed to his son. "Especially you. Shiny man toes aren't natural."

"They are too!" Marisol told him. There was no point undoing all the progress she'd made with Jacob. Every boy needed good grooming. "If you want to wear sandals—"

"I don't."

"—which come in *very* chic styles for men these days—"

"I don't."

"—you know, *mandels*, then you'll need to get regular pedicures first." Marisol paused, what he'd said a minute ago finally sinking in. "Um, did you just say, 'sleeping bags'?" She tilted her head in confusion. "Why do they need sleeping bags?"

"Campout." Cash strode purposefully toward the kitchen, with Marisol following as he dragged out a battered, broken-down cardboard box and an enormous blue ice chest. "It's our Connelly family tradition the weekend before training camp starts."

"Yay!" The kids jumped up and down. "Campout!"

Cash bent over, grappling with the ice chest. Momentarily fascinated by the fantastic shape of his backside, it took Marisol an extra ten seconds to process what he'd said.

"Campout? But—but—" In confusion, she pointed to the log cabin walls all around them. "You're *already* camping out! This place is plenty rustic enough to qualify as camping out."

"Are you kidding me?" Cash shook his head, now hauling foodstuffs from the pantry and packing them into the reassembled cardboard box with precision. It was a regular geometry lesson. "Compared with where we're going, this house is luxury."

Chills shivered down Marisol's spine. "*This* is luxury? You don't even have a concierge. Or real—you know— walls. Or decent sheets." She ticked off further proof on her manicured fingers. "Or stylish surroundings. Or professional maid services."

"Yeah, speaking of which—" Cash glanced over his shoulder, making a face. "I've been hearing some complaints about that. The girls mentioned to me that the bathroom in the loft needs work."

Work? Marisol put her hands on her hips, irked that he wasn't even listening to her. "So? Hire some contractors to do the work then. And an exterminator too, while you're at it. I'm sure bugs have been chewing on the logs all over this place, even though somebody polished over all the tooth marks."

"Those are natural flaws in the wood, and that's not what I mean." Cash's smile quirked. "The loft bathroom needs cleaning. Emily and Hannah said it's disgusting."

Marisol glanced at them. They hunched guiltily.

"We didn't mean to tell on you," Emily explained hastily. "It's just because Jacob can't aim. That's the problem."

"Yeah, he pees *everywhere*." Hannah rolled her eyes.

"I do not!" Jacob yelled, his cheeks pinkening. "Shut up, you guys! You don't even know it was me."

The sisters folded their arms. "We know it was you."

Cash patted Jacob's shoulder. "You've got to focus, buddy. That's all. Now help me find the graham crackers."

"But . . ." Marisol felt confused. Also embarrassed on Jacob's behalf, poor little guy. "Why are you telling me? You have someone for that kind of cleaning, don't you?"

"Yes." Cash nodded. "You."

"Me?" She chuckled. "No, I mean the heavy-duty kind of cleaning. Because I have been cleaning just like I'm supposed to do. I pick up all the odds and ends every day. I dust too." She winked at Cash, remembering their encounter in the hall. "And I totally have the dishwasher routine nailed now. It almost never overflows these days." Proudly, she straightened. "Actually, I've always been good at beating clutter. Maids love me. One time, I was staying at the Four Seasons in Las Vegas for my cousin's quickie wedding, and the housekeeping staff—"

"No. You're supposed to *clean*," Cash interrupted gently. "Clean everything. Scrub, scour, wash, rinse."

"Oh. Clean? You mean . . . like an actual maid?"

"More like a housekeeper," Cash specified.

He was putting it that way to be kind, she supposed. The same way she hung up her wet hotel towels to be kind to the maids and offered extra-large tips to the catering staff after cocktail parties. He didn't want her to feel bad about being an actual *maid*. But apparently that's what she was. Marisol Winston. Heiress extraordinaire. Toast of the town. Talk of L.A.

Maid. Housekeeper. Domestic laborer.

Jeremy Fordham had bested her again. When she'd told him and the Dzeel board that she was experienced at cleaning, she'd meant tidying, of course. The kind of tidying she did at her own Malibu beach house. The kind of tidying normal adults did so their maids wouldn't think they were hopeless slobs. That's it.

What kind of people actually *scrubbed?*

Not heiresses to retail fortunes, that's for sure.

Besides, it wasn't as if Cash didn't know who she was. Like Adam, he'd read her Dzeel dossier from cover to cover. She'd caught him poring over it one night, a goofy smile on his face as he'd gazed at her photo.

"You can do it, right?" Cash asked, a flashlight in hand.

She snapped out of it. "Of course." She wanted him to respect her. To give her good grades on her Dzeel evaluations. To cherish her. And okay, so scrubbing toilets probably wouldn't really lead to cherishing, but a girl had to work with what she was given. In Marisol's case, that was a scrub . . . thingie.

And maybe a gas mask. And industrial-strength gloves. Oh God. How was she going to handle this?

"Why don't you make a pass through the bathrooms while I finish packing up?" Cash threw some batteries on the pile he'd made on the countertop, then opened the refrigerator and peered in it, selecting items for the ice chest. Mustard. Relish. Jumbo-size ketchup. He stopped. "Where are the hot dogs?"

"We didn't get any hot dogs," Hannah said. "Marisol spent all the grocery money on slushies."

Marisol froze, her guilty gaze swerving to Cash's face.

"You spent all the grocery money on slushies?" he asked.

This was it—the moment she'd have to 'fess up to losing his children. The moment Cash would realize he'd have to flunk her out of Dzeel for not sticking to her list and budget and shopping journal. The moment she failed.

At least she wouldn't have to clean the bathroom.

For some reason, Marisol didn't feel cheered by that realization. She didn't want to fail and she didn't want to leave either. She really, really didn't want to leave. Unexpected as it was, she was enjoying herself here.

She decided to sneak up on the truth. Slowly.

"Not *all* of it. I actually did have enough money left to buy the hot dogs." With a nervous twitter, she reached past him and located the package behind a carton of eggs. "Here."

His gaze bored right through her. "Thanks."

He could tell she was skirting the facts. She knew it!

"A lot of the money went to bribing the kids and their friends with blue slushies." She shrugged. "What can you do? I lost track of Jacob, Hannah, and Emily at the grocery store for a few minutes, and those slushies lured them right back. Plus a few extra kids too." *Like a couple of really thirsty AYSO soccer teams.* "You know how it goes."

How it goes . . . fifty-five biggie-size slushies later.

Cash stared at her. A moment ticked past. Marisol chewed her lip, tasting the last of her lip gloss. She couldn't divine a thing from his hard-edged expression. Why did he have to be so darned inscrutable? Especially now, when it was so important?

Cash turned. "Kids, go get your sleeping bags. Chop, chop. We're getting off schedule. Get your backpacks together too."

They scurried up to the loft, feet pounding.

Marisol only stood there, watching Cash in disbelief.

He packed the hot dogs in the cooler, then noticed her standing there. "You too. The cleaning supplies are in the closet at the top of the loft stairs. If we leave the bathroom that way, we'll have raccoons nesting in here when we get back."

"But . . . don't you want to know more about what happened? At the grocery store? With the kids? I lost them!"

Cash actually smiled. "And then you found them."

"You must be mad though. Don't you want to yell at me?"

He frowned. "What good would that do?"

"Umm . . . it's just . . . what people do when you disappoint them. When you mess up, they yell at you." *Or leave. Or dodge your phone calls.*

"Hey, I'm the last person to play Monday morning quarterback. You did what you had to do, and now it's over with. The kids seem okay. We have hot dogs. We're going camping, just like we always do. That's all that matters."

Marisol didn't get it. "I did buy you a nice box of those frosted Pop-Tarts you like." She hurried to the pantry and grabbed the box—the closest she'd been able to come to a peace-making gift. She'd racked her brain to come up with something Cash would appreciate. "See? Frosted Double Berry flavor."

He looked at her as if she'd smoked a few of them. "Thanks, but you didn't have to do that." He took the box and returned it to the pantry, wincing as he crossed the kitchen. "What I need from you right now is—"

"Hey, are you okay?" she interrupted. "You look hurt."

"I'm fine." He jerked his head toward the loft. "What I need from you right now is a little cleaning. I know it's not your thing, princess, but it's got to be done. Unless you want to wait for Jacob's next puddle, which I wouldn't recommend."

"No. I mean, yes, I'll do it, but—" She frowned at his awkward gait. Cash was definitely favoring his right leg. "I thought I'd do it while you're gone."

"While *we're* gone?"

"Right. Because I'm not going camping with you."
Marisol grinned at the absurdity of the idea. "You don't
need a nanny along if you're going, right? You'll take
care of the kids."

"Yeah, but . . ." Cash gave her an especially charming
smile. "They'd be crushed if you didn't go."

Awww. That was so sweet. If she wasn't careful, Marisol
realized, she just might get attached to this family.

"Um, I'm not really the outdoorsy type," she hedged.
It was the truth, but she wanted to let Cash off the hook
too. She didn't want him to feel obligated to include her
just because she was standing there. Procrastinating on
her cleaning duties. Wondering how in the world to
scrub a toilet. "I was just telling my driver, Tom, on the
way here that I don't even like patio dining. Or playing
golf, even on a nice green. So that whole scene with real
dirt and bugs and creepy crawly things—"

Cash's smile broadened. "I'll protect you."

He probably would. A big, rugged, macho guy like him?

For an instant, she almost wanted to let him. But she
had to be strong. She was here to do a job, and she'd already had one close shave with the Shoparama fiasco.
She had to do better. She had to avoid yummy man-size
distractions.

"I don't even have the right things to wear," Marisol
protested. "And I absolutely don't own a sleeping bag,
so—"

Cash silenced her with a kiss. "You can share my sleeping bag. It's big enough for two."

Okay. She wasn't Gandhi. Shared sleeping bags? With
Cash all snuggled up next to her? Of course she cracked.

"Cool." Marisol brightened. "When do we leave?"

He smiled. "Right after you clean the bathroom."

Chapter 20

She bribed Jacob into doing the job.

"Next time, I'll do it. I promise," Marisol told him, handing over the mop, a long-handled scrub brush, and an industrial-size cleaner that promised to bubble away the grime. "But right now, I've got to figure out what to wear for this campout, and you have been wanting to hear some music, right?"

The boy nodded, his little hands clutching the supplies.

"I'll just put these on you then. Hold still." She situated her iPod's earbuds, set the volume to medium, then handed the unit to Jacob. "Voilà! Now you have an iPod of your very own."

Jacob squinted at the screen, the mop balanced against his shoulder, the cleanser at his feet. "Awesome. Thanks, Marisol."

"Here's how you choose a song." She demonstrated. "Right now it's set on my shopping playlist—songs that get me psyched up for gift hunting. But you can choose whatever you like."

Jacob thumbed the click wheel, mastering it instantly. "Wow. There must be millions of songs in here."

"Thousands at least. And look at you go!" Marisol

exclaimed. "You're like a boy genius. You're going to be a natural at cleaning that bathroom."

"You think so?" he yelled over the music, head bopping.

"You bet. You obviously have great dexterity."

"Do you think that means I'd be good at sports?"

"Absolutely." Marisol winked, then shooed him into the grungy bathroom. She was definitely going to have to get Cash to play some football with Jacob. "See you in a few minutes!"

Jacob waved cheerfully, then left Marisol free to select a choice wardrobe for the next few days.

Exactly what did a girl wear in the great outdoors anyway?

Cash steered the Range Rover down the narrow dirt road, bouncing over potholes left by the runoff from a mountain stream. Forest crowded around the vehicle, making the road appear barely navigable. Pine boughs slapped the windows.

Deliberately, Cash swerved. The kids squealed as the SUV bumped and jostled, throwing them against their seat belts in the backseat. Stuffed animals slipped to the floor.

"Daddy! Stop driving so crazy!" Hannah squealed.

"Faster, faster!" Emily yelled. "Hang on everybody!"

"Hard out here for a pimp!" Jacob sang raucously. He pumped his fists, rocking out between his sisters.

In the passenger seat, Marisol slumped, gazing outside.

"Don't bother trying to hide," Cash told her with a grin. "I know you bribed him with that thing."

She gave him a sham innocent look. "Hmmm?"

"Next time, edit the songs first."

"Maybe you can do it," she suggested, folding her hands primly atop the handbag on her lap. "After you teach Jacob how to play football. Is there a field where we're going?"

Cash fisted the steering wheel, focusing on the road.

"Because if there is," she persisted, "you can throw a few balls to Jacob. I think he'd be good at sports. The girls too."

Cash squinted ahead, pretending to need absolute concentration to find their usual camping spot. Almost there . . .

"*I* might even want to learn a thing or two," Marisol said.

That sounded promising. He could imagine all sorts of things to teach her. Except for one very obvious one.

"I don't play football on my days off."

"But why not? If you like it and it's fun—"

"It's not fun, it's work. And we're here." Cash turned the Range Rover. "Ready?"

Marisol glanced up, her eyes widening as the vehicle charged into a clearing, then stopped. Cash was already opening the driver's side door when her surprised voice reached him.

"Hey, this isn't the middle of nowhere!" She scrambled to catch up, throwing open the passenger door. "This is Happy Gecko Campground." She gestured at the camping spaces, family-friendly banners, and picnic tables. "You had me so scared too! I was half expecting to need a machete and a compass."

"Nope. The kids aren't quite ready for full-scale wilderness camping. We make do with a family campground."

"Bummer. And me with my awesome wilderness skills all at the ready too." Laughing, Marisol tromped around the Range Rover. Her sandals sank in the dirt as she joined him and the kids at the rear of the vehicle. She pointed to a nearby row of RVs. "Look! They even have star trailers here. Where's ours?"

"We're not using one." Cash opened the Range

Rover's hatch and was rewarded with a face full of doggy breath. Dump. The German shepherd wagged furiously, already scenting one of his favorite playgrounds—and probably a squirrel or two. "Everybody stand back while I get Dump out."

He wrapped his arms around the dog, speaking in a soothing voice as he got a secure grip that included Dump's front and back legs. If he didn't move slowly and hold firmly, Dump was likely to try to make the jump on his own and hurt himself. So was Cash, if he performed this maneuver too quickly with his stupid injured hamstring. He sucked in a deep breath.

"Good boy. Here we go." Cash lifted him out.

Dump wavered, then righted himself on all four paws. As though he hadn't just teetered like Grandpa Simpson, the dog trotted eagerly around the Range Rover, pursued by Hannah, Emily, and Jacob as they got reacquainted with the place.

"Hold on to Dump's leash!" Cash instructed.

He turned to see Marisol gazing at him quizzically. "What do you mean we're not using one? Other people have trailers."

"Those are RVs, not star trailers." He'd dated enough starlets during his years at USC—and logged enough make-out hours on sets—to realize what Marisol meant. "We have a tent."

"A tent?" Her eyes bugged.

"Yeah." Cash eyed the ground at the nearest campsite, checking to be sure it was as level as it had appeared from a distance. It looked good. So did the cast-iron barbecue grill and the stone-ringed fire pit. "A tent. Like they have."

He gestured to some distant campers. They sprawled happily in lounge chairs beside the vibrantly colored Happy Gecko flag that designated their site as number eleven. They'd pitched their two-person nylon dome tent nearby. A clothesline, lined with wet swim trunks, stretched between two oak trees.

The lake was only a short hike away, but he couldn't remember if he'd told Marisol about it. He hoped so.

"Did you bring a bikini?" he asked.

She wasn't biting. "A *tent*?"

"You saw me pack one."

"I thought it was for Dump to sleep in!"

"Nope." He smiled, loving the way her cheeks had turned pink and her eyes sparkled. "It's for us. About that bikini—"

"Yes, I brought a bikini." Impatiently, she waved her arms, making her flashy bracelets clatter. She put her hands on her hips. "You think I've never been outdoors before?"

He peered at her miniskirt. Then her teased-up, sexy hair. Then her bare midriff. "Well . . ."

"Don't answer that." She grinned. "Just point me to the bar. I'll have a cocktail while you get things set up."

Cash angled his head. How to break this gently to her?

"Actually, there isn't a—"

"Gotcha!" Laughing, Marisol threw her arms around him. She gave a joyful little hip wiggle, scooting closer. "I know there's no bar out here. I'll help you set up instead."

For a minute, Cash was tempted to sleep on the ground. Against a tree. Whatever it took to keep her right there next to him. The kids were occupied, the weather was sunny, and the other campers were all busy with their own fun. As far as Cash was concerned, this was enough privacy for him.

"Nah, you don't have to help. I've got it covered."

To prove it, he pulled Marisol closer, enjoying the way she smiled when he skimmed his palms over her back. Her upturned face was the most beautiful he'd ever seen. Tempted beyond all reason, he ducked his head and kissed her. Then he kissed her again. She tasted exactly as sweet as before.

She broke the kiss first. "I'll say you've got it covered."

"Don't you forget it," Cash commanded with mock sternness. Sharing that sleeping bag for two sounded better and better all the time. "Now you go put on that bikini."

He swatted her on the derrière, showing her the brick building that housed the campground facilities. She squealed.

"No, really. I was serious." Blushing, Marisol rubbed her backside. "Just point me in the right direction—the *real* right direction—and I'll get busy helping. That's what I'm here for."

He shook his head. "You're the eye candy. The inspiration."

"I mean it! I can do it." She sucked in a deep breath and threw her shoulders back. "You need somebody to hold the ruler while you do the job perfectly anyway, right?"

"Very funny." He paused. "I use a T-square."

Marisol almost looked upset. Just for an instant. Because of that, Cash relented. He even hauled his gaze away from her breasts, which had been shown to advantage by her indignant posture. He shaded his eyes as he searched for Jacob, Emily, and Hannah. They were gathering pinecones, with Dump snuffling in the pine-needle drifts beside them.

"Do you want to change first?" he asked.

"Why?" Marisol glanced down at herself. "This is my oldest vintage skirt—so it won't matter if it gets dirty. I can bleach this blouse if necessary. White, natch. And these flats are from last season, so no problem about hiking around in them. See?"

No, he didn't. "Don't you ever wear pants? Or sneakers?"

"Mmmm. Nope." Marisol shrugged. "My mom always

wore skirts too. Isn't that weird? I haven't thought about that for years. I mean, as *if* I'd want to be like her or something." She laughed.

"Why wouldn't you? What did she do?"

"Besides abandon my dad and me, shop, take advantage of the cabana boy, and marry a matador? Not much."

"Hmmm. That must make for awkward family reunions."

"Not really. I haven't seen her since I was thirteen. She sends a birthday card once in a while, but that's about it."

Cash felt sorry he'd asked. But he didn't know what to say.

"It's okay." Marisol winked. "My mom taught me how to harass the cabana boys before she left, so it's all good."

Now he was *really* sorry.

"No, seriously." Seeing his dismal face, Marisol put her hand on his arm. She gave him a reassuring squeeze. "That was a looong time ago. I'm over it, believe me."

"Still . . . it must have been hard growing up that way."

A shrug. "Sometimes. I did get to audition several bonus moms, however. Not every kid can say that. And my third stepmother, Jamie, is great. So if you ever worry about your children growing up with divorced parents . . . they can turn out okay in the end. Just look at me. I'm proof!"

She turned a pirouette, making a goofy face.

"I wasn't worried," Cash said, "until you did that."

"Har, har." Laughing, Marisol caught his arm for balance. "Also, you're a way better dad than my father ever was, so you have a leg up. Emily, Jacob, and Hannah are going to be fine."

For the first time in a while, Cash dared to hope so. Now if he could only cement his spot with the Scorpions so they could actually visit him in a good neighborhood and not worry about long-term issues like college, he'd be set.

"Hey everybody!" Jacob called, obviously spying their bent heads and closer-than-close pose. He gestured to

Emily and Hannah. "I think Dad and Marisol are going
to make out again!"

Nearby campers turned their heads. Some grinned.
Cash and Marisol stepped apart.

"Wanna put up a tent?" he asked.

"You bet," she said. "Let's go."

After the tent was set up—*with* Marisol's help—Cash
got busy arranging all their supplies inside. She doubted
the place would have much style, but she could always add
a little pizzazz later. That was her specialty. Even as she
considered a décor and theme, the kids went on setting
up, dragging in their backpacks and sleeping bags with
the air of volunteers who had done so many times before.

"Step it up." Cash crossed his arms, standing outside
the weirdly-pitched tent with its multiply peaked roof.
He waved to Jacob, Emily, and Hannah, ushering them
in through the unzipped front flap. "You know what to
do. Let's get going."

They all hunched down and duck-walked in. Jacob
flopped in the dirt and belly crawled, G.I. Joe-style. Giggling. Squealing. Cash entered too, then stuck his head
through the flap.

"Just relax," he said. "We'll get everything ready."

"Are you sure you don't want help?"

"You've already done enough." He winked, probably
remembering all the "accidental" ways they'd brushed
against one another while erecting the tent in the first
place. "Besides, out here, you're our guest. Sit tight."

The flap flopped. More giggling and rustling of nylon.
The tent's gaudy green sides bulged with their vigorous
movements.

Marisol couldn't believe the whole thing didn't topple.
Somehow it stayed in place, so she occupied herself with
finding a nice flat rock to sit on near their campsite's fire

pit. If only she could find something to brush it clean with first . . .

She was in the middle of rifling through the remaining items left in the Range Rover's cargo bay when her phone rang.

"Hello?"

"Marisol, it's Adam."

"Oh! Hi, Adam!" She pulled the phone away from her ear and looked at it. Pink. Sparkly cover plate. No messages waiting. Definitely hers. That was weird. "How did you get my number?"

"I'm an agent. I have my ways. Is Cash there?"

"Sure, I'll go get him for you."

"No! You're the one I wanted to talk to."

"Me? About what?" She found a tarp, considered it as a potential rock-duster, then dismissed it as too unwieldy to manage. More searching. "Do you need decorating advice? Is your hotel room dreary?" Adam had ended his visit with the Connellys and booked a room in Flagstaff. "Try lighting a bunch of scented candles. And put out framed pictures too. That really helps make a hotel room homey."

"Thanks for the advice." He sounded amused. "But that's not why I called."

Marisol kept searching. She would have sold her favorite Chanel bag for her feather duster right now—and if *that* wasn't a sentiment she'd never expected to experience, nothing was.

"Oh. Well, if you're lonely, you should come camping with us! We're at the Happy Gecko Campground. Do you know where that is?" She squinted, searching for identifying signs. "It's near . . . a bunch of pine trees and some mountains."

"Marisol, Cash is hurt," Adam interrupted in a businesslike tone. "That's why I'm calling. He doesn't know I know about it, but I just got off the phone with the team trainer, so I—"

"What?" She froze, gripping her cell phone. "Hurt how?" Cash always seemed so strong to her. "You must be mistaken, Adam. Cash didn't tell me about it. And he looks fine—"

"Keep your voice down. Can he hear you?"

She checked. The tent was still kind of tangoing with activity. "I don't think so," she whispered. "What happened?"

"A hamstring strain," Adam said. "During his workout today. It's relatively minor. The fight with the fullback afterward probably did more damage than the hamstring strain, but—"

"Cash got into a fight?"

How did he keep these things from her?

"Just a scuffle with another player. Nothing serious." Adam kept his voice reasonable. "Listen to me. Cash needs to rest up before training camp starts on Monday, so the camping trip is probably a good idea. It'll give him a break from training—just as a precautionary measure. At his age, Cash can't afford to play hurt."

She rolled her eyes. "He's only thirty-four."

"That's getting up there in football years. The equivalent would be . . . How can I put this? A twenty-four-year-old model."

"Uh-oh." Most fashion models were over the hill at twenty-one. Worriedly, Marisol glanced toward the tent again. She hoped all that activity wasn't aggravating Cash's injury. She should have known that something was wrong from the moment he limped past her in the kitchen. "What can I do?"

"Just keep Cash off his feet awhile. As much as possible, don't let him overdo things," Adam warned. "He's liable to be feeling pretty mulish right now. Overly emotional, maybe."

Dubiously, Marisol listened to the sounds coming from

the tent. More laughter. Knowing Cash, that probably meant tickling.

"He seems okay at the moment."

"Well, whatever you do, keep Cash busy. Don't let him mope or feel sorry for himself. Don't let him start any fights either."

"Okay. Gotcha." Marisol glanced down at herself. Sure, she kicked butt in Bjorn's advanced Pilates class, but that didn't mean much in the real world. Especially against a pro football player nearly twice her size. "Um, how am I supposed to do that?"

"Distract him. You're good at that."

She bit her lip, thinking.

"It doesn't have to be X-rated," Adam said dryly.

Too bad. "No problem. I'm on the job." Marisol gave a mock salute, then cast another anxious glance at the tent. "And Adam? Thanks for trusting me with this. I won't let you down."

Chapter 21

Cash didn't know what got into Marisol. For the next three days at the Happy Gecko Campground, she was unrelentingly cheerful, busy, and responsible. Even though they were outdoors. All the time. With no manicurists or fancy sheets in sight. It was completely surreal. If he hadn't known better, Cash would have sworn Marisol was up to something, especially given the way she pampered him. She made him rest and relax. She brought him inflatable pillows and cold drinks. She actually pushed him onto his sleeping bag when he tried to get up at dawn, then happily slept in too, along with Emily, Jacob, and Hannah.

She listened dutifully when he described the correct procedures for starting a blaze in the fire pit and for putting that fire out. She trooped tirelessly into the woods with the kids to collect pinecones and rocks, then made tree forts too. She cracked jokes and ate hotdogs on a stick and ran around in a miniskirt and white bikini top that drove him absolutely crazy.

She slept beside him—wearing a kooky pink sleep mask—in their double sleeping bag every night. She chastely snuggled her delectable backside against him in a way that was decidedly hard to deal with when the kids were wide awake and wiggly only inches away. She kissed him and held him and made him cross-eyed with unfulfilled desire.

She made every day feel sunnier somehow too.

All in all, Marisol seemed to enjoy her first foray into family camping. And Cash enjoyed it with her. He enjoyed teaching her about life outdoors, about swimming in a lake instead of a swanky L.A. pool, about watching the stars and living off the clock. He enjoyed watching Marisol put her own unique spin on all of it.

What he didn't enjoy was doddering around on a stiff-feeling log . . . and wondering what life would be like after Marisol's Dzeel-required stint with them was over.

"Hey, Gloomy Gus." Marisol nudged him, shifting her gaze from her rapidly toasting marshmallow to his face. The firelight made her features glow. "What's the matter? Did you burn yours?"

Cash shook his head. He'd had to peel off half the bark on her stick before she'd touch it—and even then Marisol had whipped out her emery board and sanded the end before she'd consented to spear a marshmallow for their nightly s'mores.

"Doesn't matter. You can have mine." She passed over a gooey, sweet-smelling marshmallow, already sandwiched between two graham crackers. Melted chocolate dripped on her fingers, making her laugh. She sucked them clean. "See? Really good. Who'd have believed I'd never tried these three days ago?" She rubbed her stomach, bared in her camping-trip getup—bikini top, miniskirt, and flip-flops. "Now I'm a bona fide expert."

Cash accepted his s'more and downed it in two bites, too preoccupied to really enjoy it. Three days of sleeping with Marisol—and *only* sleeping with Marisol—was wearing on his fortitude.

The trouble was, out here he'd started imagining what a real future between them might be like. A future where he wasn't her boss, and she wasn't obligated to spend time with him—but did so anyway. More and more, he wanted that. Wanted her.

But what did she want?

"Having a good time?" he heard himself ask.

"Sure." Marisol smiled at the kids, who'd bunched up on a fallen log at the edge of the campfire circle as they gobbled their treats. Above them, stars sparkled in the summer sky. "I like it out here. It's peaceful—kind of like the Amalfi coast in springtime."

"Yeah." He considered the place. "And you're beautiful."

She gawked, almost dropping her next toasting marshmallow. "Are you kidding me?" She tugged her hair. "My hair is air-dried and kinky, I don't have on a lick of makeup, and my manicure is chipped. I'm a mess. I'm just glad nobody can see me out here." Blithely, she bit into her next marshmallow. "The press would have a field day if I got paparazzied looking like this."

Oh yeah. To the rest of the world, Marisol Winston was a fashionable, fun-loving heiress—someone to be admired and pursued, featured in magazines and even imitated. To him, she was just Marisol. Most days, Cash forgot all about her background—her fortune and celebrity and life in L.A.

"Does that happen a lot?" he asked.

"Getting snapped by surprise?" Marisol nodded. "In L.A., I can't get a cup of coffee without photographers going crazy, shouting my name. Sometimes they draw a crowd. It's bizarre."

"Most people would like to be that famous." He grinned. "Hell, *I'm* almost that famous." Or he had been, in his prime.

"Maybe. But I never *did* anything."

Cash gave her a skeptical look. Marisol smiled wickedly.

"Okay, so maybe I did do my share of clubbing. And

there was the occasional scandalous gossip about me. But now that I'm older . . . That stuff just doesn't do it for me anymore. Plus, who wants to be known just for being part of a famous family?"

Cash shrugged, feeling unreasonably curious about her past. About her. And utterly transfixed by being with her. Maybe there was some voodoo in pine trees he'd never noticed before.

"It's not as if I chose to be a Winston," Marisol went on, jangling her bracelets. "It was an accident of birth. I haven't really done anything worthwhile yet. Besides, we Winstons aren't all we're cracked up to be, believe me."

Cash gave a thoughtful sound. "I know what you mean. Neither is football."

Surprised to hear himself admit as much aloud, he glared at his leg. Although his injured hamstring had mostly healed, he still resented having to baby it. Having to wonder about it surviving training camp next week without further problems.

"Yeah, I've been wondering about that." Marisol propped her chin in her hand, watching him. "About football, that is." She regarded him seriously. "Once you're playing professionally again, won't you be unhappy being away from the kids so much?"

Expectant silence stretched between them, broken only by the snapping of the fire as it sparked upward. Marisol waited.

Cash frowned. "They'll survive. Stephanie and I share custody. The kids have their friends. Their lives. They—"

"I'm talking about *you*. Won't you be unhappy?"

Cash slapped his palms on his thighs and rose. "Last s'mores, you guys," he said to Emily, Hannah, and Jacob. They gazed up at him with disappointed faces. "It's bedtime."

* * *

Marisol followed the trail away from the campground's ladies' rooms with her toiletries and cell phone in hand, feeling frustrated. With the phone to her ear, she passed laughing campers, playing kids, a group singing camp songs, and fires crackling so high they seemed to push more stars into the night sky. The scents of hot dogs and marshmallows and pine trees hung in the air—the unique perfume of this outdoors.

It was different from any other outdoors she'd experienced—say, at design festivals in Capri or open-air California malls or the occasional flea market browse-a-thon—but what she'd told Cash was true. She did like it. Especially with him.

At least until he got aggravating.

"I don't get it!" she told Jamie on the phone. "One minute, we're totally bonding. The next minute, Cash is stomping off without even answering my questions. Why can't I make him talk to me?"

"He's a man," her stepmother reminded her. "It's not like gabbing with Caprice and Tenley. Some men don't like to talk."

"Does Dad talk?" Marisol asked. "No, scratch that." She shuddered. "Too personal. I don't want to know. Although he doesn't talk to me these days, that's for sure."

"Your father is busy, that's all," Jamie assured her. She breathed out—probably in the middle of her usual yoga session. Again Marisol felt reminded of how easily life went on without her. "He doesn't want to distract you while you're in rehab."

"*Shopaholic* rehab," Marisol reminded her. "Which I'm not even convinced is necessary! I mean, I do wish I were in L.A. right now, so we could talk about this over a nice cruise through Fred Segal, but that's just ordinary multitasking."

"Marisol, please. We've been over this at Dzeel—"

"I just miss you, that's all." Marisol paused beneath a

pine tree, blinking back tears as she stared up at the stars. There was so much sky that it almost pressed down on a person. It made her feel small. "I don't know what to do about Cash, and I'm only guessing at what to do with the kids, and I miss you."

Jamie chuckled. "Honey, we're *all* guessing. Do you think anybody really knows what they're doing?"

"Narciso Rodriguez knows what he's doing." Marisol sniffed, then kept walking. "His clothes are absolutely brilliant."

"You are not Narciso, but I'll tell him you said such a nice thing the next time I see him. He'll be pleased." A pause. "The rest of us are just regular folks, honey. Not everyone can be a famous designer."

"Speaking of which . . ." Marisol held her breath. Was she really going to . . . ? Yes, she decided. She plunged ahead before she could lose her nerve. "I've been doing a little decorating."

"That's wonderful! Oh Marisol, I'm so glad to hear that."

"It's nothing big," Marisol said hastily, cutting off her stepmother in midgush. "Just a little rearranging at the cabin Cash borrowed and some textiles work." She pictured the shower curtain she and the kids had made together. That had been fun. "But hey, it's making the most of my meager talents."

"You have big talents. If you'd only buckle down and—"

"Dad didn't think so."

Silence. Marisol could practically hear crickets chirping. No wait. Those were actual crickets chirping. On her end.

"You have to understand," Jamie was saying. "It's not that your father can't see your abilities, because he can. It's just that he was a little wild himself when he was your age, and—"

"Never mind. Forget I mentioned it." The last thing Marisol could imagine was her sedate, responsible dad being "wild." Probably he'd neglected to fill out a Home Warehouse form in triplicate once, and had regretted his unruliness ever since.

She blew out a sigh, picking her way along the trail. Ahead, she spied campsite number seven—their campsite— and experienced an uncanny sense of homecoming. Dump trotted up to her with his tail wagging, having obviously been left out of whatever bedtime routine Cash and Emily and Jacob and Hannah practiced while she beautified herself hippie-style at the facilities. She petted the German shepherd.

"Guess what?" she asked Jamie. "I almost have a dog."

"*You*? A dog?"

"Well, he's Cash's dog, but he's special," she cooed. "He's especially good for camping. He protects our campsite."

There was an incredulous silence on her stepmother's end.

"Let me get this straight," Jamie said. "You're camping. You're walking around with no makeup. You're eating carbs by the wagon full, by your own admission. You're decorating again after a yearlong hiatus. And now you've made friends with a dog?"

"Uh-huh." Marisol nodded. "Weird but true. I'm not even scared of this one, for some reason."

"That's it," Jamie announced. "You're in love. And it's good for you too. Just look at how happy you are!"

Marisol scoffed. "I am not in love. I'm just the nanny." *And the maid*, but she omitted that. "Besides, Cash and I haven't even slept together." She sat on her rock, which she'd buffed clean since first discovering it. "Well, we've *slept* together, but we haven't actually slept together. We're sharing a sleeping bag."

"Aww, poor baby. You must be dying!"

"Oh God. Try to have a little motherly decorum, would you?"

"Decorum is overrated." Jamie laughed. "I *have* to meet this man. This miracle worker. This wonder of wonders who's got my little girl skipping spray-tan sessions for actual camping."

"No, you don't have to meet Cash. He'd only aggravate you." Marisol remembered the abrupt end to their earlier conversation about Cash's upcoming football season and still had no idea what to do. Did Cash not trust her with his feelings? The thought hurt. "I really, really like him. He doesn't even care that I'm a Winston! It's not a big deal to him."

"Then he might actually be able to handle being with you without freaking out?" Jamie asked. "That's always a plus. You've had your share of fortune hunters in the past."

"I know. But it's complicated. I mean, I'm just the nanny, and technically he's the boss, and I—oh, I don't know." Marisol sighed, still petting Dump. "Cash is very different from me, and this isn't exactly how I envisioned my life playing out."

"That's true," Jamie said cautiously. "I'll bet there's not a martini station, a raw bar, or a rack of Manolos for miles."

"I know!" Marisol saw a bug and recoiled. She stepped sideways. "But who knows if Cash even feels the same way?"

"What way?" her stepmother asked.

"Like this could be serious. Oh, what am I even talking about? All this fresh air must be getting to me." Determinedly, Marisol straightened. "Maybe I should just get through my assignment the best I can and chalk this one up to bad timing."

"No! Don't give up too easily," Jamie cautioned. "You know you have a tendency to do that. Ever since you were a little girl. Remember? With the Malibu Barbie Dream House makeover?"

"I was fourteen." A light flickered in the tent, casting four fuzzy silhouettes on the nylon. It looked cozy in there with Cash and the kids. "Too old to play with Barbies."

"You weren't playing, you were redecorating. Discovering your unique talents! Designing and imagining and reinventing. Why, you had that dream house halfway torn apart, plastic bits all over the place, before—"

"Demoed. I was demoing to prepare for the remodel."

"—before you quit on the project," Jamie finished. "All I'm saying now is, if this Cash of yours is special, don't give up before you've given it your best. Even if things get messy."

From inside the tent, an unexpectedly hushed sound caught Marisol's attention. Those silhouettes had all bunched together too. Listening, she patted Dump. He rested his gray-speckled muzzle against her knee, then gazed up at her in adoration.

"Thanks, Jamie. Something's up. I'd better go."

They said their good-byes. Marisol, her curiosity piqued, put away her phone and listened harder. The same sound reached her again—and this time she recognized it as Cash's voice.

His big, husky tone softened as he murmured the homemade bedtime story du jour, a tradition she knew he practiced. She'd never heard him tell one before though—Cash usually found something dubiously urgent for her to do at story time. This one was coming to a close, so Marisol only caught the very tail end.

". . . and that's why the two fairy princesses and the crown prince decided to skateboard home," Cash was saying. "So with two ollies and a really sick nosegrind, the three of them zoomed into the castle and lived happily ever after."

"With the king?" Hannah piped up, sounding drowsy.

"Yes," he assured her. "For as long as they wanted, they lived with the king. Because the king loved them with the strength of a million, gazillion Original Wham-O SuperBalls—"

"Hey, I've got one of those!" Jacob said.

"—and his love could never be broken. No matter what."

"Good. Good story." Emily yawned. "'Night, Daddy."

"Tomorrow they should surf," Jacob said. "Totally!"

"Maybe they will," came Cash's steady voice. "Sleep now."

"Okay. Good night, Dad."

There were a few more murmurings, but Marisol only heard Cash—Cash and the love in every word he said. It was remarkable. He still sounded manly. Still sounded sure and steady and strong. But he also sounded careful and funny and so vulnerable in his unabashed affection that she could scarcely believe this was the same man who'd cut her off so tersely when she'd asked him about missing his kids.

She'd never been within earshot of Cash's good night routine before. Had never known what went on. But now Marisol couldn't imagine why he'd ever kept her away. Because this time, hearing him, she felt something new. Something certain.

Something she should have expected but hadn't.

She felt love. She loved Cash! She loved his stubborn ways and his protective ideas and even his ridiculous method of skewering the marshmallows three at a time. Jamie had been right and she was wrong, and the only trouble now was . . .

What to do about it?

What to do about being head over heels for a man who would only be within her reach for another few weeks?

Before Marisol could decide, the tent flap flopped

open. Cash crawled out, got easily to his feet, and
stretched his big body, not noticing her yet. He smiled,
then patted the tent.

Awww. She just wanted to hug him. Probably kiss him
all over too, but the hugging was a certainty. Cash was secretly sweet! He was privately mushy and he told bedtime
stories in a soft voice that hypnotized little kids and
grown women alike.

He turned . . . and spotted her watching him.

Smitten, Marisol wiggled her fingers in a wave.

Cash frowned. Shadowed by firelight, he reached for
something in the backpack at his feet, then threw it to
her.

One of his Scorpions sweatshirts. Marisol caught it
with a curious expression, holding it against her.

"Put that on. You must be cold wearing nothing but
that bikini top."

"I'm fine." She smiled broadly. "And you're sweet."

"I'm going to pick up more firewood," Cash said, his
tone gruff. He hefted his big flashlight. "Do you need
anything?"

Marisol shook her head. "Just you. Soon."

Heat shimmered between them, searing the darkness.

Cash nodded at his oversize sweatshirt. "Put that on.
I'll be back." Then he was gone through the trees, his
shoulders sturdy in the moonlight.

Chapter 22

On the morning of their last day at Happy Gecko Campground, after a splash in the lake, a bit of hiking, and a rousing session of making shiny necklaces out of cut-up drinking straws wrapped in leftover foil, Marisol met an obstacle she could neither tackle, negotiate past, nor shimmy into submission.

"I'm bored," Jacob whined, kicking a stone.

"Me too," Emily said. "Super, fantastic, crazy bored."

"Nobody has *ever* been as bored as I am," Hannah moaned with her hand flung across her forehead. "I'm *so* sick of camping!"

It was just the opportunity Marisol had been looking for.

"Well, why don't we find out what your dad's up to in the tent? Maybe he'll come out and give us some ideas."

Emily shook her head. "I think he's taking a nap."

"Yeah," Jacob agreed. "He needed one more than we did."

That was possible, Marisol thought. Cash had been working pretty hard to get ready for training camp and the upcoming football season. He had a lot of lost sleep to catch up on. The few days' rest he'd had while camping were only a drop in the bucket. She still caught him limping a little sometimes too, as though his injured leg were stiff and slowly healing.

"Naps? Please. We're not babies." Hannah snorted, adjusting the matching princess crown she'd fashioned out of a cardboard strip and more tinfoil. "I haven't napped in *years*."

Marisol smiled at her six-year-old world weariness. "I'm pretty sure I heard somebody snoring in there."

"Probably Jacob," Emily said, studying her nails.

"Nuh-uh!" The boy craned around, yanking out his earbuds.

"Yeah, he's the youngest." Hannah stuck out her tongue.

"By twelve minutes!" Jacob said. "Big deal."

They went on bickering, their voices ratcheting up quickly.

"Hey!" Frowning, Cash stuck his head out the tent flap. His hair stood on end. "What's all the racket about?"

All three children launched into simultaneous defenses of their points of view, interspersed with grousing about how they were sick of camping, sick of pine trees, and sick of hot dogs.

Cash whistled sharply. Jacob, Hannah, and Emily snapped to attention. Grumpily, Cash climbed out of the tent.

"Cut it out, all three of you—" he began.

Hannah and Emily giggled. Even Jacob snickered.

Cash's eyes widened. In this household, he was the boss. Snickering wasn't usually allowed. Sternly, he put his hands on his hips . . . and almost dislodged the pair of SpongeBob SquarePants stickers affixed to his shorts. Marisol whipped her gaze over him, and she started laughing too.

Evidently, Emily and Hannah hadn't slept during their impromptu campout naptime. They'd improvised a craft project instead—one involving their sticker collections and their dad.

"That's better." With a scowl, Cash shoved his hand through his hair. A Blues Clues sticker drifted down from his unruly dark locks and landed on his shoulder. "No more arguing."

"We promise," Emily and Hannah said in unison.

They elbowed Jacob, pointing out a series of Dora the Explorer stickers stuck to their father's chest. Another decorated his forehead, and several more were scattered all over his torso. He wore a set of alphabet stickers down his legs.

"Um . . ." Marisol hesitated, then pointed too.

"What?" Cash scoured them all with an impatient gaze.

"You have a little . . . something . . . right there." Marisol nodded at the Hello Kitty stickers adorning his bare knee.

Cash looked down. Marisol winced, awaiting the explosion.

Instead, he actually grinned. "Aha! You got me good this time, girls. Do you have any stickers left?"

The fantastic stick-on duo shook their heads.

"Nice work." Cash rumpled their hair, then sat beside Marisol on her flat rock. He shifted her sideways with his hip, his body language completely at ease. "Well played."

"Aren't you mad?" Marisol asked. "You looked mad."

"Nah." He plucked off a few stickers and gazed at them contemplatively, then made a tiny pile on his thumb as he yanked off a few more. He motioned over Emily and gave her the stickers he'd collected, then looked Marisol square in the eye. "It's all good fun. Besides, I told them that if they can get me, next time they're allowed to come for you."

He nodded to Emily, who grew a mischievous grin. Hannah and Jacob perked up too. Next thing Marisol knew, she was racing through the woods with all four of them in hot pursuit, stickers waving in the summer-scented air.

Cash realized he was in way over his head with Marisol when he actually started to cave in to her next request. Even though it was idiotic and ill-advised and went against all his own rules. Even though it wasn't a real camping activity.

"Please," she begged, holding his hands and trying to tug him to his feet. "Please do it. For me? I really want you to."

Hannah, Jacob, and Emily stood nearby, watching avidly. He couldn't believe Marisol had ambushed him while they were within earshot. He shook his head and frowned.

"I already told you no. I'm not doing it."

"Why not? It'll be fun. You won't regret it, I promise."

"Not going to happen."

"Please? As long as you're careful, you won't get hurt. And as a bonus, you can even teach me." She gave another tug.

Cash stood firm. "I don't play football for fun."

Jacob gave a disillusioned moan. He kicked a pinecone. "I knew this wouldn't work, Marisol. Never mind."

"No, it *is* going to work." Marisol nudged her head in the boy's direction, giving Cash a *see? he needs you!* frown. She tugged down the Scorpions sweatshirt he'd tossed her, then baited him with a plaintive look. "See Jacob? Your dad's going to say yes any minute now."

Instead, Cash bared his teeth and growled.

Hannah and Emily squealed, giggling as they petted Dump.

Impatiently, Marisol marched over to the tent. She

grabbed the borrowed football that had been resting next to his sneakers ever since she came up with this cockamamie idea, then shot him an impertinent look. She tossed the ball in the air.

It fell down again, right between her outstretched hands.

Marisol slapped her thighs, giving the ball the universal scowl that blamed it, instead of the catcher, for the miss.

"You have to relax your hands," Cash instructed.

Blowing her hair from her eyes, Marisol tried again. Again she missed, muffing an easy return. Who couldn't throw a ball to *themselves*? It was pathetic. Cash decided not to watch. It was obvious she wanted to lure him into a game. He wasn't biting.

"Come on, you guys. We'll figure it out ourselves."

Marisol flounced off to the center of the Happy Gecko Campground. She assumed a determined posture, pointed Jacob to an open spot a few feet away, then threw. Underhanded and between her bent legs, like a really amateur bowler. Arrgh.

"You're not trying to land a six-ten split." Cash pantomimed making a short inside pass. "Try it like this."

Hannah scampered after the ball and recovered it from where it had rolled into someone else's campsite. Even with Cash's expert instructions, Marisol did no better the second time. Although she attempted a normal throwing motion, it was all wrong. There was no spiral. There was serious wobble. Her shoulder was twisted funny. Her foot positioning was terrible.

He cupped his mouth. "You've got no follow-through, Winston! Bring that arm all the way around."

She shot him a dire look, then pointedly glanced away.

"Hey kids, let's go!" Marisol called. "One more try!"

She clapped her hands, hunkering down to receive the

ball—now that Jacob had chased it down after another missed catch. Biting his lip, the boy hurled the football.

It landed behind him. Moaning, Cash covered his eyes.

But Marisol was just getting warmed up. "That's okay! Try again!" she yelled. "Right here, Jacob. Right here."

More attempts at throwing. Cash smelled dust being kicked up, heard the muffled *whump* of the ball hitting the ground over and over again. Marisol's voice overrode everything.

"Girls *can* play football!" she told Hannah. "It's good cardio too. Throw it to Emily. Hard as you can!"

"Ouch! She broke my fingernail!" Emily carped.

No no no. This was the worst game of catch in history. Cash wasn't even sure he was related to these kids anymore.

They just kept going, Marisol shouting encouragement, Hannah and Emily matching her in hand-holding niceness, and Jacob doing his best at trash talking.

"Oh yeah? Well you're a doody head!" he yelled.

Cash groaned. The kid lacked finesse.

More throwing. Finally, someone cheered.

A catch! Could it be? Bravely, Cash looked.

Nope. The ball was on the ground. But Marisol had removed her sweatshirt and was now playing in her miniskirt and bikini top, with lots of enthusiastic and uninhibited bouncing to go with them. No wonder there was cheering from the bystanders. Seeing her, Cash wanted to send up fireworks too.

They'd gathered a small crowd of onlookers, adults and several kids who watched the action while nudging each other and making fun. The pressure was clearly starting to get to Jacob. He wore the squinty eyes and mulish set to his chin that he'd employed since birth whenever anything had proven difficult.

Unwanted naptime? Chin jab. No TV? Chin jab. Potty training? First day of kindergarten? Chin jab, chin jab.

"Try to catch it this time, baby," an onlooker jeered.

Jacob's eyes grew even squintier. His chin wavered, and his sisters looked on in obvious commiseration. He gave a brisk nod to Marisol, wiggling his dirty little fingers in readiness.

Marisol caught sight of the heckler too. Her spine straightened as she watched him laugh at Jacob around a mouthful of Skittles. She wound up, getting in position for what was clearly destined to be a soft underhanded toss. An easy catch.

"Ha! I bet you can't even catch a throw from a *girl*, baby!"

Marisol hesitated and so did Jacob, casting her another nervous but dogged glance. *Chin jab.* Cash frowned. If that obnoxious kid had been an adult, he'd have laid him out with a ninety-mph pass to his big fat head and maybe knocked his Skittles into next week too. But since he was just one dumb kid, leading a pack of more dumb kids . . .

"Hey." Cash stood and strode to the field, his jaw set as he neared Marisol. "I'll take this one."

By some miracle, Jacob caught the hard pass Cash threw to him.

Not the first one. Not the second one. But by the time a third spiral came rocketing his way, his son actually opened his eyes and his arms at the same time and plucked the ball out of thin air. There was jubilation all around.

Marisol nearly incited a male-camper riot by jumping up and down and screaming in her barely-there getup. Hannah and Emily hollered loud enough to shake squirrels from the trees, then attempted to pick up their brother and carry him around the makeshift football field, almost earning themselves junior hernias in the process. Cash beamed, and Jacob high-fived him, and for that moment at least, all was right with the world.

"I'm never letting go of this ball!" his son crowed.

Cash remembered feeling the same way at Jacob's age. All of a sudden, he couldn't think of a single damned reason not to play football on his day off. Not when he thought about the pride and awe in Jacob's face when he'd caught that pass. If Cash could make that happen again, he'd play all day. And from that moment on, there was no getting him off the field—despite the occasional twinge from his hamstring.

By the time the sun began setting, casting long shadows over the campground, Cash was enjoying the pickup scrimmage of his life. He wasn't sure how it had happened, but he knew it had something to do with Marisol, and he knew he was glad.

"That's right!" he yelled, smiling and gesturing to Hannah with an exuberance he hadn't felt on the field in years. "Snap it. Now drop back . . . throw! Excellent!"

Flushed faces grinned at him, all part of the growing crowd of kids surrounding him. All ages, all sizes, boys and girls alike—everyone had joined in once they'd seen Jacob catch that ball. Now his entourage of wannabes trotted after Cash as he hustled downfield to coach a nine-year-old on improving the handoff he'd tried to make.

He hunkered down to meet the boy on eye level. They chatted for a few minutes, with advice given and taken, then Cash patted him on the shoulder. "Keep it up. You'll get it."

"Thanks, seven."

He'd been recognized. Not long after Cash had thrown Jacob his first real reception, two older boys who'd joined in the game dropped back with awed looks on their faces.

"Whoa! Cash Connelly! What are you doing here?"

"Camping, same as you." Then he helped Emily work on hurling a major pass, showing her how to grip the ball loosely to cut down on flutter. She grinned. "I did it, Daddy!"

And he was proud of her too.

Here his celebrity didn't matter. He was just another guy running past the pine trees, coaching an increasing number of kids on the roll out, the sprint out, and dropping back. Cash lined up everyone, big and small, and gave them short passes to catch. Then he turned over the ball and let them take turns passing to him, giving pointers and smiling at their eager efforts. To these kids, running drills was a game. Not work.

A tall, sweaty teenager in a Scorpions T-shirt cornered Cash next. He ran up, flushed and smiling. "Hey, thanks for the help on that seven-step drop. I think I get it now."

"Just takes practice. Footwork doesn't come naturally to most players, especially lanky ones like you. I know it was tricky for me." Cash sucked down a long drink of water, enjoying the rush of players clamoring as they scrimmaged just beyond him. He nodded at the teenager. "You play at school?"

"Yeah. Backup quarterback for my high school. But I don't get to play much." He stared at the pine trees, his shoulders taut. "Coach says I hold the ball wrong. I'll be in the pocket for a big play, set up for a long pass . . . then that sucker gets stripped and I get creamed." He shook his head. "I'm good, but I'm never getting a football scholarship that way."

Cash nodded, commiserating. For many high school players, scholarships were the difference between going to college and going straight to work to help support their families. Scholarships were key to landing at colleges with good teams—and eventually getting scouted for the NFL too. For a player with long-term goals like those, bad habits like inviting a strip and getting sacked were no small matter.

"Tuck your elbows in," Cash advised. He offered a few

more tips on ball control, things he'd picked up at Scorpions' practice fields and minicamps over the years. "That'll help. Look, show me what you're doing, and I'll troubleshoot."

The teenager brightened. They practiced the maneuver a while, with Cash lining up eager players from his burgeoning pool to play defense. Even as the sun slipped lower, the scrimmage showed no signs of slowing down. Hannah, Jacob, and Emily whooped and hollered their way through several good catches, and so did half a dozen other kids. Parents delayed campfire cookouts to linger on the sidelines; swim trunks and bathing suits hung unused beside disassembled fishing poles.

Nobody asked Cash for autographs. Nobody interviewed him or hinted for free tickets or took pictures. Nobody hung the whole game on his shoulders. Instead, everyone learned a little something. They played and got silly. Or they looked on and smiled. On a late July day like today, that was enough.

After a while, Cash stepped back and let the kids play alone, watching with satisfaction. He hadn't done much. He couldn't really take credit for the day. But he was pleased, all the same. All anybody needed were a few pointers, some coaching, and some practice, and eventually they would learn. They'd probably have fun too. Even Marisol had mastered the art of knocking out a decent pass—even if she'd had to ignore wolf whistles from the onlookers while trying.

He wondered where she'd gotten off to. At first she'd been right in there with him, mixing it up and laughing. But now . . .

Before he could spot her among the other campers, a squat Latino man approached him. He nodded, then shook his hand.

"Thanks for all you're doing here." The man aimed his chin toward the jovial players. "I'm George Wade. My

Hector—he's the one with the seven-stop-drop problem—has never played better. He's never *concentrated* better. And I've seen kids go from constant drops to catches today, smiling the whole time they're learning. You're one hell of a coach, Mr. Connelly."

Cash gave a grunt of acknowledgement. "Thanks, but it's Cash. And I'm not a coach. I picked up a few things over the years, but real coaching . . ." He trailed off, shaking his head.

"Real coaching is what you were doing out there. Trust me."

Doubtfully, Cash looked at the kids. He couldn't help but offer a few more shouted-out tips as they continued the last drill. The Skittles-eating kid—considerably humbled by a few athletic attempts of his own—gave him a *rock on* wave in return.

"You're retired now, right?" Wade said beside him. "I hated to see you leave the NFL, but the Scorpions' loss could be these kids' gain, I think. If you went into coaching full-time, you could really be something."

"Nah." Cash wiped his brow. "I'm a player. That's it."

"Well," Hector's father persisted, "if you ever change your mind, I know a high school in Phoenix that could use some fresh blood on the coaching staff. Or you could even work with individual players—like a trainer, you know? You could help people with the kind of one-on-one football consulting you've been doing today."

High school coaching? Consulting? Although plenty of former NFL players had segued into those fields, Cash had never even considered it. He'd been too busy playing—or trying to get resigned. But before he could answer Wade, Jacob, Hannah, and Emily rushed up, breathless and dirt-smudged and limp-limbed. They hung off Cash's arms and waist with their usual drama.

"Whew! We're exhausted!" Emily declared.

"Yeah," Hannah agreed. "We're sooo tired from playing."

"Wiped out!" Jacob lolled his tongue comically. "I could sleep for a hundred years! Like Rip Van Connelly!"

"Good," Cash said. "Maybe that means you'll sleep tonight."

And maybe I'll get a little alone time with Marisol while you're at it. Long experience as a father had taught him that when the kids slept, the adults played. There was no point in wasting time.

As if by magic, he caught Marisol's eye in the crowd. He winked at her. Even with kids hanging off him and a parent pushing him toward life as a professional PE teacher, Cash felt something special. Something sizzling. Something *soon.*

Then the crowd parted just enough, and he glimpsed who Marisol was with. He would have recognized those over-painted, empty-headed, vicious-tongued blondes anywhere. His ex-wife's former bitch posse waved at him—already gossiping, he was sure.

In that moment, years' worth of memories flashed in front of Cash—all those times he'd been dumb enough to trust Stephanie, a woman almost as shallow as her friends. He'd never regretted anything more than the bad judgments he'd made with her. He didn't want to engage in some kind of knee-jerk mistrust-by-association thing now, with Marisol. But still . . .

What the hell was she doing with those four?

"I've got to go," he told Wade abruptly. He shook the man's hand—and for the sake of getting the hell out of there, even accepted one of the business cards Hector's father pressed persistently on him. Cash shoved it in his pocket. "Come on, kids. We've got to pack up and get moving before it gets dark."

Chapter 23

Marisol slid into the Range Rover's passenger seat, feeling surprisingly satisfied and relaxed—especially for a person who hadn't touched lip gloss or hair products for days. As she gave the postsunset Happy Gecko Campground one final glance, she actually felt sorry to leave the place behind.

"Bye, fire pit!" she called, waving. "Bye, campground! Bye, pine trees! Bye, spot number seven!" *See you next year*, she wanted to add, but given the steely look on Cash's face, she didn't think she should press her luck.

Which was weird, because she'd thought he'd been having a good time too.

"Bye, barbecue grill!" the kids chimed in from the backseat, crammed in with all their gear. "Bye, lake! Bye, s'mores!"

Grumpily, Cash grabbed his seat belt and peered in the rearview mirror. "Everybody got everything?"

A chorus of "yeah!"s greeted him. Including Marisol's.

He shot her an unreadable look, then held his seat belt aloft. With his free hand, he reached toward the backseat, palm facing. Emily, Jacob, and Hannah recognized his signal. They all touched palms. Bravely, Marisol added her hand to the group.

"Okay," Cash said. "Seat belts on three. One, two, three—"

"Seat belts!" they shouted.

Everyone broke away with their arms in the air, football huddle-style. Seat belts clicked all through the vehicle. Beaming, Marisol settled back in her place. It was nice to be part of a family like this. Even if for just a little while. Even if it wasn't really hers.

One winding road and a gazillion pine trees later, Cash finally spoke. First he eyed the backseat, making sure the kids were occupied. Then, "How did you meet the fickle four?"

Marisol started. "The who?"

"The blondes you were talking to at the campground." He hooked his thumb back. "Stumpy, Stringy, Nasty, and Nose Job."

"You mean Cassie, Amanda, Ashley, and Lindsay?" Marisol shook her head, confused by Cash's sarcastic tone. "We met at the grocery store. They're football wives. They've been tutoring me in how to keep football guys happy."

"Humph." A grin. "You don't need any help with that."

That was sweet, but . . . "What's the matter? Am I stepping on your sordid past? Did you date them or something?" she teased.

"All four of them?" Cash lifted his eyebrows, shooting her a disbelieving look. "What kind of player do you think I am?"

The kind who could have four women if he wanted. The kind who could probably satisfy all of them. The kind I'd like to keep for myself. No, she couldn't say that. Particularly not the part about keeping him for herself, and particularly not when Cash was in such a strange mood.

"The kind who doesn't want to talk about his past," Marisol said instead. She waited, using her father's business technique of letting the silence stretch out. Gary

Winston swore that most people couldn't tolerate conversational gaps and rushed to fill them. Unfortunately, Cash appeared to have more patience than most. "I was surprised to see them though," Marisol admitted. "They didn't say they'd be at the campground."

"They didn't, huh?" Cash turned a corner, making the Range Rover sweep past scrubby oak trees and an abandoned-looking house. He was silent for a minute. Then, "What *did* they say?"

She shrugged. "Girl talk. Nothing much."

"I find that hard to believe." His hands tightened on the steering wheel. He didn't look at her. "They've never been the kind of women to keep their mouths shut."

Marisol gave him an empathetic glance. Cash was probably worried about what the football wives might have told her about his past. About his divorce. About his ex-wife and that other player, Tyrell. Nobody liked being the grist for the rumor mill.

But she'd already learned all those things about Cash, even before her new friends had come on the scene. There were no greater gossips than children, Marisol remembered with a smile. And Adam had done his share to fill her in during his visit too. All she cared about now was that Cash appeared to be over Stephanie and ready to move on . . . and that he might move on with *her*. Just like Christy Turlington and that hunk on the beach with the adorable children.

"Well . . . they did say they liked watching you play football today." Deciding to change the subject—and not to discuss the plans she'd made with Cassie, Amanda, Ashley, and Lindsay to have lunch next week—Marisol put her hand on Cash's knee instead. "So did I. You were impressive."

Cash scowled through the windshield, his face illuminated by the dashboard lights. Beneath her palm, his leg tautened.

"Anybody can tell you love kids," Marisol added, smiling at the sudden tension radiating from him. Could all that reaction be due to her touch? She hoped so. Innocently, she blinked as they continued zooming down the shadowy country road. "You really relate to them. They had such a good time."

"I'm not becoming a coach," Cash stated emphatically.

"Who asked you to? Although you'd probably be fantastic at it." Marisol leaned closer, stroking her fingers suggestively along his lower thigh. She skimmed the hem of his shorts, thankful Cash never wore many clothes. "All I'm saying is, I like watching you move. Other men should take lessons from you."

He smiled. Just a little. Just the tiniest crook of his wide, beautiful mouth. But that was enough for her.

She squeezed his bare thigh more firmly. It felt like granite beneath her palm. Hard, hot, flexing-to-press-the-gas-pedal granite.

Feeling those thighs of his next to hers every night in their double sleeping bag—feeling the whole strong, warm length of Cash pressing against her—had been driving her wild. The man was nothing but sex on sneakers. She didn't know why they were wasting time talking about anything except getting naked the minute they got home.

Er—home to Cash's log cabin, that is. Her temporary home.

Geez. A person would swear she was desperate to have a real home of her own, with all these slipups she'd been making. *Her home. Her kids.* Sure, she liked decorating new spaces, but that was just aesthetics—not a deep-seated yearning for anything.

"In fact," Marisol continued, trying to keep some semblance of conversation going for the sake of the kids, "seeing you today made me wish I'd seen you play football before. If not for the occasional limp or grimace, you were perfect today, so I can only imagine what you must have been like when you were in your prime."

"I'm fine."

"I know, but . . . well, you *are* still hurt, and—"

"I'm *fine*." His gaze met hers, purposeful and hot, then swerved toward his lap, encouraging her attention to follow. "Except for a little discomfort right at this second."

Marisol looked. Then she took a deep breath, wholly unable to look away. Athletic shorts had never seemed quite so intriguing before. "That looks like a *lot* of discomfort."

His grin was filled with surety. "It is. So when I tell you I'm *fine*, I mean it. When we get back home, I'll show you."

Oh wow. There was nothing she wanted more. Except . . .

Marisol nodded toward the backseat, where Hannah, Jacob, and Emily were engrossed in a cartoon on the SUV's DVD player. "What about the kids? They'll be asleep pretty soon, but—"

"They won't be asleep long enough for what I have in mind." Cash shot her another loaded glance. "This might take days."

Weak-kneed, Marisol stared. He couldn't be serious.

"You'll definitely need to bring some Gatorade." Cash nodded. "Keep your strength up and your electrolytes balanced."

Ohmigod. He was serious.

A jolt of anticipation whooshed through her. After all the time they'd spent together, after all the ways they'd gotten to know one another, after all the hours Marisol had indulged in wondering exactly what she and Cash would be like together, could this be happening? Was she actually about to find out?

The Range Rover rounded a curve, neatly gliding past the dusky landscape. Its headlights swept over a sign:

Lake Mary, 2 miles. Keeping his gaze firmly on the road, Cash punched up a number on his cell phone, then brought it to his ear.

He smiled. "Hey, Darrell. About that sleepover for the kids—we're all loaded up with sleeping bags and almost to yours and Sheryl's place. Tonight work for you?"

Marisol pressed her thighs together and gripped the Range Rover's door handle, cursing every bump and pothole the vehicle jolted over. Every last one slowed them down. Now that she and Cash had finally gotten the excited Jacob, Hannah, and Emily settled in for the night with their friends, they could not get to their log cabin fast enough for her.

"Do you think the kids will be okay?" she asked, glancing across the moonlit SUV at Cash. "They just spent so many nights in their sleeping bags at the campground. Maybe they didn't want to have a sleepover tonight. It was your idea after all."

"Did you see their faces? You were there when we pulled up at Darrell and Sheryl's." Cash patted her knee. "They almost bulldozed us getting their gear and getting inside. I could barely grab them long enough for a damned good-bye hug."

"Well, yes. That's true." Marisol bit her lip. His hand burned her thigh, making her tingle all over. Making her wonder how his touch would feel . . . elsewhere. She squirmed. "But what if the other kids make fun of their stuffed sea otters? What if Jacob forgets to brush most of his teeth? What if Hannah bosses everyone around and makes them mad? What if Emily pours on so much sweet talk that Darrell and Sheryl let them stay up all night long, and they're so exhausted tomorrow that—"

"They're kids. They're resilient. Don't worry."

Concern and desire both tugged at her. Marisol drew

in a deep breath. "Nobody will make Jacob eat the bread crusts, right? You know he doesn't like them. Maybe I should call and warn Darrell and Sheryl not to comb Emily and Hannah's hair without a really wide-tooth comb. There might be crying."

"We didn't leave the kids with a pack of hyenas. They'll be fine." Cash smiled. His fingers swept up her bare thigh, causing ripples of new sensation. "The person you should be worrying about is yourself. Are you sure you can handle this? Us?"

Marisol felt downright light-headed. "Of course." What was he *doing* with his hand? She peeked. "You only have four fingers and a thumb, right? Because that *feels* like more."

"Mmmm. Tell me more about how it feels."

Cash's voice, low and seductive, nearly made her shake. Marisol considered herself relatively experienced, but this . . . nothing she'd ever encountered could have prepared her for *this*. For Cash Connelly, bent on seduction.

"It feels . . . umm, really good."

Her voice cracked, too husky to make itself heard.

Cash laughed, his touch growing even firmer. "I like that. I'm going to make you feel incredible. Just a few more miles . . ."

Marisol gulped. Although Cash was still driving with his other hand, still keeping his attention securely on the road, she felt anything but safe or patient. She wanted to pull over. To pull off Cash's clothes. To drag off her miniskirt and her sweatshirt and her bikini top and just jump onto his side of the Range Rover, ready to have her way with him.

"Hurry up," she managed to say.

Another low laugh. Pine trees pushed at the SUV, making the darkened road feel even more remote than usual. The forest's very presence annoyed Marisol, all of a sudden. What good was the wilderness—what good was so much isolation and quiet—if a person couldn't take advantage of them?

"Right there." She pointed. "Up ahead. Pull over behind those trees. There's nobody for miles—we can park right there."

Cash didn't even look. "I'm taking you home. We've waited all this time—I'm not going to jump you in a parked SUV."

"Oh yeah? Well, I'm Marisol Winston, and I always get what I want. Please pull over."

"No. You deserve better." Cash kept on driving. "Besides, you're not the boss of me."

Ordinarily, she respected his sense of self. His unswerving integrity and tough stance. But right now, with her whole body thrumming and her heart beating fast and her breath coming in near gasps, Marisol didn't much care about Cash's inner being.

"Pull over." She jutted her chin, then wiggled in the darkened passenger seat. "I'm taking off my bikini bottoms."

Cash stared. "You are not."

More wiggling. It was a trickier maneuver than she expected. Then . . . success. With all the attitude she could muster, Marisol tossed her bikini bottoms in his lap.

Cash looked at that scrap of white fabric, then looked at her face. Ten seconds later, the Range Rover squealed to a stop in a cloud of dust, hastily but snugly parked behind a stand of pine trees. There wasn't so much as a herd of squirrels in view, much less any houses or cars. The engine clicked, then fell silent. The only sounds were crickets chirping in the darkness.

Marisol tugged down her skirt primly, then folded her hands in her lap. "Told you I always get what I want."

"Oh, you have *no* idea," Cash promised with a wolfish grin.

He pulled her close, covering her mouth with his. His kiss was crushing, intent, swoon-worthy all on its own. But when combined with his hands urgently squeezing her shoulders, then sliding down her spine, it was unbelievable. Marisol moaned and kissed him back, blindly groping his T-shirt. She got two good fistfuls of cotton and tugged, then forgot what she was doing when Cash opened his mouth wider and kissed her again. His deep moan shook her, making her want more . . . more, more, more.

"Oh! Wait, let me . . ." Squirming, Marisol raised up in the passenger seat, determined to have her way. She glimpsed the fogged windows, the moonlit darkness outside, then Cash's T-shirt. She twisted and pulled it off him with a savage yank. It landed someplace in the backseat, a vague coil of white.

"Hey, you don't waste any time," Cash murmured with his dark hair all askew and his smile all cocky.

He looked cute. He looked hot. He looked kissable. Proving it, he brought his lips to hers again.

"You don't either," she said against his mouth, loving the glide of their lips, their tongues, their hands. She grabbed Cash's hair and squashed him against her. "But I want more."

Breathlessly, she kissed him, needing to get closer. Cash obliged, sliding his hands deftly beneath her sweatshirt. His palms closed over her breasts, making her nipples chafe against her bikini top. Stupid bikini top. It was only in the way, and it definitely had to go. Soon. But first . . .

"Push your seat back," Marisol instructed. "Here I come."

Whoosh. She didn't have to tell him twice. Cash levered the seat one-handed, making more room between him and the steering wheel—room for her. The jolt separated them for an instant, a delay that felt far too long to Marisol. Still kissing him, she climbed over the console. Cash helped her, his hands on her waist. Feeling reckless and giddy, she shook out her hair.

"Mmmm." He held her upright. "Watch those knees."

"Don't worry. I know what I'm doing."

Slowly, carefully, eagerly, she lowered herself to straddle him. His shorts felt smooth against her naked flesh, but everything beneath them felt hot and hard and full, exactly as incredible as she'd imagined. Marisol wriggled, situating herself in a comfortable position, mindlessly enjoying the snug fit of their bodies. They were so close now, pulsing and ready. This would be perfect between them—perfect and *soon*.

"You're so hot." With a guttural, nonsensical sound of enjoyment, Cash stared at her. "I can feel you . . . so hot."

His hands flexed at her waist, betraying his need to regain control. Closing his eyes, Cash sucked in a deep breath.

"I've been thinking about doing this for miles," Marisol confessed, giving him a little tilt forward to prove it.

"I've been *wanting* you to do that for miles." Cash opened his eyes, and his smile lit the night.

Feeling as happy as he did, Marisol pressed her knees into the driver's seat's leather upholstery and rocked herself all the way into him. Her breasts pressed against Cash's chest, still covered by her sweatshirt; her thighs gripped his. His skin felt as scorching as hers did—it was a wonder the SUV didn't melt. The wiry hairs on his legs chafed her inner thighs, but she didn't care. Not so long as they were together like this, with only athletic shorts and agility to limit them.

"Don't worry," Marisol assured him. "I'm very flexible."

Cash's eyes widened as she demonstrated as much, his whole face growing taut with need. He cupped her jaw in his hand, stroking her cheek with his thumb in a way that belied their parked SUV, their urgency, the near-clumsiness of their desire. Tenderness suffused his expression, warming her all the way through. It was in his

eyes, in his touch . . . even in the smile he gave her next
as he reached beneath her sweatshirt again.

"Mmmm. Perfect." He touched her triangle bikini
top, seemed to get distracted by what he found beneath
it, then regrouped by sliding his fingers along its skimpy
string. With a rough yank, her bikini's tie came unrav-
eled. "Even better."

Impatiently, Cash lifted her sweatshirt and dangling
bikini. His mouth found her bare breast. Mmmm. Bliss.
Marisol arched her back, desperate to give him better
access. Anything so he would keep . . . doing . . . *that*.
Panting, she felt the steering wheel poke her spine, but
she didn't care. If anything, their inconvenient position
only added to the thrill of the moment.

She clutched Cash's head, holding him to her as her
breath came and went in a rush. Her nipples tingled as
he sucked her, sending excitement whooshing to every
inch of exposed skin. Cash's tousled hair tickled; his
razor stubble added a prickly component that was one
hundred percent male. Thrilled, Marisol moaned her
encouragement, but this wasn't enough. Never enough.

She remembered stripping off Cash's shirt and sought
his naked chest with her hands. Yes. Warm. Rock solid.
Flawless. Mmmm. His broad shoulders were an easy
target too. Ecstatically, Marisol trailed her fingers over
his muscles and down his sinewy arms, clutching at whatever she could reach. He felt hard and tough and perfect. There was no way she could stop touching him.

"I've been wanting to do this for *so* long."

"Me too," Cash managed. "Mmmm."

Their panting breaths fogged the windows even further, and the entire Range Rover swayed. Cash dropped
one callused hand to her thigh, found her miniskirt had
ridden up to nearly indecent heights, and gave a lusty
groan. His other hand joined the first, both of them cup-
ping her derrière to hold her to him.

"Last chance," Cash said, his voice hoarse as he squeezed her. "Last chance to go home and do this right."

"It will be right," Marisol said, kissing him again as she thrust herself forward. "Right here. Right now. Don't stop."

Boldly, she wriggled higher. Cash moaned, ineffectually clamping his hands on her hips to hold her in place. All Marisol wanted to do was grind herself against him, to feel him inside her, to stop the ache that gnawed at her. His erection felt huge, still covered in his sleek shorts but straining for release, and she knew exactly what should come next to make that happen. She *wanted* to make that happen. She *would* make that happen. Promising as much to herself and him, she leaned forward. She pressed her forehead to his until they were gazing into each other's eyes, caught in an oasis of wanting.

She knew Cash so well—and yet not like this. Not yet. Not enough. And oh, how she wanted to.

"It'll be good," she said. "We've waited all this time."

Cash nodded. He swallowed hard, his gaze never leaving hers. "Too long. Ahhh, Marisol. You're amazing."

His gentle tone moved her. So did the loving smile he gave her next. This would not be a hasty front-seat make-out session. Despite their urgency, their need, it would be a union between them, Marisol realized. It would be the beginning of something new and special and unique.

Feeling just as caring, just as tender, Marisol stroked Cash's disheveled hair away from his face. She paused for a breath or two, savoring the connection between them. She loved his face. She loved his eyes and his nose and his mouth . . . loved his sense of humor and his machismo and his protectiveness.

With Cash, she was safe. She was loved. And because of that, she was wholly herself.

"I don't want to wait anymore," she said. "I don't care where we are. As long as I'm with you, that's all I need."

"You're making it hard to be chivalrous."

"Be chivalrous tomorrow. Right now . . . be *you*."

Cash studied her face. Then, evidently deciding she really meant what she said—and she did—he pulled her close for a kiss.

Marisol had thought his other kisses were remarkable. But this one . . . this one put them all in the shade. Somehow, Cash made her head spin and her thighs quake and her knees gouge into the Range Rover's seat, all in a hopeless bid to find purchase in a world gone topsy-turvy. His hands were everywhere, and all she could do was moan. Her sweatshirt landed on the gearshift. Her vanquished bikini top followed. An instant later, she was in Cash's arms again, the night air cool on her bare skin.

And still he didn't stop. His hands roved over her hair, her naked breasts, her thighs as he pushed her skirt higher. Cash stared blatantly at all he'd exposed, and his intent gaze revealed nothing but reverence. With steady hands, he touched her there, making her squirm. Marisol panted and pushed against him, knowing that nothing had ever felt this good. This right.

Weak with need, she grabbed his arm. "Wait. Wait, it's so fast." She gasped, desperately twisting. "I need—"

Cash understood. Kissing her again, he shoved down his shorts with both hands, hasty and ready. Marisol levered higher to help him, her miniskirt a mere twist of inconvenient fabric bunched at her hips. She didn't care. Anything to get closer. Anything to get . . . *ahhh*.

Oh God. How had he sheathed himself so fast, protecting them both? However he'd managed it, Marisol was glad.

Desperately she clutched his shoulders, her eyes going wide at the first huge feel of him. Her body stretched,

wet and hot and ready, and Marisol eagerly slid downward. Cash met her with an upward thrust that made her
yell with pleasure.

Thankfully, he gave her an instant—only that—to re-
cover a little sanity. Lolling against him, Marisol shook
her head.

"Nothing should feel this good," she said, panting.

"It's going to get even better," Cash promised.

Then he made it so. His fingers pressed on her hips as
he struggled for control, his breath coming in gusts that
matched hers. Elated, Marisol threw back her head and
met him move for move, moaning in a husky voice she
barely recognized as her own. She savored every forceful
plunge, every slick glide, every kiss that brought them
closer and closer. The windows fogged all the way over,
something Marisol knew as she dragged her hand across
the cold surface of one, leaving a ragged impression.

This was perfect. *Cash* was perfect. Even as he squeezed
his eyes shut and surrendered to the rocking of their
bodies, even as he groaned with need, he stayed with her.
He urged her on, taking as much pleasure in her enjoyment as his own—maybe more, as Marisol begged him
not to stop . . . and he didn't.

"Yes. Yes!" she cried, never very vocal, but suddenly
unable to help herself. "Oh Cash. Don't stop. I—"

She paused, caught on the brink of an incredible
orgasm. In that moment, the world slowed down. She
saw Cash's face, tender and intent. Felt his heartbeat, as
rapid as her own. Heard their bodies coming together,
hard and fast and uninhibited.

It was all too much. With a helpless groan, Marisol let
go. Her whole body shook with pleasure, her knees gripping convulsively at Cash's thighs. He held her securely, his
skin beaded with sweat and pouring heat as he thrust again
and again, taking in her orgasm and making it his own.

"Ahhh!" His roar of fulfillment shook the SUV,

thrilling Marisol with its intensity. Eyes wide, Cash loosed himself in her, his thrusts gradually slowing as she held him tight. He squeezed her hips, gave a gusty sigh, then let his head fall back on the driver's seat headrest.

He looked gorgeous. He looked utterly spent.

He looked like *hers*.

Marisol fell against his chest, completely unwilling to move. Maybe unable to move—she wasn't sure. Her body pulsed with completion, alerting her to joyful little nerve endings she'd never even known she possessed. Her ears rang and her heart hammered. Out of breath and more than a little sweaty herself, she splayed her palms over Cash's shoulders and just held on.

They stayed that way for a while, with Cash holding her close and Marisol loving every moment of contact. She didn't want to be apart. Ever. Blissfully, she closed her eyes and relaxed completely, hardly able to believe this had really happened. She'd been with Cash. He'd been with her. And it had been really, really fantastic.

Cash blew out a sated breath. He hugged her to him, letting their racing heartbeats slow down. He smiled—she felt the movement against her cheek—then kissed the top of her head.

"You're tempting me into round two," he said.

His body swelled and throbbed, proving him right.

"Already?" Marisol grinned, feeling a genuine buzz at the idea. "All right, but this time you get the steering wheel."

"This time, *you* get the proper treatment."

"Ooh! Really? What do you call what we just—"

"A warm up." Cash's smile was dazzling, even in the dark. "Every athlete knows the importance of warming up."

A hot rush made her squirm. "Oh. Then you mean there's—"

"*More.*" He nodded, nuzzling her cheek. "So get ready."

She could hardly wait.

Chapter 24

They made it all the way to the front porch before round two kicked in. Cash sent Marisol ahead with the house keys, told her to make herself at home, then set to work hastily getting Dump out of the SUV. He awakened the snoozing German shepherd—momentarily glad the old dog hadn't been able to hear all the uproar in the Range Rover—then carried Dump to the driveway.

Finished with that, Cash turned. Marisol stood in the lighted doorway, her clothes askew and her hair wildly tumbled. She smiled at him. In that instant, his heart actually expanded, staggering him with the breadth of his feelings for her.

If he hadn't known better, he'd have thought it was love.

But he'd sworn off love and all things like it, so Cash knew he wouldn't be suckered in by the flutter in his chest, the telltale punch in his belly, the warm, tingly feeling that spread all through him. This was just one crazy night. Those were just a few crazy physical elements of that night—aftereffects of the incredible, passionate time he and Marisol had just spent together.

Parking in an SUV had never been sexier, that was for sure.

Limned by the interior lights, Marisol reached behind herself and pulled down her zipper. Her miniskirt dropped in a white puddle at her feet. She stepped out of it, barefoot, then pulled her sweatshirt over her head. Cash had loved seeing her in it—seeing her sporting his team's colors and his number—but he loved seeing her out of it even more. She looked . . .

Naked. Holy shit.

Where had her bikini bottoms gone? And her bikini top? He thought they'd both hauled on all their clothes—however haphazardly—for the drive home, but he'd been so busy trying to put himself together that he hadn't actually watched her dress.

He'd have to scour the Range Rover tomorrow. Make sure they hadn't left anything else incriminating in there. In the meantime . . . Marisol crooked her finger, beckoning him closer.

Cash pointed to himself, pretending surprise.

Marisol nodded, then slipped inside.

Cash slammed the SUV's rear hatch and grabbed Dump's collar. "Come on, boy. I've got a promise to keep."

He found Marisol in his shower, the running water sending up puffs of steam. Cash's custom-painted shower curtain billowed with her languid movements—an elbow here, a derrière there—its sheer fabric offering tantalizing glimpses of the woman beyond. It was a sight he'd never expected to see. Not here. Not now.

Hearing him, she pushed aside the curtain and poked her head out. Her long hair was slicked back and even her eyelashes were wet, a detail he found ridiculously cute.

"Are you coming?" she asked.

Cash nodded. "Yes I am. So are you, in a few minutes."

"Very funny." Her gaze skimmed provocatively over his hastily thrown-on clothes, then zeroed in on his midsection.

His chest. His shoulders. She inclined her shoulder toward the multiangled spray behind her. "Come on in. The shower's great. I thought we might want to get cleaned up after all that camping."

Yeah. The *camping* was what had made them sweaty.

"Fortification first." He held up the twin bottles of Gatorade he'd snagged from the fridge on the way here, giving her a wicked grin. "You're going to need this."

Marisol glanced behind him, eyebrows arched.

"If you're looking for fancy glassware, there isn't any. I'm a simple guy. Here."

He handed over the bottle of orange-flavored drink. Marisol eyed it dubiously, then cranked open the top with her damp hand. She hesitated, water pinging from her slick shoulders and dripping from her outstretched arm. "Are you sure I need this?"

"Absolutely." Holding her gaze, Cash chugged his.

Then he set aside the bottle and stripped.

Marisol choked, eyes squeezed shut as she coughed.

"What's the matter?"

She pointed at him with her half-full bottle, sweeping it in an arc from the top of his head to his curled-into-the-bathmat-toes. Her eyes widened. "I've never seen you so naked before. It takes a little getting used to."

Gawking, she wiped her mouth with her forearm in a gesture so unlike her it made him grin. Her gaze never left his body.

"You just saw me naked. In the Range Rover. Or do you need a reminder?" Cash took a step forward, his cock leading the way.

"Um, I know." Her gaze centered at hip height, watching his progress. "But that was different. This time you're . . . you're . . . Well, you're *right there*." She gaped, looking flushed. "All naked. All of you. All the time. Everywhere."

"Hmmm. A girl like you is good for a guy's ego."

"Um, I may have bitten off more than I can chew."

"Nah. No biting." Cash took possession of the shower curtain, covering Marisol's clenched fist with his and sliding it sideways. He stepped into the shower. "Well, no biting any place sensitive. Other than that . . . use your imagination."

"Believe me, I am!"

He chuckled, feeling so damned overjoyed to be with her, he could hardly stand it. Nothing came close to this sensation. It went beyond scoring, beyond playing ball, beyond everything.

"Go ahead and drink that." Cash nodded at her Gatorade, striving for patience. "I'll wait until you're finished."

With a single look, Marisol guzzled the whole bottle.

"Good." Cash took the empty container, flung it out of the shower, then dragged the curtain closed. Warm water sluiced over him from multiple shower heads, beading up on the pristine tiles and whirling at his feet. "But you're not properly soaped up."

"Now you're getting bossy again?"

"Be quiet and hold still."

Barely able to control his reaction to her, he grabbed the frothy bar of soap and lathered his hands. Marisol watched him with wide eyes, her earlier bravado a little shakier now. Not that he could tell by her posture. Her bearing was perfect, proud and erect at the edge of the nearest showerhead. And her voice was steady, firm and strong. Her eyes were the giveaway—wary and aroused in equal measure. Because of that, Cash vowed to be gentle with her—to give her all the pleasure she deserved.

He started at her shoulders, sliding his soapy hands over her collarbones and upward, lingering just a moment to caress the nape of her neck. He pressed a kiss to her jaw, her mouth, tasting water and smelling the remnants of his own shampoo.

"I already did that," Marisol protested. "I'm all clean."

"Shhh." Cash reached her breasts and was careful to slowly soap each perfect mound. He plucked her rosy nipples in his fingertips, loving the way they tightened just for him. "If I lose track of where I am, I'll have to start all over again."

With a low moan, Marisol closed her mouth. She tipped her head against the tiles, her wet hair swinging in a dark, twisty mass over her shoulder. Bubbles frothed over her skin, heightening its sexy sheen and washing away all traces of the days they'd spent camping. Companionably. Happily. Chastely.

Cash would be damned if tonight would be chaste.

He swept his hand lower, reaching her belly. Its curve delighted him, soft and womanly and exactly round enough to remind him that Marisol was soft elsewhere too. He smiled as he moved to her hips, the slight quaver in his hands nearly giving away how important this was— how important she was—to him.

Stubbornly, Cash shoved away those burgeoning emotions and focused on giving Marisol all the enjoyment he could. He trailed his hands up her wet back and then down again, his sudsy fingers finding the twin dimples just above her derrière and taking extra care there. He cupped her ass, his palms fitting neatly over her slippery round cheeks. As much as he struggled to rein in his need for her, touching Marisol still made him shake—still made him yearn to go faster. Faster. Faster. It was all he could do to continue his leisurely progress up her arms, then down over her breasts again, swirling the soap round each one before proceeding to lather her thighs and calves.

"Oh Cash!" She clutched his forearms, tossing her head from side to side. "This isn't fair. I want to touch you too."

"You will," he promised. "Soon."

He dropped to the wet tiles, shower spray pounding his scalp and trickling in his ears, then spread her thighs with both hands. He shook his damp hair from his face and lowered his head, eager to satisfy the *other* erotic urge he'd felt on that long, long drive home tonight.

His mouth made contact with the hottest, slickest part of her. Marisol squealed, her whole body jolting as she arched helplessly toward him. She splayed her hands to the tiles with a loud thump.

"Oh my God," she moaned.

"I know. Really good," Cash managed to say. Her response rocked him. Marisol was so uninhibited. So sweet. So *right*. Because of that, because of his need to please her, he ignored his insistent erection and held her shaking thighs steady, then just went on loving her.

"If you feel weak, hang on to me."

A muffled laugh was her only reply. Then a low, husky groan of pleasure as she shuddered against him. Long moments slid past, filled with nothing but her. Him. The warm shower and the absolute need to make this night last forever, damn it.

Soon, much too soon, Marisol quivered in his hands, fulfilling his promise to make her come. She arched against his mouth, her unrestrained moans filling his ears, and shook uncontrollably. It was good. So good. With savage pleasure, Cash brought her down from the peak as slowly as he could, gently holding Marisol against him until she went limp in his arms.

In that moment, all he wanted was her. Not only to make her shudder with satisfaction, but also to make her smile. Laugh. Even gaze at him with more of the affection he'd glimpsed out amidst the pine trees tonight. Feeling bizarrely vulnerable, Cash gazed up the wet, lithe length of her body.

Sappily, he grinned.

Marisol laughed. She burst into giggles, her cheeks pink and her body quivering, then threw her hand over her mouth.

"I'm sorry," she said, reaching for him. "It's just so . . ." She sighed. "It's never been like this for me before. Never."

Me either, Cash wanted to say. But he didn't. What kind of candy ass would come out with such a thing? Especially while naked in the shower with a beautiful woman?

He'd just made her yelp his name in a sexual frenzy. He'd made her pull his hair and scream. He'd be damned if he'd torpedo those feats by going all Hallmark on her now.

Instead, Cash threw her another grin. "You want to towel off before round three, or should I carry you to the bed wet?"

He eyed her hungrily. Fortunately for them both, Adam had pushed a jumbo pack of condoms on him before leaving for his hotel earlier in the week—a joke that had turned out to have serious usefulness. Good thing Cash had stashed the box within reach. Good thing he'd outfitted his wallet too.

A real man always planned for every possibility.

"Oh no." Weakly, Marisol straightened. She poked his chest. "This time it's *your* turn, mister. Fair's fair. I'm not letting you out of this shower until I get to soap *you* up too."

"Okay. Have it your way." Cash shrugged, then pinned her to the tiles with both arms over her head. He kissed her. "I'm happy with nailing you right here."

"You wouldn't!"

"Oh yeah. I would. Wanna see?"

Shyly, Marisol nodded. "I do."

One slippery, squealing lift, two hastily wrapped legs, and a whole lot of loving later, Cash proved it . . . to his delight and Marisol's too.

"Okay, so I didn't get a fair turn in the shower," Marisol informed Cash as they sat at the kitchen peninsula, side by side in terry cloth bathrobes sharing a much-needed snack, "but I'm *definitely* getting a crack at you after this."

"Really? Says who?" Cash scooped up more ice cream, defiantly breaking every in-training rule—hell, every rule, *period*—that he'd ever had for himself. "Open up. You need more."

He held his spoon aloft, aiming for her mouth.

"I already had more." But she scooped up some of her own ice cream anyway. With her head tilted at a mischievous angle, Marisol smiled at him as she savored it. Her eyes sparkled, making her look even prettier than usual, and her cheeks glowed, framed by her careless damp hair. "And I say so. As soon as we get back to the bedroom, I'm having my way with you."

Cash thought about it. "You were pretty in charge of what happened in the woods tonight. What do you call that?"

"A preliminary. That's a sports term, right?"

Her sassy smile made him feel warm all over. So did the way she licked her spoon, turning it over to get every tasty drop.

"It's a sports term in boxing, sure," Cash said. "But the only sport that really matters is football. And I'm telling you, you're going to need more strength if you're planning to score with me tonight. I'm not sure you're ready to take me on."

"Oh. Tough case, huh?"

He nodded seriously. "Every last inch of me."

"Hmmm." Marisol toyed with her own spoon, spinning it in her dish. Tragically, she'd opted not to try Cash's patented combo of mint chocolate chip ice cream, raspberry sauce, and mini pretzels. "I think I can break you down. I'm up for it."

He scoffed. "I'd like to see you try."

Boy, would he like to see her try.

"Okay. But first . . ." Digging into his bowl, Marisol sampled his favorite concoction. Her face puckered, then smoothed as she crunched. She smacked her lips. "Huh. Yummy. That should not be such a good combination, but it is. It's really good."

"You could say the same thing about us."

Her eyes widened. Then she tilted her head, wearing a beaming smile. *Awww,* her expression said. Uh-oh. That was the same look Marisol had worn the few times Cash had caught her mooning over his bedtime routine with the kids.

"Or you could just back up all that talk with a little action," he said. He untied his robe. Dropped it where he stood. Before long—as Cash had known it would be—his sentimental gaffe was long forgotten in a chase to the bedroom.

All right. She may have been exaggerating a little bit, Marisol realized as she caught up to Cash and found him standing beside his bed, giving her a cocksure look and a whole lot of mind-boggling nudity. Maybe she wasn't quite up to the challenge of him. But she was darn well going to give it her best shot.

She should have been exhausted. Seriously. But every time she looked at Cash, something happened. Some primal, undeniable part of her simply took over. She just couldn't help herself.

Marisol could no more resist touching Cash—or letting him touch her—than she could stop breathing. Or shopping with Caprice and Tenley and Jamie. Or giving gifts with the best, fanciest wrapping paper and bows, just to see someone smile.

Right now, Cash was smiling. But not because she'd given him a gift. Because she'd started walking toward him, untying her robe as she came. She let it trail her, then fall.

"You're extraordinary," she declared, getting right down to business. She came closer. Without her robe, the cool air teased her skin. "Do you know how special you are?"

"I'm just a guy." He gestured at his naked body, as though that would prove his assertion. "I'm not extraordinary."

"You are." Marisol touched his shoulder, helpless to prevent a low crooning sound as she encountered hard muscle and rough-textured skin. "You're every kind of extraordinary. You're like a work of art. Like here, for instance."

She skimmed her hands over his biceps. Ridges of muscle, twisted and defined, met her fingertips. Cash wasn't huge—at least not all over, Marisol thought with a naughty grin—but he was sculpted to a tantalizing degree.

Looking at him gave her the sensation that he could lift a truck if it were in her path, could hoist a mountain into better feng shui if only she asked him to. He was taut and strong and exactly manly enough to appeal to all her senses. He smelled of soap and smiled like sin and knew every dizzying way to touch her, and she could not understand why Cash didn't see how breathtaking he was to her.

"And here." She slipped her palms over his warm, hair-sprinkled chest, trembling with the impact of touching him again. "You feel fantastic. Hard and lean and— mmm." She reached his abs, then traced each muscular hollow there. She couldn't resist letting her gaze linger. "I can't stop looking," she blurted. "How do you not just stare at yourself in the mirror?"

Cash grinned, looking abashed. "This body is just a

tool." He jabbed his ribs. "It does what I tell it to do. That's all."

Disbelieving, Marisol stared up at him, both hands momentarily stilled. "You can't be serious."

"My job is physical. *I'm* physical." He shrugged. "It's not about staring in a mirror—it's about performing."

"Well, you've got that covered too." Marisol smiled, then went on exploring. Cash honestly didn't know how remarkable he was. The realization was endearing. "I'm a fan of all your performances so far."

"I meant on the field." He closed his eyes and swallowed hard, his throat working with effort. He was clearly struggling to withstand her study of his body. "Not in bed."

"In bed?" She arched her brows. "That'll be novel."

To demonstrate, she gave him a shove toward the mattress. Cash didn't even sway, but he did open his eyes.

He tilted his head, grinning. Mr. Tough Guy. "Were you trying to accomplish something with that move?"

"Don't make me get that French maid's uniform." Marisol tilted her head toward her bedroom down the hall, remembering Cash's interested reaction to it earlier. "I'll do it."

Evident, dreamy curiosity flashed across his face.

Marisol took advantage, catching him off guard with another push. This time, Cash toppled like the big lummox he was, landing with an *oof!* of surprise. Victorious, Marisol joined him on the bed. He lay on the black comforter at an angle, one tall, broad man in sharp contrast with his inky backdrop . . . all of him horizontal except for one crucial, enticing portion.

Seductively, Marisol palmed him. His body leaped with a satisfyingly immediate response, pulsing hot against her fingers. If anything, he grew even larger. Cash groaned.

"I don't know how you're managing this," she observed, hoping her voice sounded less thick with desire than it seemed to her. "You should be spent. Worn out." A slow stroke. "Bored."

"Ahhh. Ummmm . . ."

"But since you're not . . ." Again Marisol stroked him, loving the warm heft of his shaft, the helpless arch of his hips, the low sounds of enjoyment Cash made as she got acquainted with him in a whole new way. "I guess I'll keep exploring."

"Please." Tightly, he gripped the comforter with his fists, his whole body straining for more contact. "Feel free."

She did. Eagerly, Marisol went on touching him, now adding a kiss, now offering a caress, now swirling her tongue over every intriguing inch she could reach. She held Cash down with both hands and made him groan, then smiled as she consented to the merest flicker of her lips across the entire length of him.

"Oh God. Marisol . . ." Cash thrashed on the mattress, clearly at the edge of his self-control. His entire body shuddered. "You're killing me. Come here." He reached for her and missed.

"No, I'm loving you," she disagreed, smiling as she slipped sideways to touch him again. Marisol felt insatiably hungry for the feel of his skin against hers, for the sound of his pleasure and the power of his dark, hooded gaze meeting hers. "You can't make me stop loving you. I don't even think you want to."

For an instant, Cash stilled. Going motionless also, Marisol panicked, rapidly thinking over what had just happened. Had she actually said she loved him? Had she said the words? She *did* love him, she remembered dizzily, but this wasn't exactly the time to—

"I need you," Cash said. "Come here."

His rough declaration, so clear and simple, made everything all right. Weak with relief, Marisol let him drag her upward, pull her into his arms, roll them both over and across the rumpled sheets. His kiss silenced whatever else she might have said . . . and by the time that kiss was finished, seemingly a million years later, she didn't want to talk at all.

Instead, she framed Cash's face in her hands, making sure he was looking straight at her. She nodded.

He knew. Moments later, he united them again with a single shuddering thrust that communicated everything words might have done . . . and more. Gladly, Marisol lifted her hips to meet him, shoving aside yet another condom wrapper along with any doubts that Cash's sudden stillness might have raised.

She did love him. In bed at least, he loved her too. That made all the difference. Even as another orgasm shook her, even as she marveled that either one of them still had the energy to feel so blindingly wonderful, Marisol knew that nothing between them would ever be the same again.

Tonight, Cash had made her his own. Tonight, she had met him equally. She'd let down her guard, let herself fall for a man who knew her—knew all of her, for better or worse—and had the bulging dossier from Dzeel to prove it.

If this wasn't true love, Marisol didn't know what was—and she didn't know why she'd waited so long to reach for it either.

Much later and much more quietly, she turned over in bed, swerving her gaze from the stars outside the window to the man stretched out beside her. She hugged the sheets close.

"I love you," she whispered. She ran her fingertips over Cash's slumbering profile, then smiled to herself. "I really do. I only hope . . . I only hope I'm enough for you to love me back."

Chapter 25

The moment Cash awakened, he knew something was wrong. He took a quick inventory, trying to pinpoint the problem. Bed? Yes. Sleepy, satisfied feeling? Yes. Pajamas? Hell no. Of course not. But it was weirdly quiet for a summer morning—usually the kids were up and clamoring at the crack of dawn—and there was definitely something different about today.

He considered it further, shoving both arms above his head for a stretch. He clutched the headboard, making the wood squeak. It thumped back against the wall as Cash grabbed his triceps with a wince. That was strange. He felt unusually sore—and not in the normal, post-workout, athletic way he'd been accustomed to since his Pop Warner football days, but in a what-the-hell-did-I-do-last-night? way.

What *had* he done? He felt . . . he felt amazing.

Oh yeah. Grinning boyishly, Cash remembered. Marisol.

He rolled over, contemplating the first woman he'd shared his bed with in years. She sprawled asleep beside him, clasping a pillow, looking tousled and thoroughly replete. Her long brown hair was tangled. Her cheeks were flushed. Her mouth gaped open with a complete lack of restraint. The look actually suited her though. Last night, Marisol had been anything but restrained.

Damn, he'd loved being with her. He didn't know where he'd gotten the vigor, the enthusiasm, the *stamina* . . . but right now, Cash was glad he had. Last night had been good for both of them. This morning, he saw his forbidden nanny in a whole new light.

Sleepily, he stroked her hip, bared by a fold of the rumpled sheets. He eased his hand down her thigh, slowly caressing. He should probably let her sleep. After the night they'd just spent together, letting her rest would be the gentlemanly thing to do. The thing was, Cash was no gentleman.

Not when it came to this.

He added his other hand to the mix, lazily sliding his fingertips from Marisol's neck to her breast. This time she stirred, her lips puckering on a drowsy moan just as he lowered his mouth to her nipple. Ahhh. This was so good.

She clutched his head, shoving his hair against his closed eyelids. She patted his skull. "Mmmm. What are you doing?"

"Shhh. You're dreaming. Just enjoy it."

"Dreaming?" A wide, beautiful smile crossed her face. "I never dream like this. Except that one time . . ."

Ending on an incoherent murmur, Marisol wriggled in bed, making the sheets whisper against her skin. She rolled toward him, then opened her eyes. She smiled more widely.

"Hey, you're real," she accused.

"Guilty." Lustily, Cash palmed the apex of her thighs, taking possession. At the warmth he found there, he couldn't hold back a moan of his own. She felt so good. "Good morning."

"I'll say it's a good morning." Marisol pulled him to her, pressing kisses to his cheek, his jaw . . . his shoulder. Nope. That was a nibble. "I can't believe you're still here."

"I'm not going anyplace."

"You might have to." She spread her legs, nestling him cozily between them, then swept her hands over his shoulders. Another smile, then a kiss. "I think we're out of condoms."

"It's a jumbo box," Cash assured her. "We're all set." *Mmmm.* He could stay here all day with her. Just loving her . . .

"No, seriously." Turning her head on the pillow, Marisol glanced at the nightstand. She stretched out her arm and shook the empty box. "See? All gone, stud."

"Nooo." With a moan of disappointment, Cash reached for the box, planning to take it from her. Just because they couldn't go all the way didn't mean she couldn't have a good time. He could make sure of that. "We'll just have to improvise then."

Grinning, he plucked away the box and tossed it aside. At the same moment, his gaze landed on the bedside clock.

He froze. "Oh shit. This is bad. I've got to go."

"What? *Now?*" Marisol looked puzzled as he leaped from the bed. She clutched the sheet, sitting up. "But we—you—I don't mind if we're out of condoms. I'd be happy with snuggling!"

"No time. Sorry." It was no use. Shit, shit, shit. Cash pressed a hasty kiss to her mouth, then bolted for the shower. "Pick up the kids this afternoon. We'll talk tonight."

After a single glimpse at Marisol's startled face, Cash slammed the bathroom door and hurried to get ready. His future was waiting. He'd be damned if he'd screw it up again.

Now more than ever, he had reason to succeed.

After all—a genuine Winston heiress would *not* want a ho-hum life in the 'burbs. And he meant to give Marisol— *his* Marisol—exactly what she wanted.

* * *

Fifteen minutes later, Marisol stood at the window, wrapped in a terry cloth robe, watching Cash drive away down the long, forest-edged road. She couldn't resist sneaking one last glimpse of him—or remembering the sweetly erotic way he'd awakened her.

Not with fanfare. Not with a dozen hothouse orchids. Not with impeccable room service in a five-star hotel suite and a promise to call her after his next business meeting or nightclub opening or European trip. But with gentle kisses and a swoon-worthy smile capable of making even the most jaded home-improvement-super-center heiress giggle like a girl. Which (for the record) Marisol had.

Unlike the other men she'd dated—men who'd been desperate to impress her—Cash hadn't needed to do anything except be himself. He hadn't needed to do anything except love her. And for that, she loved him. The truth of that—especially now—was undeniable.

If only he hadn't had to leave so quickly . . . but one glance at the big crayoned family calendar near the pantry explained the reason for that. A big green swoosh encircled today's date, with a childish TC written inside the square beneath.

Training camp. Officially, today was the beginning of Cash's second chance at football. But for Marisol, it felt more like the starting gun at the beginning of a race. Starting today, she had only a few more weeks with Cash and the kids. No matter what else she did, she had to make the most of them.

Rapidly formulating a plan, Marisol let the curtains fall. She strode across the family room, evaluating all she saw there. With Jacob, Emily, and Hannah still enjoying their sleepover, she had a real opportunity for the first time since she'd arrived. An opportunity to show Cash that she could do more than struggle with making PBJs, carpooling, and getting bubblegum out of hair. An opportunity to make him love her back.

But only if she were lucky—and very, very good.

You brought you, didn't you?, Leslie had said when she'd first come here. *That's all you need.* Now more than ever, Marisol hoped she was right.

Time to get busy!

Cash hurried across the NAU campus, his gym bag in hand and his face stony. He reached the Scorpions' training zone and increased his pace. Moments later, the door to the designated training camp meeting room slammed shut behind him.

In the sudden silence, dozens of players, several front-office eggheads, and an assortment of offensive, defensive, and special-teams coaching staff members glared at him.

Head down, Cash strode to an empty seat.

"You're late." The team's head coach, Ed, crossed his arms, bellowing the words across the room. "You're not going to be a problem again this season, are you Connelly?"

There was nothing to do but man-up. "Sorry I'm late, Coach." Cash grabbed his Scorpions playbook, three inches thick with at least fifty passing plays and more than two hundred running plays—all of which needed to be committed to memory before the preseason. He slammed it on his lap, then dropped his gym bag beside his chair, ready to go. "It won't happen again."

"You're damned right it won't happen again. This is the first fucking day of training camp, number seven!" Ed paced, flinging out both arms. He spun to glare at Cash, his features compressed with ire beneath his gray hair. "What the hell is wrong with you? You get a second chance and you screw off?"

Every player turned his head, watching as Ed lit into him full-bore. A few slumped in their seats. Several chairs away, Darrell looked on with an unreadable expression. Football was a team sport. Any man who couldn't handle himself was a liability.

Cash met his coach's gaze head on. "I'm ready to go."

"Oh, *are* you?" Ed's sarcastic tone bit into every word. "Well, the rest of us were ready to go forty-seven minutes ago."

A muscle ticked in Cash's jaw. He tapped his pen on his playbook, fighting an urge to hurl the whole thing across the room. He owed it to his teammates to stick this out. He'd been chewed out before, and worse. The only consolation today was that being with Marisol had been worth it.

"Nothing to say for yourself?" Ed goaded.

Cash compressed his mouth and remained silent.

"Fine. But that idiot fight of yours was strike one, Connelly." With a hard glare, Ed studied the fullback Cash had tangled with, then looked back again. "And this is strike two. One more and you're out—remember that." Moving to address every man assembled, the head coach jerked his chin up. "Just to make sure our returning backup quarterback is up to speed with the rest of us, we're ditching this meeting. Instead, all this week, we'll have two-a-days. Starting now."

An assembled groan went up. Two-a-days were just what they sounded like. Two punishing, heavy-duty practices every single day—one in the morning and one in the afternoon. They were hard, sweaty work, universally loathed by the players.

"Get the fuck on the field, you jerk-offs!" Ed yelled.

Eighty-five burly men, some rookies and some veterans who Cash had sweated beside for years, grabbed their things. Chairs scraped and the floor shook as they shuffled off to suit up for the football practice field . . . but not a single man among them met Cash's eyes.

* * *

"So what do you think?" Marisol asked Tenley during their usual cell phone confab as she drove along Lake Mary Road to pick up the kids. Trees rushed past and the lake sparkled just beyond them, shallow this time of year. She was really getting a grip on this carpooling thing—it was downright suburban of her. "Everything was so great up until this morning, but then Cash left so quickly . . ."

"Well, sex changes things. You know that," her friend pointed out. For once, Tenley was not shopping. Instead, she was on her way to interview for a position with an event-planning company—just more evidence of things moving on without Marisol in L.A. "Probably Cash was a little freaked out to have felt so close to you, and he needed to get some distance. Plus he *was* kind of going to work, so—"

"Yeah." On the third line of their conference call, Caprice snorted, calling in from her appointment at the Jonathan salon in Beverly Hills. Caprice believed in frequent color touchups and masterful blowouts from her favorite stylist, and always got both. "Either that," she said blithely, "or Cash is at the hospital having emergency medical care for his P.O.U."

"P.O.U.?" Marisol spotted Darrell and Sheryl's house.

"Penis Overuse Syndrome," Caprice specified with dead seriousness. Chortles came down the line from her colorist. "I once heard about a guy whose dick got permanently bent like a swizzle stick because he got too rambunctious at a B&B in Napa."

"Marisol's guy just went to football practice," Tenley interrupted in her usual sensible way. "That's all. I'm sure he's not built like a swizzle stick, right Marisol?" Without waiting for a reply, Tenley rushed on. "Look, I'm here. I'm sorry, but I've got to run. Wish me luck on this interview, you guys. I'm *so* nervous."

"Good luck!" Marisol said. "Let me know how it goes."

"You'll be fab," Caprice added. Foils crinkled against

her headset. "And Marisol? Don't worry about Cash. Unless you saw an actual swizzle to his dizzle, you're probably okay."

"Gee, that's really comforting. I have a cocktail accessory for a boyfriend." Hmmm. *Boyfriend.* Or maybe more. She liked the sound of it. Her ex, Chad, wouldn't have believed the turnaround she'd made. Marisol pulled into the driveway and parked just as Tenley signed off. "I've got to go too. I've got kids to pick up. It's weird—I'm actually excited to see them again."

"Huh. That *is* weird," Caprice weighed in. "But you know, even with a swizzle, things might be okay." Breathlessly, she rambled on. "Sometimes you can work around that. I swear, those Kama Sutra positions sometimes require a swizzle-stick dick."

"Okay," Marisol said breezily. "I'm going now. Bye!"

"Bye, Marisol," Caprice said cheerfully. "Good luck!"

Sweaty, exhausted, and probably bruised all over from taking hits in scrimmage after running innumerable passing and handoff drills, Cash strode into the locker room. He dropped his helmet on the bench near his assigned space, ignoring the glares his arrival caused. After all, he deserved them.

Around him, players stripped for showers, dropping pads and practice jerseys and cleats; others returned from showering with towels wrapped around their waists, grabbing for street clothes. There was talking and swearing and laughing—mostly from veterans. The rookies surveyed the locker room with guarded eyes, grimy and tired from learning new plays, trying to fit in, and pushing for permanent spots on the Scorpions' roster.

The NFL was a big step up from college; some of them would wash out when the Turk came around with cuts in the upcoming weeks. Out of more than eighty players, only sixty-five would survive the first cut. In the end, only fifty-three—newbies and veterans alike—would make the team, plus a few developmental players for the eight-man practice squad. Football wasn't a game for the weak. Cash knew that all too well.

The exterior door opened as a few players left. From outside came a swirl of voices and activity—the press.

"Cornering 'em early this year," Darrell observed.

"Yeah." Cash jerked his chin in welcome as the offensive lineman approached. "You'd think they'd have real news to cover, besides us meatheads beating the hell out of each other."

"Same old seven. Still not a fan of the media, huh?"

"Nah, I love 'em." Cash tossed his elbow pads into his locker. "As long as they stay the hell away from me."

His friend nodded in commiseration. Much of the brouhaha surrounding Cash's early retirement, his break with the team, his feud with Tyrell, and even his divorce from Stephanie had been fueled by the media. Before long, the Scorpions' management had gotten fed up with being the subject of so much bad press.

So had Cash. He knew better than to push his luck again.

This is strike two. One more and you're out—remember that.

"You going out there?" Darrell gestured toward the door, his pinkie ring flashing. In street clothes, the big man was a snappy dresser, favoring suits, bright ties, and British shoes. He stood out, especially in training camp in small-town Flagstaff.

"No." With his mouth tight, Cash reached for a tube of liniment. His hamstring still hurt. If he was going to survive two-a-day practices, he might need a visit to one of the team's trainers. Today, though, a checkup might raise more questions than it answered. Especially given the delicate bite marks on sensitive—but usually private—parts of his anatomy.

He'd see a trainer if his leg still hurt tomorrow. Right now, Cash had his hands full just getting through the day. His impromptu pick-up games at the Happy Gecko Campground may have put the fun back in football for him, but today's punishing schedule of practices, drills, and meetings had sucked a lot of it back out again. Now it was just work. Same as always.

"I'm going home." Cash didn't look up as he smeared on the liniment. "Marisol and the kids are waiting for me."

Silence fell. At least as much as was possible in a room full of testosterone-charged, head-butting men and clanging lockers, with a whole cadre of local and national media outside.

"Good for you, seven," Darrell said. "Kinda nice, isn't it?"

Cash glanced up. There was no mistaking what his friend meant. Darrell was a family man—a goodhearted man—all the way. His family—especially his wife—stuck by him through everything.

"Yeah," Cash admitted. "It is nice."

If he could manage not to screw it up, he'd be golden. But first he had to salvage some goodwill with management. To do that, he had to perform.

On the other hand, Cash Connelly had always excelled at performing—both on the field and off, he remembered with a grin. And if his mojo *off* the field translated into good things *on* the field . . . well, he was going to have one hell of a season.

Grabbing a towel, Cash headed for the shower. He wanted to be nice and clean when he demonstrated a little of that prowess for Marisol later. Because now that he'd caved in a little, he saw no reason in hell not to enjoy life to the fullest.

Chapter 26

"It sounds as if you're making great progress, Marisol."
Imelda Santos shuffled her paperwork, stacking everything neatly in a Dzeel folder with a green *oniomania*
label. "Your work-placement evaluation forms are excellent, as always—if somewhat sketchy on the housekeeping details." She smiled. "But I'm a bit concerned
about this growing relationship of yours."

Uh-oh. Newly alert, Marisol sat up straighter.

For more than a month now, she'd been making required weekly visits to the rehab center, taking part in as-
sessments and exercises and group counseling sessions,
fitting in all of that around her nanny and housekeeping
duties—and making the most of her time with Cash and
the kids too. But this was the first time since the faux
Jake Gyllenhaal sighting that Imelda had actually drawn
Marisol aside for a one-to-one talk.

"As we've discussed in sessions," Imelda continued
with a kind look, "oftentimes our patients develop their
disorders in an attempt to overcome pervasive feelings
of inadequacy, or as buffers to avoid fears of abandon-
ment. I'm very glad you're happy with this interpersonal
development, Marisol, but we don't usually suggest starting new relationships while in treatment."

"Wow, you're a real buzzkill, Imelda."

Her counselor shrugged. "I'm not trying to be."

"Is this because Cash is my work-placement boss?" Marisol asked. "Because if so . . . Please. That's *so* provincial! I don't know how it is out here in Hillbillyville, but in the rest of the world, people often meet each other at work. I mean, hello? How else are you supposed to meet someone?"

"It's not because Mr. Connelly is your 'boss,'" Imelda disagreed in her sedate counselor's voice. "As a matter of fact, I know Mr. Connelly personally, and I feel confident he has the integrity to handle the situation. It's you I'm worried about."

Suspiciously, Marisol peered at her. She plucked a Native American sculpture from Imelda's desk and turned it over in her hands, admiring the workmanship. Something like this would look fantastic on Cash's fireplace mantel. She'd rearranged the whole log cabin house now—part of her efforts to impress Cash with her sole area of expertise that didn't require a Platinum Visa—but she was having a hard time resisting the urge to buy new accessories and furniture. Those were her areas of expertise.

"Me? I'm fine. I've never been better," Marisol insisted.

"Well, I'm glad you're happy. I really am." With an uneasy smile, Imelda took off her glasses. She rubbed the bridge of her nose, then replaced her horn rims with a scholarly gesture. "I have to remind you, though, that it's important—especially for someone in recovery, like you—not to derive your feelings of self-worth and satisfaction from another person."

"Oh, I'm not." Marisol replaced the sculpture. "I mean, sure. The sex is absolutely *incredible* and all, but I know that a healthy woman takes charge of her own satisfaction. It's not up to a man to make me feel desirable or sexy. It's up to me. And believe me, I'm definitely getting that one nailed."

Imelda's mouth quirked. "That's admirable, Marisol. Here at Dzeel, we value all forms of self-expression, along with a healthy appreciation for sexuality, of course. But that's not quite what I meant when I said—"

"And seriously, even though Cash is *the* most skilled lover I've ever had, I can honestly say that I'm giving my fair share too!" Marisol gushed. She'd never had such an exhilarating talk with staid old Imelda before. It felt right though. After all, the counselor knew all her other secrets. "With Cash, I feel positively inspired," Marisol confided, leaning over her counselor's desk. She tapped it. "Over the past few weeks alone, I've explored more areas of my sexuality than I even knew I *had*. I didn't even know I was capable of such remarkable—"

"That's fine." Imelda cleared her throat, fingering the counselor badge pinned to her blouse. She gave Marisol a frank look. "What I'm trying to say is that being loved by someone is wonderful, but it's not a stamp of approval."

"Right." Marisol felt her forehead pucker. This was not as much fun as talking about sex.

"It's not a replacement for real self-solidity," Imelda went on, "any more than a shopping spree is a panacea for feelings of inadequacy. You can't buy enough items to fill that void. Similarly, you can't be loved enough to close those gaps. You have to take care of filling them yourself, first."

Marisol thought about it. She sat back in her chair, mimicking Imelda's taut posture, breathing in the bracing scents of pine forest and antiseptic floor cleaner (kudos to her for actually recognizing *that* smell!). She nodded. It made sense.

"Well," she said slowly, "I guess I could try filling those needs myself. I mean, sometimes Cash is tired after training camp, so he might like it if I lent a hand . . . so to speak."

She perked up, remembering their latest rendezvous. She still hadn't tried the French maid outfit. Maybe later tonight, after their usual dose of Flagstaff nightlife—aka, stargazing.

Marisol couldn't believe how mature she'd become. How happy.

"My friend Caprice swears by those bunny vibrators," she mused, getting back on track. "Too bad I'm not allowed to buy—"

"I'm not talking about self-gratification!" Imelda looked exasperated—and maybe a little flustered too. She smoothed her short haircut. "Although that's fine too. You know what? Maybe we should revisit this topic another day. In the meantime, is there anything else you'd like to share?" Patiently, she steepled her hands on her desk blotter. "Feel free."

"Well . . ." With that opener, Marisol was off and running. She chatted about the past several weeks with Cash and the kids, described her redecorating activities at Dozer's house, her explanations of them to Cash and Adam, and her love of good design and unique furniture.

"When I lived in L.A.," she told Imelda, "I only liked really avant-garde stuff. You know, esoteric designers with an ultramodern bent—totally *not* the whole Home Warehouse aesthetic. Totally *not* kid friendly either. But these days . . . I don't know, it's weird. I'm starting to appreciate fabrics that can withstand grape juice spills."

Imelda nodded.

"Did I ever tell you? I once wanted my own home furnishings boutique. I even approached my father for the funding, but—" Marisol broke off, smiling. "Never mind. In other news, I actually mastered Go Fish yesterday."

She described the game, making Imelda laugh over her descriptions of Hannah's ultracompetitiveness, Emily's attempts to sweet-talk Marisol into showing her cards, and Jacob's inability to sit still for more than two rounds without running around with his new Nerf football. Feeling proud of all the changes she'd made, Marisol told Imelda about the dinners she'd cooked, the football passes she'd learned—even the friendships she'd formed with Cassie, Amanda, Ashley, and Lindsay.

"They're my own personal insiders," Marisol said, picking up speed. "We meet for coffee or lunch or a play date a few times a week, now that their kids are here in town. The four of them are football wives too, and—"

She broke off, slapping her hand over her mouth.

Football wives too. Too!

Imelda's perceptive gaze made her slipup all the worse. Not that her counselor looked unkind . . . only that she looked knowing, filled with so much more insight and serenity than Marisol could ever hope to have. Especially while learning so many new things.

"I mean—" Hastily, Marisol backtracked. "Of course Cash and I aren't *that* kind of couple right now, but—"

"But someday you might be," Imelda finished. Her tone was soothing, her manner understanding. "It's all right to hope for that. Everyone dreams about what might lie ahead—it's the way human beings try on their future selves."

"Hey, I do that! Or at least I used to." Marisol brightened. "When I was shopping, I'd bring these crazy outfits into the fitting room and just go wild. Like playing dress-up."

"See? There's nothing wrong with experimentation."

"Exactly. Unless you've grabbed a leather bustier." Marisol shuddered, making a face. "That's too much."

"It *is* important to know your limits," her counselor agreed sagely. "For any relationship to be successful, you have to come to it as a whole, happy person first."

"Like shopping with your hair done and some makeup on," Marisol agreed, nodding. "At least mascara.

Unless you take care of the essentials first, *nothing* is going to look good on you."

Imelda smiled. "I think you're starting to get it."

Marisol beamed. "You know what? I think maybe I am."

Astonishingly, Imelda reached for her hand. She gave it a squeeze. "You've been a unique guest here, Marisol. Only one more week to go! We're going to miss you when you've finished."

Warmly, Marisol smiled. "I'm going to miss you too."

They sat that way for a second, two women having fully bonded over the power of sexual freedom and fitting-room tips.

Then Marisol pointed. "Um, would it be against the rules for me to buy that sculpture of yours after my program is up? I think Cash would really like it."

"Ohhh! I can't believe it!" Cash sat back in his chair at the dining room table, working up his best—and most exaggerated—sad sack loser face. "Hannah wins again!"

"Yes! Money, money, money, money." Gleefully, Hannah swiped out both hands to gather arms full of the stuff in every color. Perched on her knees, she scooped up a fistful and kissed it with a loud pucker. "You're all busted, suckers! Yippee!"

"Take it. Just take it!" Emily sighed dramatically.

Jacob groaned. "No matter what I do, she gets everything."

"Get used to it, Junior." Adam pushed an errant scrap of Monopoly Junior money toward the victor. "Women are like that."

"Hey, I object." Marisol gave him a nudge. "Maybe the women *you* meet are like that, Mr. Overdevelopment King, but some of us are more interested in *other* attributes besides wallet size."

The playful glance she threw Cash made it clear exactly

what attributes she was talking about. Happily, he squeezed her fingers, laying their clasped hands in plain view on the table. To his relief, Hannah, Emily, and Jacob hadn't had any trouble accepting their nanny in her new capacity as daddy's . . . playmate? Special pal? Future (you never knew) wife? So far, Cash hadn't defined what was going on between them. But he sure was enjoying it. And he was glad the kids were okay with it too.

Adam glanced toward their joined hands, then stretched. "Well, this has been fun, gang. But I've got team reassignments to negotiate for released players tomorrow, along with a huge pile of exhibition game scheduling to deal with, so I guess I'll be saying good night."

Smiling, he tipped an imaginary hat to Marisol.

"Do you have to leave so soon?" She pouted, still cleaning up the game. "It seems as if you just got here."

"Time plays tricks on you out here in the boonies." Adam winked. "Once you get back to L.A., you'll realize only three days have gone by since you left." He stood. "Bye, kids!"

Clamoring their usual giddy sendoff, the three of them surrounded him. Giggling, Jacob, Emily, and Hannah offered up their current specialty—squishing hugs meant to squeeze the life out of any adult, child, dog, or stuffed animal within reach.

"Oof!" Adam played along, staggering toward the door with Emily, Jacob, and Hannah still clinging to him. He bugged out his eyes. "Must—crawl—toward—car. Must—get—away. Arrgh!"

The kids collapsed in laughter. Right now, this was their most hilarious and cherished maneuver. "Gotcha!" Jacob cried.

"All right, enough strangling Adam." Sternly, Cash pointed toward the loft stairs. "Use some of that energy to brush your teeth and get ready for bed. It's getting late."

"Awww, Dad!" they chorused, disappointed. "Do we have to?"

Now they'd be foot dragging. Strict reminders. A late bedtime story. Anticipating all of it, Cash shared a look with Marisol. She shrugged, knowing the routine as well as he did.

Cash sighed. What the hell. They'd only live once right?

"If you hurry up and get your pajamas on, you can stay up late to look at the stars with me and Marisol," he relented.

"Yippee!" the three of them bolted upstairs.

As they vanished, the sound of Emily's impromptu "we get to stay up late" song-and-dance boogie number got quieter too.

Turning, grinning, Cash caught Adam staring at him. "What's with you?" he demanded.

"Nothing." Wearing a knowing smirk, Adam fisted his car keys. "'Night Marisol. Thanks for the deep-fried Twinkies."

"It was my pleasure." She beamed. "We were lucky that Dozer already had that Fry Daddy in the cupboard. Tomorrow I'm going to make deep-fried Snickers bars. Jacob told me they're 'awesome.' He had them at the fair with Tyrell."

Tyrell. He'd arrived at training camp a while ago. Even franchise players needed to learn plays for the upcoming season, and Tyrell had wanted to see the kids too— a visit Cash had grudgingly consented to. Since Tyrell's arrival in Flagstaff—without Stephanie, who'd traveled from Venice to Paris for a few weeks' vacation with some girlfriends—Cash had felt the probing gazes of his teammates and management on him more than ever.

Everyone expected him to play rough with Tyrell, to work out their personal history on the field. But with Marisol on his side, Cash hadn't felt the urge to do much more than make it home as early as possible each day. Tyrell's posturing didn't mean a thing to him these days. Neither did Adam's goading. He knew damn well his manager was making a point about Cash's new laxness with the kids. But hey—it was summertime, right?

Marisol had showed him exactly how fun summertime could be. Now Cash wanted it to go on and on.

"See ya, everybody." Adam held up his palm in farewell. His gaze caught and held Cash's. "Hey, I think you left some paperwork in my car." He angled his head toward the door.

"I haven't been in your car." Cash leaned toward Marisol, happily slinging his arm around her shoulders. Upstairs in the loft, the kids bumped around, slamming drawers and doors. Contented, he rubbed her bare arm with his fingertips, gazing down at the mayhem of the Monopoly Junior board. "Drive safely, you loser."

Maybe tonight he could talk Marisol into wearing that French maid's uniform, it occurred to him. He nuzzled her neck.

Adam cleared his throat. "Yeah. I'm pretty sure you left something in there."

"So go get it. I'll wait here."

"I can't," Adam insisted. "I—uh, don't know where it is."

"Then quit bugging me about it."

Marisol laughed, poking him in the ribs. "Cash, clearly Adam wants you to go outside with him. Can't you see? He's giving you that telltale eyebrow waggle of his."

"Humph." Adam crossed his arms, looking amused. "Remind me not to play poker with you," he told her. "Come on, Cash."

"Whatever you have to say to me, you can say in front of Marisol." Cash kissed her upturned face, hugging her against his side in a way that had become increasingly necessary to him. "We're a team. We don't have secrets from one another."

Adam shafted a look between them. He weighed his options.

"Okay, Cash," he said. "Here it is then. I've been watching you all night, and clearly you're in love with Marisol. *Crazy* in love with Marisol. I'm happy for you. So don't take this the wrong way when I—"

"Right. Outside it is." With lightning speed, Cash whipped his arm around, freeing Marisol, then hustled his manager to the front porch. "Tell me what's on your mind . . ."

Smiling to herself, Marisol carried the repackaged Monopoly Junior game to its designated shelf. It had been her first time playing a board game—her various stepmothers had been more interested in collecting party invitations than in entertaining a bored stepchild, so Marisol had never had a chance to get up to speed on Candy Land or Trouble. By the time Jamie had come along, Marisol had moved on. Tonight though, she'd had as much fun as she'd ever had club hopping in L.A.

Probably it all had to do with who you were playing with.

Footsteps thundered downstairs. "Marisol! Jacob squirted toothpaste on me." Emily plucked her shirt, showing the damage.

"I did not!" Jacob exclaimed, following close behind. "It was Hannah! She was showing how she used the *most* toothpaste of everybody, and squirted it all over the bathroom."

"It wasn't me!" Affronted, Hannah thundered down the loft stairs with one shoe on and one shoe off. "I can't help it if you're a big baby who can't even get the tooth-paste on the brush. If Emily hadn't been singing that dumb song, we—"

"Okay, time out!" Marisol teed her hands the way she'd seen Cash do. "Stop it right now. You're all three behaving like tattletales. Do you know what tattletales grow up to be?"

Wordlessly, they shook their heads.

"Tabloid reporters." Marisol nodded, making sure they caught her appalled tone. "Do you want to spend your grown-up days reporting on the exploits of Mary-Kate and Ashley Olsen?"

There was an appropriately horrified hush.

Then, "What are exploits?" Jacob asked.

"Never mind. Just trust me, you don't want that job."

"But—" Emily began, still clutching her stained shirt.

"Nope." Marisol cut her off, gently but firmly. "Just rub on some of that stain remover stick from the laundry room and throw your shirt in the hamper. It'll be fine."

"I'm *not* a baby," Jacob protested. "I'm big."

"You're not bigger than me," Hannah argued.

"Yes I am! Because I'm a boy, and boys are bigger!"

"Nuh-uh. See?" Hannah swiveled back-to-back, her one shoe clumping on the floor. She leveled her hand between them at head height, sloping steeply upward on her side. "I'm taller."

"I think you might be right, Hannah," Marisol mused. "That means you're tall enough to reach all the toothpaste spatters and clean them up. It should only take a minute. Use those glass-cleaning wipes I stashed under the bathroom sink."

Hannah shot her a dismayed look. Jacob gloated.

"Did you give the toilet a swipe with the antibacterial wipes?" Marisol asked him pointedly. "I left them out for you."

That was the compromise they'd reached, now that Marisol was cleaning the bathroom regularly for her Dzeel work placement. She'd learned to buff, scrub, and polish more than just her complexion at a spa or her toes during a pedicure.

"I'm going, I'm going." Jacob followed Hannah upstairs.

Feeling satisfied, Marisol watched the three of them leave. She was really getting good at this whole nannying thing. If she'd possessed this kind of diplomacy during her regular life, she might have been able to coax more trust fund money out of her father. She might even have been able to open her dream boutique and show the whole world her fantastic finds.

Thinking about it, she grabbed a bottle of sparkling cranberry-grape juice from the fridge, then went to the cabinet for five plastic tumblers. It wasn't fine wine in cut crystal, but it would do. Marisol had actually grown to enjoy it.

She wandered toward the front door, intending to peek outside and see if Cash and Adam were done talking yet. Instead, just as her hand hit the knob, she heard Adam's raised voice.

"Look, I've got to level with you," he was saying. "You're on thin ice with the team, Cash. The fighting, the hamstring injury, those times you were late—"

"I made up for those," Cash said irritably. "Believe me."

Marisol nudged the curtain aside and looked out the window. Both men stood on the porch, clearly at odds, their posture rigid and their faces flinty. She didn't want to listen, but the next thing she overheard made it impossible to step away.

"You're expendable." Adam jabbed Cash in the chest. "You hear me? It's as plain as that. You're dividing the team—just like before—and the other players aren't happy. There's talk. You're not my only client, you know. I've met with Ed and the Scorpions management too. Their positions couldn't be clearer. If there's one more incident—"

Cash swore. "There won't be another incident."

"One more incident," Adam persisted, "and you're out. If it comes down to you versus Tyrell, you know who they'll pick."

The silence felt laden with meaning. Dire meaning.

"Oh screw you." Cash turned away, his expression pained. His shoulders were stiff as he slammed his palm on a porch post. "This isn't a contest between me and Tyrell. Not this time."

"All the same, management won't tolerate divisiveness. There are players on that team who think you were the asshole for retiring after a winning season. They won't back you."

"So? I don't need them to. Not now. Not ever."

"You just might. Don't do this alone, Cash." Adam stepped closer, staring at him earnestly. "Don't be that guy. I'm saying this as your friend. If you want another season in the pros—"

"You know I do," Cash gritted out.

"—you've got to buckle down. Stay out of trouble. Make a good impression on Ed and the front office. Watch yourself at the scrimmage tomorrow, because *they* sure as hell will be. So will the media. They want to see the Cash Connelly they love."

"Fine. I'll kiss babies. Whatever. Are you done?"

A long look. "You're not taking this seriously."

"The fuck I'm not."

"All right." Adam put up both palms. "I get it. I've done all I can do. Don't say I didn't warn you."

"I won't," Cash said, then headed for the door.

The knob turned. Panicked, Marisol stared at her sparkling cranberry-grape juice. Her fistful of plastic tumblers. Her incriminating, eavesdropping-ready position next to the window.

Even Dump threw her a *how-could-you* look as the dog padded nearby. Marisol bolted for the middle of the room just as Cash came back in, his face a study in darkness and obstinacy.

He looked at her . . . and he knew. He *knew* what she'd heard.

But he didn't say anything. Instead Cash only took the

tumblers and juice bottle from her, taking charge as usual, then trod toward the back patio. "Ready for some stargazing?"

"Cash—" Marisol tagged after him. She grabbed his arm, hastily catching up. "Are you all right? Do you need help?"

"No. I'm fine."

That didn't mean anything. He always said that.

"If your head were on backward, you'd say you were fine." She stared at him, exasperated. "Right before you attempted some on-the-spot head-repair job."

His smile looked dimmed. "I'm fine."

"But . . ." Marisol scurried in Cash's wake as he walked further. "Well, it's just that I couldn't help but overhear what Adam said." She cast a glance to the loft, making sure the kids wouldn't overhear her. "It sounds as if you're in trouble."

"I'm fine." Cash opened the door and stepped outside.

Marisol pursued him. "That scrimmage thing Adam talked about—what is it?"

"A practice game—offense versus defense, but all of us are on the same team. Offense scores by making first downs and touchdowns. Defense scores by causing three-and-outs, getting interceptions, and recovering fumbles."

Okay. Marisol felt pretty sure that wasn't even English. More importantly: "Is it open to the public?"

Looking distracted, Cash nodded. "At the NAU field."

He sprawled on his usual deck chair, staring at the darkened tree line instead of the sky. He seemed to have forgotten all about the juice and cups in his hand.

Gently, Marisol took them. She opened the juice. "So you'll be playing then." She watched him nod. "Can the kids and I go?"

"The kids don't come to games. Sometimes on TV—"

"Stephanie didn't take them? No wonder you never felt supported!" Marisol said, indignant on his behalf. "Emily, Hannah, and Jacob *love* seeing you play!"

Cash only grunted noncommittally. He stretched out, looking around for the first time since coming outdoors. "Hey, come over here." He patted her usual deck chair. "Sit by me."

Marisol did. She poured them both some juice, then set the bottle aside until the kids joined them. She sat back, her head tilted upward to the amazing jeweler's case of stars overhead.

After a while, Cash sighed. "It might be nice if you came."

That was all Marisol needed to hear.

"Maybe sometime we will," was all she said.

Chapter 27

The moment Marisol pulled onto the highway leading into Flagstaff, she realized that Adam had been right.

This scrimmage thing *was* a big deal.

Evidently, other people could understand that gobbledygook Cash had spouted last night, because the route to town, lined on both sides with pine-tree forest and the occasional cluster of houses, was jam-packed with cars—all of them headed toward NAU. Ordinarily Marisol enjoyed the meandering drive into town—a nice breather from the hair-curling, traffic-clogged L.A. freeways—but today there was nothing but free parking on the road.

"What's going on?" Hannah asked, peering through the windshield. "Why are there so many cars today?"

"I think it's got something to do with your dad's scrimmage." Biting her lip, Marisol inched forward. She hadn't left enough time for this delay. Most days, getting to town was a speedy, breezy trip. "Unless there's an accident up ahead."

"Nope." From the backseat, Jacob piped up, filled with six-year-old certainty. "It's definitely Dad's scrimmage. Look."

He pointed to the car ahead of them. It sported three

Scorpions bumper stickers, a team banner, a stick-on antenna flag (currently wilted in the stalled traffic), and an assortment of player bobbleheads lined up along the rear window. Its driver and passengers all sported Scorpions gear too.

Marveling, Marisol looked around. The pickup truck in her rearview mirror was similarly outfitted, its occupants wearing jerseys with the distinctive Scorpions team logo and colors. A beat-up convertible two car lengths ahead—yay, they were moving again!—had even been painted with the team colors in stripes. Another car had *Super Bowl this year!* painted on the side.

"Wow, these people really like the Scorpions," Emily said.

"Well, we do too," Marisol pointed out. She nodded at the kids' assortment of Scorpions gear—hats, child-size jerseys, pom poms on sticks, banners, flags, drink coolers, and more. "I have to say, you guys look fabulous. Your dad will go crazy!"

"You look the *most* fabulous," Emily said. "I've never seen anyone who's so nice, with so much style and great hair too."

"You think so?" Marisol checked the mirror. "I'm going for a football-is-chic look today. I think I make it work."

"You do!" Hannah chimed in loyally. "Really pretty."

In the rearview, Jacob wrinkled his nose. "Hey, Marisol? How long are you going to be our nanny?"

"Um, a little longer." Marisol snaked forward. Ahead, she glimpsed police officers directing traffic, guiding everyone to alternate routes to the NAU campus. "I wish it was forever."

"Long enough till our birthday?" Emily asked.

"It's exactly twenty-three days away," Hannah informed her.

"We're having a big, *ginormous* party!" Jacob whooped

from the backseat. "It's going to be at my dad's house this year, with monster trucks and mud fights."

"Are not! It's going to be a tea party," Emily protested.

"Yeah," Hannah added, "with flowers and big hats."

"Yuck. That's stupid," Jacob said. "Hats are stupid."

"They're cool!" Emily argued. "Right, Marisol?"

Marisol, stricken with the reality that she would *not* be the Connellys' nanny twenty-three days from now, stared straight ahead. She picked up speed, following the traffic. As usual, she hadn't thought about the future at all.

"Right, Marisol?" Hannah nudged.

"Um, you could have monster trucks *and* hats, I guess."

The three of them groaned, launching into an immediate squabble about the ins and outs of kids' birthday parties.

"Either way," Hannah broke off with a sense of importance a few minutes later, "Marisol's got to be there. Right?"

A hush fell. Marisol felt their gazes pinned to her as she navigated through the congested streets to a parking lot near the NAU field. People streamed past the car, walking to the Scorpions scrimmage in shorts and sports clothes. Several carried coolers and blankets, creating a festival atmosphere.

Seeing the crowds, Marisol felt twice as glad she'd decided to come here with the kids. Cash would be *so* happy to see some familiar faces in the stands. And no matter what he said about being fine, she was positive he needed help. Big time. Just look at that dire warning Adam had given him last night.

Sensing Hannah, Jacob, and Emily waiting, Marisol paused. Their birthday was almost a month away. A lot could happen in that time. She didn't want to make promises she couldn't keep.

On the other hand, things were going so great between her and Cash—so great between her and the kids. What could it hurt?

"You bet," Marisol said with a nod. "I'll be there for your birthday party—whatever it turns out to be. I promise."

Then, beaming, Marisol gathered all their things and followed the crowd as it streamed into the football stadium.

In the locker room, Cash stood in front of a sink, his toothbrush in hand. Looking like a rabid dog, he grinned into the mirror, then went on brushing. One, two, three . . .

"Fourteen, twenty-two, six," Darrell said. "Hut, hut."

"Aww, hell. What'd you go and do that for?" Cash complained. Now he was off count. He'd have to start again.

Resignedly, he brushed as Darrell laughed, knowing damned well what he'd done. Players milled around them both, going about their usual pregame rituals. All of them were warmed up, suited up, and ready to go, but that didn't stop superstitious players from indulging their own personal good luck charms.

Some prayed. Some paced. Some listened to special music or ate particular foods. Case in point was the Scorpions' kicker, who always noshed on spicy kielbasa before games.

The scrimmage wasn't an official regular-season game—it wasn't even a recognized exhibition game—but it was an annual tradition, all the same. It was the players' first shot at a public arena this season, and everyone took it seriously. So did their fans who'd driven from Phoenix and elsewhere to see it.

The sound of the crowd filtered into the locker room, then a roar of approval. Likely, the Scorpions' cheerleaders had hit the field for their introductions and were doing their part to rev up the fans. Already today, Cash had had to fight through throngs of media, dodging network satellite vans as he'd arrived this morning and slipping past

ESPN reporters with only terse remarks. Adam's warning had spooked him—not that he'd admit it.

Cash spit out foamy toothpaste, then rinsed.

"All ready now?" Darrell grinned.

"Bite me." Cash jabbed the lineman in the sternum. "I know damned well you're wearing a freaking locket with a picture of your kids under those pads."

"Touché." Darrell gave a hearty laugh, then slapped Cash on the shoulder. "Ready for that receiving line?"

He meant the mass of reporters, camera crews, and print journalists who'd be waiting on the field when they emerged. There'd be a meet-and-greet first, including autographs and photo opps with fans, then the scrimmage, then a halftime routine with prizes, a Scorpions' cheerleader show, and more interviews, followed by the rest of the scrimmage.

It was set to be a tough afternoon.

"Damned straight, I'm ready." Cash grabbed his helmet.

"Do you see him?" Marisol strode past the bleachers with her Scorpions cap and sunglasses on, grateful she'd worn low-heeled sandals for this excursion. Anything higher and she'd have gotten stuck in the grassy field for sure. "Is that him?"

She pointed toward a corner of the field, where a Scorpions player could just be seen in the middle of a huddle of people.

"I don't know." Hannah shaded her eyes, peering past the fans surrounding them. "It's hard to see past the reporters."

"Those are reporters?" Marisol stilled. "Here?"

She hadn't counted on there being media here. And she'd been so focused on finding Cash and making sure he knew they were there to support him that she hadn't

noticed much else. But now that she looked around—
yup—she could see all the signs. Cameras. Notebooks.
Voice recorders and earnest, pseudoprivate conversations. All the things she usually strived to avoid.

On the other hand, it was unlikely she'd be recognized, Marisol reminded herself, given her nonheiress
getup. She glanced down at her outfit, plucked from the
pages of the Cash Connelly fan club—baseball cap and
all. She'd never appeared in public looking *less* stylish,
that was for sure.

But it was for a good cause. For Cash. Marisol straightened her oversize number-seven jersey and kept going,
holding Emily's hand.

"Hold up that banner, you guys," she instructed,
waving her pom-pom on a stick. "Let's make sure everybody sees it!"

Enthusiastically, the kids raised their *Cash Connelly #1*
banner. The four of them tromped across the field,
dodging other fans and the Scorpions team mascot,
looking for Cash. Marisol wanted to let him know they
were there. Their show of support would mean a lot to
him. But if they couldn't find him . . .

Jacob perked up. "Hey, there's Tyrell!"

"Look at all those reporters around *him*," Hannah
said.

"We're going to go say hi," Emily said. "Back in a
minute."

They ran off, headed for the broad-shouldered, grinning man who was the subject of multiple TV cameras.
Reporters hung on his every boastful word, looking en-
raptured.

"Come right back here when you're done!" Marisol
called.

She kept a close watch, not wanting to interfere with
the kids' time with Tyrell. Hannah and Emily reached
the big man first, greeting him with smiles and jumping-

up-and-down hugs. Jacob came last, but no less boister-
ously, with a tackle hug.

It was sweet. It was better for them, Marisol knew, if
they loved Tyrell too. After all, he was practically their
stepfather already. Their mother showed no signs of
moving on the way she'd done with Cash.

Reminded of him, she turned . . . and spotted him at last.

Cash stood only a few yards away, his gaze pinned on
his children as he watched them greet Tyrell. A pained
look flashed over his face, erasing the smile he'd worn
earlier to take a photo with a fan. He nodded the woman
off, saying good-bye.

He hadn't noticed Marisol yet. She was about to go to
him—to reassure Cash that the kids loved *him* most of
all—when four women rushed over to her in a giddy,
perfumed mob.

"Hey, Marisol! We're here. Check us out!"

Cassie, Amanda, Ashley and Lindsay surrounded her,
all four of them performing model turns to show off
their outfits. Each of them wore at least one item of Scorpions regalia—a hat, a T-shirt, a replica jersey, or (in
Cassie's case) an unofficial sequined halter top that
made the most of her implants.

"Now *this* is what I call high/low," Lindsay said, gesturing to her designer jeans and Gucci shoes. "I'm a thousand dollars on the bottom and thirty-seven fifty on top."
She giggled. "You look cute too, Marisol. Wow, you really
went all out!"

"Yeah, that's wild. Where did you get all that stuff?"

"It was in the log cabin's attic," Marisol told them,
striking a pose. "Two boxes of Scorpions gear, still
wrapped."

"Hmm. When Dozer got traded to the Chargers, he
must've put that stuff in storage." Amanda waved to her
husband, a Scorpions running back. "But it's a stroke of
luck for you, right?"

"Right," Marisol said firmly. She hadn't even had to break her no-shopping rehab plan, and she was proud of it. "Now if I can just get the kids back here, we can get started . . ."

Official player introductions came next. Cash stood in the tunnel, waiting for his cue, watching his teammates run onto the field to riotous applause. He clenched his fists, feeling unaccountably nervous, trying to stay light on his feet.

"And now, number seven . . . quarterback Cash Connelly!"

He ran out, adrenaline pumping through him. At the same time, someone else sprinted onto the field. A flashy banner caught his eye, waving in the breeze. Wait a minute. Was that . . .

It *was*. Marisol and his kids raced across the field diagonally, whooping and hollering, making a complete spectacle of themselves. Fully outfitted in Scorpions' gear, they pumped their pom-poms in the air. Marisol broke off and performed a miniskirted cartwheel. The kids cheered, then kept going, their faces wide with grins—the grins of people doing something crazy.

In the booth, the announcers stuttered and stopped, undoubtedly wondering what the hell was going on. Then one of them started narrating the movement of "the fans on the field."

Jumping around, Marisol, Emily, Jacob, and Hannah hoisted their banner higher, then pointed to it with their pom-poms. It was hard to read because of their jiggly progress, but he'd swear it had his name on it. His picture too. Oh Christ.

Given no choice, Cash kept running to his assigned place, ignoring the murmurs and jostling of his teammates. He waved to the crowd, but most of them were following the spectacle of one leggy brunette and three irrepressible children gallivanting across the field. Now security was in pursuit too, revving their carts as they gave chase.

Not noticing, his miniature fan club reached the sidelines, their pom-poms waving madly. Marisol and Emily and Hannah and Jacob jumped up and down, still showing off their banner.

Cash Connelly #1, he read. *Oh man.*

Two security guards stopped them. The whole crowd groaned, booing security's intervention. Taking advantage of the moment, two beer-bellied middle-aged men broke from the stands and hurtled themselves toward the Scorpions mascot. They tackled him, then jumped to their feet in jubilation.

The crowd roared. Cameras flashed. The mascot got up, waving his fuzzy suited arms in a *what-the-hell?* gesture.

Marisol actually blew Cash a kiss, then waved.

Disbelieving, Cash ducked his head, too infuriated to wave back. Couldn't she see what kind of mayhem she'd caused? Nobody in professional sports had much patience when it came to antics like those. He was surprised Marisol hadn't been handcuffed and escorted out already—along with his kids.

Damn it! What the hell was she thinking?

This was his second chance. His final chance. More cuts were coming to the roster, and Cash couldn't afford to be turked. If this had happened during a regular-season game (and he doubted Marisol knew the difference), his team would already have been slapped with a huge penalty because of her stunt.

Because of Cash allowing it in the first place.

The coach stomped across the field, giving a signal to the referees. Ed stopped beside Cash, his face a mask of annoyance.

"What the fuck is this, Connelly?" the coach growled,

pointing to Marisol. "Another one of your stupid stunts? Because your goddamn 'fans' are out of control."

"No! Jesus, Ed. I didn't have anything to do with that."

Skeptically, Ed eyed Marisol and her gang of three. "If you're pissed that Tyrell's getting all the media attention today, you can damn well grow up. Lay off your feud already. It's game time."

"I know. I'm ready." Clearly his head coach was fired up for the scrimmage and spoiling for a fight. So was Cash. A lot was riding on this. Irritably, he jabbed his hand toward Marisol and the kids. "I didn't even know she'd be here today."

His coach gave him an aha! look. "Then you *do* know her."

Cash shut his mouth, mad at himself for his slipup— and just then remembering what he'd said to Marisol last night too.

It might be nice if you came. What the hell had he been thinking? *Feeling* that way was one thing. Admitting it out loud to a woman was something else entirely. Something idiotic.

Ed shook his head, looking disgusted. "I might have known. That one's just your type." He looked at Marisol, currently flirting with the security guards—probably in a bid to be set free. "Leggy, ditzy, and capable of scrambling your brains." *Just like your ex-wife* hung in the air. "Look, Connelly. You're a good player, and I was happy to give you another shot at the pros. But you've got to pull it together. Right now."

"I'm already on it."

He'd have to find a way to get to Marisol. Tell her to get the hell out of here before she caused any more problems. But dealing with this was the last thing Cash needed with his game face on and the whole team—and management—looking on.

"Just take care of it," Ed said. "We have a game to play."

With a curt nod, the head coach stalked away. As order was restored and the player introductions continued, Cash risked another glance at Marisol and the kids. She actually gave him a beaming thumbs-up sign, pointing to the cameras hovering nearby.

She was hopeless. Did she think he liked being bawled out by his head coach—and filmed while it happened? Did she think he liked inadvertently delaying the scrimmage? Stealing the focus from all his teammates? Cash didn't know what the hell Marisol was doing here, bringing the kids and his home life and football together—again—but so far the effects were disastrous.

It had to stop.

Chapter 28

"Things are going awesomely! We've *definitely* got to keep it up," Marisol gushed, hugging the kids to her. The security guards had escorted them to their seats beside Cassie, Amanda, Ashley, and Lindsay, then left them alone with a hasty warning—thanks to their more urgent need to deal with the mascot tacklers. "Did you see your dad's face when we ran onto the field? He was *so* stunned!"

"Yeah," Emily said. "I'm not so sure he liked it."

"Me either. I told you spectators aren't supposed to go on the field," Hannah chimed in, ever the stickler for the rules.

"Nobody's going to forget my dad is back!" Jacob crowed.

"That's right," Marisol agreed firmly. "And now they know he has a bunch of eager fans too. Even the head coach noticed. Did you see him talking to your dad?"

Jacob nodded exuberantly. They exchanged high-fives.

"Really, all your dad needs is better PR. He's not in the spotlight enough! It's no wonder the team management is worried about working with him. He's got to bring more razzle-dazzle to the experience."

That's what Caprice and Tenley would have said for sure.

"I don't know, Marisol," Cassie hedged as the scrimmage

got underway. "The Scorpions management and owners are pretty conservative. They don't like controversy or negative press."

"Well, they clearly like the press in general, because there's tons of it here." Marisol pointed to the media on the sidelines, not far from their seats. "And you've got to believe what people do more than what they say. Whoops—that's my phone."

She picked it up. Adam's voice blared over the line.

"Are you crazy?" he yelled. "What are you doing?"

"Helping Cash." Marisol shielded the receiver with her hand, trying to keep their conversation private. "I heard you two talking last night, and I decided to come support Cash—to show the team management that he's way too popular to cut."

"That's sweet, Marisol, but stop it."

"I can't do that, Adam." Marisol smiled. "I love him. You're supposed to stand behind the people you love. That's one thing I learned from Cash, you know. He's always there for the kids—and he's been there for me too. Now it's my turn."

"Marisol—"

"Anyway, where are you? You should join us. The girls and I—and Jacob—have prime seats for the action."

"I have work to do. This is work for me, and Cash too."

Now he was just being silly. "I know, but it's also a game. Come on over." She scanned the crowd. "You can hold the banner."

"No more stunts," Adam warned. "I'll see you afterward."

"Okay, bye." Cheerfully, Marisol hung up. When Adam realized how much she'd helped Cash—how much she'd bolstered his spirits and helped his performance and demonstrated his popularity with the fans—he'd understand everything.

In the meantime, the scrimmage picked up speed,

with players putting all their energy into a process that looked incomprehensible to Marisol. They'd line up, then there'd be running and some kind of mad scramble for the football—sometimes with shouting from the fans—then all the players would stop while the referees vogued on the sidelines. Worst of all, no matter how long it went on, Cash didn't even get to play.

She scowled as the second quarter continued and one of the other quarterbacks took another snap—a term she learned from Ashley. This was getting Cash nowhere. If he didn't even get to play, how could he impress the coaches? Marisol cupped her hands around her mouth and mimicked the boisterous fans near her.

She stood. "Hey! Put in Connelly! Put in Connelly!"

"Yeah!" agreed a tubby guy next to her. "Put in Connelly!"

Soon other fans joined in. So did the kids and the football wives. They even started a wave, sitting down and getting up in a giddy pattern with their arms overhead. It was really cool.

"Put in Connelly!" Marisol yelled again, grinning.

This was totally working. She was making a difference. She was helping Cash, rallying the fans!

A horn blew. For an instant, Marisol thought this was it—the coach was putting in Cash. But then all the players trotted off the field, and the cheerleaders pranced on instead.

"What's happening?" Marisol asked, confused.

"It's halftime," Cassie said. "The game's stopped for the halftime show, and probably more interviews on the sidelines."

"But Cash didn't even get to play! Didn't they hear all of us"—she waved her arm at the fans nearby—"yelling his name?"

Emily shrugged. "Maybe the coaches don't care about that."

Marisol frowned. She couldn't believe nobody was listening to her. *Everyone* listened to a Winston. Winstons

were like American royalty or something! Even if they
were temporarily in shopaholic rehab. Besides, the
wishes of so many regular fans should mean something
to the coaches and team management.

She pondered the problem as the halftime show continued. Off the field, she spotted at least a dozen camera
crews and even more journalists milling around, all of
whom had their microphones or notebooks aimed at a
few chosen, sweaty players.

None of those cameras were aimed at Cash, Marisol noticed. None of the reporters were talking to him either. Despite her efforts to show fan support for number seven
with her banner parade, her pom-poms and shout-outs,
her "wave" and her fan rallying, the media huddle was focused elsewhere—on Tyrell, for instance. No wonder Cash
was having a tough time with the team management! He
was being completely (and unfairly) overlooked.

Marisol had had enough.

Determinedly, she examined that crowd of reporters.
There was bound to be a familiar face among them—
after all, she'd been hounded by the paparazzi all her
life. In L.A., she couldn't step outside her front door
without cameras whirring. It would be too ironic if
now—when she actually needed and wanted them—the
members of the press were inaccessible to her.

Besides, what good was being a Winston—what good
was being *her*—if she couldn't use those things to help
Cash?

Finally, Marisol spotted someone familiar. Leaving
Jacob, Hannah, and Emily with the football wives for the
moment, she trooped to the sidelines, tugging down her
miniskirt as she went. Imperiously, she motioned over a
reporter.

At first he dismissed her—then his eyes bugged as she
took off her sunglasses and he recognized her beneath

her Scorpions baseball cap. He scurried over, camera at
the ready.

"Hey, Joe," Marisol said breezily. "How's it going? How
come you're not covering my favorite player, Cash Connelly?"

The reporter—a regular contributor to L.A. media—
shrugged. "He's old news. The big story now is Tyrell."

Marisol glanced at the wide receiver, who was whole-
heartedly hogging the spotlight. Although she was happy
the kids liked Tyrell, he was no Cash. Not even close.

And time was wasting.

"Tell you what, Joe." She leaned on the fence, offering
up her trademark Winston smile—the one that had
earned her red-carpet status and cover treatment on a
million magazines. "Are you still interested in doing that
interview with me?"

"You bet." The reporter nodded. "Right now?"

"Sure. I'll trade you an interview . . . if you'll help me
out and give some coverage to Cash Connelly."

"No dice. I'm next up to talk to Tyrell."

"You and a million other reporters." Marisol waved
her hand dismissively. "Tell you what—how about an interview plus exclusive pictures of me instead? I know you
can sell those."

"I don't know . . ." Obviously torn, Joe hesitated.

"They'd be the first in over five years where I'm not
wearing my signature color, white," Marisol coaxed.

Pivoting, she showed her jersey. When negotiating, it
was always a good idea to let people see what they stood
to gain.

"Okay, it's a deal." Grinning, Joe hoisted his camera.
"We'd better get busy though. There's not much halftime left."

Relieved, Marisol sealed their agreement. They talked
briefly, with Joe firing off questions and Marisol explaining her Scorpions gear, her number-seven jersey, and her

newfound appreciation for football. As they talked, players lined up on the field again, getting started on the third quarter.

"You're going to have to interview Cash after the game," Marisol said, gesturing to the players' bench. "Give him good coverage too. Don't forget, we have a deal."

"Sure, whatever. No problem." Joe motioned for her to step back a few paces. "Let's get those pictures now."

"Make *sure* you get good coverage of Cash."

"I will, I will." Joe snapped a photo. "Good. Yes!"

Resigned to fulfilling her portion of their deal, Marisol struck a few poses, making sure her Scorpions' replica jersey was featured prominently. Hey, it was all good PR for the team, right? Whatever benefited the team benefited Cash. She was practically a Cash Connelly goodwill ambassador.

"Cash is a terrific player," Marisol said between shots. By rote, she took off her Scorpions cap and shook out her hair. More poses. "He's really dedicated. And very fit. And he's great with kids too. Did you know he does coaching as a hobby?"

Joe muttered a response, still snapping away. This ought to just about do it for the photos, Marisol thought. Then, just as she struck what she figured was her final pose, a shout went up from the assembled reporters nearby.

"Hey! That's Marisol Winston."

"Marisol, over here!"

"What are you doing in Arizona, Marisol?"

They mobbed her. Rushing over in twos and threes, with cameras already trained on her, the entire media throng forgot the game altogether. They smelled an exclusive, a story in the making. Any news item about one of the most photographed, most talked-about, most well-known heiresses in the world trumped a preseason football scrimmage any day.

Especially when that heiress had been out of the spotlight—mysteriously—for months now.

"Where have you been, Marisol?"

"What's with the getup, Marisol?"

"Smile this way. Marisol! Marisol! Over here!"

The noise and rush of reporters surrounded her. Caught amid the mayhem, at first Marisol thought she'd *really* succeeded this time. She would use the attention her celebutante status gave her to promote Cash, and everything would be great.

Then reporters started running across the field in midplay. Someone drove a network news van down the twenty-yard line, narrowly missing a gawking referee. Spectators in the stands caught wind of what was happening, and they mobbed the sidelines too. The announcers squawked over all of it, clearly at a loss.

Nothing like *this* was what she'd had in mind. This was mayhem! Cameras and microphones were shoved in her face, and no matter how hard Marisol tried to steer the subject around to the topic of Cash, all anyone wanted to do was snap her picture, film a sound bite, and find out where she'd been all these weeks. Marisol stood on tiptoes, trying to locate Emily, Jacob, and Hannah in the stands—hoping that Cassie, Amanda, Ashley, and Lindsay had scooted them off someplace far from the mêlée.

She couldn't see them. She couldn't see anything except shoving reporters, busy cameras, and hordes of gawking people. It was actually kind of nerve-racking. Usually in L.A. she had a getaway plan in mind, or friends to help shield her until she got to her Mercedes. Here . . . she had nobody.

Where was Cash? She tried to spot him amid the players, but the scrimmage seemed to have been stopped. Several players pointed and scowled at her. A few more clustered on the field. In its center, a quartet of coaches hunched around a player—an injured player on the ground. She could just glimpse the man clutching his ankle, then being helped unsteadily to his feet.

Appalled, Marisol tried to shove away from the reporters.

"Thanks, everyone." Shakily, she flashed a smile. "That's all for today. I really have to go—"

Nothing. They only pressed closer, making her feel seriously claustrophobic. All those faces, all those voices, all of them pushing, tugging, wanting something from her. Someone even grabbed her jersey and wrenched it as though trying to tear off a souvenir. Someone else trampled her Scorpions hat.

"Don't forget to talk to Cash Connelly!" she said, valiantly trying to stick to her plan. But her voice sounded shaky and her knees felt that way too. "He's really fantastic!"

Suddenly someone grabbed her. A male someone, judging by his size and strength and the no-nonsense way he wrapped his arm around her waist. Someone big too. It had to be Cash. Stiff-arming the reporters, he forced a broad-shouldered path through the crowd, partly dragging a panicky Marisol with him.

They reached the tunnel leading from the field to the locker rooms. Its semidarkness closed around them—and no one followed either, not inside the exclusive domain of the team. At least there were still some boundaries left.

Thoroughly relieved, Marisol sagged. "Oh my God, Cash! I—"

"I told you, no stunts," Adam said.

Roughly, he deposited her at the concrete wall. His face was hard with anger, his eyes dark and his whole demeanor rough.

"Where are the kids?" he demanded.

"I don't know. How did you . . . ?" Marisol struggled for breath, feeling on the verge of tears. She'd *so* wanted him to be Cash—so wanted all this to just go away. With a mighty effort, she regrouped. Where were the kids? "I left them with the football wives. Um, Cassie, Amanda,

Ashley, and Lindsay. Our seats were right on the side-lines, but when the reporters came—"

"Which side?"

"Well . . ." Faltering, Marisol put her hands in her hair, trying to think. "All sides, really. They just kept coming!"

"No, which side were you sitting on?" Adam de-manded.

"Um, the side by the scoreboard?"

"Close enough. Stay here."

"But—I need to go get the kids!" Realizing the prob-lem, Marisol tottered toward the daylight at the tunnel's mouth.

Adam stopped her. "If you go out there, you'll only make things worse." He gave her a harsh look, one unlike any she'd ever seen from him before. "You've al-ready done enough."

"But there must be something else I can do!"

Adam's expression suggested several possibilities, none of them polite. "I'll find the kids."

He hurried out, intent on his mission, leaving her alone.

So much for her rescue. And for her attempts at help-ing Cash. The whole thing had turned into a fiasco—and it was still going on, judging by the clamoring crowds she heard. In all the turmoil, Marisol had no idea what had happened to the scrimmage.

Uncertain what to do, she looked around. At one end of the tunnel was the football field; at the other, only shadows.

Well, maybe there was a phone down there. There had to be. She could find it, call one of the football wives, and make sure Hannah, Jacob, and Emily were all right. Heading that way, with her heels clicking and her fan wardrobe tattered, Marisol felt sorrier than ever for not bringing her handbag—and with it, her cell phone—to her disastrous meeting with Joe.

Halfway down, a thundering sound made her stop.

She turned around. The entire football team—players of every size, coaches, trainers, staff, and all—was headed her way. Evidently, they'd called off the scrimmage or postponed it, because the players carried their helmets in taped-up hands.

Cash trudged in the middle of the pack, his head down and his face bleak. His eye black made him look defeated somehow. But the sight of him was a balm to Marisol's spirits. She rushed to him, grabbing his arm while the other players streamed around them both, giving her an extra-wide berth.

"Cash! I'm so sorry! I had no idea—" Futilely, she waved her arm. "I was only trying to help, I swear."

He shrugged off her hold, not looking at her. "I can't talk to you right now."

"What? Of course you can, I'm right here. We *have* to talk." Frantically, she hustled after Cash as he kept following the team down the tunnel. "What happened to the scrimmage? Aren't you ever going to play?" She gulped. "Have you seen the kids?"

This time, he did meet her gaze—and his end of it was scary. Marisol stepped back, her heart pounding.

"You don't know where they are?" Cash asked. His voice was raspy, his tone fierce. He grabbed her arm and shook her. "You don't know where they are?"

"No!" Marisol gulped, feeling her eyes bug. "Adam went to look for them, but I left them with Cassie and Amanda and—"

Cash thrust her away, making her stumble.

"They were okay when I left!" Marisol cried. "I wasn't even going to be gone for long. I went to get press coverage for you! So you could stay on the team. I didn't think—"

"No, you didn't think." Cash looked disgusted. So did

several of his teammates who trod past. "I'll find them myself."

"But I can help you." Marisol choked back the tears that threatened, hardly able to believe he was being so mean to her. Yes, she'd screwed up. But she wanted to make everything better now. Didn't that mean anything? "I can fix this! I can call in a helicopter search, a whole police force, whatever we need!" she babbled. "I'm a Winston. I always get what I want. I *always* do."

Cash shook his head. "Not this time, you don't."

"What do you mean?" Marisol sucked in a deep breath, her whole body trembling. She'd never seen Cash look so dire—had never seen him appear so fed up with everything. With her. "I lost the kids before, remember? In the grocery store. And you didn't freak out then. No Monday-morning quarterbacking, you said. You forgave me, because I found them. I can find them this time too. It'll only take—"

He held up his hand. "Stop it. Just stop it."

Apparently, she'd used up all of Cash's easy forgiveness.

"No, listen," Marisol blathered on, desperate to make him understand. "You just haven't seen me in action, that's all. As soon as I find a phone, I promise I'll—"

"Keep your promises," Cash said. "All I need you to do is stay the hell away from me."

Then he fisted his helmet and walked away from her, far into the shadows where Marisol couldn't follow.

Chapter 29

After the disastrous scrimmage, Cash arrived home to an empty house and the sound of the phone ringing. Ignoring it, he slung his gym bag and equipment on the floor, then stepped aside as the kids barreled past him through the front door.

"Dibs on the TV!" Jacob yelled, jumping on the sofa.

"You were first yesterday," Emily complained.

"I think we should flip a coin." Hannah barged bossily in between them. "That's what would be fair."

Bickering ensued, competing with the electronic drone of the answering machine as it clicked on. Cash stilled. Marisol's voice came over the line, leaving a frantic message.

"Cash! Where are you? Adam said you found the kids. Whew!" She gave a shaky-sounding laugh. "Way to pull a fast one, kids! I heard Cassie, Amanda, Ashley, and Lindsay took you to Peter Piper Pizza and gave you about a million tokens to play with while the scrimmage wrapped up. I guess you lucked out, huh?"

Cash made himself move again, heading to the kitchen. Dump trotted up for a head scratch, a maneuver Cash completed woodenly. He murmured to the dog as Marisol's voice kept chattering away. They hadn't

spent enough time apart for him to realize she was a
person who left lengthy phone messages.

"Anyway, I'm headed home . . . um, to your place," she
said to the accompaniment of car-door slamming. The
Prius's engine revved. "So if you're there, I guess I'll see
you soon. Bye!"

Instantly, *stupidly*, anticipation rose inside him. Stubbornly, Cash shoved it back. He couldn't be happy to see
Marisol. Not after everything that had happened.

"It's mine!" Jacob shouted. "Gimme!"

"Why don't you take it, stupid head?" Emily taunted.

"You guys, cut it out!" Hannah said. "Just take turns."

Cash glanced their way. Jacob and Emily were having
a knock-down, drag-out tug of war over the remote control. Hannah refereed in the middle, pinwheeling her
arms. Their shouts rose to new heights, inciting Dump
to romp creakily over, barking.

"Everybody, shut up!" Cash yelled.

All four of them—children and canine—gawked at
him.

"Upstairs! Right now. Things have been too lax in this
house for a while now, and it ends today. Get moving."

"But—" Emily began.

"Now!" Cash's roar shook the rafters.

They dropped the remote and bolted, Hannah looking tearful. Even the dog slunk off to one of the bed-
rooms, casting Cash a reproachful look. Too on edge to
care, Cash paced across the kitchen as the sounds of children settling in the loft subsided.

That was better. Order restored, at least a little. Things
were almost getting back to the way they used to be—the
way they were supposed to be, when he was in control.
Really in control.

He stopped at the answering machine. His finger hovered over the flashing play button, one gesture away from
hearing Marisol's voice again. Cash hesitated, then swore.

He stomped off to the other end of the house. There were other things to be done today, and the sooner the better.

Cash had just snapped shut the last suitcase when Marisol rounded the corner to her bedroom, looking flushed. Her hair flew around her face as she hurried into the room.

"Ohmigod, I'm *so* glad you're here. Are the kids okay?"

She reached him and threw her arms around him, hauling him close for a hug. Or at least trying to. She didn't have the strength to budge him, and Cash made himself stand like a stone.

"I was going to go upstairs to see them, but I wanted to find out how you were doing first, so—hey, what's the matter?" Marisol pulled back, peering into his face. "Why are you so . . . Are you still mad at me? But you found the kids, and I—"

"I'm not mad at you." Cash moved her arms down, then away.

"Oh good. I didn't think you would be. I mean, you've always been very forgiving." Marisol watched blankly as he picked up the suitcase. "You didn't even get mad when you had cartoon stickers all over you at the campground, right?"

She gave a stilted laugh. Cash only stepped away, sliding the suitcase he'd just packed to join the pair of tote bags on the floor. They stood in a neat symmetrical row, ready to go.

"Hey, that's my suitcase! And my tote bags." Marisol rushed forward, her expression changing. "What are you doing?"

"Packing. You have to leave."

It came out less firmly than he wanted. Nevertheless,

Cash crossed his arms and stared her down. He couldn't afford to weaken—not again. Not now. He'd done enough of that already.

"*Leave?*" Marisol asked. "Now?"

Grimly, Cash nodded. "This was a mistake. I thought I could handle it, but . . ." He swore. "This never should have happened."

"What shouldn't have happened? *Us?*" Marisol grabbed him, trying to make him look at her. Something in his face must have gotten through, because she spoke more urgently. "Cash, you were the best thing that ever happened to me! Because of you, I found the whole *rest* of life—the *real* life—the stuff I'd never encountered before. Because of you, I fell in love! I—"

"You have to leave," he said again. Maybe if he kept repeating it, it would hurt less. "Just go." He gestured roughly to her suitcase. "I packed so it would be easy."

"Easy?" Marisol boggled at him, her eyes filled with tears. "You call this easy?" Visibly, she rallied, lowering her voice. She drew in a deep breath. "Look, I know I messed up. I know I shouldn't have left the kids with anyone else today, and I'm sorry for that. So sorry. It'll never happen again, I promise."

"No, it won't happen again," Cash agreed. "I won't let it."

From now on, he'd be in control. He'd be himself again.

And he'd be alone too. Believing it could be any other way had been a mistake—a mistake he might as well deal with right now. It would only hurt Marisol more if he let her stay.

Forcing himself away from her, he picked up the envelope and file folder on the bureau. He offered her their bulky contents, newly—if hastily—filled out and signed with his scrawled signature. "That's your Dzeel paperwork. Consider your work placement finished. I'll call Fordham to explain why it's ending early, if you want, but you should get full credit."

"I don't want full credit! I want you."

"I rated all your work as excellent on the evaluation forms," Cash continued doggedly. His eyes burned. "Including the final one. There's no reason you should pay for my mistake."

"Your mistake?" Looking utterly baffled, Marisol took the paperwork. She set it aside without so much as a glance. "What are you talking about? Cash, come on. You're scaring me."

He didn't mean to do that. Jesus, this was hard. Steeling himself, Cash offered the only explanation he could.

"I shouldn't have let you get to me. It was a mistake." A pause. "I'm not cut out for . . ." He gestured feebly. "This."

Marisol's face softened. She came closer, trying to hug him again. "Of course you are. And of course you let me 'get to you.'" She chuckled softly, attempting to duck under his arms for that hug. "That's what people who love each other do."

He blocked her. "I can't love you."

She stepped back as if he'd punched her.

"I can't love you, and I should have known better than to come close to it." Damn, but he'd come close to it. Until today, he'd actually thought . . . Closing his eyes, Cash swore. Why had he allowed himself to lose control? To let her in? He should have known better—especially if he wanted his second chance to work out. He shook his head. "That stunt you pulled today—all those freaking reporters—"

"I didn't know that would happen!" Marisol protested. "I had a deal with one reporter. One! Then all of a sudden—"

"One of our halfbacks is questionable for the season," Cash broke in. "He wrecked his ankle dodging that damned news van that drove across the field to get to you."

Marisol's gaze was solemn. "I'm sorry for that. I'll visit, I'll get him the best rehab care, the best doctors and trainers, whatever it takes. But Cash, I was only trying to help. I was trying to help *you*, because I love you and you needed me."

"Stop saying that." He couldn't listen to this. He had to do something. He turned away from her and snatched the Dzeel paperwork, then picked up her luggage. He carried everything to the front door, where the bags landed with a final-sounding thunk. "I never asked you to help me."

"Of course you did," Marisol insisted, doggedly following him to the foyer with her high heels clicking. "You said 'I'm fine,' but then you gave me that look—the one that says, 'make me macaroni and cheese.' I'm a sucker for that look every time. It means you need me . . . and God knows, nobody else really does."

She was crazy. Cash Connelly didn't give anyone that look. Maybe Marisol could read Adam like a damn book, but she couldn't read him that way. No one could. No one ever would—not if he were smart. He should've known not to let "love" interfere with his life again. Not to let himself need someone again.

He had, and now he was paying for it.

"You didn't help me." Cash slapped the Dzeel paperwork atop one of the suitcases. "I got cut from the team today."

Marisol stopped. She gaped at him, her eyes all sparkly with unshed tears, then stepped forward. She hugged him.

For an instant—only that—Cash let her.

"I'm so sorry," she murmured. Another squeeze. "So sorry."

Cash shrugged. "Three strikes. I'm out."

His damn voice almost gave out on the words. Jesus. It had been bad enough when Ed had given him the news, not even bothering to chew him out first. Just, "You're out, seven."

Numbly, Cash had turned in his playbook, taken one last look at that number-seven uniform, and left the team for good.

Now he didn't know where he was going to go, how he was going to make a living . . . how he was going to break this news to Stephanie and the kids. His hopes for expanded custody were a dead issue now. So were his dreams of going out on top.

This time, he didn't even have his ex-wife or Tyrell to point the finger at. He had only himself to blame. He'd lost focus. He hadn't stayed on top of things. He'd screwed up.

He'd fallen in love. Again. With a woman he couldn't trust.

Aching all over, Cash pushed Marisol away.

Tenaciously, she came back to his side, looking so cute in her Scorpions jersey he could hardly stand it. It had been sweet of her to wear his colors—to rally the kids into getting tricked out too. But those were small details next to the havoc she'd wreaked. Now more than ever, Cash had to stand firm.

"I'm really sorry," Marisol said, her voice gentle. "What are you going to do now?"

He couldn't begin to consider his future. "In the next ten minutes? Watch you leave."

She didn't so much as budge, but she did give him a sympathetic look. Oh hell. This was going to be harder than he'd thought. He had to push Marisol away—push her far away, whether he wanted to or not. Determinedly, Cash braced himself.

"No, seriously. Maybe this is a good thing," Marisol persisted, sniffling. "Right? I mean, kind of a blessing in disguise. After all, you *did* get hurt not too long ago, remember? You retired once before, and now you're even older than when you did that, so—"

Cash glared at her. "I'm not too old to play football."

"But if you don't love it the way you used to—" Marisol broke off, probably thinking the better of kicking him when he was down. Then, incredibly, she just kept on. "Maybe there's something else you can do. Something new. Something better."

"I've never done anything else." He looked away. "The one time I tried—" Awww, hell. This was too brutal. "Never mind."

"I'll help you," Marisol announced to his disbelief. She nodded. "You can't keep a Winston down, you know. That's what my dad always says, at least. I thought that particular gene had dropped off the family tree when it got to me, but I guess mine just kicked in late. After I met you and the kids."

She strode across the family room and grabbed her handbag. When she turned around again, she had her cell phone in hand.

"What are you doing?" Cash asked.

"Calling Adam. We'll have a strategizing session. As soon as the Scorpions realize how much you want to be on the team, they'll reconsider. Or maybe I can donate new uniforms or a stadium or something. The Winstons are loaded, you know—"

"Stop it." Cash closed his hand around her phone, gently snapping it shut. "I'm finished. This is it."

Marisol gazed up at him, her face tilted and glowing with hopefulness. With determination. She was a little red around the eyes, and her nose was still kind of scrunched up, but overall, she actually seemed to believe she could accomplish something.

"I know money can't solve everything," she said, laying her hand on his arm, "but I would do anything for you,

Cash. *Anything.* Just tell me what you need, and it's done.
I promise."

This was it. He couldn't have asked for a better lead-
in. So why did his throat hurt so much right now? Why
did his whole body rebel at what needed to be done?
Cash felt as if he'd been tackled hard, hit again and
again—and he hadn't even played.

"I need you to leave," he said, "and don't come back."

Marisol stared at him, her forehead crinkled as
though she didn't get the joke. Then the jovial determination in her face gradually faded. "Are you serious?"

Painfully, Cash nodded.

"But I—I'm offering you all I have." A tear dropped to
her cheek, then another. Marisol gulped, sniffling. "All
I am. It's yours, if you want it. Can't you see?"

Once again, Cash nodded. Her hurt was so naked, so
undeniable, it nearly killed him. But he didn't have the
words to explain anything else, and he didn't dare touch
her either. If he did, he might lose his resolve. Then he'd
have nothing.

Marisol straightened, swiping her cheeks. Her lips
trembled. "Can I at least say good-bye to the kids first?"

Cash glanced over his shoulder, and they were already
there—Emily, Jacob, and Hannah sat on the loft stairs,
draped over the banisters with solemn faces. He didn't
know how much they'd heard, but he hoped never to
see them look so sad again.

He murmured his agreement and stepped aside. His
chest ached as Marisol strode briskly to them, shaking
out her hair and clearing her throat with an indomitable
air. She plastered on a smile—a wobbly, sparkly-eyed
smile—then stood at the foot of the loft stairs. She held
out her arms.

"Hey, you guys." Her voice cracked, hoarse with emotion. "It looks as though I'm leaving a little sooner than
we thought. Why don't you come on down here for a—"

All three of them arrowed downstairs, homing in on Marisol with pale faces. The moment they reached her, she dropped to her knees and hugged them close. Soon all four of them were sobbing.

"I don't want you to go!" Emily cried. "Please don't go!"

"I promise we'll be good." Hannah buried her face in Marisol's arms, her hair tangled as it fell over their matching jerseys. "We won't argue at all, and we'll eat all our vegetables, and we'll brush our teeth six times a day!"

Jacob only nodded, snuffling loudly as he hung on Marisol's shoulder. He patted her back with his little hand, clearly trying to comfort his weeping nanny. He jabbed his chin, once and then twice, in that characteristic gesture of his, looking determined not to bawl out loud. "You've got to stay!"

Marisol raised her head. "You guys are really, *really* good. This isn't because of anything you did. It's just time for me to go, that's all." She sniffled mightily. "We all knew this wouldn't last forever, right? Soon you'll be back in Phoenix, starting second grade, and you'll forget—"

"I don't care about second grade!" Emily cried.

"Well, sometime you will," Marisol said gently, still on her knees as she hugged them all close to her. "And you'll see your friends, and you'll have fun, and your mom will be back from Paris soon, and you'll forget all about this summer."

"I won't!" Hannah declared. "I won't ever forget."

"Me either." Manfully, Jacob raised his face to Cash's. "Tell her she doesn't have to go, Dad. Just tell her!"

"I do." Marisol patted them all, then got to her feet. She gave them another unsteady smile. "I do have to go, but thank you for being so wonderful to me. I really loved . . . this."

Appalled, Emily, Hannah, and Jacob stared at Cash.

"Tell her, Daddy!" Emily urged. "Make Marisol stay!"

"It's not your dad's fault." Marisol grabbed the tissues

from the side table and pulled a handful from the box. She distributed them with very nannylike efficiency, saving herself for last. There was much nose-blowing. "Take care of yourselves, okay? And if you ever get to L.A., just look me up."

The kids stared from her to Cash, their faces tear-streaked and their expressions accusatory.

"We never go to L.A.," Hannah said peevishly.

"Yeah, why don't we ever go to L.A., Dad?" Jacob demanded.

Uh-oh. They were really getting mad now. Before Cash could think up a reply—before Emily could translate her injured expression into another accusation—a car horn sounded outside.

Startled, Cash jerked. "That's your ride." He gestured to the door. "I called Tom at Dzeel, so he could pick you up."

Marisol looked at him. "That was very efficient of you."

He shrugged, feeling . . . not a damn thing. He pushed everything away except what needed to be done. "I'm an efficient guy. This summer was just an aberration. It's over with."

Looking sad, Marisol came nearer. "I guess neither one of us changed as much as we hoped. I'm no nanny, I'm just an heiress. And you're no comeback kid . . . you're just you."

That hurt. Getting mad too, Cash tightened his mouth.

"I love you that way though." Marisol touched his face, gave him a wry look, then let her hand fall. "If you ever think you can do the same thing for me . . . let me know."

Curtly, Cash nodded. It couldn't hurt. It would never happen anyway. Romance didn't mesh with him and never would.

The car horn blasted again. Marisol picked up the suitcase. Cash pushed past her to grab the tote bags and the paperwork from Dzeel. He shifted his burden and opened the door.

Dump trotted over, shoving his muzzle beneath Marisol's hand. She gave a choked laugh and petted the German shepherd.

"I guess you want to say good-bye too, huh, boy? You've been a good dog. You watch over these guys, okay?"

Dump pressed his head against her leg, wagging his tail.

Marisol glanced up, smiling at them. "Geez, I nearly believe he understands what I'm saying. You can almost—"

Then her whole face crumpled. With a muffled sob, she pushed out the door, her suitcase thumping awkwardly on the jamb. She clattered down the steps with Cash in her wake.

Tom greeted her. He gazed with suspicion and not a little hostility at Cash when he saw Marisol's tear-streaked face, then set to work helping load her luggage. He took the paperwork.

Marisol slid in the front seat, crumpling her wad of tissues, her head down.

The kids filed out too, standing on the porch. Marisol raised her hand in a wave, trying to smile. They waved back.

The last thing Cash remembered was raising his own palm in good-bye, then seeing Marisol finally turn away as her car bumped down the road out of sight, leaving him alone in a way he'd absolutely demanded . . . and didn't want at all.

Summer was over. Squaring his shoulders, Cash went inside to pack up everything and head for home.

Chapter 30

"What the hell is this?"

At the sound of her father's irate voice, Marisol glanced up. Through her disheveled bangs—courtesy of her emergency broken-heart haircut—and against all reasonable expectations, she spotted him striding into her Malibu living room.

She had to be hallucinating. Gary Winston did not make beach-house house calls. He did not shout. And he especially did not take special pains to visit his only daughter.

Marisol decided to play along. "How did you get in here?"

"I pay the mortgage. I can damn well visit if I want."

She raised her eyebrows, then just gave up. It didn't really matter anyway. "Fair enough."

"Actually, the maid let me in. Can I sit down?"

Her father hovered nearby, gesturing awkwardly at a chair. He didn't commandeer it, or rearrange it, or insist that it be burned as a statement protesting "hideous modernism." He just . . . stood there, waiting. Apparently for her permission.

That was new. Perplexed, Marisol nodded. "Go ahead."

"Thanks." He tossed the newspaper on her prized Le

Corbusier coffee table. It landed amid empty martini glasses, overflowing ashtrays, a cast-off pair of diamond earrings, and other holdovers from last night's welcome-home soirée. "So . . ." Her father blew out a breath. "How have you been?"

Oh. This was an official visit then. A Winston status check. The Home Warehouse board of directors was probably waiting outside to make sure the family heir hadn't gone around the bend due to heartache and an excess of football-related publicity. Grudgingly, Marisol levered herself up on one elbow. She wrapped her silk robe tighter—it was pretty, but not as warm as terry cloth—then thrust her chin toward the newspaper.

Her state of being was beside the point anyway.

"Your hair was practically on fire when you came in here," she said. "Aren't you dying to know what the hell *is* going on?"

Looking abashed, her father fiddled with the collar of his golf shirt. He'd been on the links when she'd come home from Dzeel a week ago, a straight-A student with absolutely no interest in her diploma, and she hadn't seen him until today.

"Uh, that was just my way of getting things kicked off." Her father shrugged. "There's nothing in the paper—not today. But confrontations are efficient at getting the ball rolling. You should remember that for future business dealings."

Right. As if she'd ever have any. Marisol yawned, then reached for her art deco silver cocktail shaker. "Want a drink?"

"It's ten o'clock in the morning."

"So?"

"So I'm starting to see why Jamie insisted I come here."

"Ah." Bleary-eyed (and teary-eyed), Marisol poured herself a room-temperature Gibson. The onions would be solid food at least—more than she managed to eat most days lately. She took a sip, made a face, then nudged a file folder across the coffee table with her toe. "Well, you can rest easy. I finished my program at Dzeel with flying colors. Take a look."

Her father didn't even budge. "I'm glad to hear it. But you're dodging the question, and I won't have it." His voice was gruff and businesslike. "How do you feel?"

As if my heart dropped out someplace along I-40, and I'll never find it again, Marisol thought. *As if nothing matters now.*

"Just peachy." She saluted him with her glass. "*Salud.*"

He squinted at her. "Jamie says you've had four welcome-home parties in a row now. Don't you think that's a bit much?"

Marisol shrugged. "Says who? I'm a globe-trotting, style-setting, swinging-single heiress—I have a lifestyle to maintain. Certain things are expected of me. Besides, I have to do something besides shopping. This week, it's partying and drinking."

"I see. Do you miss it?"

Startled, she lowered her cocktail. "Do I miss . . . ?"

"Shopping." Her father nodded, his hands hanging between his knees. He looked kind of careworn, she noticed upon closer reflection. His golf shirt was wrinkled. His hair was messy too.

Was it possible she'd actually worried him?

"You know what I mean." Awkwardly explaining, he gestured toward her collectibles, her perfectly designed furniture, her accessories. She'd always been so proud of them. "Do you miss shopping, the same way a person who quits smoking wants to light up again when things get stressful?"

With a vague movement, he patted his shirt pocket.

"Sometimes I miss it," Marisol admitted. She swirled her Gibson, watching the onions bob together in a perfect pair. "But not when I see a cute skirt or a fantastic chair. It's not about that." Thanks to Imelda, she understood that now. "Mostly I still want to give people wonderful gifts, and now I can't. All I have left is myself." She sucked in a deep breath, trying to sound lighthearted. "Apparently, *I'm* not in demand right now."

Her father cleared his throat, fidgeting. *Whoop, whoop. Emotional nakedness alert!* He looked around uncomfortably, then flexed his hands. Meaningful heart-to-hearts weren't exactly Gary Winston's speed. As his famously devil-may-care daughter, Marisol should have known better than to expect an empire builder to come down to her (heartbroken) level.

"Well. That's no reason to sit around drinking yourself into a stupor," her father announced. He leaned over and snatched her glass. Vodka splashed as he plunked her cocktail out of reach, then gave her a defiant stare. "You're my daughter, and I won't see you give up on yourself."

"Oh right. You've got exclusive dibs on that."

"On giving up on you? Since when?" He blinked, seeming taken aback. "Marisol, why do you think I sent you to Dzeel?"

"I don't know," she said breezily. "To make me miserable? If so, mission accomplished." She saluted. The gesture would have been much more sassy and effective with a cocktail in hand.

A moment passed, during which her father appeared to contemplate leaving her alone in her sarcastic funk.

Then, "I don't think you're miserable because of Dzeel."

Clearly he knew about Cash—probably thanks to Jamie. Despite his gentle tone though, Marisol didn't want to hear her father's diagnosis. Or be pitied either. She didn't want to be caught up in needing him—in needing anyone—anymore.

Silence descended, broken only by the tick of her

1958 Nelson sunflower clock and the distant sound of surf outside.

Marisol shifted on the sofa, buffed a coffee table ring, then perfected the tabletop arrangement. She glanced up.

"I wasn't really going to drink that whole Gibson," she confessed. "*Liquor* is what really gets the ball rolling, Dad. Not imaginary confrontations. You might want to remember that."

Startled, he laughed. "Like father, like daughter, eh?"

"Well . . . I was afraid you'd leave if I didn't do something attention grabbing." A new geniality popped up between them, green and delicate. Perking up for the first time in days, Marisol gave him a wan smile. "You're not the only one who needs an excuse to get the conversation started sometimes."

As though her admission had loosened something between them, her father slid to the edge of his seat. He eyed her seriously. "A while ago, you asked me for start-up money for that home-furnishings boutique of yours. Remember?"

Marisol made a wry face. "I want my cocktail back."

"But I didn't think you were ready to own a business," he continued. "You'd never done anything serious before—"

"Hey, that mambo contest was no walk in the park!"

"—and your spending was out of control. Jamie was concerned too. There was only one way to find out if you were ready for the next stage of your life, and that was—"

"To stage an intervention and make me a *maid*?"

"—to throw you in the deep end of the pool and make you swim. That's why I sent you to Dzeel—with Jamie's help and your friends' too, I might add. And now I'm glad I did. I'm proud to say . . ." He hesitated, an unfamiliar expression on his face. "I'm proud to say, I'm proud of you, Marisol. I know the oniomania program wasn't easy for you."

"Come on, Dad. You couldn't even be bothered to call

me." Marisol couldn't hold the words back. "Two phone calls in three months? That's it. Did you ever stop to think that maybe I *needed* you? That maybe that's why I kept calling you? Or did Sophie not give you my messages?"

Her father stared at his shoes. "They told me not to call."

"Right." Marisol scoffed, hurt all over again. "That's a really easy out, isn't it? I don't exactly have Imelda Santos and that string bean Jeremy Fordham here to confirm that, do I?"

"Call them. Ask them."

She shook her head. "I don't even want to think about Arizona. Everything there is over with for me."

Whether she wanted it to be or not.

"Well, I met them all. I took the helicopter there for bi-weekly sessions." Her father lifted his gaze to hers. "I learned that I'm part of the problem, Marisol, and that's why I did what they told me to do. To make sure you got better."

Incredulous, she stared at him. "You were there?"

"Yes, and I'm sorry. I'm sorry for everything." He sighed, shaking his head. "The way you grew up, your mother, all the stepmothers you had . . . most of all, my inattention. I don't have any excuse except that I was a businessman who had no business being a single father."

Marisol didn't know what to say. Their problems went back a long way, but this . . . well, it felt a little like a fresh start.

"I didn't do a very good job," her father told her, his voice strengthening on the words, "but I always loved you, Marisol. Right from day one, when you looked at me and cried your bald baby head off from that hospital bassinet. I love you very much, and I always will."

"Oh Dad." Tearfully, Marisol shook her head. So he wasn't perfect. At least he was here. "I love you too."

They both stood, nearly colliding. They stepped closer, almost tangoing. With a gruff exhalation, her father embraced her around the shoulders; Marisol showed him how to give a proper squeezing hug, the kind she'd learned from the Connellys.

Sniffling, she stepped back. A tear trailed down her father's handsome, patrician face. Marisol thumbed it away.

"You look too good to be sixty-one," she said, hugging him again. "I suspect Botox. I hope you're getting a good deal."

"Of course I'm not. I'm a Winston. I always overpay."

They both laughed. With a much more relaxed atmosphere between them, they sat again—this time together on the sofa. Her father grimaced at her cocktail shaker, frowned at her party remnants and last night's robe, then sighed.

"Is this *really* what makes you happy?" he asked. "Going out, being seen in the papers, sleeping until noon?"

"Well, it's not that bad." Trying to keep their optimistic vibe going, Marisol shrugged. "And I've got to do something. Tenley has a job at a PR firm now, and Caprice just got a book deal to write an L.A. exposé." Incredibly, her gossipy friend had secretly been writing a much-read, tell-all society blog online, and had been scooped up by a publishing company. "So they're both pretty busy these days, but I . . ."

I miss Cash. And Jacob, and Hannah, and Emily.

A day didn't go by when she didn't think of them.

Of course, those remembrances always ended with Marisol recalling the abrupt way Cash had practically shoved her out the door, so that part kind of put a damper on the rosy glow.

"But . . . you're not ready to move on yet?" her father asked.

Marisol glanced at him. "From Cash? I will. Eventually."

Her dad shook his head, patting her knee in commiseration. "Don't worry. I've never been very good at love either."

"Until Jamie," Marisol reminded him.

"Of course. She's wonderful—more than I deserve."
Her father smiled, then his determined expression returned. "Do you want me to make Connelly suffer? Because I can do it, you know. I'll buy the Scorpions myself, bring him back on the team, then cut him all over again. Just say the word. I'll do it. Twice."

"Geez, you're really bloodthirsty, Dad."

"If somebody hurts my little girl, I am."

Aww, that was sweet. Twisted and goofy, but sweet.

"No, I don't want you to do anything to Cash. It's not his fault. I just . . . wasn't enough, that's all."

"Bullshit."

"Dad!"

"Well, it's the truth. If you can drink before noon, I can swear. The gloves are off." Her father smiled. "You're more than enough, Marisol. And if Cash can't see what a catch you are, then he doesn't deserve you."

Marisol sniffed. "Thanks, Dad. But I'm trying to move on here, you know? I've already had the bad haircut, the wild partying, and the girl talk with Jamie. All I need now is . . ."

Cash, her heart supplied.

"To be happy," her father announced. "And that's all I want for you too. I want you to be happy again. Tell me what I can do to make it happen, and I will. We Winstons don't mess around."

From out of the blue, it came to her.

"Loosen up my trust fund," Marisol said. "Give me the money for my boutique."

Dubiously, he examined her.

"Look, I know this ambition of mine came out of nowhere," Marisol admitted. "But I want to stay busy, and opening my dream boutique will keep me from wallowing in misery. And from getting more vodka stains on my coffee table too."

Her father sighed. "If you think it'll make you happy—"

"It will." *I hope.*

"Then I'll do it," he said.

They had another hug, then decided to head to the bank together.

Saturdays were the best days for Shoparama appearances. The grocery store was packed with shoppers, the managers were all on hand to make announcements, and nearly every aisle sported an end cap with a sample table of freebies. Standing beside his favorite one, Cash smiled at a middle-aged woman.

"Thanks for stopping by," he said. "Don't forget your coupon for new Alpine-Scented Tidy Wipes!"

"Whoops! You're right. I'm going to want that."

"Now with twenty percent more scrubbing power." Cash handed her a bright preprinted coupon, then winked. "It's Tidy-tastic."

The woman wiggled her fingers in a wave, then left.

Cash put his hands on his waist, looking for his next target. The feisty-looking senior choosing pork chops might be perfect. Experienced shoppers always wanted to save money.

"Miss? Have you tried new Alpine-Scented Tidy Wipes?" He fluttered his coupons enticingly. "They're Tidy-tastic."

Whack! Somebody smacked him.

A familiar voice came next. "What the hell are you doing?"

Frowning, Cash rubbed his shoulder. He turned and wanted to groan at the sight of Adam standing there, looking cranky.

The man would not leave him alone lately. He'd been underfoot ever since the Scorpions scrimmage had gone wrong.

Maybe Adam needed to get laid, Cash thought. He sure as hell was obsessed with *his* love life for some reason.

Now that it was over with. Now that Marisol had gone . . . Screw that. Cash jutted his chin defiantly.

"I'm working," he informed his erstwhile manager with a poke to the chest. "Which *you*, if you were doing your job, would already know about. I had to do all the leg-work for this damn appearance myself, just like the last two I did. You're not getting a cut of this, that's for sure."

Adam shook his head. "Keep your cut, dickhead. I told you, I'm not setting up any more personal appear-ances for you. Not until you get normal again."

"I am normal." Cash flagged down a passing customer, then handed over a coupon and sample. "Remember, it's Tidy-tastic!"

"Arrgh." Adam covered his eyes.

Waving good-bye to the customer, Cash offered up his most happy-go-lucky expression. "See? *I'm fine.*"

Looking aggravated, Adam snatched Cash's bundle of coupons. He grabbed his arm and hustled them both sideways toward a pyramid-shaped display of canned tuna, pinning Cash in the canned goods pocket like a blitz off the corner.

"You're not fine," Adam insisted, "and this is not normal. Handing out coupons for Tidy Wipes is not normal. Not for you. You hate personal appearances, remember?"

"That was the old Cash Connelly," Cash said breezily. He pointed down the aisle, peering past throngs of cus-tomers. "Hey, today's mini sausage patty day. Come on. Edna's all set up in aisle four with her electric skillet and those toothpicks—"

"Fuck the toothpicks! What's the matter with you?"

"Nothing." Cash gave him a steely-eyed stare. "So why don't you just leave me the hell alone? The season's in full swing. You must have real football players to deal with, right?"

Adam clenched his jaw. "Right."

"Then get out of here. You're screwing up the traffic flow." Cash reclaimed his coupons with a savage grab, then leaned sideways. "Ma'am? Here's a handy coupon."

"Ooh! Thank you, young man."

"My pleasure. They're Tidy-tastic!"

Adam turned purple. "Yes, I've got work to do," he said, jerking his head and nearly stepping on Cash's toes. "But those are just players. They're not my friends. They're not you."

"Wow." Cash rolled his eyes. "I always knew you were a candy ass, Sullivan. The Hallmark cards are in aisle seventeen. The Midol, in case you're feeling crampy, is in aisle twelve."

"Oh yeah?" Adam jabbed him in the chest. "Can you point me to the self-respect aisle, asshole? Because you need some."

"Oh yeah? Fuck you."

There was a gasp from a nearby table.

"Sorry, Agnes." Cash offered the detergent-sample lady an apologetic wave. "This guy brings out the worst in me."

"*You* bring out the worst in you." Adam shoved him. "Ever since Marisol left, you've been impossible to deal with."

Cash shrugged. "Like I said. Leave me alone."

Marisol definitely had.

A part of him had hoped she'd put up more of a fight. A stupid part of him, granted. But he'd still hoped. Was *still* hoping, some days. Which was why he had to stay busy.

"You should call her," Adam said. "Talk to her. Straighten this whole thing out. I know she lost the kids during the scrimmage fiasco, but we found them again. They were fine. No harm, no foul, right?"

"Yeah. It's not about that."

"What is it about then? Enlighten me."

Mulishly, Cash shut his mouth. Adam stared at him. For a moment, the only sounds were squeaky shopping carts, an announcement of a special on tomato sauce, and the usual Shoparama Muzak. Then his manager spoke up again.

"You can feel sorry for yourself all you want, pal. She wouldn't have left if you hadn't made her go."

Feeling agonized, Cash scowled at the tuna cans.

Here it came again. The recriminations. The I-told-you-sos. The browbeating. He felt bad enough without his so-called friend pestering him every damn minute.

"Look, I did what I had to do, all right?" Cash fisted his hand. "It was for her own good."

"Hmmm. How do you figure that?"

He couldn't believe Adam didn't know. "Your smart-ass routine is really getting on my nerves, you know that? Just get out of here." He shouldered past him. "I've got coupons to give out. I promised Eunice I'd help her get rid of these."

Adam stopped him with a hard stare. "You loved her."

"It didn't work out."

"She loved you. I know it."

"That wasn't enough." *He* wasn't enough. Especially now. Without football, what did he have to offer? He'd used part of his signing bonus for a down payment on a fixer-upper house in a good neighborhood—a place where Jacob, Emily, and Hannah liked visiting. Other than that . . . it was Shoparama appearances and selling his old gear for cash on eBay. "It's over."

"No." With annoying certainty, Adam followed, ducking beneath a CASH CONNELLY APPEARANCE TODAY! banner to stand beside Cash's autographing table. "It doesn't have to be over."

Cash stopped. "Yes, it does. Hell, look at me. *I'm* over." Trying to laugh, he shook his head at the stack of glossy publicity photos awaiting his indecipherable autograph. "By this time next week, I'll be demoing floor wax."

A fresh crowd of people approached his table, including two excited college girls and their beefy frat-house boyfriends. Cash shook hands, smiled for photos, then waved them off with autographed replica jerseys—and Tidy Wipes coupons too.

"Thanks, Cash!" Eunice waved from two aisles over, giving him a geriatric wink and a thumbs-up sign. "You're a natural."

"No problem, Eunice!"

Adam stepped in. "I've got offers lined up for you," he said urgently. "People have been calling. The Chargers can use someone. The Ravens too. Plenty of teams are still rejiggering their lineups, filling in for injured players and—"

"Not interested. Football's over with for me."

Adam looked incensed. "Really? Nice of you to fill me in. So I've been working my ass off for . . . what, exactly?"

"Look, I'm sorry." Cash squeezed Adam's shoulder. "Getting back in was a mistake. It just took me awhile to realize it."

Marisol had known it though. *Once you're playing professionally again, won't you be unhappy being away from the kids so much?* she'd asked him that night over s'mores and firelight. And she'd been right. He would have been.

He didn't know why he hadn't seen it before.

"You always said I was a stubborn son of a bitch, right? I guess you had it nailed." Grinning, Cash broke off and signed another autograph. "I'll come up with something else," he said afterward. "In the meantime, pass out some of these coupons."

He pushed a handful toward Adam.

The whole lot of them fell to the floor instead.

What the f . . . ?

"Do it yourself." Adam dropped a wrapped package on the autographing table, obscuring several eight-by-ten versions of Cash's smiling face. "I just came by to give you this. And maybe talk some sense into you, but I can see that's pointless."

Cash turned over the package, its plastic wrapping crinkling beneath his hands. Through it, he glimpsed his former team colors. Several lumpy objects. And the number seven.

"It's from Marisol," Adam said. "She didn't have your new address, but she wanted to make sure you got that. It's all the stuff she borrowed from Dozer's attic, dry-cleaned and packed."

Barely listening, Cash reached past a pair of pom-poms and a Scorpions baseball cap and pulled out the jersey. He held it up, some strange emotion making his hands clench on the fabric.

It didn't smell like her. It didn't look quite like her (since it wasn't white, skimpy, or sexy), and it sure as hell wasn't as soft as her. But Cash hugged it to his chest anyway.

For an instant, everything else faded.

He'd be damned if Dozer was getting this particular jersey back for his collection. Cash would replace it himself, if he had to. He glanced up. "Hey, thanks, Adam. This is—"

But his manager was already gone.

Cash fisted the jersey, missing Marisol intensely.

But hell . . . If even Adam had given up on him, what chance did he have to set things right? Resigned, Cash folded the jersey and stuffed it back in the package.

"Miss, have you tried new Alpine-Scented Tidy Wipes?" he asked the next woman passing by. "They're Tidy-tastic!"

She shook her head and kept going.

Damn. All his mojo had deserted him.

What was he supposed to do now?

Chapter 31

Marisol stepped into a vacant retail space near La Cienega Boulevard, followed by her real-estate agent and her father, who'd taken the day off to help her assess the latest contender for her dream boutique. She stopped in the middle of the all-white sales floor, squinting at the street-side windows.

"The light is quite good in here," she said.

"It's a southern exposure." Her real-estate agent strode toward the plate glass with a practiced smile. "Very nice for creating an upbeat atmosphere for your customers."

"That's true. Although such strong sunlight might fade the fabrics on the upholstered pieces." Frowning slightly, Marisol took a few paces toward the rear wall. She ran her hand along the chilly surface of the sales counter there. "Is this removable? I'd really prefer a more intimate sales area—maybe a desk. I have a very nice French provincial piece in mind."

Her real-estate agent's smile turned a little grittier. "I'm sure everything is adaptable. You're in luck with this space—the owner is in a hurry to lease it again."

She offered an overview of the leasing terms.

Marisol wandered farther, her footsteps echoing in

the emptiness. "I don't know . . . I can't quite picture myself here."

"It'll look different when it's been retrofitted." Her father glanced at her real-estate agent. "I have all the contacts you need to help you make this your perfect shop."

"I know, Dad. It's just . . ." Marisol hugged herself, feeling both of them staring at her curiously—and not a little bit impatiently. "The walls look crooked to me. And it's too sunny."

It was so sunny, it almost made her want to cry.

"Too sunny?" her real-estate agent repeated. "I thought you just said you liked the sunlight. Really, Miss Winston, we've been over this. If you're not sure what you want, then please stop wasting my time. I'm one of the best agents in the city."

Her father held up his hand for quiet.

Patiently, he followed Marisol, then slung his arm around her shoulders. He gave a jovial squeeze. "The walls are fine. And you like sunlight! Your place in Malibu is bathed in the stuff. You could get a tan in your living room."

"I know . . ." Helplessly, Marisol gestured. "It's different."

"Don't be nervous," her father said. "We've looked at over fourteen retail spaces now. One of them must be close at least."

Pressing her lips together, Marisol took another look around. He must be right. Maybe she was being too picky. The space didn't have to knock her socks off. It just had to work. *She* just had to work. She was going crazy thinking about Cash.

"What's back there?" she asked, pointing toward a closed door painted in the same blank white. "Back-office space?"

She raised her chin and headed that way. She'd never

realized exactly how *bare* white seemed. Here, with nothing but icy white all around her, she felt its starkness strongly.

"What this place really needs is a few little handprints, right about here." Marisol nodded at the doorknob. "And maybe a grape-jelly stain over there. With some dog slobber on the floor, just to make things seem homey and approachable."

Her father and her real-estate agent looked appalled.

"Kidding! Sheesh." Briskly, she opened the office door.

Four people were already standing inside.

"Surprise!" Jamie came forward with her arms wide.

Marisol stopped, staring in astonishment at Jamie, Caprice, and Tenley. "What are you doing here?" She spotted the lone man in the group and pointed at him. "*Adam?* Is that you?"

"Guilty as charged." He smiled at her, coming close for a hug. "Hey, Marisol. I hope you don't mind. I was in town on my way to meet with a 49ers player and decided to stop by."

"Really? But the 49ers play in San Francisco, Adam."

Everyone gawked at her, particularly her dad. Adam grinned more widely, as though her blooper were adorable somehow.

"So I learned a little football," she grumbled. "Shoot me."

"Okay, well, first of all, we're glad you're here." Jamie put her palms together with a serene, yogic gesture, her bracelets jangling. "And second of all . . . please don't be mad."

"Mad? Why would I be mad? What's going on?"

Trying to get her bearings, Marisol looked for her dad and her real-estate agent—both of whom were blocking the exit with their arms crossed over their chests, Mafioso-style. Hmmm.

Something about this setup seemed strangely familiar . . .

"Don't even think about leaving," her father said.

"We've been patient with you long enough. Now we're having our say."

"Yeah," Tenley said. "We want to help you."

"You have a problem," Caprice added. Everyone nodded.

"A serious problem." This, from Jamie. "And we're here to help you face it. To help you get off your butt, go out there, and wrestle true love to the ground, once and for all."

Get off her butt? That was laying things on the line.

Marisol blinked. "This is a *love intervention*?"

They nodded solemnly. That was all she needed.

"You guys are the nosiest bunch of —" Marisol broke off, looked at them closely, then closed her eyes. They were right, and she knew it. Things had gone on long enough. "All right, I'm listening." She sucked in a deep breath. "Let me have it."

Even his ex-wife wouldn't get off Cash's back.

Stephanie ambushed him when he arrived to pick up the kids for their weekend visit—a tradition whose boundaries had loosened somewhat, thanks to some inexplicable softening on Stephanie's part. She opened the door to greet him, backed him into the corner of the porch, then let him have it.

"Hey, how's your love life?" she demanded.

"Fantastic," Cash shot back, lying his ass off. "Is that an invitation, or are you just feeling nostalgic today?"

"Same old Cash." Her gaze softened as she shook her head. "Our love life was never our problem, and you know it."

"Yeah. Now that we've skipped down memory lane together, are the kids ready? I've got to hit the road." He hooked his thumb toward his parked Range Rover. "Traffic's bad today."

"I mean it." Giving him a measured look, his ex-wife leaned against the overly ornate porch pillar, effectively penning him in. "What's going on? I thought you really liked Marisol."

Cash stared down his former street. Silently.

"Boy, you're more broken up than I thought. Not shaving is bad enough"—she nodded at his stubbled jawline—"but going all strong-and-silent macho man with me? You mean business."

He looked at her. "Why do you care?"

"The kids like Marisol. They've been talking about her for weeks." She shrugged. "And I wouldn't mind seeing you happy."

"Right." That's why she'd divorced—and nearly bankrupted—him two years ago. Cash gave her a skeptical look.

"It's true, Cash. I'm not evil—I'm just me."

"Yeah, well . . . I'm just me too."

"And Marisol didn't like that?"

"Marisol liking me wasn't the problem, believe me." Cash couldn't help but grin. They'd *really* liked one another. He hesitated, then—for better or worse—found himself sucked in by his ex-wife's commiserating expression. He shrugged. "I'm just not cut out for this stuff, I guess."

"What, the way you weren't cut out to take care of the kids when they were babies?" Not unkindly, Stephanie shook her head at him. "You're the only one who thought that, Cash. You weren't instantly an expert at it, so you checked out. Period."

That was bullshit. "I didn't take care of them more because you criticized everything I did. And because I had to make a living playing football. It's not the same thing."

"Yes, it is. And now you're pushing away Marisol because you think there's something wrong with you"—his ex-wife jabbed him in the chest, flashing an engagement ring he hadn't noticed before—"the same way you did to me. You think you can't handle a relationship, so you're bailing out. Don't make the same mistake twice, Cash. You've got another shot here. You should take it." Her expression lightened. "Adam says she's cute too."

Jesus. Next Tyrell would be offering him freaking love-making advice. Cash couldn't stand it. He leaned sideways and bellowed into the house. "Kids? Daddy's here. Let's go!"

They barreled out, hollering past their mother with backpacks and blankies. Cash dropped to his knees, then pulled Emily, Jacob, and Hannah close for the best hug of the week.

Right now, this was all he lived for.

And if he never discussed relationships with his ex-wife again, it would be too soon.

Marisol sat on an industrial-size ten-gallon bucket of white paint, arms and legs crossed, surrounded by people who wanted to badger her to death. Why had she agreed to this again?

Even Jamie—sweet, lovable, yoga-practicing Jamie—had turned into some kind of mad-dog love advocate. Her stepmother paced across the room, brainstorming while dodging the rest of the love intervention crew, then came to stand in front of Marisol.

"Did you insist on staying and fighting?" she asked. "You know you have a tendency to give up too easily sometimes."

"No. I told you, Cash was practically shoving me out the door!" Marisol said. "I couldn't leave fast enough for him."

"So? Maybe his feelings were hurt. Maybe he was having a bad day." Her stepmother gave her a serious look. "Maybe he was still dealing with having his entire career ended, and he wasn't thinking straight. It happens."

In her peripheral vision, Adam nodded somberly.

"Not to Cash," Marisol insisted. "He's strong."

"Aww, honey." Jamie shook her head. "The strong ones need help the most. They're the ones who can't bear to ask for it."

"That's right." Her father jumped in, nodding vigorously. "He's probably not superhuman, you know."

"Yeah. Swizzle dizzle or not," Caprice said, "he's just a man, right? Cash is fallible like the rest of us."

"I know, but . . . come on, you guys." Marisol put on a brave face. "I have to face facts. I just wasn't enough for him. That's all. Otherwise, he would have wanted me to stay."

"Did Cash *say* that?" Tenley asked, hands on her hips. "Did he actually *say* you weren't enough for him?"

"Yeah, did he?" Caprice prodded.

Her father and stepmother arched their eyebrows, looking fully prepared to ruin Cash Connelly for good if he had.

Caught in the midst of their haranguing, Marisol swiveled on her paint bucket. If she took this space, the first thing she planned to do was paint it something besides white.

"Well . . . no. He thinks it's all his fault," she said.

"See?" Jamie said. "Maybe *you're* the only one who thinks you might not be enough for him. None of us feels that way, that's for sure. We think you're wonderful."

Everyone nodded, especially her dad.

"Have you considered that maybe Cash thinks he's not enough for *you*?" Her real-estate agent stepped forward, catching Adam's eye. They smiled at each other. "Men can be sensitive. Maybe he needs *you* to be strong and show him he's wrong."

"Hey, you haven't even *met* him!" Marisol said.

A shrug. "I know, but I've been single a long time. I've known a lot of men." She sidled closer to Adam. "Have we met?"

"Arrgh." Marisol stared up at the lot of them, even as

her real-estate agent and Cash's manager had a private tête-à-tête in the corner. "I know you all mean well. I honestly do. But how can this really help? I mean, say you're right. Say *I'm* afraid I'm not enough for Cash, and *he's* afraid he's not enough for me, and that's why things didn't work out. But what then? Knowing what happened doesn't change the fact that we're apart now."

"And that you're miserable," Adam said. "I can't speak for you, Marisol, because you look great. But Cash is a broken man."

He told them something about coupons and Tidy-tastic.

Her father spoke up. "That's nothing. Marisol has water rings on her Le Corbusier coffee table, I've seen them myself."

There were gasps all around. Caprice even looked teary.

"It's not that big a deal," Marisol grumbled.

"On our way in here, Marisol suggested dog slobber as a décor item," her real-estate agent added, nodding.

Her family and friends practically whimpered with concern. They all stepped forward, patting her back and offering hugs.

"Look, you guys. Stop it. Just stop it!" Marisol stood in the center of the circle, defiantly holding out her arms. "I don't need pity! I'm perfectly capable of handling this myself. If there's one thing I learned at Dzeel—and at the Connellys' house—it's that I'm more competent than I realized. Okay?"

They all stepped back, murmuring to each other.

"Okay," Jamie said. "I agree. And it sounds as if you've made a decision too."

"Yes, I have." Marisol nodded. She pulled her handbag closer, then shook out her hair. "I'm leasing this space. I want the paperwork finished as soon as possible. Dad, I'll need referrals to a few contractors for the interior work too. Tenley, I want you to handle the PR, and Caprice, if you could mention my boutique in your blog sometime, that would be great."

"Consider it done," her friend promised.

"Good." Marisol studied them all, eyed the paint bucket, then raised her chin. "I'm also painting the whole place pink."

Then she headed out, ready to get started.

"Are you absolutely sure this is what you want?" Cash asked. "A monster-truck tea party is pretty unique."

His children, assembled around his old kitchen table in his messy new kitchen, nodded in unison. Even Dump wagged his tail.

"It's the coolest idea ever," Jacob said. "I like it."

"As long as there are big, fancy hats too," Hannah said.

"It's what we really want," Emily confirmed, coming into the kitchen with a multicolored bundle tucked beneath her arm. "And because you're the best, smartest, most wonderful dad ever, we know you'll make it happen perfectly!"

Dubiously, Cash examined them. Usually Stephanie planned the birthday parties, but somehow he'd been drafted this year.

"Okay. Then we'd better get started on the invitations."

Hannah went to collect supplies. Cash grabbed the blank invitation cardstock and envelopes he'd bought—Stephanie's one concession to spilling her party-planning secrets—and put them on the counter. When he turned around again, Jacob was there.

"Here, Dad." He handed him a familiar, plastic-wrapped package. "You'd better move this off the table."

Cash found himself holding the jersey and Scorpions gear Marisol had sent. Ever since he'd brought it home, it had been all he could do not to sleep with the damn stuff. But he didn't want to weaken in front of the kids. Gruffly, he set it aside.

A piece of paper fluttered out.

Jacob caught it. "Look, there's a note."

"I'll take it." Carefully, Cash unfolded the paper.

Cash, I hope you can get all these things back to Dozer. Thanks for my favorite summer ever. Marisol's handwriting was steady and expansive, with lots of loops. Seeing it again made him smile. *I'm sorry about the way things ended. You forgive everyone else so easily. How about trying to forgive yourself?*

He glanced up, momentarily struck by Marisol's uncanny ability to recognize—and accept—things about other people.

She'd understood Emily, Jacob, and Hannah almost instantly. She'd charmed his hard-boiled mother-in-law, Leslie, on sight. She'd made Adam her own personal fan club. She'd made Cash fall in love, despite all his efforts not to.

And all because she was so giving. So understanding. So willing to look past flaws and embrace people as they were.

He guessed that was what came of having the best of everything. Or maybe just of having enough *dzeel.*

Take care of yourself, Cash. Don't eat too many s'mores! the note concluded. *Love always, Marisol.*

"What's that, Daddy?" Emily gave a curious peek.

"Nothing." He shoved the paper in his pocket. "A note from Marisol about this stuff she returned." He shook himself, determined to ignore his daughter's suddenly wide-eyed look and get back to the job at hand. "Nothing important."

"Did she ask about our birthday party?" Hannah trotted in, carrying a whole armful of crayons, markers, glue, ribbons, shiny stickers, and glitter. "Because I've got everything ready to make a really super special invitation for her!"

Cash's heart sank. He hadn't counted on this at all.

"You want to invite Marisol?" he asked.

"Of course." Cheerfully, Emily fluffed out the multi-colored thing she'd brought. It billowed in the air, then settled.

Cash stared at her impromptu tablecloth. Artistic blobs of finger paint stared back at him, daring Cash not to remember Marisol and the kids painting his shower curtain—*this* shower curtain—with their Jackson Pollock-esque design.

"Where did you get that?" he blurted.

"From the cabin." Smiling, Emily smoothed it in place. "Don't be silly, Daddy. You're the one who packed it."

"Yeah." Looking absorbed, Jacob spread out the blank invitations, then snagged a crayon. "You said we couldn't ever leave it behind. You said you'd buy a new one for Dozer."

"Besides, we can't reach high enough to take down a shower curtain." Hannah chuckled as though the idea were ridiculous, then snatched some glue and glitter. "We'll do the decorating, Daddy. You do the writing. Let's do Marisol's invitation first."

He gazed at them, nonplussed. He didn't remember packing that shower curtain, but then he'd been pretty wrecked when they'd left Dozer's place that day.

"It'll be *so* great when Marisol gets here." With her tongue sticking out, Hannah squirted on a glue border. "I can't wait."

The other two nodded. Frowning, Cash stood nearby. He'd hoped they'd let this idea drop. But since they hadn't . . .

"I'm sorry, you guys, but Marisol isn't coming."

He waited for the inevitable explosion.

Nada.

"You'll feel better when Marisol gets here." Nonchalantly, Emily passed the glitter to Hannah, then picked up a pack of Wonder Woman stickers. She started sticking them on. "You were lots happier when she was around, Daddy."

Jacob and Hannah nodded, still drawing and gluing.

"Marisol is all the way in Los Angeles now," Cash said. "She isn't coming to your birthday party."

"Hey, maybe we can make invitations for your wedding too!" Jacob glanced up, his little face bright. "It'll be so cool!"

They weren't even listening. Man, his children were obstinate. Cash strode closer.

"Marisol and I aren't getting married," he said in his most patient voice. "Marisol isn't coming to your birthday party."

The only sounds were markers scratching and glue squirting.

"But she promised she was coming," Hannah said.

"We even told her the day," Jacob added, drawing smilies. Neither of them seemed the least bit worried.

"I wouldn't be surprised if Marisol came first!" Emily sprinkled on more glitter. "Plus, I think your bed here is bigger than your sleeping bag, so you guys can share again!"

He wished. "Marisol isn't spending the night here," Cash said firmly. "Marisol isn't coming back. Ever."

The words hurt. So did seeing his children's faces when his statement finally sunk in. They looked crestfallen.

"Well, she probably wouldn't mind staying at a hotel, I guess," Jacob said finally. "Especially if it's like the one Grandma goes to, with a swimming pool."

Emily and Hannah nodded, going back to work.

Damn. They were even more stubborn than he was.

A few minutes later, the three of them happily pushed their creation toward him. Based on white invitation cardstock, it reeked of scented markers and sparkled with gobs

of glitter. It was covered with crayoned flowers and hearts
and stars and smiley faces, each squiggly decoration
drawn with painstaking six-year-old care. In the center was
a blank spot—left free for writing the invitation details,
Cash assumed—directly above a childish drawing of five
hand-holding stick-figure people.

"That's us and you and Marisol." Hannah pointed to
their smiling faces. "Go ahead. Time for your part,
Daddy."

"Yeah, write the invitation," Jacob instructed.

"Spell it right and use good handwriting," Emily
added. "Not like you do when you sign an autograph
on someone's shirt."

Duly chastened, Cash looked down at Marisol's invitation. One of his children shoved a magic marker in his
hand. All three of them watched him expectantly.

You were happier when Marisol was around. The words
boomeranged around in his head, making him feel weird.

What the hell. It couldn't hurt to see Marisol for a
single afternoon, right? It didn't have to be a big deal.

He printed a few lines. Added a few details, double-
checked the date and time on the family wall calendar, re-
considered the whole damn thing, then wiped his brow.

"Don't be scared." Hannah crowded closer, peering
over his shoulder. So did Jacob and Emily, their faces
rapt. "I worry about my printing too, but yours looks
pretty good, Daddy."

"I think she'll like it," Emily announced.

"Maybe enough to try some more kissing with you,"
Jacob said eagerly. "You know, lock lips and play tonsil
hockey."

They all gaped at him.

"Hey, I didn't say I was going to do it!" Eyes wide,
Jacob held up his arms in horror. "Getting lovey-dovey
with Marisol is Dad's job!"

Emily and Hannah nodded thoughtfully, agreeing.

Cash only shook his head. He'd say one thing about his children—they never gave up.

This time, maybe he wouldn't either.

Maybe. If he could only bring himself to mail that invitation. He addressed an envelope, copying the information from the package Marisol had sent before he could talk himself out of it. Carefully—so as not to knock off all the glitter blobs—Cash slid the special invitation inside.

Then, frowning, he set it aside until later. He made a joke for the kids and got started on the next invitation.

Chapter 32

The kids' birthday arrived on a sunny Saturday afternoon, bringing with it over two dozen manic five-, six-, and seven-year-olds, a handful of friends, relatives, and neighbors, bundles of balloons and streamers, an inflatable Jupiter Jump in the backyard, and one seriously overdue clown.

On the lookout for tardy Bozo, Cash pushed a HAPPY BIRTHDAY banner out of his way, then navigated through his packed house. He wouldn't have believed so many people could fit inside its relatively modest layout, but everyone seemed to be having a good time, talking and eating snacks and drinking punch.

At the table, several kids—including Hannah and Emily—sipped tea from an elaborate play set, all of them wearing huge flower-covered hats. In the living room, Jacob knelt with a pack of his buddies, making *vroom vroom* noises as he staged a pint-size monster-truck rally. In between, party games were set up at stations throughout the house, with adult helpers to supervise each one. Outside, for those kids who didn't want to bounce themselves silly, there were games of catch with a pair of Nerf footballs, and there was a piñata for later too.

With a wave for his kids, Cash checked his watch. Adam should be here with the birthday cake soon, and

Stephanie and Tyrell were due any minute too. Where was the clown, damn it?

He peered out the window. No floppy shoes. No rubber nose.

No clown. Emily, Jacob, and Hannah would probably survive without corny jokes and balloon animals, but Cash wanted them to have everything they'd asked for this year. It wasn't every day a kid turned seven years old. It wasn't every day their dad planned a party—his first-ever attempt at doing so.

"Hey there, hotshot. Nice shindig."

He turned. Leslie stood there, resplendent in the biggest possible flower-covered hat, holding a mini monster truck.

"What's up with you?" she asked, adjusting her hat with a backward glance at the girls. "All that pacing and checking your watch. You're making *me* nervous, you're so nervous."

"I'm fine," Cash said.

His mother-in-law made a face. He realized he was doing it again—shutting people out, the same way he'd done with Marisol.

"The clown I hired is a no-show," he admitted. "I don't want the kids to be disappointed."

"Aww, they won't be. Just look at them!"

They did look pretty happy, Cash had to admit. Still . . .

"Look everyone! The cake's here!"

"Yay! Cake, cake, cake!"

Adam made his way between the cheering partygoers, wielding a gigantic rectangular bakery box. For possibly the first time ever, Hannah, Jacob, and Emily had agreed on the same cake flavor—chocolate with sprinkles—so Cash had been able to order one large sheet cake. Relieved, he went to meet his manager.

They settled the box between them in the kitchen.

Leslie and the kids gathered around, eagerly awaiting the unveiling.

Cash lifted the bakery box lid. Sugary, chocolaty smells wafted out. Nestled on a lacy liner inside, expertly decorated with a variety of colored icings, lay the cake. The big, long, insanely lifelike cake, with a massive shaft and two round—

"It's a schlong!" Leslie burst out.

They all stared. Adam recovered first and slammed the lid.

"Somewhere across town right now," he said, "there are a dozen *really* disappointed bachelorette partygoers."

Cash bit back a swearword. "You got the wrong cake."

Emily and Hannah pushed nearer. "We want to see!"

"What's a schlong?" Jacob asked.

Leslie took another peek at the cake, then tittered. "I really think the bow on top is overkill."

Ding, dong. The doorbell saved the day.

"We'll have cake in a few minutes, you guys." Cash hustled to the door, praying for a grease-painted, Bozo-style miracle. "In the meantime, who wants to see a clown?"

"I do! I do!" came several excited shouts.

Kids lined up, pushing toward the living room with Jacob at the lead. Vowing never to rehire this guy, Cash opened the door.

The brightly painted, unshaven, and more than a little unsteady clown on the other side tipped his teeny-tiny cartoon-style hat. He hiccupped. "Toodles the Clown, at your service."

He held up his bag of tricks. A few uninflated balloons dropped to the floor, bouncing off his floppy shoes, along with a rubber duck. He bent over, whacked Cash in the midsection, straightened awkwardly, then gave a bright beaming smile.

"Hey, Toodles. Glad you could make it." Cash grabbed

the clown's polka dot bowtie, dragging their faces together. "You reek of tequila, pal. What's the matter with you?"

"No worries. That's because of the bridal shower I appeared at before this." Tottering, Toodles gave an exaggerated wink. "In my spare time, I'm also Officer Toodles. I arrest naughty bridesmaids for body shots infractions. Sometimes they share."

"I didn't hire a drunk clown."

"I'm not drunk!" In his defense, Toodles held up both palms. "I didn't have time to shower and shave, that's all. And I may have had one or two *itsy-bitsy* shots, but that's—"

"Daddy, is that the clown? I want a seahorse!" Emily said.

"I want a poodle, please!" Hannah called.

Other kids started shouting out balloon animal requests. From just beneath Cash's elbow, Jacob spoke up. "I want cake."

Oh yeah. The cake. Shit. He still had to deal with the pornographic birthday cake. Cash let go of the clown, then patted down his silly striped shirt in apology.

"Watch yourself," he said. "I have a cake to deal with."

"You go, Betty Crocker!" The clown waved, then reached for his sack of balloons as he came all the way inside. Jovially, he settled in the middle of the clamoring kids. "Who's first?"

Cash stomped into the kitchen, wanting to pull out his hair. Tipsy stripper Bozo was in the living room making balloon animals, kids were overrunning his house, and he had to find a way to serve a penis cake to a bunch of grade schoolers.

"Sorry about the cake." Adam stared at it, looking perplexed. "There must have been a mix-up at the bakery."

"It's fine. It's over with now. We just have to find ourselves another cake." Cash glanced at Leslie. "Hey . . ."

"Don't look at me." His mother-in-law shook her head. "I use my oven to store extra gardening pots in."

Cash looked at Adam. "You'll have to get another cake."

"Hang on. I've been studying this cake, and I think we can make it work." His manager opened a drawer, then pulled out a knife, two spoons, and a pancake turner. "Here, hold this."

Cash balked. "What are you going to do?"

"Settle down, nervous Nellie. I'm just going to perform a little home surgery on this cake." Adam hunkered down.

Kids clamored in the background. Several jumped in and out of sight in the bouncy tent. A few feet away, Toodles got increasingly boisterous. "Look! It's an octopus!" he said.

Cash groaned, sticking his head around the kitchen corner to supervise. He paced a few steps each way. He sighed.

Silence fell. Adam and Leslie gawked at him.

"Geez Louise, you *are* a wreck." His mother-in-law gazed at him curiously. "What's the matter now?"

"Yeah. I've almost got this cake patched up. Just a few more tweaks." Deftly, Adam held one frosting-covered mound between two spoons. "What's going on with you?"

Mulishly, Cash shut his mouth. He checked his watch.

Adam and Leslie exchanged glances. They crossed their arms.

Seeing their expectant stares, Cash finally caved. "Fine. I invited Marisol to the party. She probably won't come anyway, but the kids made this extra-special invitation, and I'm—"

"Oh, Cash! That's great!" Leslie crushed him in a hug, cutting off everything else he'd been about to say.

"Finally!" Wearing a broad grin, Adam put down his cake and spoons. He shook his head in amazement. "I wondered how long it would take you and your thick head to come around, jackass."

"Nice. That's touching," Cash said. He was an idiot for confiding in them. None of it would matter if Marisol didn't make it. He endured another hug from Leslie, then some especially aggravating high-fives from Adam. "Quit dancing around the kitchen and fix that damn cake, you knucklehead."

His manager sobered. "I'm on the job. Here we go."

Wielding the knife, Adam sliced the twin mounds into quarters (a move that made both him and Cash wince), then rearranged the resulting pieces along either side of the shaft. He smeared around the icing, covered the whole cake generously in multicolored sprinkles, then added a pair of M&Ms at the top.

"Voilà!" He stepped back, offering a view.

Cash frowned, assessing the job.

So did Leslie. "You made a fuzzy worm with feet?"

"It's a caterpillar! It's cute!"

"It's good enough." Cash poked in some candles, grabbed the whole thing, then carried it to the kitchen table. "Let's get the birthday kids over here. It's cake time, everybody!"

It took Marisol a good six minutes to work up the courage to get out of her rental car. First she parked on a Phoenix street and double-checked the directions she'd looked up. Next she stared at Cash's front porch and reminded herself how important this was. Then she yanked the keys from the ignition and made sure her fab boots and favorite lip gloss were in place to give her courage. Finally, she . . . just . . . chickened out.

There was no doubt this was the house. Several cars parked at the curb. Crepe-paper streamers twisted along the porch posts. A bunch of balloons floated above the strings tied to the mailbox. Dump even snoozed at the edge of the yard, and the sounds of revelry and kids' music drifted from the open windows.

Straining for a glimpse of Cash, Marisol spotted only children and other partygoers. Her heart pounded and her hands shook as she made herself open the car door and gather the things she'd brought. She wasn't at all sure she'd be welcome here. Cash might toss her out like yesterday's tabloids.

But she'd come all this way—cheered on by Jamie and her dad and Caprice and Tenley (and her real-estate agent)—and somehow she had to find the *dzeel* to carry on. If she didn't give this a try, she'd wonder forever how things might have turned out . . . if only she'd been a little braver. She simply had to do it.

Maybe he needs you to be strong and show him he's wrong, she remembered, and the words finally prodded her into getting out of the car. The Marisol Winston who'd bailed out of handbag-resistance therapy might not have done it, but she'd learned a lot since then. So the Marisol Winston who'd actually taken a commercial flight to get here today? She tried harder.

Traipsing up the front walk was scarier than she'd expected. Actually ringing the doorbell nearly gave her heart palpitations. By the time a kindly elderly woman let her in, Marisol was entertaining serious thoughts of coming back with a set of much grander gifts—say, a gold-plated Tonka truck for Jacob and two real diamond tiaras for Hannah and Emily.

Instead, all she had were the very simple things she'd brought . . . and herself. Nervously, she stepped inside.

The kids spotted her first, even in the birthday mêlée. Emily and Hannah perked up and shoved their way through the crowd. Jacob grinned and tossed down his monster truck, then made his tousle-headed way across the room to greet her too.

It was *so* good to see them again. Not caring what anyone thought, Marisol dropped everything she'd brought as though it were nothing. She opened her arms wide, then fell to her knees.

She wound up at perfect kid height. Jacob, Hannah, and Emily crashed into her, shouting hellos and squeezing her hard.

"Hold on, you're toppling me over!" Marisol cried, but she couldn't bring herself to move an inch. Instead she only hugged them all closer, burying her face in their dark, shampoo-scented hair and inhaling the fragrances of crayons and Play-Doh and something sweet— probably birthday cake. "Happy birthday!"

"You came, you came. You really came!" Emily said.

"Of course I came!"

Marisol couldn't tell them how hard it had been. How much she was risking just by being here. Her heart still felt fragile, and so did her new sense of strength. But as Bjorn always told her when they trained together in Malibu, the only way to get stronger was to work at it. So here she was.

"*I* knew you would come," Hannah said. "I told everybody."

"Are you staying in a hotel with a swimming pool?" Jacob leaned back, peering into her face earnestly. "Because that's the best kind. That's where my grandma always stays."

"Do you like swimming pools?" Marisol asked. "I don't think I told you this before, but I have a great, big, deluxe infinity pool at my beach house in Malibu. You should—"

They tilted their heads. She caught them gazing strangely at her, and realized she was doing it again— trying to make people like her because of what she could give them, not because of who she was. Just the same way she'd always done.

"Never mind." Marisol offered another squeezing hug. "I'm so happy to see you three again, I can't stop smiling!"

They all started talking amid the hubbub of the party, with Hannah and Emily taking her by the hand to show her around. Jacob patted her arm every few minutes as if to reassure himself she was really there, and Marisol wanted to pinch herself to affirm the same thing. She really was here. Where she belonged.

Intensely curious, she looked around at the small, cozy house. She didn't see any trace of Cash. Come to think of it, she didn't spot Adam or Leslie or anyone else she recognized here either. That was weird. Feeling let down, Marisol steeled herself to ask the one question she'd delayed.

"So . . ." *Keep it casual.* "Where's your dad?"

Jacob, Hannah, and Emily exchanged knowing glances.

"He had to call a cab for Toodles," Hannah said. "He's a clown, and funny too, but he fell asleep in the birthday cake."

"Dad got mad. Like this." Jacob clenched his teeth.

Emily nodded. "There was cake *everywhere.* Adam yelled. And Grandma made Daddy take Toodles out through the backyard, so we wouldn't hear the swearing while he waited for the taxi driver."

"That's very smart of him." Smiling, Marisol craned her neck, trying to see past the kitchen table through the patio doors to the backyard. "Has he been gone long?"

Jacob shrugged. "Since right before you got here."

They must have just missed each other. If that was a sign, then she probably shouldn't even be here . . .

No. She wasn't giving up that easily. Broadening her smile, Marisol grabbed her things. "Well, until your dad comes back, I have a few birthday presents someplace in here."

"Ooh, yippee!" Hannah rubbed her hands. "Presents."

"Yay, birthdays!" Emily scooted closer. "You're the best."

"I hope they're good," Jacob said. "What'd you bring?"

Apparently polite demurrals were passé among seven-year-olds. They were all about the goodies—a tough crowd for her.

"Well, they're not that fancy," Marisol said as she handed out each hand-wrapped package, "but I picked them all by myself, and I wrapped them too. I really hope you like them."

With her heart in her throat, she watched as they yanked off the ribbon and ripped off the paper. The bows weren't artistic, and the corners weren't square, but they'd been the best Marisol could do without her professional gift-wrapping staff on hand. She'd given them all bonuses and sent them on their way, determined to shape her new life around really giving, not just impressing people.

"Wow! This is so neat!" Emily held up handfuls of lipsticks—professional brands Marisol had been given as party swag or tubes she'd been offered in the hope she'd endorse them. "And a coupon for playing dress-up together too? I love it!"

"Look at mine!" Hannah squealed. She put on the hat Marisol had made, pulling it over her ears before performing a model turn. "And skiing lessons too! This is great. Thanks, Marisol."

Muffled by the girl's impetuous hug, Marisol patted her. "I took trendy nouveau-knitting lessons a couple of years ago, but I never really used them for anything until now. And I'm an ace skier, so if your dad agrees, we're in business."

"Awesome!" Jacob yanked away the last of the wrapping paper to reveal a gourmet ice cream maker that had gone sorely unused in Marisol's sleek bachelorette kitchen. His eyes widened with a pint-size version of guy-style gadget admiration. "Can I really make ice cream in this? All by myself?"

"I'll show you how," Marisol told him. "There's a certificate in there for an ice cream party with me. You can make up all the ingenious ice cream flavors you want to."

"Sweet." He hugged her. "First up, strawberry-hot dog!"

The girls made faces, then progressed to gagging noises.

"I suspect you'll have a lot of that particular flavor to keep for yourself," Marisol said. "But you never know— it just might be a winner."

"I dare you to take the first bite," someone said.

Marisol glanced up, and Cash was there.

From this vantage point, he towered over her, looking so good and so right that it was all she could do to catch her breath. He smiled at her, and breathing went out the window too.

"Well, I'm game for trying it," she managed to say, bravely getting to her feet. *Boots, don't fail me now.* "But it can't possibly be as good as mint chocolate chip with raspberry sauce and mini pretzels."

His eyes darkened. Probably he was remembering their crazy midnight snack on that crazy, romantic night they'd shared all those weeks ago—just like she was.

"Yeah, that combination shouldn't have been so good together," he said. "But it was. It really, really was."

For a long moment, they only gazed at each other. Marisol couldn't believe how much she'd missed seeing him. His eyes, his nose, his mouth, his ears . . . everything. She wanted to lick him up and down, then hug him close to her so he couldn't get away.

"Hey, kids." Cash nodded toward the patio, clearly king of this birthday party domain. "Grandma's looking for help with setting up the piñata. Why don't you give her a hand?"

"We get it, Daddy," Hannah said. "We'll leave you alone."

"Don't be too handsome, Daddy," Emily added.

Jacob only tittered. "Here comes the kissing!" he murmured.

They all left, giggling behind their hands, leaving Marisol and Cash alone. Really alone. Alone in a way she hadn't quite planned on. It made her nervous all over again.

"So . . ." She gestured to the house, with its comfy furnishings and warm feeling. "This is a nice place."

"Yeah. Thanks." Cash stuffed his hands in his pockets, offering a shrug. His gaze stayed on her. "After I left the Scorpions, I made a few connections. Adam did too. I just started working as a special quarterbacks coach for the ASU team. One of the campers from the Happy Gecko helped set it up."

"Oh Cash. I'm so glad. You like it then?"

He nodded. "It's only been a couple of weeks, but I've got a knack for coaching. Football is fun again. And the job lets me be here for the kids more too. You were right, Marisol. I would have been unhappy, being away from all . . . this."

He nodded toward the mayhem all around them, the kids running past and the grownups drifting by with punch and birthday cake, trying to give them space. Marisol and Cash smiled at each other, but he still kept his hands in his pockets, his posture stiff, his body half turned away.

Why was this so awkward? Why weren't they kissing already?

This was not the movie-style happily ever after she'd been hoping for. Worrying, Marisol barely heard Cash's next words.

"You kind of saved me from myself, in a way." His tone was light—deliberately so. "So I guess you got your invitation?"

"No . . ." She tilted her head. "Did you send one?"

"I had to. I needed to see you," he said.

"You *wanted* me here?" she asked at the same time.

Cash looked abashed. And handsome. And wonderful.

She wanted him so much it almost hurt. And maybe, just maybe . . .

He blinked. Then nodded. "We all wanted you here. But if you didn't get your invitation to the party, then why . . . ?"

"I couldn't stay away any longer," she admitted. "That's all. I'm a lot braver now, Cash, and the way we left things—"

"Was a mistake. I was an idiot." His gaze begged her to understand. "Sending you away was the hardest thing I ever did. But now that you're back, now that you're here—"

He broke off, shoving his hand through his hair. He glanced up at her, flashing a self-deprecating smile that was no less devastating for all its unexpected humility.

Cash, Marisol realized, actually looked embarrassed.

"Hell. I had this all planned," he said. "If you came, I was going to be so cool. I even practiced, but now I—"

"For me? Oh Cash. That's so—"

"Lame, I know."

"No, it's sweet!"

"But now that you're really here, all I can think is that I'm sorry." He leveled her with an anguished look. "I'm so sorry for hurting you. I never meant to do that."

Marisol waved her hand, fighting back tears. "I'm fine."

"No, you're not fine. Adam told me about the dog slobber incident. And the coffee table rings." Cash brought his hand to her cheek, shaking his head. "It's all because of me, and I'm sorry. I know I screwed things up pretty bad, but I need you, Marisol. Without you, I'm only half a man. And I don't want to live the rest of my life without feeling my heart beat the way it is right now, because of you."

"Oh, Cash." Sniffling back tears, Marisol captured his hand and squeezed it. He was so big, so strong, so tough.

But now, if she were very lucky, he might be hers. "All I've really got to give is me, but now I know . . . that's a lot."

"It's all I've ever wanted." With a hoarse cry, Cash pulled her into his arms. "All I've ever wanted is you," he said, resting his forehead against hers to gaze into her eyes. "From the first time I saw you up in that tree, from the first time you smiled at me, you bowled me over. And then I was lucky enough to have you, and I knew it couldn't last. I knew it. But I started to hope it would. Because I love you, Marisol."

She laughed and cried, both at the same time, hardly able to believe she was hearing everything she'd felt coming from Cash. They were the same in that way, and she needed him too.

"I love your laugh," he said, picking up speed now, "and your sexy walk, and that kooky little thing you do when you brush your teeth and do squats at the same time—"

"Bjorn says quadriceps strength is very important."

"—and I love your determination, and I love your weird way of whittling s'mores sticks with a nail file, and I love waking up with you and going to sleep with you." With both hands, Cash framed her face in his palms, his rugged, supermacho expression wavering just a bit. "I know there are a million more things—damn it, I rehearsed them all, so this would be perfect—but then I thought it was just a dream, and now you're here, so—"

"So everything's perfect again."

Unable to resist, Marisol kissed him. She also dripped happy tears on his cheeks, but she figured that was okay, given the circumstances.

"I love you too, Cash. I love you, but I never thought you could love me back. So every time you smiled at me, I tried to remember it. Every time you touched me, I tucked it away for later. Every time you helped me or teased me or just snuggled up to me, I tried my hardest to keep those moments close, because I knew they wouldn't last. But then I realized—this *could* last with us. It could last if I could be brave enough to come and get it. And you know what? I am brave. If I could tackle that dishwasher and that Dumpster, I can tackle this."

Solemnly, Cash nodded.

"So here I am, with nothing but me to offer. No shaving cream, no fancy gifts, no helicopter rides or shopping sprees. Just me. And if that's something you're interested in—"

"How soon can you move in?"

"Then I'm yours!" Giddily, Marisol threw her arms around his neck. Softly, she pressed a kiss to his lips. Not the least bit softly or hesitantly, Cash kissed her back. "Look out Phoenix, here I come!" she yelled.

"Yay!" Cheering came from the open patio doors. Emily, Jacob, and Hannah ran over and threw themselves into the hug.

"Does this mean you're staying?" Hannah asked.

"Yes." Marisol nodded, grinning broadly.

"Absolutely," Cash confirmed, looking equally buoyant.

"It's about time!" Leslie burst out.

The five of them gawked at her. The entire houseful of partygoers beamed back, poised in carefully circumspect eavesdropping positions around the room. Even the piñata and birthday cake had been abandoned.

"It looks as if you have a bunch of new friends to meet," Cash said. "Everyone, this is Marisol. The woman I love."

"Hi, Marisol!" everyone boomed, even the little kids.

She waved. "Sorry to crash the party, you guys."

"Nonsense. It's for a good cause." Suddenly Adam was there, looking suspiciously red-rimmed around the eyes. He punched Cash in the arm with a gruff gesture. "Good going, smarty-pants."

Leslie hugged Marisol. "I knew you'd be just what this family needed. Cash has been waiting for you."

"I've been waiting for him too. I just didn't know it," Marisol said. "I've been waiting for *all* these guys!"

Wrapping her arms around Cash again, she squished Hannah, Emily and Jacob into the hug too, making sure she held everyone close. Because the ultimate family—like the ultimate bargain and the perfect love—didn't come along every day. When it did, a girl had to grab it with both hands, hold on tight, and never let go.

"Yippee!" Jacob shouted. "Who wants more schlong cake?"

Utterly baffled, Marisol stared. He couldn't mean . . .

"It actually looks more like a caterpillar," Adam said.

"Or a fuzzy worm with feet," Leslie hastened to add.

"We may have accidentally created a freaky family tradition." Cash slung his arm around her shoulders, cozily steering her toward the kitchen. "Getting cold feet yet?"

"In these fab boots?" Marisol slanted him a playful look. If this was a test, she planned to nail it. "With you? And these kids? Never. Lead me to it. The schlongier, the merrier."

"Ladies and gentlemen, we have a winner!" Cash pulled her arm in the air like a championship prize fighter. As everyone filed into the kitchen, he leaned nearer and whispered in her ear. "Lucky me—I'm the one who's down for the count."

Then he waggled his eyebrows and gave her a grin that promised love and laughter and so much more . . . like Pop-Tarts with omelets, and all the happiness she could hold.

Chapter 33

For the third time in two weeks, Cash came home from his coaching job to find a camping tent set up in the living room.

Everyone was quiet, even Dump, but he wasn't fooled. He knew what this scenario meant. Any minute now, he'd hear Emily, Hannah, and Jacob giggling. There'd be indoor s'mores, sleeping bags on the floor, a special expanded story time (performed upon request by yours truly) . . . and one more night when he didn't get to sleep beside Marisol in their big double bed.

Dropping his gym bag, Cash tiptoed closer. His role was to pretend not to see the tent, be extravagantly surprised when the kids all barreled out shouting about it, then grumpily agree to another indoor campout. Getting ready, he put on his game face.

One pseudogrouchy dad, coming up.

Anything less than surly would have led them to believe he was going soft—and after only six blissful months of marriage too. He'd be damned if he'd disappoint anyone—although these days, Cash had learned that apologies and trying new things and talking about problems (as wussified as that sounded) went a long way toward keeping everyone happy.

Thanks to Marisol, he was no longer shouldering everything himself. Slapping on a scowl, he moved closer to the tent.

At his approach, Marisol stuck her head through the zipper opening. She smiled widely at him. "Hey, big boy. Welcome home. Come on over and visit my tent sometime, why don't you?"

Her saucy delivery made him grin. "You've got to get off the family camping kick," he told her. "The kids are going to forget what it's like to sleep in a normal bed."

"Hmmm. Maybe you're right." She motioned him closer, still not opening the tent all the way. "Maybe that's why I sent them to Stephanie and Tyrell's tonight."

Lately their custody agreement had loosened even more, and now Cash had all the time in the world with Jacob, Hannah, and Emily. Still, there were times when a man wanted to be alone.

Times like now, when his favorite wife was giving him that very special smile of hers. "Tonight?" he asked. "All night?"

"Mmm-hmmm." Marisol nodded. "All night. So come on in. I've got something to show you, and I think you're going to like it."

Like it? He loved it already, and he didn't even know what it was. The dreamy look in her eyes told him it would be good.

He kicked off his shoes, squinting as he gave his first guess. "Is it another fancy designer chair for your shop?"

It hadn't taken Marisol long to take the Valley by storm. Her new home-furnishings shop—a twin to her retail space in L.A.—was a big hit in its recently opened Scottsdale location.

"Nope. It's not a chair."

Cash stripped off his shirt. "Is it a froufrou pillow?"

"Nope. It's not a pillow."

Stalling with his hands on his belt, Cash peered at the ceiling to muster up another guess. He didn't want to rush things. Anticipation was half the fun. "I know. It's one of those weird, artsy kitchen tables made out of glass and jumper cables, isn't it?"

"Those aren't jumper cables." Looking on the verge of laughing, Marisol shook her head. "And it's not a table."

She wrapped her hands around the tent's opening. Interestedly, Cash watched.

"It's this." She revealed herself. "Surprise."

"Oh man." Thrilled to the core of his suddenly snug pants, Cash stared at her. At her sassy black miniskirt, sexy high heels, demure little lace cap, and sheer white apron. At her hot-hot-hot French maid's uniform. "I can't believe it."

"Believe it. Touch it." Marisol arched her brow, giving him a tempting look. "Take it off. Whatever you want."

Cash didn't need to be told twice. Filled with love and need and whole lot of desire, he crawled into the tent. He caught a giggling, sexy Marisol in his arms, angled her head back, and kissed her. He had both hands full of French maid's lace before either of them got upright again.

"All I want is you," he said, dipping his head for another kiss. It was hard to do when he couldn't quit smiling—a frequent problem of his lately. Manfully, Cash managed to make Marisol swoon and moan with interest, all the same. "Morning, noon, and night. All the time. You, you, you."

"You've got me." She gazed into his eyes, giving him that special smile that never failed to make his heart feel twice as big. "Now what are you going to do with me?"

He growled, nuzzling her neck. Damn, she looked good. Felt good. Smelled good too. "First? Rip off this outfit."

Marisol gasped. "Nice plan. And second?"

"Second?" He offered up a cocky smile. "The usual—make you beg me for more."

"Ooh." She helped with his fly. "And third?"

"Third?" Cash pretended to think about it, but there

was really no need. He stroked her cheek, nodding. "Third, I'm going to love you, baby. And it's never going to stop."

Then he closed his eyes, tipped her backward, and made both their dreams come true.

Twice.

Dear Reader,

Thank you for reading *Let's Misbehave*! I really hope you had a good time. When I thought up Marisol and Cash's story, I absolutely couldn't wait to write it, so I'm very happy to be able to share it with you now.

With every book I dream up, my goal is to tell a story that will make you smile. So if there's a grin on your face, hurray! Please tell a friend that *Let's Misbehave* made you smile—or go ahead and share this book with them. Maybe they'll enjoy it too.

In the meantime, you're invited to drop by my Web site at www.lisaplumley.com, where you can sign up for my reader newsletter, read sneak previews of upcoming books, request special reader freebies, and more. I hope you'll visit today.

Are you wondering what's next? I'm already hard at work on my next Zebra Books contemporary romance, so please be on the lookout! *Home for the Holidays* should be arriving in a store near you sometime next year.

Finally, I'd love to hear from you! You can send e-mail to lisa@lisaplumley.com or write to me c/o P.O. Box 7105, Chandler, AZ 85246-7105.

Cheers,
Lisa Plumley